CW01163110

Rising Son

By R.L. PACE

FIRST EDITION

ISBN: 978-1-961545-06-9
Copyright © 2024 Robert L. Pace & Deep7 Press
All Rights Reserved Worldwide
Cover design & formatting by Todd Downing
Editing by Nancy Pace

Deep7 Press is an imprint of Despot Media, LLC
1214 Woods Rd SE Port Orchard, WA 98366 USA

WWW.DEEP7.COM

*For Nancy,
who married me for
my potential so many
years ago*

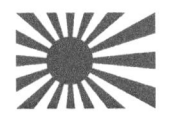

AUTHOR'S NOTE

This novel is based on two simple questions; what was the coming to America story like for Japanese emigres and what if the attack on Pearl Harbor wasn't the first idea for initiating hostilities with the United States? The idea presented itself to me while randomly thumbing through *Jane's Fighting Ships of WWII* in a public library. In particular I was intrigued by Japanese submarines designed to carry airplanes, either fighters or bombers. The more I contemplated them the more likely it seemed they were specifically for clandestine missions and thus I was inspired to begin writing.

In this novel, historical figures, locations, dates and accounts are as accurate and timely to the period as I can make them. All the newspapers, periodicals and journal entries are quoted verbatim with no fictional content.

While I put words in their mouths and thoughts in the heads of historical figures even those reflect my research into their actions and their own accounts of events as they unfolded. Any errors are solely my responsibility.

I grew up living less that twenty miles from the Minidoka War Relocation Center in Idaho yet not a single moment of my public education in history included even a mention of the forced relocation endured by Japanese Americans. It wasn't until my father died five plus decades after the events, that I discovered while going through his effects that he had driven a bus for Greyhound that transported incarcerees throughout the western U.S. The events had been thoroughly scrubbed from the pages of history and buried deep in my father's living memory. In some small measure this book seeks to restore those lost entries and honor the lives affected.

In 1983 a Federal Court vacated the decision of the 1942 Supreme Court in *Korematsu v. U.S.* acknowledging the obvious; racism played a central role in the original conviction and subsequent incarceration. It was 1985 before Congress authorized token reparations to all surviving people who had suffered internment and for the illegal seizures and forfeitures incurred as a result of Executive Order 9066. President Ronald Reagan issued a formal apology as part of the legislation.

Finally, this is a work of fiction. There is no evidence that a single act of disloyalty or Fifth Column activity ever took place among Americans of Japanese descent. The stain of illegally imprisoning 120,000 loyal Japanese Americans deserves a place in our history books and eternal vigilance to ensure nothing like it ever happens again.

Robert L Pace

Part One

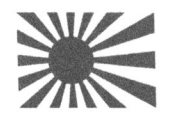

United States Trade Dock

Shimoda Harbor
Shizuoka Prefecture, Japan
May 12, 1890

A spring breeze carried white cherry blossom petals from trees nearby and deposited them on the bamboo sandal clad feet of Toshio Sakai, as he stood with perhaps two-dozen other young Japanese men on the loading dock. Slightly built but sinewy and strong, he regarded the petals absently as a representative from the Hawaiian Sugar Planters Association droned endlessly through an interpreter.

"When you arrive in Lahaina," the interpreter said, pausing for the American to speak before continuing, "you will be met by the plantation overseer. He will transport you to your new home and help you with any special needs you may have."

Toshio adjusted his simple work clothes and pulled his woven bamboo hat, which looked vaguely like an inverted funnel, onto his head as a shield against the sun. His wide-set black eyes peered into the rigging of the old converted whaler, then to deckhands unloading a cargo of cheap machine-made cloth and a few cases of small tools. His perusal wandered to the bow of the ship and lingered over the foreign letters spelling out the name of the vessel, *Hawaiian Sunrise.*

The old wooden ship was past her prime, too small and too slow to compete with the smoke belching coal steamers that plied the Pacific trade these days. The master was an old man on his forty-first, and last, sailing and could be seen treading the deck in a sort of sentimental haze, perhaps recalling his youth harpooning humpbacks and wrestling lustily with the naked island girls that used to swim to meet the boats in Lahaina harbor. The bawling of protesting livestock held in pens on deck added to the cacophony around the port. Stevedores and crewmen could be seen brandishing all manner of convenient weapons and heard swearing at each other in half a dozen languages as cargoes were loaded or discharged. Japanese *okinakashi* guided nets with crates marked "Porcelain ware—Destination Boston" aboard and disappeared down the hatch, reappearing moments later heading down the gangplanks for another burden. Toshio did not understand that the cargo coming off this and dozens of other foreign ships was what was driving him on board.

In his lifetime, Toshio hadn't been beyond the fields, hills and plains surrounding his village. When the agent for the plantation had come looking for contract field hands, his family saw a glimmer of hope for relief from the grinding poverty they endured. Only recently, an Imperial Order had been forthcoming that made it legal for Japanese citizens to emigrate to other countries. Toshio's blind grandfather had spoken in favor of working for the plantation. His father, too old now to go himself, had then sternly instructed Toshio about his duty as eldest son and the first in the family to read and write.

Toshio recalled his youthful fascination with the brushes and strokes of the calligraphy used by the Buddhist monks—so spare yet so beautiful. His *sensei* was a bald, emaciated old man who had spied the youngster peeking into the transcription room of the monastery. With the permission of his father, the cleric had patiently revealed the magic of the written word to the child. The epiphany that followed as the young student saw the world exposed in written language was a source of pleasure to the old monk. Eventually, Toshio began reading everything: old newspapers, scrolls of poetry, religious volumes. He became the village reader, explaining Imperial Rescripts to his family and neighbors and translating the occasional letter for some member of the small community. With the blossoming of his connection to the outside world, so came his vague discontent. There is more than just the village. There are more than just farmers and carpenters and tradesmen.

Of course there had been consternation in the village when it was learned the reader would be leaving, but that was allayed when Toshio-san revealed that he had been instructing his younger brother and even his worthless sister in reading and writing. Actually, his sister was more facile in mastering the language in its written form and thus became an acute source of embarrassment to everyone. Eventually the village worked out an elaborate ruse where letters and proclamations would be loudly presented to the remaining brother for translation. He and his sister would do the work and then he'd equally loudly present the result. Over time, since she was not the first or even the second to learn to read in the family, the villagers would ignore the fact she was a girl. But it would take a long time.

Toshio was to arrange to send money when it was possible and to save some each month. Grandfather lectured against foolish purchases and gambling, Father and Mother both admonished him to take a Japanese wife when the time came, preferably from this district, and certainly not an unclean *Eta*. Above all he was reminded he was Japanese and to do nothing to dishonor or disgrace the Emperor, his family or homeland. This also meant he was to return to his home as a rich man. "Five hundred Yankee dollars would be enough, then you come back," his father had insisted. For him it seemed like an impossibly huge sum of money.

Toshio listened to each speaker in turn, giving polite and properly deferential attention to each. He fully understood his obligation to his family and his village, yet he was uncertain of his feelings. That night he was restless on his simple *tatami*, weighing his duty against his sentiments. After a Spartan breakfast of rice with bits of fish and pickle, he headed for the fields with his friends and neighbors. All through the day, he tended the crops, using a bamboo hoe to divert water from a series of small canals into rows of green tea bushes or delicate pebbly streambeds planted with *wasabi*. As each terrace flooded with water, it brought with it from the Kawazu River a few eels, the largest of which he would collect to take back to the village to sell.

By evening, he had made his decision, and on the walk home past the Seven Falls of Kawazu he took in the details of the countryside with great care, committing each important element to memory. He spoke cordially, but at a distance, with two *Eta* men returning from a successful boar hunt. The wild pig was slung from a pole between the shoulders of each man and swayed rhythmically with their easy gait. Everywhere he looked there was order. The terraced fields, distant from the central village clinging to the steep hillsides were each tended with great precision as they had been for two thousand years. The pathways were swept and then raked each day. As he entered the village he noted the ramshackle homes huddled together. Each had a family that accepted tradition and was steeped in duty and obligation. From the beginning of remembered time these families had been farmers. They paid honor to the Emperor by never speaking his holy name, observing his birthday and paying the taxes imposed. At home Toshio made a lingering mental note of the earthen floors partially covered only with soiled and frayed *tatami* mats. Slowly he surveyed the cracked earthenware cook pots, worn bamboo kitchen utensils and the remaining meager implements of poverty.

Once he had been to the home of the *shoshu* of the prefecture to sell eels to the cook. While waiting at the back door of the house, he peeked inside. The polished wooden floors, jade carvings, porcelain vases and beautiful screens were emblazoned in his memory, and from that time forward, he entertained decidedly un-Japanese thoughts. Toshio pressed into his memory the monochromatic sameness of each of the huts in the village. He could not remember a time when anyone had improved their position in the community or risen above their circumstances. He could not recall anyone ever suggesting they even had a hope such a thing was possible. In Japan you were born into your station and there you remained for the entirety of your life. He understood the necessity for such traditions. It maintained orderliness in the world. He could not help thinking though, that in a new place perhaps it would be different. In a new place perhaps he could escape. Escape, never before considered, now became a partner to hope.

"If you can read, come forward and sign your name to the contract," the interpreter intoned, breaking the young farmer's introspection, "then go aboard and wait for instructions from the crew."

Toshio Sakai did as he was told, as he had always done, as was his duty. He picked up his small reed satchel containing his best rice bowl, a clay cooking pot along with two pair of chopsticks, a small brazier, a bamboo cup, his precious writing brush and a tiny white ceramic ink pot sealed with beeswax. Also inside were a few scraps of paper, a portrait of the Emperor presented by the village mayor, several paper folders of medicinal herbs and a small cache of seeds from various plants and flowers villagers thought would be useful in his new home. Those items, the clothes on his back and a sleeping mat were all his worldly possessions. He made his way forward and signed the contract. Since it was written in English he could not read it, but he had been assured that he would be provided with a wage of seventy-five cents per day and his food and lodging. This was in exchange for his three-year commitment to work ten hours a day, six days a week. Four religious holidays were allowed in each year. Toshio climbed the gangplank to the deck of the ship, and when he reached the top, he paused to look back to take in the sights and sounds of this port just a few miles from his home.

As he gazed back toward shore he was grabbed from behind and dragged on board by a deckhand. The sinews on the seaman's neck were taut and his face red as he shoved Toshio roughly to the deck brandishing a belaying pin. He pointed to the opening on deck leading to the hold. Toshio was motioned by an armed crewman to a ladder.

Gathering his few things he descended from the warm spring sunshine into the claustrophobic darkness of the hold. Many faces looked up at him. Faces like his, filled with hope. Faces filled with fear.

Having boarded its mercantile and human cargo, the *Hawaiian Sunrise* weighed anchor and sailed on a retreating tide into the vast expanse of Pacific, bound for an archipelago of tiny islands known collectively as Hawaii, protruding defiantly from the restless waters of the Pacific Ocean.

At Sea

Pacific Ocean

Sakai had never been to sea or even on a boat and was terrified as the wind whistled through the rigging and the tall ship shuddered through the waves of the first squall it encountered. Within hours of departing from the homeland, among the group of young farmers, apprehension had been replaced with wretchedness. Most began vomiting as seasickness overtook them. That, mingled with the overwhelming smell of rancid whale oil and spilled latrine buckets, was rendering life in the 'tween deck generally abysmal. By nightfall rats crawled among the miserable men gnawing at any exposed skin. The men organized themselves to sleep in shifts, with someone wielding a stick and always awake to keep the vermin at bay.

As the days passed the crippling stomach cramps, weakness and sickness abated for most and Toshio and his countrymen began to adapt to the mind-numbing boredom of shipboard life. The Captain was a humane man, uncommon in that regard among most of his peers, and sent buckets of seawater down to clean the hold. This the men did with great vigor for it helped dissipate the overwhelming stench of the deck.

To while away the hours some men gambled and many lost all their meager possessions to unscrupulous cheats. Toshio had been warned of such things by his grandfather and so avoided the games. One man named Watanabe had brought fine woodworking tools, a gift from his village. With his chisels he carved a figure on one of the beams. It was a handsome dragon, a sign of luck and good health. To block the sounds of livestock bawling on deck and the groans of the few men with persistent seasickness, Toshio would concentrate on listening to the wind moaning through the enormous sails with their infinite lengths of hemp rope rigging. He tried to imagine what his new home would be like. Some of his companions had been at sea before and told outrageous tales of monstrous sea creatures that could eat ten men with a single bite and storms with waves taller than the Emperor's Temple in Tokyo. He did not entirely believe them but kept a weather eye nonetheless.

When the skies were fair and the breezes benign the first mate of the ship would allow a few of the voyagers to come on deck in shifts under guard. The men would clamber up from the hold and set up a brazier to serve as a makeshift stove. A small iron pot was produced in which they would cook rice. This, along with dried fruit, fish and pickled vegetables provided by the sugar plantation was served once daily for the duration of the journey. One third of each man's ration of water was dispensed at this time under the watchful eye of the Master at Arms.

One day in the early evening, he was eating his rice and watching with great amazement as porpoises raced before the bow of the boat, their white flanks flashing as they leapt gracefully out of the water. A sailor in the basket high on the mast yelled out to the Captain below and pointed at the horizon a few degrees off the bow to starboard. The old salt took up his telescope and peered in the direction the sailor had indicated. Everyone on deck turned their eyes that way as well. Toshio squinted against the sub-tropical glare of the sun and saw a black speck in the distance. He thought perhaps it was another ship then realized it was much too far away to be any vessel.

"Sakai-*san*!" an excited voice called out.

Toshio turned away from the rail to look at the owner of the voice. It was his new friend Soshi. He was a small, slightly stooped man about twenty-five years of age with deep set coal black eyes. A sparse beard covered his face and a ragged mustache drooped around his mouth, an odd contrast to his bright smile. Muscular and deeply bronzed by years of toil in the sun, his persistent optimism had been the counterpoint to Toshio's naturally taciturn demeanor. Soshi came from the village of Shuzeji, even smaller and much farther north in the prefecture than Toshio's home. Astride the Katsura River, Shuzeji was known principally for its hot springs, but like all of Japan, farming was carved deeply into the countryside and the culture. Soshi had taken a journey of many days to reach the dock at Shimada and had befriended Toshio effortlessly even before he had fully descended the ladder into the hold on the first day.

"*Hai*, Soshi-*san*, come and see! I think this is our new home," Toshio said.

Although neither man could read, write or understand English both had begun to master a few spoken words, one of which they were hearing from many members of the crew, Hawaii! The two men clung to the railing. The trade winds filled the sails, blowing strong, relentlessly pushing the ship forward slipping the waves beneath the hull. The porpoises racing before the bow were forgotten now as water-weary eyes strained to catch a glimpse of the island rising from the sea before them.

Near the Tropic of Cancer
Pacific Ocean
Early June, 1890

From experience, the veteran Captain of *Hawaiian Sunrise* had a good idea of the distance to the island, but he had the navigator measure the dip angle anyway and grunted with self-satisfaction when the number returned was eighty-five nautical miles. At the current rate of six knots he would reach Kaulakahi Channel between Kauai and Niihau Islands in about fourteen hours. He would tie up at Pearl Harbor by this time tomorrow and with luck and a speedy dock crew, would put out for Lahaina before midnight.

Early the next morning, the hatches were thrown open and ladders extended into the hold by order of the Captain. Crewmen hollered down into the hold and motioned for the men to come up. The Captain appeared and actually climbed down into the foul 'tween decks smiling broadly and gesturing for the men to climb up. Toshio was the first, followed by the old sailor and then everyone else in turn.

As Toshio clambered onto the deck and began to survey his surroundings he was suddenly struck dumb by what he saw. The Captain, having regained the deck, derived great amusement from the reaction of his cargo, which was the principal motivation for allowing the men topside.

The surge of his countrymen pushed Toshio Sakai toward the port side railing and he gawked at what he saw. Looming three thousand feet above the ocean were wildly rugged escarpments and deep jagged canyons disappearing miles back from the shoreline. Slashes of bright red, iron-laden volcanic earth were exposed where eroding cliffs had recently plunged into the sea.

Cascading waterfalls appeared randomly atop the cliffs, tumbling toward the shoreline below, finally melting into gossamer clouds of mist. Almost every visible inch was covered in a profusion of lush green vegetation. Kauai was an emerald in a turquoise setting of sea and sky and was unlike anything he had ever seen before. It took his breath away. The virility and wildness, the sheer grandeur and scope overwhelmed him.

"There you are, boys," the Captain gestured grandly toward the island with a sweep of the arm, "your first glimpse of Hawaii. Enjoy the view now. Once we put you ashore, you poor bastards will never see the like again." The deck crew laughed raucously and although they understood nothing that was said, the Japanese laborers began to smile and laugh as well.

Hawaii! Toshio thought. *This is where hope begins!*

Lahaina Harbor

Maui, Kingdom of Hawaii

Two days later

When the cattle had been offloaded, the workers who had continued from Honolulu to Lahaina were brought up from the hold and herded off the vessel to the wharf. After weeks at sea, standing on *terra firma* suddenly seemed unfamiliar. Their bodies, continuing to adapt to a motion that was no longer present, could be seen rocking gently as they stood. They formed a desultory impromptu lineup on the coral quay, wondering individually what their lives would now be like, and collectively what to do next.

That unspoken question was answered almost immediately as a coconut-husk-brown, shriveled, bespectacled little man walked swiftly down the quay.

"*Hai*, you men come by me, we process. You come ova be betta faster." He was Portuguese but his language was an amalgam of Portuguese, English, Hawaiian pidgin and Japanese. He rapidly motioned with his left arm, "An now wat you waitin' fo? No make da boss man mad."

The tiny band of men, having no real idea of what was said to them, nonetheless followed the little man down to a narrow frontage street along the harbor. Their path took them past a massive banyan tree with its multiple trunks and the crumbling two foot thick coral brick walls of the old fortress built for missionaries to protect themselves in the early settlement days.

The practice of naked native girls swimming out to meet, trade and otherwise commingle with sailors aboard whalers anchored in the bay was summarily ended shortly after the arrival of the first Congregationalist missionary family. One Captain in particular took drunken umbrage to the meddlesome cleric and proceeded to lob cannon fire into town. A riot ensued on and offshore, and when finally quelled, fort construction commenced soon thereafter.

A two-storied, white plastered building stood in mute testimony to New England sensibilities. It was square, squat and functional. Sparsely decorated it featured a square stoop built out from the main entrance, flanked only by Doric columns with a second floor balcony above. The hip roof was covered with palm thatch, undoubtedly awaiting the arrival of proper shingles from the United States. There upon the porch, seated bolt upright at a battered Shaker secretary with a large ledger book in front of him, sat a pinch-faced clerk wearing a pince nez and a once fashionable black frock coat. An inkwell stood to his right side and the book was open to about the halfway point. A huge native man, the largest human Toshio had ever seen stood nearby his massive arms folded across his naked brown chest. He wore only a brightly painted cloth wrapped several times around and folded into itself at his waist.

"Welcome to Lahaina," the clerk said perfunctorily in a clipped New England accent to the first man to present himself to his station. "I will enter your name and the date you arrived in Hawaii before you go to your assigned plantations. Please have your contract ready for inspection." The interpreter did his best to make the instructions understood and, after several attempts, almost everyone was prepared to comply.

"Name and contract please," the clerk asked without a trace of interest or emotion. Each interpreted response was duly mulled, then the steel pen in the ink stained fingers of the clerk scratched the information on a line in the ledger. As the queue moved forward and the questions were translated, the frayed cuff of the tattered frock coat dragged across the page with each entry. Toshio was fascinated by the writing instruments because they were so different than his own brush and ink pot. Most men inferred key words farther down the line so it moved forward with increasing speed as each interviewee came along.

"Name and contract please," the clerk intoned again.

"Sakai Toshio" was the response as he handed his document to the man behind the table.

The man wielding the pen was familiar with the Japanese custom of placing the family name first, but the overseers and plantation owners didn't know or care about that and making life easier for them made life easier for him.

"Toshio, hmmm, not too hard to say but still sounds foreign. Toshio, Toshio; he mulled it over for a moment, Toshio, Tom, Thomas; *Thomas*, that's not too bad." The clerk looked at the man before him, "Okay, Toshio, starting today your name is Thomas; Thomas Sakai. Next in line please."

When the clerk had processed the last worker, the wizened Portuguese man began addressing the two groups that had been formed at the direction of the massive Hawaiian. "You mo betta listen me. You belong to da haole boss men now. You hard work, dey like. You no works, dey get mad send Lunas find you."

The assemblage struggled to understand what they were hearing, but for most it was a total loss. Finally, the little man finished, pointing first to one group motioning it to climb into a horse-drawn wagon, then to Toshio's group indicating they should follow the Hawaiian who had been dividing the men from the clerk's table at the Custom House. The giant barefoot man spun around casually and ambled off down the dusty road into town, his ragtag group trailing behind at a respectful distance.

After a walk of less than half a mile, the group was halted along a narrow railroad track near a long row of immense sheds alive with noisy, smelly activity. Two shiny rails gleamed in the midday sun winding through the village toward the interior of the island in one direction, running adjacent to the buildings nearby in the other. Sitting on a siding next to the building was the *Ko'oko'o,* a diminutive 1886 vintage Baldwin Locomotive Works 0-4-2T engine. It wheezed serenely, steam escaping from its two drive cylinders and smoke curling skyward from the stack. She patiently waited while swarms of men unloaded her sugarcane from trailing cars, which looked oddly like giant overturned cockroaches on wheels.

Toshio and Soshi, now dubbed Sammy by the clerk, exchanged nervous glances. Everything about this place was so different from home. It was hot with sub-tropical sun beating down; the water was bluer, the sky brighter and the plants and animals mostly foreign. And there were so many different people! Until Toshio had arrived at the docks in Shimada Harbor, he had scarcely seen any but Japanese people. Now everywhere he looked strange people speaking alien languages abounded.

Soshi nudged his friend, "Listen, Toshio, far away. What is that sound?"

Toshio listened intently to the far off song of a steam whistle. As all the men listened, others began looking in the direction of the sound from up the tracks, which led inland. Soon, in the distance, another locomotive hove into view. This train, the *Ahi Alamihi,* which Toshio later learned meant fire crab, had come around the Cape from Philadelphia only a year ago and was sister to the *Ko'oko'o*. As it neared the refinery, the *Ahi Alamihi* sent three long blasts from its whistle and was answered by a short, a long and a short blare from its counterpart. Slowly the *Koko,* as the haoles called it, began to pull away from the sheds clearing the siding and then halted next to the collection of workers milling about.

The giant Hawaiian spoke for the first time now "You climb bettah on ka'aahi train. Lunas fix you home some later. Two days you work." With that he motioned the men to climb aboard the empty cane cars, made a laconic turn and ambled away in the direction they had all come. The moment the *Ahi Alamihi* cleared the siding, the engineer threw the tracks and scampered back to the *Koko.* The narrow-gauge saddle-tank engine began sending steam to the pistons, driving the four little wheels that provided the motive force.

In the beginning, the train ride was an excursion through Lahaina. Nearby workers moved cargo steadily in and out of a few large warehouses crafted from coral hewn from the harbor. Then the train ran out past the mission where houses ranged from little more than poor palm frond huts to magnificent Victorian mansions built with the abundant sugar money.

Everywhere the men looked, they saw a profusion of exotic vegetation. Surrounding one house grew a hedge of croton introduced from Indonesia. Around another, poinsettias imported from Mexico formed a fiery enclosure. As the train moved away from town and into the surrounding countryside, little patches of taro planted in carefully flooded plots among the abundant palm trees rotated their huge emerald green, heart-shaped leaves to follow the sun. They reminded Toshio of rice paddies back home.

Gradually the caravan moved beyond the outskirts of town, past the taro and palms, and began a shallow climb through acres upon acres of sugar cane. With a two year growth cycle, cane fields could be seen in all phases of production. To the west, smoke billowed from fields ablaze to set the sugar in the cane and eliminate vegetation that impeded harvest. To the east, the stalks in mid-growth towered over the train, and ahead some of the passengers strained to see what other workers were doing.

The train chugged by field laborers, past the fields and slowly clanged its bell as it slowed by a huge mansion set on a bluff overlooking the ocean below. The house was set back about three hundred feet from the rail line and a suggestion of a road meandered through the grounds among carefully tended trees and exotic plants. Given the sub-tropical climate of Maui, the large glass conservatory adjacent to the main building was surely superfluous, built simply to demonstrate that financial wherewithal was available to the owner. Peacocks and hens made stately parades, occasionally piercing the air with their eerie childlike screams. Marble statuary guarded a large central fountain and several men could be seen tending to the extensive gardens on the grounds.

A mile beyond the estate the train finally ground to a halt near a rudely constructed shack erected in a clearing at the edge of a cane field. A man riding a horse and wearing a white shirt waved to the passengers. Carrying the few possessions each had brought with them, the new crop of farm hands disembarked and walked to the rider. After everyone had cleared the tracks the *Koko* chugged away leaving the men at the edge of the field.

Perched regally on a bay stallion, his blousy white cotton shirt fluttering in the trade winds, the horseman waited as the men gathered around.

"I'm Gustav, your overseer." The phonetically pronounced Japanese words were rendered with a barely intelligible thick German accent. "On this island we are called Lunas. Does anyone here speak English or German?" he asked. No one did, so the next question was, "Does anybody here *read* Japanese?" Of the present group only Thomas Sakai raised his hand.

"Read this to the group," Gustav said, handing Thomas the paper. Gustav had exhausted most of the Japanese he knew and sat back in the saddle to listen to the reading.

Thomas examined the paper, reading ahead a little, then began: "From Jedediah Whitehead, *Shuyo na* Master of the plantation to the new workmen arriving today..."

Clearing his throat, Sakai continued more formally, "...welcome to the Maui sugar plantation. The man who gave you this letter is your overseer, your *bosu*. He will manage your daily work assignments and see you get paid on payday. The overseer will arrange for food to be delivered and for medical attention if necessary. His instructions should be followed as if they came directly from me.

"Your contract requires you to work ten hours per day, six days per week for three years. Workers who are fifteen or more minutes late to work will be docked one half a days' pay. Workers who miss work for a day will be docked two days pay. Four holidays will be granted each year in addition to the Sabbath.

"The buildings here have been built for you to live in while working on the plantation. They will be your home while you are here. Please take the rest of this day and tomorrow to make your living arrangement amongst yourselves. Your overseer will be back to guide you to your first day of work."

Thomas finished the document, and then handed it back to the Luna on horseback. Gustav took the paper then used the last Japanese word he knew, "Understand?"

"*Hai*," Thomas replied, bowing from the waist. The overseer nodded then nudged his horse and rode away leaving the group alone.

"Well, Toshio-san," Sammy said, "we'd better take a look around and find out where we live now."

After weeks at sea together the twenty-three men standing at the edge of the clearing, were, if not all friends, at least well known to one another. Most had exchanged their stories during the long hours at sea and the usual squabbles, disagreements and reconciliations that occur in gatherings consisting of more than one human presence had come to some sort resolution. The result of this winnowing process had produced a group that already had a de facto hierarchy in place upon arrival. Although he had not sought it, and in fact was uncomfortable in a leadership role, Toshio-san (now

Thomas) by virtue of being the only reader in their midst, was a kind of quasi-mayor in the tiny community. In Japanese a single word in differing contexts conveys a sense of place geographically like a village or district, or of rank or discipline as an individual. A *Shichou* can be a mayor, teacher, high-ranking official or a man of prominence and, like it or not, young Thomas had become most of those things to these men.

Thomas looked around him. Twenty-two other faces stared back at him as if waiting for some signal about what to do next. Inside he squirmed with anxiety but outwardly his emotion was unreadable. He turned to Sammy and said, "We cannot live in a mess like this. Let us get to work turning this place into a home."

Sammy returned a sly grin. "*Hai*, you are right Shichou Thomas. We must begin." Upon hearing himself called 'Mayor', Thomas began to protest but before he could Sammy barked out instructions to the men; "Shichou Thomas has spoken wisely. You four men clean up the clearing and find some firewood. You three, see if there is any water and food to prepare." Sammy waited to see if the men would actually obey, and when they did, he was further emboldened. "You, take five men and make a latrine at least fifty paces downwind. Make that sixty." Everyone laughed. "The rest of you get started on the barracks."

As the last of the men headed off to their assignments Shichou Thomas, nascent Mayor of Maui Plantation Labor Camp 14, stood in wonderment and *Sanbouchou* Sammy, his self-appointed Chief of Staff, beamed a crooked smile back at his friend.

"So, Toshio-san, you shall see, the morale of the farmer soldiers will be very high and we will become very rich."

Thomas shook his head in disbelief and without a word picked up his little bamboo case and walked down a slightly worn path toward the barracks, his new assistant bringing up the rear.

Though inexpert at such things even Thomas could easily tell the building was rudely constructed of inferior materials. Lumber was expensive and imported from the great conifer forests of the Pacific Northwest, thus most of the workers shacks were made with salvaged scraps, rejects or green wood that had warped and cracked. Like most of the small houses in Hawaii, this one was built with the floor starting about eighteen inches above the ground. Every ten feet around the perimeter of the twenty-by-forty-foot building a palm log protruded twelve feet or so upwards from where it had been shoveled into a hole in the ground. Rough timbers spiked to the logs served as ledger boards to which floor planking was nailed and a similar arrangement at the top of the logs acted as headers. Boards were then simply butt-joined together vertically and nailed in place to form walls.

Glassless windows of varying sizes appeared randomly, apparently placed when short pieces of wood were used along a section of wall. Crude shutters had been formed with scraps that were otherwise too small and were fastened with leather hinges. The roof was rusted corrugated tin that sloped from the leeward high side to the windward low side of the building. Most of the material was of dubious pedigree; in addition to the rough unfinished wood, some planks were painted yellow, a few were whitewashed, mixes of brick-red, green, black and even orange were occasionally evident. It looked like a livestock lean-to crossed with a patchwork quilt.

As he climbed the steps to the shelter and went inside, Thomas was for the first time entertaining serious doubts as to the wisdom of his decision to leave home. Even his poor home in Japan was superior to this creaky mess. Walking deeper inside, the floor planks sank dangerously beneath him. Even his slight weight created sway because no joists supported the planks. Clearly this was not going to hold twenty or more men and all their accommodations.

"Soshi-san," he said. "Have a couple of the men look for long logs from the strange trees or some heavy planks. Then find Watanabe. We may be able to use some of his tools to cut the wood. If an overseer or Gustav rides by, try to get him to stop so we can show him this problem."

"Should I send someone to look for the Luna?" Sammy asked.

"No, not now," Thomas replied. "No one among us knows where anything is yet. He'd probably just get lost."

"Okay, Thomas. I'll get started."

Left alone for the first time in months, Thomas Sakai took a moment to survey the dim interior. Stacked upon each other were bed frames with wire springs, rusted from exposure and damaged from prolonged use elsewhere. Attached to the walls in four places were old kerosene lamps, three of which actually still had smoky globes in place. Just inside the door stood a potbellied stove with a cast-iron teakettle on top. In the daylight he could see all the holes and cracks in the walls where the sunlight poured through illuminating the fine red dust suspended in the air.

Gingerly he made his way across the floor, testing each board before placing his entire weight on it, then moving to each window to open all the makeshift shutters. The bright tropical sunlight streamed in, revealing two small tables crafted from packing crates and a few chairs with broken parts or missing cane seats.

At the very back of the room were several enormous bags filled with copra from the coconuts harvested on the island. The coarse brown fibrous shreds reminded him of the packing material he had seen in crates being sealed in Shimada. Next to the copra was a pile of sugar sacks, which Thomas counted. Then he clicked off the bed frames and when the numbers were the same he surmised that they must be the elements of mattresses for everyone.

As he pondered his next move, the room suddenly darkened. Then the roof exploded in a cacophony of noise sounding as though someone were pouring buckets of gravel on top. The din was incredible. He looked out the window and could see the men racing for the building while rain poured from the sky as if they were fighting through a waterfall. No sooner had the last man entered, the floor creaking ominously, than the sky cleared, the sun came out and the breeze returned. In fifteen minutes everything was dry again.

Watanabe the carver, came swimming upstream against the tide of exiting workers. He was looking for Shichou Thomas and found him staring out the window at an intense rainbow that had formed. Watanabe had never seen so bright a rainbow, and for a moment was as transfixed as Thomas. The carver was a practical man though and things needed to be done.

"Shichou-san, we have found a few old logs. Not as good as bamboo or pine but pretty strong, I think. What should we do with it?"

"We must build a support for the floor," he muttered to himself. Let's look under the house to see what is there," Thomas said as he headed out the only door and down the steps. Once outside he got down on his hands and knees and crawled under the building. The ground hadn't even been cleared before construction, so shards of harvested cane protruded from the ground scraping mercilessly at carelessly placed flesh.

"We can do most of this with what we have found around here." Watanabe asserted. He crouched down sitting on his heels peering into the gloom under the house. "We have three old tree trunks and some short plank pieces. Let me show you what we can do."

The carver was already drawing a picture with a stray bit of charcoal on a board scrap while Thomas crawled out and dusted himself off. "Look here, we can make a smooth, level place for this flat wooden piece. Then we make a pillar like this," he said, indicating a drawing of a cylinder flat on one end with a concave sort of half-pipe carved at the top. "If we split the logs in quarters and put a length between two pillars, we can hold up most of the floor with what we have."

"We are very lucky today, Shichou Thomas," Sammy said as he joined the conversation. "One of the men found part of a cask of nails and an axe. That should speed things up. We found rice and pickled vegetables, but no water."

"Okay, Sammy, take three men from the cleaning and have them start stuffing mattresses. Watanabe, you take everyone else except two men from the latrine and start on the logs. I'm going to find water."

The two subordinates headed off to their assignments, shouting for men to gather and giving orders like foremen on a construction site.

Thomas could see the men nodding and heading off toward their new assignments. He could sense that for these men, accustomed to working from dawn to dusk, doing *something,* anything really, after being cooped up aboard ship was welcome relief.

Putting on his bamboo hat, Thomas walked the short distance back to the railroad line. A trail ran beside it and recalling he had not seen any water along the way in he struck out in the direction Gustav had ridden down the tracks. At first it seemed as if all were a sugar cane desert. Cane stalks rose eight feet tall in every direction with the path and rail line carving a narrow straight path through the fields as if reluctant to relinquish even a square foot to unplanted land. After a mile or so, he came upon an expanse that had been recently burned. Harvesting was under way and shirtless men wielding odd-looking machete-like knives with a hook at the end toiled under the tropical sun, their skin burnt to a deep russet hue. Rhythmically, the knives chopped the stalks. These were then stacked in bundles, which were carried off to the train, whose cars waited patiently for the next load to be completed before trundling back to the refinery in a neverending cycle.

Directing ash-covered workers from horseback was a man in a white shirt. Thomas thought it might be Gustav, but even if it wasn't, he might be able to tell him where to get some water for his campsite, so he began walking in his direction.

The *haole* Luna spotted Thomas, and seeing him without a knife and apparently without anything to do rode in his direction fully prepared to deliver a few timely blows with his quirt to get the sluggard moving again. He charged up hard on his horse, stopping just short causing Thomas to flinch. The Luna raised his arm and was about to strike when a voice with a thick German accent stopped him.

"Wait!" Gustav said as he rode up. "This one came in today; he starts later. Go back to your crew and get them to work."

"What are you doing here?" Gustav asked, turning his attention to Thomas.

Thomas looked at him helplessly, not comprehending a single word, but understanding an answer was expected. For a moment the two men regarded each other across the language barrier in silent frustration. Suddenly the Luna seemed to have an idea. Reaching into his saddlebag, he extracted a small notebook and a pencil and handed it to Thomas with an expectant look. The Mayor paused for a moment then realized what his boss wanted. He thought for a moment and began to draw. Elegantly, he sketched a quick landscape with a river running through it and tracks leading to a small building with several stick figures nearby. He handed the drawing back pointing to the canteen Gustav had on his saddle. Gustav looked at the sketch and laughed. Nodding in understanding, he made a crude depiction of the horizon and the sun where it now stood in the sky and showed it to Thomas, pointing to the sun. He then drew a second sun lower in the sky and handed it back for review. Thomas studied the image. The dawning of comprehension crossed his faced and he too smiled. Later that afternoon the Luna would send water to the camp.

With the problem solved, Thomas bowed to the man on horseback before turning to start back to camp. Gustav stopped him with a word and a gesture to follow him toward the train. At the back of the last cane car was a barrel with a dipper hanging from it. The German overseer indicated Thomas should drink and he barked a few orders to the engineer. When he had finished, Thomas peered questioningly at Gustav. The absolute picture of his Teutonic background with a huge brown handlebar mustache, Gustav glanced back at Thomas with deep blue eyes and made an indication for him to get aboard the train. Farther ahead, the engineer was beckoning him to the front. The cars were fully loaded now and Thomas understood he was to ride the train back to his camp.

The engineer was a Filipino man about the same size as Thomas, sweating profusely and covered with the grime of coal dust, soot and ash from the burnt cane. He smiled widely at his unexpected assistant and handed him a shovel, indicating a small tender containing coal then pointed to the firebox of the engine. The newly appointed fireman of the *Ko'oko O* tentatively threw in a couple of small shovels of coal. Several more followed at the encouragement of the engineer. The little Baldwin quickly built up a head of steam, and after a blast from the whistle, the pistons labored to move the drive wheels and began backing up the train. When the engine had cleared the temporary spur laid in the field for the harvest, the engineer hopped out, ran to change the switch, then started the ride on the main line to the refinery.

After about ten minutes Thomas realized the train was probably going to make a big loop back to Lahaina and not go anywhere near his camp. He handed the shovel back to the engineer and prepared to jump from the slow train to begin the walk back, but the Filipino grabbed his arm and shook his head vigorously.

"Luna says you bettah stay with me," he said in that strange pidgin that everyone seemed to understand. "We bring water your camp on da way back. More bettah you stay, you see good."

Thomas had only the vaguest notion of what was intended, but one thing was clear, he was expected to remain on board, so he went back to his coal shoveling. It took the train nearly an hour, at the blistering pace of thirteen miles an hour, to work through the serpentine of tracks laid throughout the cane fields to make the return to Lahaina and the refinery Thomas had embarked from early that morning. She whistled her arrival and received the customary response as her counterpart headed again into the fields in an endless cycle on a closed track. *Koko* pulled ahead to the siding by the warehouses as the morning swarm of workers began unloading the cars.

The engineer twisted a few knobs and set the brake, then left the cab. He went directly to a man who seemed very hot and uncomfortable in a black suit wearing a wilted starched collar and ribbon tie and exchanged words with him. Thomas could see the engineer point back to him, then listen to the response from the man. After a moment, both men seemed to come to agreement as they nodded heads at one another and the Filipino hastened toward the engine. He scrambled aboard the front of the locomotive opening the saddle-tank cover as he pulled down the fill pipe from a wooden water reservoir overhead. A torrent cascaded down the pipe into the inlet. The engineer doused himself thoroughly, rubbed away some of the grime vigorously, then rinsed himself again.

When he had finished, he scampered into the engine cab and indicated Thomas should shovel more coal. As he did so, Thomas noticed that all the cane had been unloaded and several large barrels were being rolled toward the first car. With much pointing, shouting and arguing, it was finally decided one side of a car would have to be removed to load the barrels. So tools were produced and one of the stake sides was taken off and tossed into the next car. The carpenter stayed with the car since he would have to reassemble it when they got to the cane fields. Now the imported oaken kegs were loaded, six in all, and the engineer slowly inched the train forward till the fill-pipe of the water tank was directly above each outsized canteen. The workmen brought the pipe down filling each in turn and rolling it away till all were topped off. They nailed down tin lids and slung a rope around the lot tying it off on the stakes of the opposite side. Full of water, each weighed over five hundred pounds, and Shichou Thomas was already wondering how in the world they would unload them at the camp.

Watanabe and Sammy had divided the workers, Sammy taking his group to clear and smooth spaces down the centerline under the shack. Using whatever they could find they hacked at the cane stubble then hammered at the red volcanic earth to compact it as much as possible. Meanwhile Watanabe had fashioned large wooden mallets with his carving tools and the axe. Then he made a few quick wedges from scraps and had his men rhythmically splitting the trees into makeshift floor joists. While they worked on splitting palm logs, he worked on the stout piers upon which they would rest.

"Watanabe-san," Sammy called as he emerged from under the building covered in sweat and red gritty volcanic dust, "we are ready to begin putting in the beams. Will you be ready soon?"

"*Hai* Soshi. First you must place the short planks in the space you cleared every two arm lengths. Then measure the distance from the floor to the plank. I will cut supports to the measure."

By the time Thomas Sakai returned on the train, all the piers had been set and nailed in place and Watanabe and Sammy were directing the placement of the final stringer stretching to the last pier. One of them called out from under the building when the board had been set, and immediately a worker inside pounded the last few nails. Wearily, he stood up and surveyed the completed work before him. From the inside there was almost no evidence save the shiny nail heads in the flooring, but when he walked, it was on a firm floor that did not sag. Outside, the two men emerged from the crawl space, and though tired and dirty, they smiled at one another and headed for the crowd that had surrounded Thomas as he stood near the train.

Actually it was relatively easy to remove the makeshift cisterns, the men simply used the rope and lashed them firmly one at a time to two long surplus staves left from the construction project and carried them to the side of the building, easing them down gently. One of the men traded the carpenter from the train two Japanese coins and a hand-carved ivory cigarette holder for a hammer, and the top was carefully removed from one of the barrels.

The first water, smelling faintly of molasses, went to the cook so he could start the rice. Then each man drank his fill, some greedily, others savoring every drop. It had been twelve hours' work in the sun since their last water and some men had been overcome with exhaustion. Their friends tended to these few. A third of a barrel of water was placed in a big black cast iron kettle found under the copra and a fire was set underneath. From this, each took his turn to wash and clean himself. It was not a proper *yokujou*, but until they could figure out how to build a hot bathing tub, it would have to do.

In the failing light of a Maui sunset, most of the men munched on rice and pickled vegetables, alone with their thoughts. The copra mattresses were arranged on the floor, the iron bed frames with the foreign springs were ignored by men who had slept on the ground all their lives. Men were leaning against trees sitting in a small group around a guttering campfire or shaping mattresses for comfort as the warm tropical breezes caressed the new settlers. Some thought longingly about the home islands, others about families, friends and girls left behind. Thomas thought about tomorrow until he finally drifted off to sleep, his body still believing it was swaying in the gentle swells of the Pacific.

"Kouin ya no gotoshi"

Time, like an arrow, flies fast

Japanese Proverb

It had been three years since Sammy had first stepped off the train in the bright Hawaiian morning sun. Now, along with his coworkers, he did so again striking off in the direction his day's labor would take him. He carried a small can of coal oil and in his pocket a tin with stick matches. Today was burning day in these fields. Smiling his broad smile he waved cheerfully to a dour luna directing the efforts of another group. The luna glowered at him briefly before returning his attention to some unfortunate worker falling behind the others.

"Sammy-san!" Thomas called out from behind, "don't lose your head among the clouds!" Thomas knew well his friend's predilection for daydreaming during the long hours of work.

"No, Shichou Thomas, I will be back before your canteen is dry!"

Sammy made his way about half a mile to the edge of the upwind corner of the field. As he had done dozens of times in the past he studied the sky, noting dark thunderheads coming in from the northwest. The wind was normal but rain was not common this time of year. He waited while others positioned themselves to start the fire. In the distance he could see the luna moving workers upwind and mentally calculated the rate at which the flames would burn. As he waited, a mist began to fall, lightly at first, then becoming a heavy downpour, soaking him to the skin in moments. These cloudbursts rarely interrupted work because they came and went so quickly and the blazing tropical sun dried everything in minutes.

Finally after waiting about twenty minutes, Sammy saw smoke curling up from several locations in the field. The downwind firebreaks had been started; that was his cue to begin. Taking his little can of fuel; Sammy made his way into the cane stalks about fifteen feet and poured a small amount on the crop. He struck a match and touched his incendiary to life. An oily orange-yellow flame immediately began producing dense black smoke. He moved about fifty feet further into the sweet grass and set another and repeated this several more times.

Unlike others he had set, these were slow to take off. The rain dampened the cane so it burned slowly and the wind had slackened and began to swirl aimlessly. Sammy tried to make his way out of the field, but it seemed everywhere he turned was choked with dense gray-black smoke. His instincts told him to work his way away from the heat and circle toward the clearing in the adjacent field, but he couldn't find the edge, and was becoming disoriented.

After some hesitancy the tinder dry section began to shed the moisture and the wind sprang up again from the northwest. By this time, Sammy was hopelessly lost in the fields. Suddenly the little starter blazes sprang to ferocious life and burned with menacing intensity. They raced together creating a single immense wall of red and yellow cutting off any escape and bearing down on the terrified worker as he scrambled helplessly through the dense growth.

Sammy could feel the fury of the heat on his back as the fire raced toward him. He was swiftly overtaken flames lapping at his legs. Cinders and red hot ashes rained down on his head setting his clothing afire.

His tortured screams of anguish could be heard across the distance by dozens of helpless workers. Immediately everyone began running toward the sounds of his screaming, risking their own lives to enter the smoldering stalks to search for the missing man. When they finally found him moaning and horribly burned, he was rushed back to camp on the train with Thomas refusing to leave his side. Stubbornly he clung to life for hours as Doctor Davidson was summoned from Lahaina.

Upon arrival the doctor made a brief examination and took Thomas aside to deliver the news: "Thomas, I am sorry, but your friend will not live through the night."

"Is there nothing to be done?" Thomas asked the question even though in his heart he already knew the answer.

"No, Thomas, he will not survive." the Doctor said. "But I can end his suffering. It would be the humane thing to do."

"I understand, Doctor. I will speak to my friend."

Thomas knelt at the bedside of his friend trying to remain stoic, but his voice faltered as he whispered in Sammy's ear, "Sammy-san, it is Toshio."

Through his agony Sammy managed an uneven smile for Thomas, his eyes yet bright even as he faced his own death. "I am undone, Thomas my old friend."

"The doctor says you will meet your ancestors this day."

Davidson prepared an injection of laudanum and cocaine and Thomas leaned over to hear a whisper.

"I will miss you, Toshio-san," Sammy whispered. "*Rakka eda ni kaeraza.*"

"I will miss you too, Soshi-san." Thomas's eyes brimmed with tears. "Please to go peacefully to join your ancestors." The doctor injected the solution into Sammy's veins.

"Goodbye, my friend," he whispered to Thomas with his last breath.

Thomas gently touched his friend's forehead with his hand and then stood, the tears now streaming down his face, his body racked with sobs.

The doctor stood by silently. Witnessing similar events many times in his career never quite removed the sting of the moment. Finally he asked quietly, "Thomas, what was it he said to you at the last?"

Choked with emotion Thomas replied, "The fallen blossom does not return to the branch. It means what is done is done, don't cry over me."

It was a great blow to Thomas to lose his best friend and most able helper and he mourned his friend, refusing food or to return to the fields. Even the lunas left Thomas alone, for in truth they too missed Sammy's broad smile. On the fourth day everyone in Labor Camp 14 was given the day off without penalty for his funeral. In the Buddhist tradition, Thomas cooked the first meal and served it, then made and started the pyre upon which his friend rested. Hours later when it had burned itself out, he used his best chopsticks to collect the bone fragments. He would pass each bone to the chopsticks of a member of the camp, who in turn would pass it to the next, until the last man would place it in an urn. Thomas then served a second meal and collected the small honorariums due from each guest. On behalf of Sammy's family he gave each guest a scroll with a favorite poem he had transcribed as a token of remembrance.

After he finished the day long ceremony, he wrote a letter to the family. With it he sent the money Sammy had saved, the urn containing his bones, the honorariums collected, and two poems Soshi had written. He saved one poem and a drawing for himself. For thirty-five days, incense was burned continuously and Sammy's name was never again spoken out of respect for the dead. Thomas would recall his old friend many times in the years to come and always he remembered how fond he was of his grin.

"I no nakano kawazu taikai wo shirazu"

A frog in the well knows not the great ocean

Japanese Proverb

Social and economic change raged around the isolated workers of Camp 14. Conflict increased between the Hawaiian Royal Family, wealthy and influential haole growers and merchants (called the "missionary men" with contempt by the Hawaiian natives) and American businessmen all sought to manipulate the government so they could further control the economy.

Purposely segregated by the plantation owners, the Japanese workers were mostly unaware of the struggle by Chinese and Filipino workers on other islands and the fierce debate arising from the overheated politics of the tiny kingdom.

Eventually the men of Labor Camp 14 built their hot-bath tub, grew their own vegetables, fell into a routine of pitiless grinding physical work as a group and relaxed or entertained their own private indulgences in off hours. Some would frequent brothels and waste their money on *sake* and gambling. Others became merchants, artisans and gardeners as their contracts expired and they invested their savings. A few returned to Japan homesick, lovesick, or both and some moved on to California.

Watanabe found himself carving decorative furniture and *objets d'art* for rich merchants' wives long before his field contract had expired, and now he had his own shop, carving, ironically, dragons and other icons for Chinese customers.

One day, Gustav sought out Thomas to talk. By now Thomas spoke passable English, a bit of pidgin and even a few words of German. Gustav had improved his Japanese, and between them conversations would flow in an odd amalgam of four languages.

"Thomas-san, there is much sickness on the other islands."

"Sickness?"

"Yes, Thomas, cholera."

Thomas shivered as he recalled the tales of horror he had heard as a child of the deadly white man's disease sweeping across entire villages in his homeland, decimating young and old alike. The memory of the vivid descriptions of corpses piled into enormous funeral pyres struck fear deep into his heart.

"What must we do, Luna Gustav?"

"Dr. Davidson says we must clean the work camps and clean up Lahaina. Master Whitehead wants all the workers to clean the camps today and kill rats and burn them. Then tomorrow everyone will come to Lahaina instead of the fields and we will clean the refinery and the streets."

"I will bring the men back to camp as soon as the train returns," Thomas said. "How shall we catch the rats?"

"The doctor says not to touch them. The train will bring tools for everyone to use." Gustav paused before continuing. "This is very important, Thomas. Don't become ill. You are important to your friends."

"Thank you, Luna Gustav, I will stay healthy and so will my friends."

When the *Ko oko O* reappeared, Thomas and the rest of the workforce returned to their camp. Armed with long sticks with nails pounded into one end they searched throughout the building and surrounding grounds killing any vermin they could corner. Any garbage that would burn was piled in the center of the compound yard and set alight. The few Norwegian browns they killed were tossed on the fire, but most of the varmints simply disappeared into the dense growth of sugar cane surrounding the camp.

The next day, an army of field workers descended on Lahaina armed with their makeshift spears prepared to do battle with rats and garbage. This alarmed many of the citizens for fear of insurrection, especially when the workers began to invade the yards of every residence and business in their zealous quest for rodents. The anxiety began to abate when Lunas could be seen directing the efforts of the workers and government doctor, Charles Davidson, explained the prevention methods he was employing to ward off the cholera.

By the end of the night, fires of burning garbage and rats dotted the little community from one end to the other. These measures and the suppression of any cargo being landed on the wharves of Maui provided victory. Not a single case of cholera was reported on Maui in 1895.

"Less haste, more speed"
Japanese Proverb

As he hurried down the spotless corridor of the Tokyo Imperial Palace, Oishi Akagi grappled with his problem. For years, Akagi's father, bidden by the invisible manipulators of the crown, had been propping up the right hand of Emperor Mutsuhito, who dubbed his reign *Meiji,* the enlightened rule. Akagi recalled in his childhood when former President Grant winked at him in the palace garden, having unwittingly put his executive imprimatur on the new constitution. Modeled on the Prussian example, the document given to the citizens granted them no real power and retained a final veto power for the Emperor in all matters he chose to consider. After little debate, and no real consideration by the Imperial Deity, his 'advisors' presented their new political canon. It granted the Emperor, like the Kaiser, ultimate royal authority. In truth the new Japanese version granted no real power to anyone but the Emperor. It was noted that the German and Japanese people shared similar traits, not the least of which was a culture that respected hierarchy and expected orders to be followed without question. It was the orderly modern way to run a government, but more to the point, it left governance in the hands of the throne, ergo the *zaibatsu* houses that had always retained power.

In the end, the Emperor had been a feeble, dissipated old man. His friend and confidante, Ito Hirobumi, who had written the new constitution, became the first Prime Minister. Then he was forced from office as the shifting tides of power had drifted toward a different shore. The 'Elder Statesmen' of Kyushu, led by the 'Three Heroes' had been more powerful and in political leadership for years, but militarists and nationalists were asserting their jingoistic rhetoric. Now they were pinching off the avenues of power long held by others. Succeeding his father in the royal court, Akagi now served as the go-between. When the time came, Oishi would send his own son into the world to be his eyes and ears in the United States.

Eventually this Emperor too would be supplanted by treachery, murder or enfeeblement as had all his predecessors. What was important was that the Oishi line would continue its powerful role. When his son reached adulthood he would travel along the entire West Coast to learn about agricultural advances. For now, though, it was enough that he assuaged, advised and occupied the ego of the deity currently occupying the Chrysanthemum Throne. Though increasingly difficult, he was also lubricating the wheels of practical administration.

Akagi in his own way had quietly prepared the path for the Emperor Taisho Yoshihito for several years, but was now uneasy with the powerful military man Aritomo Yamagata. Yamagata had been instrumental in bending the Emperor to create an Imperial Rescript establishing the newly modeled constitution and as a hero of the Japan-Quing War wielded outsized influence in the palace. The canny soldier was portraying the new royal leader as a drunken buffoon. It was not true, of course, but even so, the narrow path winding between the Imperial Court, elders who counted General Arimoto among their members, and an increasingly belligerent military was growing fraught with peril. Manchurian army officers, manipulated by generals and princes and goaded by greed at the plunder of China, arrogantly ignored orders from senior officers in Tokyo, and military high commanders began to demand more Imperial territory.

Oishi was worried; already Japan's armed forces had defeated the Chinese dragon in a war for the Korean peninsula. Now a sly Russian bear was fixing a gaze on Port Arthur in China while dragging a reluctant France and Germany into a power play to force Japan to return the Liantung Peninsula to China. Japan had been forced to retreat, but managed to forge a treaty with reparations from the Chinese that actually made the war profitable. Still, the army maintained a presence in Korea to ensure Chinese payments would continue.

Relations with the United States were increasingly strained too, as Washington sought to reverse Japanese gains on the Asian mainland. They began militarizing islands in the Pacific far from the shores of America, ostensibly for a war with Spain but, Oishi suspected, for designs reaching much farther than that. His task of being the lubricant was increasingly dangerous, and it was nearing the time he would have to choose between the old guard and the Emperor. The *genro* had executed an ambitious plan of modernization for the last forty years, but it was the Army ultimately that had consumed an alarming portion of the national budget. The military was increasingly arrogant and suspicious with regard to those with imperial connections. *Such a change is not without risk, but failing to change could also bring disaster*, he thought.

Whitehead Sugar Plantation

Maui, Kingdom of Hawaii

Buddhist monks would occasionally appear as representatives of the Emperor. They would give impassioned patriotic speeches enjoining the laborers to send money back with them to help the Emperor defend the home islands. The monks would recount the difficulties in China in florid detail, not the least of which was the problem of the Russians building a great railway from Moscow to Vladivostok with a long spur from Manchuria to Port Arthur: The object of which, from the Imperial viewpoint, was to threaten Japanese interests and gain control of the vital Korean Peninsula. Grave threats to the brave men of the Imperial army, as they held off invading hordes threatening the ancestral home islands were often a centerpiece of their commentary and a compelling case was urgently made for building another warship. And although they had never heard of many of the problem areas, some of the men, overwrought with patriotic fervor, often gave all or most of their money to these itinerants. Thomas never spoke either for or against Japan and always contributed a token amount so as not to appear unpatriotic.

Privately, he wondered why money should be sent to support a regent that had done nothing to intervene on behalf of beleaguered countrymen living in Hawaii. Many times Thomas had written entreaties to the Japanese ambassador in Honolulu to agitate in favor of workers being brutally exploited by growers. The envoy responded to each letter politely. An investigation was promised but never begun, and a formal protest was assured, but never lodged. This studious neglect slowly convinced Thomas he would never find the help he needed from his government. If he yearned for freedom, he would have to make it for himself somewhere else.

For years, planters had imported laborers from other countries to work the cane and pineapple fields. The New England descendants who owned almost everything had found the native population wanting in willingness to do back-breaking labor for almost nothing. Because of this, they began bringing in Chinese laborers. These people worked hard, complained little and tolerated living in abysmal conditions, keeping mostly to themselves.

When the Chinese began educating themselves to become merchants, lawyers and shop owners and had a sense of collective strength, they agitated for better wages and living conditions, greater opportunities for their children and more equality. In short, they wished to be citizens of their new homeland. Plantation owners responded by plotting an act by which they eventually overthrew the Hawaiian monarchy in favor of a lofty sounding Republic. In truth this was nothing more than an oligarchy of wealthy businessmen. Most of the "Missionary Men"—so called because they were descendants of the first New England Christian missionaries that settled the islands for the church—favored becoming a United States territory with the implicit promise of future statehood. They graced the Chinese protesters with slightly better wages and promptly brought in a flood of Filipino workers who would work for lower wages in wretched conditions.

Thus the cycle repeated itself when the Japanese field hands were imported. They too toiled for low wages and endured the endemic of worldwide racism as reflected in the microcosm of Hawaiian culture and politics. Unlike many who had preceded them, some chose not to live in squalor. A few camps, however poor, were organized, fairly clean and well maintained.

Over the years men came and went from the camp, grew strong and prospered—or weakened and died. Young firebrands from other camps or plantations sneaked past lunas into Camp 14 and held clandestine labor rallies arousing anger at the racial disparity in wages paid field workers. Strikes were contemplated by workers. Lunas would assault organizers. Planters would make a few minor concessions. Mostly life continued largely unchanged.

Thomas Sakai was a well-respected *shichou*. For years now he had steered a middle course. He worked hard and was regarded as a fair and honest leader by his camp mates. Lunas knew they could count on him to keep men working through labor troubles, and they knew his word could be trusted. His name was even known among the plantation owners and his influence with Japanese labor was grudgingly respected and a little bit feared.

For himself, Thomas had always kept his goal in mind: Freedom! Four times a year he had sent modest amounts of money to his family along with short letters about his life in Hawaii. He had earned extra money writing letters for coworkers to friends and families in Japan, and as his pidgin and English skills improved, he even began simple translating for the Nippon merchants seeking to advertise to a wider customer base. Even-tempered, diligent, hardworking, sober, well-respected twenty five year old Thomas Sakai had saved the substantial sum of two thousand seven hundred sixty-three dollars and fourteen cents from his various efforts over the past seven years. On the twelfth day of September, in 1897, he decided it was time to take a wife.

On the surface this seemed simple enough. Find a suitable Japanese girl and court her in the traditional manner. After proper negotiations with the family he would marry her. However, in 1897 in Hawaii it was not so easy as that. Of every one hundred Japanese people, eighty were men. Of the remaining twenty, fifteen women were already married, two were betrothed, one would be a child, one would be too old and the one remaining would be pursued by sixty-five single Japanese men.

Being a practical man, Thomas concluded that the best way to obtain a bride would be to employ the services of a *nakahodo*. In preparation, Thomas went on his day off to a small tailor shop where he purchased some new clothes. He was careful to buy only what was needed: A properly fitting jacket and a shirt with a collar and a necktie. He borrowed a hat from Watanabe and got a real haircut from a man from Camp 6 that had opened a shop in Lahaina after his labor contract had expired. He took his new apparel (shoes and pants not needed for this purpose); a scroll he had made that said *"Shichou Thomas Sakai, Lahaina, Hawaii"* and went to the local photographer. He explained he wanted a photo of himself from the waist up in his new clothes and borrowed hat with the scroll visible and that he would need four prints.

When the photos were finished, Thomas negotiated with the photographer to trade the now unnecessary togs for his new portrait. He explained to the shutterbug that he could then rent them to Japanese men who could not afford such items. He assured him that with Thomas' referrals to the men in the camps, he could make all his investment back in a short time. He also suggested the photographer buy a hat for the ensemble and order a scroll with the subject's name in calligraphy in the photo. For a nominal fee, he said, he would even make the scrolls.

When he left the small shop to return Watanabe's hat, he had arranged for another source of income, left his new clothes behind, and would receive four pictures next week worth more than he had paid for the clothes.

After each working day during the week while waiting for the photos, Shichou Sakai composed a letter to send home. In it he made arrangement for directing money to the go-between, the *nakahodo,* his family would employ in his behalf. He also informed Gustav that when he was notified his picture bride was on her way, he would be moving out of Camp 14 and into Lahaina. He expected this would be in about eight to ten months. He further explained that when his current contract expired in 1899, he would likely not renew for another term.

Gustav understood, and in fact had planned to move on as well. Over the years, the two men had come to an understanding; while not exactly friends they had come to respect one another. After the first few months, Gustav let it be known that no luna was allowed to discipline or touch any worker from Camp 14. Thomas handled misconduct. Lunas would explain the problem and discipline—if deemed justified—was meted out. The *shichou* was uniformly fair; never punitive and never corporal. Punishment was usually extra duties around the camp or the loss of a privilege such as the hot bath. The worst that could happen was banishment from the camp, and no one wanted that.

However Spartan—harsh even—the conditions in Camp 14 were, it was uniformly worse in every other camp. When Gustav and Thomas parted that day they both realized that the old ways on the plantations were almost over. The breezes of change were blowing across the islands like the trade winds that swept in from the north each season.

Village of Kawazu
Shizuoka Prefecture, Japan
October 23, 1897

"My son Toshio is a very important man in his village in Hawaii. He is very rich and sends his family money like a good Japanese son! Someday soon he will return home and will be respected even by the Emperor." Toshio's father, now the senior Sakai with the passing of his own father two years earlier, was boasting among the other senior men of the village.

"Sakai Toshio will not return here. Why should he?" The village blacksmith was challenging Sakai. "He is a rich man leading a life of leisure in a tropical paradise."

"He will return because he is a good Japanese son," Sakai reiterated.

"He will stay because he is a smart Japanese son," the smithy countered.

"I have another smart son at home," Sakai retorted. "And even a smart daughter going to school." He instantly regretted making such a public announcement, although he was secretly proud of his daughter. In spite of the Imperial Rescript making education of all children mandatory regardless of gender, most of the older generation, especially the men, found this an unsavory departure from tradition, certain to lead to future mischief.

"It is better for him to stay away," the *omawarisan* added, graciously ignoring the reference to Sakai's daughter. "If he came home, he would just be sent to the army and his money taken for the Emperor to build the navy," the village constable concluded. The forge glowed dull orange as the men stared at it pensively for a moment.

"Better he should be an important man living far away than another soldier at home," the blacksmith said simply. Hardly anyone ever spoke against the Emperor, for to be overheard by Yamagata's Secret Service spies would surely be considered fatally treasonous but these men were all friends and privately many agreed with the sentiment.

"He will come home," Sakai insisted stubbornly, but with less resolution in his voice.

From down the street a great hubbub could be heard moving toward the blacksmith shop. The constable drew himself up ready to quell the disturbance as it grew near, and suddenly the door was flung open and a young man of twenty burst inside.

"One thousand pardons, Nakamura-san, for this unseemly intrusion," he said bowing breathlessly to the blacksmith. "Great news from Toshio," he spoke to his father rapidly. "He has sent another letter!"

"*Hai*, there, you see," Sakai said to the group which now including many villagers who had followed the younger son to hear the news. "My son writes to say he is coming home."

"No, honorable father, he writes to say he wishes to take a wife!"

The astonishment on the face of the elder could not have been more complete if his second son had announced Toshio had become Emperor.

Lahaina Post Office
Maui, Republic of Hawaii
October 18, 1897

"So Thomas, sending more money home to your parents? You are a faithful son. Are you planning to return home?" The hawk-nosed questioner behind the counter squinted through wire rimmed glasses at the letter he had been presented.

"No, Mistah Jensen, I stay here in Hawaii at least till contract run out." Then, as an afterthought, he added, "I am sending money for a wife."

Mr. Jensen peered over the top of his glasses with raised eyebrows. "Really! Well, that's great news. Is this a girl you've known since childhood?"

"Oh, no, Mistah Jensen, my family will hire a *nakahodo* to find a suitable wife. I have told my father to choose a good family and my mother to teach her about keeping a proper house."

"A *nakohada*?" The postman looked at the letter addressed in both English and kanji.

"*Nakahodo*," Thomas corrected, "is woman who finds bride for young men."

"Ah, a matchmaker, an arranger," he said, placing three colorful stamps on the letter.

"Exactly so—she will bring several choices to my family. They will choose one or two and I will select my wife."

"So you *will* go back to Japan — for the wedding I mean." The clerk rubber-stamped the newly affixed postage and placed the letter in a bag marked "Honolulu."

"When the proper time comes, the priest will hold a ceremony in my village in Japan. After the wedding, my wife will live with my family for some months. Then she will come to live with me here. I will not go back to Japan."

"You mean, when your wife arrives here next spring or summer, you will have never met?"

"That is correct, Mistah Jensen. Of course I will send letters and a picture of myself, and she will send a picture of herself to me. She will be Japanese; she will know what is expected of her."

"But what about love, what about romance?" The question hung in the air like a smoke ring. After a long pause Thomas replied.

"Tradition and law different here. We will live together and work together. She will have many strong baby boys for me. Love will come with time."

"I suppose, Thomas. I suppose." Mr. Jensen was still shaking his head as his customer left. He had known Shichou Sakai for several years, posting his letters to home, sending responses with the sugar train on its run to the labor camps. He had affection for the laborer, not unlike the feelings a man might have for his pet dog.

Village of Kawazu
Shizuoka Prefecture, Japan
November 12, 1897

The village square had filled with people in spite of a cold drizzle and biting wind. Old women wrapped in winter *sho ru* peeked from under colorful umbrellas and gossiped among one another. Children ran about playing hide and seek or splashing in puddles only to be admonished by a parent or older sibling. Dead leaves skittered among the stones at the feet of passersby. A fishmonger, ever prepared to take advantage of a sales opportunity, had set up his cart at the edge of the crowd. The important men of the town stood with arms folded across their chests and waited patiently in positions of honor. Their wives and children held bamboo and painted paper umbrellas over their heads.

From around the corner came the procession. The elder Sakai was followed by his son, Tanazaka, and his wife, with his daughter bringing up the rear.

The *omawarisan* in addition to his negligible duties as Constable was also more or less the town Master of Ceremonies, presiding over gatherings such as these and as the entourage approached he was first to speak.

"So Sakai-san, this is an important day for our village. What has your important and rich son written this time?"

"He has written of his wishes for a bride. He has sent ten United States gold dollars for the *nakahodo*." There was a murmur that such an extravagant sum should be paid for the service. "He wishes for a beautiful wife that works hard and will grow boy babies."

"Hmmph," grumped an old farmer in the front row, "so did I." His unattractive wife of many years adjusted the umbrella over his head just slightly, sending a cascade of cold rainwater down his neck. The crowd laughed heartily and the man's face reddened with embarrassment and anger, but he said nothing further.

"Read the letter, son," the proud papa said.

The young man glanced at his sister, who in truth had done the reading of most of Toshio's letters at home. She shrugged blandly and he stepped into the small clearing left by the crowd pressing forward to hear. He cleared his throat and took the letter from the envelope with three stamps and ceremoniously opened the pages.

"Honored Father," he began reading nervously, "I am still well, living in Hawaii. Where you are at home I am sure it is cold and rainy now, but here the days are warm. The wind blows more strongly this time of year.

I am desiring a wife to come and live with me. Please arrange for a *nakahodo* to find a suitable match. The weather is pleasant and she will get used to the food. I am desiring of a wife who will not shun hard work. If she could read and do arithmetic it would be better, as those skills are highly prized here. She should be not frivolous or frail or ugly and should be strong and obedient. I am sending a picture of myself taken one month ago." Tanazaka paused for a moment then held the photo aloft for people to see before he resumed his reading.

"I am desiring of a picture of my bride so I may know her when she arrives. I am wishing you to tell the villagers that I pray for peace and prosperity to visit their homes. Your obedient son, Toshio."

The reader carefully refolded the letter and placed it back in the envelope, having omitted the parts that Toshio always included meant only for himself and his sister.

"We should go home now, before we all become frozen statues in the square," the Constable said after a moment of indecision and the crowd began to drift away.

"Sakai-san," the town tea merchant called out. "Jimmu has blessed me with three daughters who are strong. My oldest is nineteen and can read every page of the *Asahi Shinbum*. Please to have the *nakahodo* call upon my household."

"Just so, Hisaichi-san, I will do so." *So already the campaigning begins!* he thought. In the five hundred feet back to his home he was politely entreated no less than five times by fathers seeking consideration for their daughters and twice by old women seeking the ten dollar fee as the go-between. Finding a wife for Toshio was not going to be a problem.

In his carefully written letters over the years, Thomas had never really dwelt on the difficulties of adjusting to the racism, intolerance and grueling labor of the cane fields. Instead, he had described the wonder of the islands, new friends he had made, the exotic foods and mild climate. He alluded to occasional problems with workers and how he had solved them, but he had never characterized himself as any kind of leader. The money he sent quarterly had made a measurable difference in his family's lifestyle, but hardly enough, he thought, to be imagined important. *Shichou* had become an affectionate nickname over the years, an honorific really, not a formal title. He also had no idea that all his letters home were read aloud in the village.

Of all the young men that had left the village, mostly to join the army where social status was not a barrier to advancement, Thomas was the only one who wrote and sent money regularly. These things were not unnoticed by the elders, and by subtle unintentional misunderstanding and the assumption he was being overly modest, Toshio-san had risen to the level of rich and important in the estimation of his hometown. All this time he imagined himself exactly as he was: A frugal field laborer with a small talent for negotiation and a keen eye for a bargain. When the scroll and fine clothes in his photo confirmed his high status, the transformation was complete.

Thomas was seeking a wife to help him grow vegetables and children on a farm he was hoping to buy. His village was scrambling to find a suitable consort for a rich and influential leader in a Hawaiian city halfway across the Pacific Ocean.

Outside the Post Office

Lahaina, Maui
Republic of Hawaii
December 24, 1897

Thomas studied the photos before him very carefully. Along with a letter from three potential brides, his family had sent their pictures each made in the same studio seated on the same bench in front of the same *shoji* screen depicting cherry tree limbs. The young women stared out at Thomas from the photos wearing their best kimonos. All were attractive and all appeared strong.

Is this easy because they all seem so similar, or more difficult, he wondered. He read the letters in turn, occasionally peering closely at the accompanying photo of the correspondent. They all spoke demurely of honor and tradition and were uniformly hopeful of a new life in Hawaii expressing a desire to raise a family. All read and wrote Japanese, although one letter looked suspiciously like his sister's calligraphy. Two demonstrated simple arithmetic. One wrote haiku and had done so for him in her letter. One could also speak some English, having learned from a missionary some years before. *It is more difficult,* he concluded.

As he walked back down the shortcut by the refinery to the train, he heard a strange sound—strange because he had never heard western melodies sung in Japanese. As he listened he realized they were coming from the new church not far from the old mission. It was Christmas Eve so there was no work tomorrow. He understood it to be a religious holy day for the white men and their families on the islands. Many homes were decorated in a festive manner each year for this event, but he was uncertain of its significance. At any rate, he was drawn to the music and soon found himself standing outside the church near the front door.

In the seven years he had lived on Maui he had never entered a Christian church or a *haole* home by the front door, so he was startled when a Japanese man inside spied him listening to the music and came outside to invite him in. He started to resist but his curiosity got the better of him and he went inside to a back pew to listen. As he looked around Thomas saw all the congregants were also Japanese.

After the singing stopped, the congregation sat down as a man at the front of the church strode purposefully to the pulpit and placed his hands on either side. Reed thin and well over six feet tall, Pastor Ambrose Foster Pearson cut a curious and imposing figure. He was dressed in the traditional liturgical garb of a Presbyterian minister. His pale, sallow skin sharply contrasted with the simple black pulpit robe. A seasonal purple stole draped over his neck hung down either side of his chest. Even from the back of the church, his deep-set blue eyes seemed to pierce through to a person's soul as if he were God's interrogator on earth. His dark brown hair was combed straight back and showed a touch of gray at the temples.

"And Mary brought forth her firstborn son, and wrapped him in swaddling clothes, and laid him in a manger; because there was no room for them in the inn." Pastor Pearson's rich baritone easily filled the little church as he continued in Japanese.

"And there were in the same country shepherds abiding in the field, keeping watch over their flock by night. And, lo, the angel of the Lord came upon them, and the glory of the Lord shone round about them: and they were sore afraid. And the angel said unto them; Fear not, for behold, I bring you good tidings of great joy, which shall be to all people. For unto you is born this day in the city of David, a Savior, which is Christ the Lord."

Thomas sat transfixed by this man. Never had he heard a white person speak so eloquently in his native tongue, nor had he ever heard this particular story.

The Seattle-born missionary continued recounting the story of the birth of Christ as written in the second chapter of the Gospel according to the physician Luke. He spoke of angels and shepherds, wise men with gifts and a duplicitous and venal king. The preacher told of an infant sent by God to save mankind. For over an hour he recited the story of Christmas, never once referring to the book open before him or breaking the gaze of the assembled congregation. When he had finished, the group arose once again to sing more hymns, then heard a prayer and an admonition to leave the church with the spirit of the season in their hearts and bearing no ill will to any man.

As he rode the train back to Camp 14, he pondered the photos and the letters. One of these women would be his wife soon, but how to choose. And what did the words of the preacher mean to him? It was a restless night for Thomas Sakai, and Christmas Day came and went in a quiet but indecisive way.

Parlor of the Mercantile Club
Honolulu, Oahu
Republic of Hawaii
January 5, 1898

"The annexation isn't moving fast enough, Isaac. The treaty is stalled in the Senate and doesn't even figure to come to the floor out of committee. We're going to have to push harder, a lot harder—and soon, too," James Templeton said as he exhaled a cloud of blue smoke from the cigar clamped between his teeth. Templeton was a short, rotund man with political ambitions and a sugar fortune to protect.

"Look, Jim, I agree with you, but the timing on this is delicate. Remember that with territorial status comes United States law, and while that certainly will be good for fending off ambitious European governments, it may be a disaster for us on our labor contracts." Isaac Newton, a principal investor in a pineapple plantation and saddled by his father with the famous mathematician's name, sipped the brandy from a snifter in his left hand.

"Dammit man, sometimes you just have to bite the bullet! If we put this off too long, McKinley and Congress are going to get an earful from guys like James Kaulia. Did you read what he said to Senator Morgan? Listen to this..." Templeton took out his reading glasses and perched them perilously at the end of his nose. Clearing his throat, he referred to an old newspaper he held in his hand:

"*James Kaulia, President of the Hawaiian Patriotic League, in a rebuttal to visiting Senator Morgan of Alabama, Chairman of the*

Committee on Foreign Relations, stated, 'The destiny of Hawaii, situated in the mid-Pacific as she is, should be that of an independent nation and so she would be, were it not for the policy of greed which pervades the American Legislators and the spirit of cowardice which is in the breast of those who first consummated the theft of Hawaiian prestige.' My God, Isaac, he wants to return to the Monarchy, and if we don't do something pretty significant, he may well get it. And I know this too; a politician responds to voters, especially rich ones. We're rich and we would like to be voters but we have to be a territory first. This is a big risk to delay. Hell, we can work something out with the Japs. We'll talk to that guy on Maui who works for Jed."

Upon hearing his name, Jedediah Whitehead looked up from the *Harpers Illustrated* he had been reading.

"You mean Sakai. Thomas Sakai," Whitehead offered.

"Yeah, that's it," Templeton recalled. "The Mayor of Camp 14," he snorted. "We'll set him up with some money and a new title and see if he'll agitate for us with the Japanese."

"Don't underestimate these people, Jim," Isaac said. "They work hard and some of them are pretty smart with good instincts. When they recognize they are in a powerful position they will take advantage of it. The Chinese have already demonstrated that."

"Then it seems our job is to make sure they never figure that out, doesn't it?"

Whitehead, sitting on an oxblood-colored leather ottoman with his magazine, had been eavesdropping on the conversation. The bronzed muscular man, sporting an enormous mustache, was owner of three huge pineapple farms and two sugar plantations. He downed the whiskey he had been swirling in a glass and arose.

"You're a fool, Jim," he said. "Start saving cash now. Lots of it. When Hawaii becomes a U.S. Territory, and it will soon enough — all of our labor contracts will be subject to American law, which means they will be void. The Chinese Exclusion Act will apply and all those workers will suddenly be free to unionize, strike, demand higher wages—and probably most important, in a few short years they will figure out that they might become voters. Do you think they're going to vote for you? Tom Sakai might be the real Mayor of Lahaina before you get the chance to be Territorial Governor."

"The Japanese will control these islands someday," Isaac asserted.

"Maybe so," Jim confessed, "but not today, not tomorrow and not before statehood."

"You're a fool," the owner reiterated. "Take my advice, sell your plantation while you can and move back to California. Be a rich Senator and forget about Hawaii." Putting his glass down on the sideboard he nodded to Isaac, arose, and walked out of the room.

"Drink your brandy, Isaac," Jim said after a moment. "Jed has always been an alarmist. Everything will turn out fine."

"He has also been correct every time," Isaac observed dryly, draining his snifter.

Labor Camp 14
Maui, Republic of Hawaii
February 7, 1898

In the fading light of a Hawaiian sunset, Thomas lay on his copra mattress atop the iron bed frame and springs he and most of his coworkers began using to adapt to western ways. When it was discovered the biting black centipedes couldn't climb the frames, the adaptation proceeded with alacrity. The flickering yellow light of the oil lamps made the sepia-toned face staring back at him from the photo appear to glow.

His wife (or at least she would be, after his latest letter reached home) sat modestly in the picture looking directly into the camera. It created the illusion that her eyes followed his from every angle. He could not say why he had chosen this particular girl. Perhaps it was the bit of English she said she spoke—that would certainly be useful here—or maybe it was the elegance of her calligraphy. Thomas was by now pretty good at writing and reading English but possibly she could take over this task of aiding illiterates who wished to write home in Japanese. He enjoyed the notion of being envied by his camp mates, for Moriko, as seen in the photograph was by consensus uncommonly beautiful.

While his thoughts wandered, Thomas absently noted the everyday sounds of camp life. Occasionally the fire heating the hot bath would hiss and sizzle as one naked man would step out dripping water and the next in line would step in for his opportunity. Outside, in the near distance, the clucks, crows, honks and oinks made by the camp farm animals at feeding time mingled with the sharp rap of *goh* stones on a tabletop playing board. This would be followed by jovial shouting and imprecations as the combatants were alternately praised and pilloried by competing kibitzers gathered around. With the winds soughing through the trees and cane fields, it made for an impromptu concerto featuring an unlikely natural orchestra.

"Thomas-san?" it was Morimoto, a young man just about to finish his first contract.

"Yes, what is it?" Thomas sounded a trifle irritated at the disturbance.

"Thomas-san, is it true you will leave the camp when your new wife arrives?"

"Yes Mori, camp is no place for a young bride. Where would she sleep? Where would she clean herself? How could she make a proper household?"

"But Thomas-san, we cannot all leave the camps. Most of us are not rich like you are. What shall we do?"

"Do about what?" Thomas asked absently.

"Our picture brides," Morimoto stated simply.

Thomas regarded the man blankly for a moment; then the import of what he said began to sink in. He had lost track of the number of scrolls he had provided the photographer for men seeking wives from Japan and realized he served only one photographer on a small island. *Tsunami!* He thought; *a tidal wave of new brides coming from Japan!*

"I don't know," Thomas stated honestly. "But I shall discuss the matter with Gustav tomorrow." Then, as an afterthought: "How many wives are coming?"

"Eleven this year for this camp not counting yours." Morimoto turned to leave. "Thank you, Shichou Thomas. I will tell the others," he said and walked outside to discuss the matter further with his friends.

The haoles won't spend the money for new houses. Not with so many talking of strikes for higher wages, Thomas mused. He thought about how he might inform Gustav tomorrow and finally drifted off to an uneasy sleep filled with dreams of what feelings he would try to convey to his new wife when they met for the first time.

Sakai had followed the same workday morning ritual for nearly eight years. Arising at 4:30 a.m. he would answer the call of nature, then dress in his work clothes for the day. He had three sets of clothes. Two were for work and one for occasions when he would go to Lahaina on business. Each night after the hot baths were finished, he would wash the clothes he had worn that day and hang them to dry from a rope strung between the barracks and the lone palm tree in the camp. Then he would eat a hearty breakfast of rice and fruit with a small piece of meat or fish. He would drink a small pot of tea. He had also acquired a taste for coconut water which he indulged whenever he could.

After eating, he turned his attention to whatever calligraphy the photographer had ordered. As the rest of the camp stirred, he would write letters to his family and for a small fee write home for other men in the camp who could not do so for themselves. If any important letters or news had arrived he would open them and read. By 5:45 a.m., he was finished. The last thing he did was wrap some rice and pork in a ti leaf and fill his canteen. Then he walked up the small slope where he met the train that would take him and his fellow camp mates to the field for the day.

This morning's routine had varied little from others and from all outward signs there was no evidence that anything was the least bit unusual about this day. The truth was different for Shichou Thomas, however. He was agitated after a restless night of fretful dreams and wondering about his conference regarding the flood of wives about to hit the islands. Gustav had risen from luna to Plantation Manager over the years but had uncharacteristically protected Thomas and his Camp 14 coworkers from other lunas. In return, Sakai had reluctantly assumed tacit management of an orderly camp and acted as an intermediary in disputes among Japanese laborers from most of the camps on Maui. Their relationship had benefited all parties for several years, making life for this camp the exception rather than the rule. Virtually every other camp throughout the islands had foreign overseers and squalid, fetid living conditions.

The field labor was equally harsh and most of the contract toilers resented the conditions and the low pay. Thomas' camp was relatively tidy and well kept, mostly peaceful and enjoyed a slightly higher living standard because of the negotiations and small favors traded back and forth between him and Gustav. It had also made possible profitable side work for Thomas without interference, and small 'bonuses' quietly added to his pay for using his persuasiveness in keeping field hands mollified.

Recently though, events seemed to spin farther from the control Thomas had enjoyed. Challenges to his unofficial authority were becoming more frequent and harder to fend off peaceably. There was disgruntlement in the air from the workers and harsher rhetoric coming from the plantation owners. The *Pacific Commercial Advertiser,* the unofficial Honolulu newspaper of the sugar cartel, carried more stories about competition from the mainland and other tropical regions.

Pineapple growers had been beset with crippling blights. Stories circulated of beet growers in the United States complaining about how imported produce, specifically Hawaiian sugar, was depressing the market. There was discussion about cane sugar being more pure or sweeter or better tasting, but the truth seemed to be that there wasn't much difference except cost. Cheaper to produce, cheaper to transport, and most important, the sugar beet farmers in the United States were actively lobbying Congress for protectionist tariffs and Members were listening.

Into this volatile mix of unrest, sharp debate about annexation and territorial status for the Republic of Hawaii, ethnic conflict and declining profitability for growers, Thomas was about to inject the influence of an influx of Japanese picture brides. This would swell the demand for separate new households with children—lots of children most likely.

When the diminutive Baldwin Locomotive discharged its riders at the designated field for the day, Thomas, for the first time in months, stayed aboard. He rode with the engineer and fed coal to the firebox so he would still earn his pay as he rode around the line to the front of the plantation mansion. The train slowed and he stepped off onto a grassy apron that served as an informal platform. He stood for a moment staring at the grand structure in the distance with the fountains and a swarm of gardeners attending to carefully manicured grounds.

He removed his hat, took a deep breath and exhaled slowly. Looking back down the track, he saw the last of the cars rounding a bend to disappear into the swaying green oceans of cane. Thomas sighed and began the walk toward the main house, a manifestly worried man.

Parlor of the Mercantile Club
Honolulu, Oahu
Republic of Hawaii,
February 23, 1898

"Well, the fat's in the fire now for certain!" Isaac Newton was reading a week-old account of the sinking of the U.S. battleship *Maine* in Havana harbor. The *San Francisco Examiner* contained a lurid account of the tremendous explosion and the loss of 266 American sailors. The Hearst newspaper suggested sabotage by the Spanish and editorialized with calculation to do two things: Increase circulation and inflame the American people, in that order. "McKinley will have to do something pretty dramatic after this."

"War, I should think. What else makes any sense?" A pensive Templeton contemplated the chessboard situated between himself and Newton. "You can't have some third-rate power like Spain sinking our ships without any consequence."

"I hesitate to point out that technically they aren't really *our* ships just yet. We are still the *Republic* of Hawaii for the time being." Newton moved his black knight.

Templeton picked up a pawn and was about to execute an *en passant* on the board when a small smile played over his face. "Isaac, my friend, Spain may have just become the architect of territorial status for our islands." He completed the move now threatening a bishop.

"How so?"

"By demonstrating what a dangerous world it is for tiny little countries isolated in the middle of huge oceans. I can hear the debate now," he said, lowering his voice to a stentorian baritone and proceeding in a slow speech-making cadence, "Mr. Speaker, in the defense of freedom for all peace loving countries we must come to the aid of little Cuba. We have no ambitions of global empire, but neither can we sit idly by while one-by-one, defenseless people worldwide succumb to the threat of imperial expansion. Let us together be reasonable, friends, and bring under our strong eagle's wings the little fledglings of democracy floating freely in the oceans."

"Do you suppose McKinley might be tempted to send out the fleet?" Isaac asked as he imperiled Templeton's queen.

"Not doing so would be political suicide without Spanish capitulation, and patience is not an American virtue." Jim slashed his bishop, capturing an errant rook. "Check," he said. "He'll send out the fleet after diplomatic niceties are observed. Count on it."

"Then what?" Isaac asked, interposing a knight. "Where are we in all this?"

"Spain loses a short war and is forced to sign an unfavorable treaty. To the victors go the spoils. You watch; he'll end up with the Philippines, Guam, Wake Island, Puerto Rico, probably Cuba and poor little Hawaii." Templeton moved his queen down a rank capturing a pawn. "Checkmate."

Newton tipped over his king and made a note to start buying land around Pearl—lots of coal, too. *The fleet will need both,* he thought, *who better to supply it?*

**Executive Building
(Formerly Iolani Palace)**

*Honolulu, Oahu,
Republic of Hawaii
March 8, 1898*

"Under 'Old Business,' gentlemen, you will note the first item is a request made early last month by Consul General Haywood, representing the United States, for the use of property near Pearl Harbor for the storage of coal." Sanford P. Dole paused. After a moment of silence he prompted, "Well, is there any discussion?"

"Mister President," Jed Whitehead attracted the Chair's attention, "since we are honored with the presence of Consul Haywood, perhaps it would be useful to hear from Bill exactly why the U.S. wants to store coal."

"Oh, for Heaven's sake, Jed," Templeton said with exasperation from the other end of the table, "there's going to be war with Spain and the Navy wants a coaling station for the fleet in the Pacific. Good grief, man, it's just the opportunity we've been looking for."

"You've been looking for," Jed corrected. "Nonetheless, it hardly seems unreasonable to hear it from the requesting party. Mr. President?"

"No, no, or course not. Bill, if you don't mind, perhaps you could explain exactly what the United States has in mind."

"Well, to put not too fine a point on it, Jim summed it up pretty well," Haywood said. "President McKinley has already put the Navy and Army on a preparation for war footing, and the Secretary of

War believes it prudent to have a mid-Pacific coaling station for the American Asiatic Fleet." Bill Hayward continued, "There is concern that Spain may back away from Cuba at the same time she steps up activity in the Philippines and may even make a grab for other islands, perhaps even Hawaii. With the build-up of the Japanese navy and its tensions with Russia, a forward port would leave our fleet in a better position to defend the western U.S. and put others on notice that these islands were off limits to expansionists."

"So, if we grant this additional access and war is declared between Spain and the United States," Whitehead asked, "how could we credibly maintain the assertion of neutrality?"

"That's a policy question, Jed, and I don't have the authority or frankly the desire to influence that," the Consul said. "The Republic of Hawaii must make that decision when the time comes. All I'm really here for is to get permission to lease a few acres for a coal pile. Beyond that I cannot go."

"Jed, we talked about this for most of the month," Josiah Hale put in. "If we support the U.S. now, it will most likely bust up the logjam in the Congress holding up our territorial status. Your position against becoming a territory is well known, but if the States end up with Cuba, Puerto Rico and the Philippines as territories and we are left out, our sugar business will dry up and blow away with the trades."

"McKinley is on record as a protectionist in favor of high tariffs," Templeton chimed in, "especially on imported items that compete with American producers. All that Caribbean sugar would suddenly be 'Made in the U.S.A.' If we miss this opportunity, we may as well plant taro and start getting used to eating poi on banana leaves. We'll all be broke in ten years."

"Look, Jed, if it will help this go down any easier, I'll make an informal canvass of folks around the island and get a feel for what they think we should do if war comes." Continuing, Sanford Dole—President of the Republic of Hawaii—urged reasonably, "It can't really hurt us to lease a few acres. If the Spanish fleet starts bombing Hilo or Lahaina, would it be a bad thing if the U.S. Navy fired back?"

"Bill, have you identified what property you would like to lease?" Jed knew when he was beaten but with bulldog tenacity he was determined to take it to the end.

"I have. There are four lots marked on the map on the wall there. Those would be just what we are looking for."

"Who owns those lots?" Jed asked.

"Actually, I do," said Isaac Newton. "I bought those lots last week. And the ten thousand tons of coal stored there, too."

"Good guess, Isaac," said a junior board member. A chuckle circulated around the room. "Get a hot tip somewhere?"

Isaac shrugged offhandedly with a quick sidelong glance at Templeton.

"The Chair will entertain a motion," said Dole. The resolution was passed unanimously with two abstentions: Isaac because he was a principal in the transaction and Jed because—in principle—he was opposed to the transaction but was smart enough not to say so on the record.

Village of Kawazu

Shizuoka Prefecture, Japan

8:00 a.m. March 9, 1898

Moriko entered the Shinto shrine dressed in a vintage white kimono painstakingly decorated with elaborate stitching and beads. The *obi* tied at her waist was a masterpiece of delicacy in design and embroidery and the new *zori* upon her feet clacked against the stone flooring of the temple. Her long black hair was done in a traditional upswept style, and an elaborate white headpiece secured it with beautiful lacquered bamboo combs. She was demurely radiant on her wedding day, a beauty by any standard as she arrived with her family to be seated.

Already present in the shrine was the family of Toshio Sakai. Papa Sakai was dressed in a worn but tidy black kimono bearing the recently acquired family crest, a visible symbol of the wealth they now enjoyed from Toshio's quarterly tithe, embroidered on the breast. Each other member of the family was dressed in his or her finest ceremonial clothing. Additionally, only the *nakahodo*, her husband and the Shinto priest were invited to the ceremony, as was the custom.

Beaming with pride, Hisaichi Gom brought his daughter forward. She knelt and bowed first to the priest then to Sakai and finally to her own father. The priest said a prayer, and then they all sat at a low table to continue the ceremony, Moriko in the center next to the photo of Thomas. A *miko* serving girl placed three sake cups stacked one upon the other before the bride who in turn sipped from the cups in the proper ceremonial fashion, offering each in its turn to the photo and then the elder Sakai who drank in proxy for his distant son. At the conclusion of the ritual, Hisaichi took on the new name of Sakai and was the proper bride of Shichou Thomas Sakai. For his part, Thomas was sweating, hard at work in a cane field several thousand miles away, ignorant of the moment.

After the wedding, the group departed for a banquet customarily served to honored guests. In this case the entire village was invited, so using money sent by Thomas combined with money from Moriko's father, a temporary pavilion had been hastily built in the town square and most of the women in town were cooking all day. There was great feasting, speech making and toasting to the union of the most beautiful girl in the village to its most important absentee citizen.

In Camp 14, Thomas and his twenty-seven workmates feasted sparingly on rice and chicken gizzards, boiled in cabbage broth and washed down with lukewarm rainwater smelling faintly of molasses.

The White House
Washington D.C.
March 26, 1898

"Good morning, Mr. President. I trust your breakfast was satisfactory."

"Yes Robert, it was just fine. What do we have today?"

"Spain sir," the presidential secretary replied, "followed by a gaggle of congressional members wishing to express their opinion before you do anything about the Spanish situation."

McKinley groaned. "Mr. Porter, kindly inform the assembling hordes that the President has exceeded his capacity for Congressional opinion for the duration of the century and instead will entertain only those members who have no opinions to express on any subject. I look forward to a morning of idle chitchat about rose gardening or horse grooming. But only if they have no opinion regarding how or when either should be done."

The secretary grinned wickedly. "Yes, sir, I shall see to it immediately. In the meantime, I have prepared your communique to the Spanish Consul. It is awaiting your signature on the desk." He became somber and asked, "This will mean war, won't it, sir?"

"Let's hope not, Robert. Spain can still back down. Back away from Cuba and the Philippines. But the Spanish are a proud people with a long heritage of sea power and colonialism, so we must be prepared for the worst." The President strode to the desk and opened the portfolio containing the document. He picked up the pen and dipped it in the inkwell on the desk. He signed the paper, blotted it and then brought it back to his secretary. "Send this by courier to the Spanish Embassy tomorrow and have it cabled to the Ambassador in Madrid today to be presented tomorrow. The deed is done. Give me fifteen minutes, and then begin sending in all the people to whom I must explain myself."

Lahaina Post Office
Maui, Republic of Hawaii
March 30, 1898

Thomas sat on a low coral block wall holding the unopened letter in his hands. It was clearly a packet containing much news because it was thick and had many stamps upon it. He had been sitting there holding the envelope for over half an hour, yet he could not bring himself to open it. What was inside was known to him (or at least guessed). He was married.

His new bride was living with his family at his ancestral home and would do so for several months before she was legally allowed to join him here in Maui. His mother would have her doing menial tasks to teach her proper humility; his father reminding her every day of how unworthy she was to be marrying his son. His brother sought to ignore her. *Now that I'm married, he is free to marry as well, and probably has a match in mind already.* Only his sister could show compassion. She would help his new wife adjust and pass the ensuing endurance test to follow. *Endurance will be an important lesson,* he thought, *for life is a long, hard struggle.*

"Good morning, Thomas."

Sakai looked up into the face of Reverend Ambrose Pearson.

"Good morning, Pastor," he replied.

"A letter from home, my son?"

"Yes, from my family."

"Well, I hope it is good news. It's always nice to have pleasant news from home."

"Yes, I am sure it is news that I am married, Father," Thomas said.

"You're not certain that's what is in there?" the Reverend asked.

"No."

"Well, for Heaven's sake man, open the letter! Find out! God favors marriage in very special ways. It is a cause for celebration and great rejoicing."

The exuberance of the tall missionary overcame Sakai's reluctance and he opened the packet carefully. He extracted several sheets of paper, and upon opening them, a photo fluttered to the ground at the feet of the minister. Pearson stooped over and scooped up the photo. Before handing it back to Thomas, he scrutinized it carefully.

"A handsome family and a radiant bride. *Houga, Thomas-san.*"

"You are most generous in your congratulations, Father. Thank you."

"I'm hopeful of seeing you in our church again, Thomas. In fact I have a gift for you." He reached into his pocket and withdrew a small volume. "These are the words of God as told to followers of Jesus Christ nearly two thousand years ago. There is much wisdom and peace within these pages. All people are the same standing before the throne of God, rich or poor, strong or weak, all races. All people are the children of Him. Don't search for peace or freedom on this earth, Thomas. It will elude you always. Place your faith in the one true God." The gaunt minister handed the book to Thomas. The red leather binding was stamped in kanji with the words "New Testament". "Read it, and I will answer any questions you have if I am able. I have marked a few passages which are especially important to Christians in the next couple of weeks. Read them, then ask me about the meaning of Easter."

The newlywed took the volume and arose. He bowed deeply to the frock-coated man who returned the bow.

Thank you, Pastor, I will read them as you ask. But I will read my letter from home first if you don't mind."

Reverend Pearson laughed as he walked away "By all means my son, by all means," he said. "Goodbye, Thomas, and congratulations once again. I hope to meet your wife when she arrives."

Sitting on the low wall once again, Thomas began reading his mail. The first letter was from his sister. In it she recounted in great detail the wedding ceremony and the celebration that followed. He thought it very unusual the entire village should be invited and odder still that a pavilion would be erected for the occasion. Perhaps his sister was mistaken. The pavilion was undoubtedly built for some other occasion and merely used as a convenience for the celebrants. The second letter was from his new wife Moriko.

Respected Husband Toshio,

Yesterday we were married in the Temple up the hill at the edge of the village. Our fathers were very proud and spoke loudly in praise of our new family union. Tomorrow I shall bring some of my belongings to my new home and begin to learn from your honored father and mother the traditions of your family.

When I come to Maui in a few months time I will prepare myself to be the respectful servant of my husband and to keep a proper household for a man of such high station. It is widely known in the village that I have been lucky to be matched with a rich and important shichou in a faraway place. I tremble that I may not be worthy of notice but I will work hard and learn from your family.

I would ask most humbly that you take some time from your important and busy work to write a letter to me once each month that describes what I will need when I arrive in October.

Your obedient wife,

Moriko

On the train back to the camp Thomas mulled over what he had read, and the more he thought about it the more unsettled he became. He couldn't be certain from one letter, but he suspected that somehow the people of the village of his ancestors had gotten the wrong notion about what it was he was doing in Hawaii. By the time he got back to his cot he could feel the walls closing in as he tried to imagine how he would paint an accurate picture of his life without bringing shame to his family. For the first time, he began to worry about the disparity between his reality and the village vision of heightened expectations.

DEWEY SMASHES SPAIN'S FLEET!

"You may fire when you are ready, Gridley."
Commodore commands
New York World *headline*
May 2, 1898

Captain Charles V. Gridley had spent most of the Battle of Manila Bay commanding the U.S.S. *Olympia* from inside the cramped armored control center. Stricken with dysentery and liver cancer, he shouldn't even have been aboard, much less acting as Captain. He was still in charge only because of his strong protests to Commodore Dewey when the latter had broached the subject of relieving him of command.

The tropical sun beat mercilessly on the exterior of his metal conning tower creating a tiny oven from which he directed the firing and maneuvers of *Olympia,* the flagship of Dewey's Asiatic fleet, currently raining death and destruction on the Spanish navy trapped in the harbor.

After the battle, when the fleet had retired some distance and communiques were being exchanged between Dewey and Spanish Commander Montojo, an exhausted and gravely ill Gridley slumped into a deck chair to pen a letter to his mother. Too weak to walk the thirty feet to his cabin for pen and ink, he wrote the following:

My Dear Mother,

Excuse pencil, but I am writing on the deck aft, under the awning, and ink is not handy. Well, we have won a splendid victory over the Spaniards. We left Hong Kong on April 25, Mirs Bay April 27 and arrived off Manila Bay at midnight on April 30. We steamed in with our lights all out, and by daylight we were off Manila, where we found the Spanish fleet, or rather, at Cavite, seven miles from Manila. We attacked them at once, the Olympia *leading, and, being flagship, she was of course the principal target, but we (our fleet) were too much for them, and after fighting two and a half hours, hauled off for breakfast, giving them another hour of it afterward. We succeeded in burning, sinking and destroying their entire force. They were also assisted by shore batteries. Their loss was very heavy, one ship, the* Castilla, *losing 130 killed, including the captain.*

And now as to ourselves; we did not lose a man in our whole fleet and had only six wounded, and none of them seriously. It seems a miracle. Everybody fought like heroes, as they are. The Olympia was struck seven or eight times, but only slightly injured, hardly worth speaking of.

Stickney, New York Herald *correspondent, and a former naval officer, was on board by permission of the department and acted during the battle as Dewey's secretary. His account in the* Herald *will be full and complete, so you had better get it. His reports will go in the same mail as this.*

We have cut the cable and can only communicate via Hong Kong. The McCullouch *will go over in a day or two, carrying Commodore Dewey's dispatches and this mail and bringing our mail I hope. I am truly thankful to our Heavenly Father for His protection during our battle and shall give Him daily thanks. Manila, of course, we have blockaded. We can't take the city, as we have no troops to hold it.*

Give my love to all and accept a large share for yourself.

Your loving son,

Charley

Gridley clung to command for three more weeks, grimly carrying out his duties, but clearly with increasing difficulty. Finally, Dewey would hear no more protests and released the ailing man from the burden of command. On May 25th, Gridley, whose name was now famous across America by virtue of the Commodore's imminently quotable order, was finally headed home. Lieutenant G.T. Tisdale recorded his impression of the moment in a journal entry:

He came up out of his cabin dressed in civilian clothes and was met by the Rear Admiral who extended him a most cordial hand. A look of troubled disappointment flitted across the Captain's brow, but vanished when he stepped to the head of the gangway and, looking over, saw not the launch but a twelve-oared cutter manned entirely by officers of the Olympia.

There were men in the boat who had not pulled a stroke for a quarter of a century. Old Glory was at the stern and a captain's silken coach whip at the bow; and when Captain Gridley, beloved alike by officers and men, entered the boat, it was up oars and all that, just as though they were common sailors who were to row him over to the Zafiro.

When he sat down upon the handsome boat cloth that was spread for him, he bowed his head and his hands hid his face as First Lieutenant Reese, acting Coxswain, ordered, "Shove off; out oars; give away!" Later in the day, the lookout on the bridge reported, "Zafiro under way, sir," and the deck officer passed on the word until a little twitter from Pat Murray's pipe brought all the other bos'ns around him, and in concert they sang out, "Stand by to man the rigging!"

Not the Olympia *alone, but every other ship in the squadron dressed and manned, and the last we ever saw of our dear Captain he was sitting on a chair out on the* Zafiro's *quarter deck apparently listening to the* Olympia's *old band play.*

Dewey, the hero of Manila Bay who had wrought vengeance on the Spanish for the *Maine* had been advanced to rear admiral and had recommended that Gridley be advanced on the promotions list by ten places. The six places his name was advanced still constituted substantial recognition for his leadership, but he would never know of it. *The Bounding Billow,* ship's newspaper for the *Olympia* ran the following article three weeks later:

Captain Charles V. Gridley

It is with indescribable sorrow and regret that we hear of the untimely death of our beloved Captain, Charles V. Gridley. He died on board the O. & O. steamer 'Coptic,' at Kobe, Japan, June 5th. Owing to a serious illness, he was ordered home on sick leave, taking with him the sincere respect and esteem of every man in the fleet. He left on the Zafiro, *escorted to sea by the* Concord, *amid the cheering of the entire fleet. He was taken to the steamer by a boat's crew of officers with First Lieutenant Reese acting as coxswain. The news of his death came like a thunder-bolt, filling our hearts with grief and pain. We respectfully extend our sincere sympathy to his relatives and friends.*

Gone a-head, to the Heav'nly land

Across the mighty River;

Gone to join the angel band:

Gained peace and joy forever.

A Letter
May 28, 1898

Dear Moriko-san,

Today I am writing on the 28th day of May. It was sunny and very warm today as I worked in the sugar cane field. I am very tired this evening and will take a long on'yoku before I sleep. I will wait till the others have had their baths so I may spend extra time in the water.

It is so warm here that the air dries me before I can even put on a yukata.

I have inquired in the town about renting a house where we might live but the haoles won't rent to Japanese. I am still inquiring and I am confident I will find a suitable house.

When you come to Hawaii you will not need ceremonial kimonos. I am sending money for you to buy American-style clothes. A woman's suit, hat and shoes and two dresses of moderate price and light weight would be proper. Please bring such other things as a woman should need that I do not know of. My friend Morimoto knows a merchant who buys from the Beniya Western Clothing Shop in Hikone in Shiga Prefecture. It would be a long train ride to get there and I think Tokyo is closer.

Before you get on the ship, visit an apothecary for herbs for seasickness. Bring a houchou knife in your bag as they are very expensive here.

My father is stern but he is fair and in time he will soften. Life here will be very different from Japan and I hope you will like living here for a while.

I have met a man who is a priest in the haole church in Lahaina. He speaks Japanese very well and tells me stories of a man called Jesus who lived two thousand years ago. This Jesus man was son of the white man's God but he was killed.

It is customary among the whites to speak the names of the dead without disrespect. To them his death was important, but I do not understand why. He says we should get married again when you get here to be protected by his God. We will talk about this when you arrive.

Please tell my father I am honoring our family name here. Tell my mother she is doing a good job preparing you to be my wife.

Please tell my brother I am filled with joy that he has found a girl to marry. Please tell my sister to study hard but to look for a husband.

Please write to me again.

Respectfully,

Your husband Toshio

Report of Ranking Naval Officer on Transfer Ceremonies (Abridged)

Pearl Harbor, Honolulu, Oahu
Territory of Hawaii, U.S.A.

U.S. FLAGSHIP PHILADELPHIA
Honolulu, Hawaiian Islands
August 14, 1898
Sir:

I have the honor to submit the following report on the participation of the forces under my command in the ceremonies attending the change in sovereignty of the Hawaiian Islands, which took place at noon on Friday the 12th instant:

The forces under arms from the Philadelphia *and* Mohican *attending the ceremonies consisted of four companies of infantry and two sections of artillery.*

The Hawaiian National Guard met our force at the landing and escorted them to the front of the executive building, where they took position in column on the driveway leading to the front of the building, the head of the column being close to the official stand.

The official stand was in front of the executive building, one side for the Hawaiian officials, the other for the United States minister and his attachés and the officers of the Navy and Army.

All the officials having been seated, a prayer was offered by the Reverend G. L. Pearson, of Honolulu. Minister Sewall then rose and addressing President Dole, formally communicated to him the text and purpose of the joint resolution of Congress annexing the Hawaiian Islands to the United States. President Dole then formally tendered the sovereignty of the islands, with all the public property of the Hawaiian Government, to the United States through our representative, Minister Sewall, who accepted it in the name of the United States Government. The actual ceremony of exchanging flags was then begun by the Hawaiian band playing "Hawaii Ponoi," the national anthem. Colors were sounded and a 21-gun salute was fired by the shore battery and by the Philadelphia and Mohican, after which the Hawaiian flag was slowly hauled down.

Colors again were sounded, the flagship band played the "Star-Spangled Banner" and the United States flag was slowly hoisted on the flagstaff of the central tower of the executive building. Twenty-one guns were fired by the Philadelphia and Mohican and the shore battery when the flag had reached the truck.

I am gratified to be able to report to the Department that the ceremonies throughout were a complete success in every particular, and were rendered very impressive and dignified by the simplicity and lack of ostentation of the carefully prepared program. The battalion from the two ships presented a fine appearance and it gives me great pleasure to congratulate the Department on the opportunity given the Navy to take such a prominent part in an important event in the history of our country.

Very respectfully,

J.N. Miller, Rear Admiral U. S. N.

Commander in Chief, Pacific Station

A Letter
August 31, 1898

Dear Toshio-san,

Last week, I went to Shimado and purchased second-class passage on the Shunyo Maru to Honolulu. It will depart from the dock at 10:00 a.m. on September 19th and arrive sometime on September 28th. Since your last letter, I have visited an herbalist in Shimado and purchased the items you requested. I also purchased a root to chew upon if I feel seasick. He tells me it works very well for most people but that it stains the teeth. I may make tea with it instead.

Your mother has been most patient with me, even when I am slow, and your brother tells me father Sakai boasts in the village about his oldest son's new bride. I blush when he tells me this as I am yet unworthy of praise. Your sister is most kind. She helps me in my chores and we study together writing and arithmetic. There is a missionary in the next village and sometimes I can try to speak some English from him. It is very difficult to learn but I am trying very hard.

Each day, I study your face in the picture you sent to our wedding so that I will know you when we meet in Honolulu.

My father says I will have many boy babies for you. My mother says grandfather said that about her, too, but he was wrong; I have two sisters instead. I am hopeful that our family will be large with many strong children.

Next month, I will begin to pack my belongings and the gifts the villagers wish to send to you. I will heed your advice and carry a small case with me and place the rest in a suitcase for storage. I will bring my ceremonial kimono to wear in case your friend Reverend Pearson wishes us to perform our wedding ritual for his God, too.

Your obedient wife,

Moriko

Thomas folded the letter and placed it carefully back in the envelope and then with the others she had written over the months. He looked at her photo again, marveling that the image had not been worn away by his simply staring for so long. He had studied it in great detail, examining the shape of her mouth. He knew where every strand of hair was placed, the kindness of her lovely almond eyes, her ears and chin and nose. Not coarse and broad and flat like so many, but small and in perfect proportion.

Time was running short now; he was yet to find a proper place, and since the annexation had been made official, there was much upheaval in the camps. Conflicting reports in the newspapers left workers uncertain about their status. Some believed their labor contracts were void and they were free to go. Lunas and plantation owners disagreed and times were very confusing; dangerous even. Angry shouts were heard every day among the men in the camps as disagreements erupted over the most trivial things, and Thomas had finally given up trying to mediate. For now, he contented himself with dreaming about his new wife and the freedom soon to come.

Aboard the *Shunyo Maru*

Four days outbound from Shimado
September 23, 1898

Moriko stood on deck sipping her tea. Looking out at the vast expanse of the Pacific, a shiver of fear and anticipation ran through her. Like Toshio, nearly a decade earlier, she had never been much farther than the next village, although new trains in Japan were beginning to make metropolitan areas more accessible. She tried to imagine what her new home would be like from the vague description in her husband's last letter. It was exciting to be finally going, but what kind of man would she find when she arrived? Would he be like his father, gruff and stern on the outside but proud and tender inside? Would his high status among his co-workers have placed an undue burden on his heart? How would he touch her? Tenderly, she hoped, like a flower, not hard like pulling out an old weed.

She was grateful the tea was working. Several of her picture-bride shipmates were overwhelmed with nausea and hadn't been out of their hammocks for more than twenty minutes in the last four days. The food was greasy, mostly fried by Chinese cooks hired in Shanghai, but it was edible and with only four girls to each second-class stateroom, it wasn't all that crowded. It was, however, hot, and each day it got hotter as they neared the Tropic of Cancer. *I will be home soon, my husband,* she thought as the ship sped through the deep blue waters toward Hawaii.

Railside Coal Shack
One mile outside Lahaina
Maui, Hawaii Territory, U.S.A.
September 27, 1898

With less than a week to go before his new bride arrived, Thomas was anxious to get going on fixing up the shack. After lengthy negotiations with Gustav, he had finally secured a promise that he could rent the abandoned shack for a modest payment. Now he stood facing the daunting task before him and felt discouraged.

The tiny building, which had held coal for the sugar trains, had fallen into disuse and disrepair since a second coal tender had been added. Rudely constructed to begin with and never intending to be inhabited by humans, the ramshackle structure seemed to peer back at Thomas, challenging his ingenuity. Merely ten feet by fifteen feet with three walls and no floor, it stood only ten feet from the tracks. No provision for sanitation was present, nor was a water source or even a tree. *I don't want to live here, how can I expect my bride to be satisfied?*

He sat on an old oil can pondering his first step when he heard the train in the distance coming from Lahaina. It would carry the supplies he had purchased; used lumber, an old door from a house being remodeled, a window with two broken panes and four sheets of corrugated tin for the roof. As the train neared, he sighed and got to his feet preparing to attempt the impossible.

Soon the *Ahi Alamihi* hove into view, sounding its whistle madly, with Watanabe waving to Thomas. On board were a dozen men from Lahaina and camps all over Maui. Reverend Pearson was aboard waving as well. When the train stopped, they swarmed over the sides carrying tools and materials. Watanabe began pointing toward the time worn shack then sending men to begin the complete remodel.

Thomas was dumbstruck. Men poured over the tiny structure to begin its reconstruction. Others began hacking at the ground preparing a place for a porch and floorboards. Reverend Pearson walked over to Thomas with a grin on his face, wielding a hammer and carrying a small cask of nails.

"Thomas-san, we heard you could use a little help," he said.

"How is this possible, Father?"

"It is possible because you have been a friend to everyone on this island. These are your friends, Thomas. People are trying to repay their debt of *on* to you for your kindness and hard work. Jedediah Whitehead told me you were the only Japanese on the island who had earned his respect as a truthful man who worked hard every day."

"I am so unworthy of this honor. There are others who are stronger and have worked harder than I. They are more deserving."

"Thomas, I don't know another man that deserves this small thing more than you. Look over there next to Watanabe. Isn't that Frank Matsasuki? Didn't you stay by his bedside every night for two weeks when he broke his leg, bringing his food and helping him with his call to nature? Joe is on the roof. Haven't you written letters home for him for five years and managed his affairs without pay because he is backward by nature but kindhearted. And Robert there: Weren't you his first customer when he opened his grocery in Lahaina after his contract expired? These are all men that honor you, Thomas, and I would be honored to call you my friend if you will permit it after all these years."

Thomas colored deeply in embarrassment. His head down, he studied his toes sticking out from his sandals. He noted a weed underfoot and the oil stains from the train along the tracks. How could he ever repay this *on*? "I am honored beyond words to call you friend, Reverend Pearson," he choked out.

Pearson reached over and lifted the young man's chin until their eyes met. "Reverend to you no longer, Thomas," he said searching the face before him. "I am just your friend, Ambrose."

Immigration Dock
Pearl Harbor, Oahu
Territory of Hawaii
September 29, 1898

There had been a flurry of activity in the rooms carrying the picture brides as the ship entered Pearl Harbor. Some girls, still queasy, needed help getting their things together. Others were organizing the sheaf of documents they were required to carry through Customs and Immigration.

Moriko had carefully rechecked her papers the day before. Included was a birth certificate issued in the capital of the prefecture, proof of marriage to someone living in the islands, a health certificate and permission to emigrate issued by the Office of Citizenship in Tokyo. With all her chores done, she now gave herself one last quick assessment in a mirror. She wanted to be certain to look nice for her husband when they first met. The image staring back at her seemed hardly anything like the photo she had posed for over a year ago. The kimono was replaced with a long-sleeved, white blouse with starched pleats in front and a high collar with lace edging around her neck. A floor-length, black skirt with buttons down the front rested just above the floor on uncomfortable black leather shoes that laced up four inches above the ankle. Topping the ensemble was a round, natural-colored straw hat with a wide red ribbon as a band perched on a head of thick black hair worn down in western fashion. Except for the trace of ochre in her skin and her lovely Japanese features, she could have passed as a schoolmarm in any town in Kansas.

"Moriko-san, quit admiring yourself and come along, the other girls are already in line!" Tatsuyo admonished her friend, "Don't worry, you will find your man somehow."

"*Hai*, it is time to go," Moriko admitted. She looked around the stateroom one more time to be certain nothing was left behind and stepped out into the companionway with her friend.

The aisles were clogged with young women. Some were dragging heavy cases others carrying only their papers. Excited voices were jabbering away, creating an awful din. An aging Japanese steward, cast adrift by his shipmates amid all these women, swam upstream like a dying salmon trying to get past a phalanx of grizzlies. As he passed Moriko and Tatsuyo they heard him mumble "*onna sannin yoreba kashimashii.*"

They looked at each other and giggled. If ever the old proverb "wherever three women gather it is noisy" was applicable it was certainly here. Trapped in the crush of bodies, the two friends simply allowed themselves to be swept along by the human tide. As the line inched forward, the girls would peek out the portholes trying to see what was ahead, but all that was visible was a line of unclaimed brides snaking down the dock disappearing into a building at the end of the wharf.

Separating the docking area from the frontage road in the harbor was a series of warehouse buildings. Any spaces between the buildings were fenced off, and pressed four or five deep against every opening were Japanese men searching the line of faces leaving the boat for the one that matched the photo in their hand.

Converted Railside Coal Shack
One mile outside Lahaina Maui
Hawaii Territory, U.S.A.
September 29, 1898

While falling well short of a mansion, the little shack by the tracks had undergone an amazing transformation. Now there were four walls, two with windows, a proper door with a small covered porch and a step-down that led to a path. An outhouse stood at the other end about one hundred feet away.

Inside the house was a new wooden floor and a tiny black-iron potbellied stove parked in one corner. It would serve as a rarely needed heating and cooking appliance as most cooking was done outside. On one wall were three wooden shelves and six long nails for clothing. Crammed next to a tiny table and two perilously rehabilitated chairs stood a single iron bed with a mattress stuffed with cotton, and a pillow, stuffed with *nene* feathers. Thomas had found an old calendar with a lithograph reproduction of a painted Japanese landscape. He had cut the numbers off the bottom and tacked the poster to the wall opposite the door.

The roof was newly covered with shingles scavenged from repairs to a mansion built in Lahaina and the tin he had purchased had served to create a small outdoor enclosure for bathing. A fire pit with an old iron pot sat about twenty feet away from the door. A damaged molasses barrel had been cut down and turned into a small rudimentary tub. His friends had even taken the time to turn a small area into a garden, planting cabbage, cucumber and Chinese long green beans. As Thomas surveyed his new home he was grateful for all his friends had done. He was relieved that he could bring his new bride to a proper—however humble—home.

As he made his way back to camp he knew tonight would be the last spent living among his friends. He would mediate his last argument and share his last meal. Tomorrow would be the start of his new life, as he had been dreaming of for years. The last part of the puzzle of his life was a family of his own, and a farm where he would be the Luna. He would plant his own crops and take an extra day off if he chose.

That night, Thomas was feted by his fellow camp dwellers. Home-brewed *sake*, forbidden in the camps, magically appeared and flowed like water. The guest of honor, naturally temperate by nature, was out of his element but polite, and he drank a toast with each man who proposed one. By the end of the festivities, Thomas had to be helped to his bed by his drunken cohorts. Within minutes he and most of the party goers could be heard snoring from a hundred yards away. The celebration was considered a complete success.

Naturally when the entire crew of Camp 14 failed to board the train and report for work the following morning, some great calamity was feared. Among all the camps, Shichou Thomas had always had every able-bodied man ready to work on time at the correct field. The luna who had taken the daily duties of Gustav got the other crews working, and then rode back along the train line to the camp. By the time he got to camp, there was beginning to be some activity, principally in the outhouse. No breakfast fire had been started and the few bleary-eyed combatants from the previous night bore silent testimony to what had befallen the inhabitants. The luna smiled, made a few notes on a small pad and rode away. He didn't even bother to talk to anyone.

In all his days, Thomas had never felt like this. After heaving his guts out sometime in the middle of the night, he had felt a little better and fallen into a dreamless sleep. But now, in the morning, the world was still spinning slightly and his head was viciously pounding out a painful rhythm. His mouth was drier than the copra that filled his mattress. When he drank a little water, the sour taste of his vomit came back to him and filled him with nausea again. The principal architect of this set of circumstances made his way over to Thomas sporting a painful grin.

"It was a good celebration Thomas! I am glad to see you feeling so well this morning." Harry Tsuda, a longtime worker and legendary debaucher, clapped his friend on the shoulder. "Come on, have a little more *sake*, it will make you feel better."

"I'd rather die," Thomas admitted.

"Well, whether you have the *sake* or not, you won't die. But if you don't you will certainly wish you were dead."

"Even so, this morning I will not have any more *sake*. I will pretend I am dead and maybe my head won't be able to find me."

"You can't pretend to be dead today," Harry said. "Today is when you sail to Honolulu to fetch your wife. In fact, you better hurry to the dock so you don't miss the sailing. The ferry won't be back for four days."

Thomas suddenly went ashen with a stricken look on his face. He ran back to his bedside, snatched up his best clothes and ran out the door headed for the dock.

Honolulu Customs House
Processing Residence
Honolulu, Oahu
Hawaii Territory, U.S.A
September 30, 1898

It had taken Moriko hours to finish the process yesterday. Hawaii was only recently U.S. territory so the President and the Congress hadn't had time to put any bureaucratic structure in place. Instead, they had simply renamed it by executive fiat the Government of the Republic of Hawaii. Moriko's documents had been checked three times and her luggage inspected briefly by a bored clerk.

She had been shuttled into a large room with a few chairs and tables and most of the incipient brides she had traveled with from Japan. Milling about in the room were Japanese men of every age and description, most wearing worn work clothes or tattered suits, each clutching a picture of his bride and searching each new face as it entered in the room. Occasionally, a grunt of recognition could be heard and a self-introduction would occur.

Tatsuyo had been spotted by her husband almost immediately and she was shocked to discover he was at least twenty-five years older than his photo appeared, and rather than the prosperous business owner he had proclaimed himself, he was obviously a broken-down field worker. A fierce argument ensued, with Tatsuyo refusing to go with her husband as she sat stubbornly on her lacquered trunk, her arms folded tightly across her chest. Every effort by her husband to lure, coax and cajole her into coming along was met with stony silence. Finally, when she had heard enough she stood up. Icily staring the man in the eyes, she glared defiantly.

"I will divorce you and find another man who is not a liar. I will go back to Japan and never send a picture to anyone again. Go away old man!"

Accepting defeat the man turned, his shoulders sagging and a weary countenance etched in the lines of his face, and walked out the door. When he had gone, Tatsuyo broke down. Sobbing inconsolably, she sat on her little trunk, hands fidgeting restlessly in her lap.

Moriko had witnessed most of the exchange and had noticed similar scenes played out to a greater or lesser degree among several of her shipmates. Most were disappointed in the initial contact with their new mates and it filled her with fear. Moriko worked her way through the crush of people in the room over to her friend to comfort her, all the while suppressing the dread that now filled her heart.

"What am I to do?" Tatsuyo wailed. "It is so far from home and I have so little money."

"Maybe when my husband comes you can stay with us in our house," Moriko said. "I'm sure it is a fine house."

"But without a husband how will I live?"

"You will find a new husband. Maybe Toshio knows a good man needing for a pretty wife like you."

"Maybe," she sniffed. "But what will your husband say when he finds two women to take home instead of just one?"

"I don't know," Moriko answered honestly, "but I think he is a good man."

Aboard the Inter-Island Ferry
Entering Pearl Harbor
Honolulu, Oahu
Hawaii Territory, U.S.A.
October 1, 1898

With his head throbbing from the previous night and his heart pounding from the dash to the ferry, Thomas scurried aboard as the last boarding whistle was sounding. Throughout the day as he drank many ladles of water and ate little, the effect of his celebratory night ebbed. This morning he was concentrating on trying to clean himself up a little. He'd forgotten his razor in the rush to get to the boat and hadn't had a real haircut in weeks. His 'best' clothes were just work clothes in good repair with only a few small stains and one small tear in the shirt. He had been so busy in the last week preparing a place for the arrival of his bride that he neglected to prepare himself and admitted he probably didn't make the best impression. *Nothing to be done for it now,* he thought, *I'll just try to explain it all to Moriko when I find her.*

When the ferry docked, he rushed off the vessel. It was half a mile to the Immigration Building and he began the walk down the harbor road past the warehouses and piers lining the bustling street. He'd forgotten Moriko's photo too, but he wasn't concerned about that. He had studied her image until it was etched in his memory. *I will know her the moment I see her,* he reassured himself.

'Waiting House' Mission
Women's Bedroom

Honolulu, Oahu
Territory of Hawaii, U.S.A.
October 1, 1898

From the second-floor window, Moriko sat in a chair staring out the window at the street scene below. Drab drayage wagons pulled by giant dapple-gray draft horses hauled cargo from docks to warehouses and thence into the community. Sacks of sugar, barrels of molasses and crates of pineapples rolled in from outlying plantations. There was a beehive of activity as ships came and went from the docks across the street from her vantage point. Stevedores swarmed over vessels of all descriptions. Wealthy merchants dressed in silk finery stepped down from shiny black carriages with matched horses and entered and left waterfront offices, their clerks, drivers and servants buzzing around like flies over some necrotic piece of flesh. Chinese and Japanese merchants could be seen bargaining for goods to sell in their shops. Moriko scrutinized each face she saw looking for her new husband, thus far to no avail.

"He will come for you, Moriko-san. Remember you said he lives on a different island," Tatsuyo recalled. "He may not know you have arrived yet."

She did not answer her friend. She was lost in thought, doubt and fear gnawing at her. *I am so far away from home and I am frightened.*

"Moriko, come away from the window," Tatsuyo scolded. "He will come along soon enough!"

She sighed and came back to the table. As she sat there, her friend chatted away about home and how untrustworthy men were. Then she began to gossip about the other girls who had come with them and how shabby were the husbands who came to pick them up.

Only half listening, Moriko pondered what had happened since yesterday. As the hours wore on in the Immigration Building, most of the brides were met by their husbands. While most seemed startled by the disparity between what they expected and what they got, with Tatsuyo's single exception each left with her man. They were Japanese, steeped in a patriarchal society that required sacrifice and obedience from women, and in the end, their disappointment could not overcome two millennia of cultural mandate.

Eventually the crowd had dwindled until by dark only three, two unclaimed brides and Tatsuyo, remained. The customs clerk came in and told them in Japanese they would have to stay in the mission until their husbands arrived and they could not leave. The three girls crossed the now-deserted harbor street to the Mission and went into the parlor.

They were met by a kindly, spinsterish woman who gave them exhaustive instructions in English on the rules and regulations as she showed them to the room they would all share. That the instructions were rarely understood and mostly incomprehensible to her guests seemed inconsequential. Finally Moriko used some broken English and sign language to indicate eating and drinking. It had been nearly all day since they had eaten. The spinster seemed perplexed then a momentary glimmer of comprehension crossed her face. She nodded and left the girls to settle in for the night. Minutes later, she returned with a large platter and a huge tea pot, set them on the table and departed, locking the door behind her.

On the platter were thick slices of roast pork and chunks of pineapple, mango and bananas with baking soda biscuits, butter and passion fruit preserves at one side. Except for the pork, nothing on the platter was familiar to them, but being famished, they tentatively tasted each item and, discovering its palatability, ate a hearty supper.

This morning, the husband of the third girl had arrived and claimed his bride. That left Moriko as the only one whose husband had not appeared. Tatsuyo was different of course. Her husband had come and pleaded with her, but she still refused to go. In her village the scandal would be complete making it unlikely she could return. Even if accepted back by her family, she would be shunned by others and eventually it would become unbearable.

A loud knock at the door startled the one girl from her gossip and the other from her reverie.

"Young ladies, there is a gentleman to see you in the parlor," a Japanese-speaking voice called through the door. "He says he has come for Moriko Sakai."

The parlor was outdated Victorian, ornate and heavily draped. A small corner display was cluttered with *chinoiserie*, a popular trend in the British Empire twenty-five years earlier and only recently reaching the islands. He was too nervous to sit, and unaccustomed to being in the front room of any haole building, Thomas fidgeted and paced, peering occasionally up the stairs. After what seemed an eternity, he heard the squeaking hinges of a door opening on the second floor, and as he sneaked a peek up the stairwell he got his first glimpse of a Japanese woman coming toward him down the stairs.

That she was not wearing a kimono was a little disorienting since it was the only image he had of her, so he searched the face for details he had been so certain he had committed to memory. Somehow the mouth didn't seem quite right and the nose in three dimensions seemed different than the nose in the photo. When their eyes met a sort of panic set in. *This is not the bride in the photo! They sent the wrong girl!*

As Tatsuyo made her way down the staircase and looked at the field hand waiting at the bottom of the stairs, her heart sank. *He will not be able to find a husband for me. He is barely a husband himself.* She inspected him and could see confusion on his face. *He thinks I'm Moriko!* She reached the bottom step and walked over to Thomas and extended her right hand to him in the western manner they had been taught aboard the ship.

"I am Tsuda Tatsuyo, friend of Moriko," she said. "You are Sakai Toshio?"

"I am," he said simply. Not being quite sure what to do with her extended hand, he bowed at the waist. His relief was palpable and clearly worn on his face.

"Moriko-san is coming in a moment." She casually dropped her arm and returned the bow graciously.

From the second floor, Moriko had viewed the scene below by peeping around the corner like a schoolgirl. The man in the parlor was certainly the man in the photo but didn't look prosperous or important at all. To her eyes his clothes were soiled and torn. A sparse week-old growth of whiskers sprouted from his face and his hair was overlong and appeared to have been hacked with a kitchen knife weeks before. His sandals were run down at the heels and sweat circles were beginning to appear under his arms. *He's like all the rest we saw yesterday, just a field worker. What am I to do?* For the moment, however, she knew there was only one thing, and that was to meet the man who was her husband. Swallowing her fears, she stepped forward and began to descend the stairs.

She is beautiful! Thomas recognized her instantly, not the least fooled by the western clothes or style. *She is the most beautiful woman I have ever seen!* Then he had a moment of doubt as he thought, *what must she think of me?*

Moriko crossed to the parlor where Tatsuyo and Thomas stood. She bowed deeply and her husband returned the gesture. They stood for a moment gazing at one another without speaking, searching for the person in the photo, recalling every word of every letter exchanged and all the hopes expressed for the future. When their eyes finally met and held each others', they saw what they had seen in the photos and written in the letters, and Moriko knew she would go home with this man wherever home would be.

Finally it was Tatsuyo who couldn't stand the silence any longer. "Toshio-san, this is Moriko, your wife."

"Hai, this is Moriko," he said, a dreamy quality to his response.

"Toshio-san, your father sends you his approval," Moriko said. "He doesn't say so in the house but he boasts about you in the village."

Now there was a voice attached to the picture. A soft melodious voice like a fine bamboo flute and it transported Thomas to the clouds.

Suddenly the front door rattled open and the moment was shattered. A shipping clerk from the warehouse burst in with a handful of papers and a passel of questions.

"Are you Thomas Sakai? Which one of you ladies is Tatsuyo? What should I do about these boxes of personal goods? Anybody here speak English?"

The trio was taken aback by this rude intrusion, the betrothed a little frightened. Thomas had grown accustomed to the abrupt, even aggressive mannerisms of westerners, particularly Americans, and so answered his last question first."

"I speak English a little and I am Thomas Sakai. This is Tatsuyo, she does not speak English. If you have a question for her, ask me and I will ask her."

"Well, I need to know if she's gonna go back on the next boat so I can load her crate again."

Thomas translated this wondering to himself why anyone would come here only to return one day later. As he did, tears welled in her eyes and she looked pleadingly at Moriko.

"Toshio-san, my honorable husband, Tatsuyo needs your help."

There ensued a long polite discussion in Japanese. The shipping clerk watched, trying to gather something from the tenor of the discussion but was quite at a loss for understanding. Thomas would say something, the other woman would say something considerably longer and Sakai's eyes would widen in surprise. Tatsuyo would offer a brief emotional comment or two. This went on while the clerk shifted his weight from one foot to the other, thumbed through his papers importantly, stared around the room and rattled his papers again impatiently.

"Have her boxes put on the ferry to Lahaina to the attention of Thomas Sakai," he finally said.

Now it was the clerk's turn to have wide eyes. "Are you the husband of both these women?" he asked. "She's gotta have a husband to stay on the islands."

"No," Thomas bluffed, "she must have a sponsor. I am that sponsor."

"Okay," a thoroughly confused junior clerk capitulated, "but you —or maybe she—has to sign these papers. No, I'm pretty sure it's gotta be you."

"I will sign the papers," Thomas said. After carefully and slowly reading the documents, he signed his name in English and the clerk retreated to his loading tasks.

Sakai Residence Outside Lahaina
Maui

Hawaii Territory U.S.A.

October 3, 1898

*K*o'Oko'O waited patiently on the tracks dripping oil and water as Thomas struggled to load the cargo boxes. In a decade of service now, her paint had faded and was flaking in the fierce Maui sun. The arched wooden roof over the engineer's compartment was cracked, so when it rained errant drops dripped hissing against the hot boiler door. Rust streaked the boiler tank and drive pistons. Hand wheels and levers were burnished with use, and over the years, a patina of oil and dirt had accumulated around all the lubrication points. The cane cars were falling into disrepair with broken side staves and creaky floorboards.

Thomas had ridden the train, aging with it over the years, not noticing the changes as they gradually occurred. The young bride and her friend, however, were keenly aware of the pint-sized trains' shabby condition as they waited to board in Lahaina. With the cargo loaded, Thomas helped the girls up and pulled himself into the cane car. Others climbed into cars behind them—some of them new field workers with eyes wide with anticipation, others—veterans of the labor camps—immediately settled in for the ride, a few trying to catch a nap.

Finally loaded, the *Koko* wheezed into action as the engineer shoveled coal into the firebox. Smoke poured from the stack and gritty black soot rained down on the passengers. The train slowly moved down the tracks headed for its various stops along the circuitous route.

Thomas had usually ridden in the engine and helped shovel the coal, but today, he rode in the car with the women. Each was sitting on a cargo box rather than the floor and all were observing the landscape around them. Lahaina was still a village, but haole houses had inched farther out on the fringes and other communities on the island were growing as well.

The new arrivals were taking in the lush views of exotic plants and countryside as the train creaked and groaned along. Some of the veteran workers had taken note that Thomas had two women with him and, if not scandalized, were at least envious of his good fortune. Thomas, on the other hand, found the extra person to be a difficult complication to an already touchy situation.

The return from Honolulu on the ferry had been awkward. Conversation had focused principally on the situation Tatsuyo found herself in and what might be done about that. Clearly she couldn't marry someone else while still married to the rejected husband. For the time being she was attached by some invisible cord to Moriko. Thomas had not spent so much as a minute alone with his bride. Trying to find the right time to explain what she could soon expect to find eluded him, as did any effort to become privately acquainted with the woman he now called his wife.

When the train finally reached the former coaling station Thomas called home, its asthmatic huffing came to a stop. He helped his charges off directing them to the tiny shack while he and a couple of other laborers removed the cargo boxes and hauled them to the back of the building.

Standing on the threshold of the converted coal shack, Moriko and Tatsuyo could not find words to speak their shock and disappointment. Though both were from humble—even impoverished—backgrounds, this was far worse than either could have imagined. Even the poor Sakai ancestral home in the village of her birth, with its earthen floors, was better than this minuscule space. The train sounded its whistle and chugged away leaving the three strangers alone.

Now, finally, thousands of miles away from home and family, the two women began to grasp the enormity of the change in their lives and looked at each other wordlessly.

"Moriko-san," Thomas called, "let me show you where everything is."

Still numb, her head reeling with the disorienting circumstances in which she found herself, Moriko turned her head toward the sound of her husband's voice and started down the path, her friend trailing closely behind. She found him beside the rude tin enclosure surrounding the molasses barrel bathtub and followed him in a daze as he explained where the outhouse was and when the vegetable patch would need tending. Water would come from a recently built cistern nearby, and coal would be used in the tiny indoor stove. Wood could be used to start a coal fire under the iron kettle for the bath and the oil for the lamp was in a can alongside the house. When the tour was complete they all ended up back in the little house. Tomorrow, Thomas explained, he would return to work, but as soon as he could he would begin to work on Tatsuyo's problem, for although he didn't say so, he knew her presence would be an insurmountable obstacle to beginning a life with Moriko.

By evening, the initial dismay the women felt had begun to dissipate. Granted, the shack was tiny, and hastily constructed, but it was clean and the sparse furnishings were in fairly good repair. Anxious to get started on the right foot with his bride (and her traveling companion as well, it seemed), Thomas had laid a fire for a bath. He knew it was unlikely either woman had enjoyed a proper bathing opportunity since leaving Japan and he hoped it would relax them and relieve the tension in the air.

Three weeks earlier, he had purchased two towels from the Japanese mercantile in Lahaina. They were fine towels made from cotton imported from Egypt and had cost him eighty-seven cents each. That was a days wage and an extravagance he wrestled with for many minutes before making the purchase. Originally he had intended one for himself and one for Moriko, but now, of course, each woman would have the use of a new towel.

The small size of the barrel made traditional communal bath a physical impossibility, so it was Tatsuyo who washed herself first, standing on a small wooden rack outside the barrel behind the tin tub surround. She lathered herself and her hair, then rinsed away the soap. When she had finished, she stepped into the bath and began a long hot soak. As she did so she marveled at how such a simple luxury in such a strange setting could be so relaxing.

Thomas, meanwhile, took the opportunity to be alone with his wife for the first time since they met three days ago. This was the first private conversation they had enjoyed and he was anxious to hear about her and his own family. As she recounted how his letters home had been read among the villagers and the money he sent raised the living standard of his parents, he began to realize what a distorted picture of his life in Hawaii he had ignorantly created over the years. The woman across the tiny room had been duped by misperceptions and half-truths. He was not at all what she expected to find and this was not the life she had been expecting to lead.

"Moriko-san," he said hopelessly, "how you must despise me. How you must wish to return home and be rid of this adventure." His voice choked with emotion "I have waited for this moment and dreamed of you. I have imagined your voice and memorized your face. In my heart I have touched your skin and felt our babies grow in your stomach. I have seen in my heart our own farm and planted a vigorous tree for each child. I have dared to dream of happiness in a quiet life with you." He lapsed into a painful silence and stared at a knot in one of the floorboards beneath his feet.

His words were so simple and honest, his emotions so evident, that Moriko felt a little guilty for her feelings. *This is a man I can respect even in poverty. There is tenderness in his heart and kindness in his eyes. I can grow to love him.*

Wearing a light, informal bathing kimono, Tatsuyo drifted in languorously, fully relaxed and oblivious to the emotions hanging heavily in the air.

"It's your turn, Moriko. Your husband will need to reheat the water, though."

"Thank you, Tatsuyo." Moriko rose, crossed to her husband and placed her hand on his cheek. "Come along my husband and heat the water for my first bath with you."

Shimano River Bridge
Niigata City
Niigata Prefecture, Japan
November 4, 1898

The frigid waters swirled under the bridge and worked their way toward the Sea of Japan as a cold autumn drizzle fell on a solitary figure staring out upon the harbor. A stiff breeze blew in from the northwest bringing a biting sting and a portent of winter. Isoruku Yamamoto stared at the vessels at anchor in the harbor. Small boats and fishing vessels were tied up along the pier against the impending storm; larger vessels at anchor swung around their chains bending to the will of tides and winds.

Times were changing in Japan. Poor rural farmers had begun to migrate to urban centers seeking employment in the ever-increasing industrial boom. The war in China and confrontations with the Russians along the Chinese leg of the Trans-Siberian Railroad were taking a serious toll on the financial resources of The Empire of the Rising Sun. Though the solitary young man on the bridge could not know it, the military was spending a perilous amount of revenue on arms, particularly naval vessels, in a near-frantic effort to enlarge its sphere of influence in Asia while boxing out European and American expansionism.

Isoruku Yamamoto was small of stature and temperamentally unsuited to the army, but his samurai breeding called to him even at age sixteen. So it was that standing on the bridge over the Shimano River he made a decision for the life of a naval officer.

Sakai Residence
One mile outside Lahaina
Maui, Hawaii Territory, U.S.A.
November 14, 1898

Reverend Pearson had devised a way for Tatsuyo to end her marriage honorably and legally, at least in Hawaii, so recently things had moved along swiftly. Pearson intervened with local authorities for an annulment on the basis there were neither two consenting parties nor a consummation under Hawaiian law; therefore, a marriage did not legally exist. The local magistrate thought it to be a novel interpretation of international law but granted it nonetheless, principally on the reputation of the good reverend.

Shortly thereafter, Thomas made a formal introduction of Tatsuyo to his friend Watanabe the carver, and after a very brief courtship, the two were betrothed. They were united in an unusual blended ceremony. Thomas acted as best man and Moriko matron of honor, roles unfamiliar in Japanese tradition, as well as witnesses, and Reverend Pearson performed the ceremony in Japanese while Marie played the reed organ as little Joshua slept in a cradle nearby.

After the wedding, Tatsuyo moved out of the little home by the tracks she had shared with the Sakais and moved in with her new husband. That had been a week ago, and finally there was privacy between husband and wife.

Some semblance of routine began to develop as well. Thomas would arise at his customary hour and perform his chores. His writing chores now were mostly confined to English, Moriko having taken on most of the Japanese calligraphy aspect of his little cottage industry. Requests for their services were in decline, as more workers learned how to read and write and fewer sent letters home. The influx of picture brides was reducing the need for the scrolls for the photographer as well. Thomas was concerned about his dwindling revenue stream, but still he went to work each day for the plantation.

Moriko started a fire under the iron pot in the bath enclosure, something she did each morning after her chores were completed and her husband had departed for work. She would bathe and soak in the morning, then have it ready for Thomas when he returned from the fields. As she tended the flames and poured water in the pot, she hummed a traditional tune and planned her activities for the day.

Riding along the railroad tracks headed for the cane fields, a recently hired young luna heard the humming from behind the tin enclosure and it piqued his curiosity. He reined up and slid noiselessly off his horse hitching it on the siding switch, which had fallen into disuse. Quietly he made his way along the path toward the bath.

The water was a little too hot and Moriko was filling the old molasses barrel with the water. By the time she had washed and rinsed, the water would be just right for a nice hot soak. Removing her light kimono she hung it on a nail, splashed herself with warm water and began lathering her hair and skin.

Hearing the splashing water, the luna crept to the opening of the small space and peeked around the corner. Moriko, her eyes closed against the lather as she washed her hair stood naked on the little wooden platform. His greedy eyes took in every detail of this beautiful woman. Her rich, full breasts glistened with water. Rivulets of soap traced a path down her body over the low swell of her stomach disappearing into the black hair of her nether regions. She turned to rinse away the soap revealing the rounded curves of her buttocks to her undetected observer.

Breathless, the unseen intruder watched as she rinsed her hair and body with the steaming water and, with her back still toward him climbed into the molasses tub. She settled in and the luna retreated a few steps. His lust and cruelty inflamed, he crept silently away and waited in the tiny house.

When the water began to cool, Moriko stepped out of the tub and dried herself with the new towel her husband had provided. She slipped on her kimono and bath sandals and began brushing her hair with a boar bristle brush that had been a wedding gift from a villager. Still humming she walked back along the path to the house and stepped inside, closing the door behind her. She started to shrug off the kimono as her eyes adjusted from the bright sunshine to the darkened room when suddenly she noticed the sharp tang of unfamiliar sweat.

Before she could react, she was grabbed around her neck from behind in a choke hold. The assailant's other callused hand tore the flimsy fabric of the kimono aside and grabbed roughly at her breasts.

"You like, Pietro, eh, little flower?" the brutish luna mocked "Pietro like you! Pietro pick little Japanese flower of his own today."

Moriko tried to struggle but his grip around her neck got tighter and she began to feel lightheaded, her brain deprived of oxygen. Finally she passed out.

The young attacker swept up the limp body and tossed it on the bed. He roughly pulled aside the remainder of the kimono baring the object of his attack. He unfastened his belt and dropped his khaki pants to the floor, revealing his rampant member engorged with blood and lust.

Moriko came to her senses at that moment, and seeing her attacker for the first time screamed loudly. From this position she was better able to resist and she kicked and flailed frantically while the young rapist attempted to pinion her to the small bed. He pushed her down, placing one huge hand in the center of her chest, and forced her knees open with his own. Her strength and ability to resist the brutal assault was waning, but she continued to scream as he positioned himself for the consummation of his licentiousness. He pressed his advantage, placing his penis against her warm moistness in position for a ravaging thrust.

An enormous roar reverberated in the room and the air around her was instantly filled with a fine red mist as her assailant collapsed on her. Bright sunshine streamed in through the open doorway and silhouetted in the frame was the familiar figure of Gustav, acrid smoke still curling from the barrel of his pistol.

It took a moment for Moriko to grasp what had happened. As reality began to set in and the horror of the moment overtook her, a low, keening wail emanated from her throat. The corpse of the lifeless luna oozed blood from the ghastly wound onto her chest. She began to shake uncontrollably and pushed ineffectually at the body still holding her down on the bed.

Gustav crossed the room in three strides and hoisted the body onto his shoulder. He carried it outside, flung it over the saddle of the horse tethered nearby and returned to the house. Inside, Moriko had managed to sit up. She was still naked, covered in blood and bits of gore and bone fragments. She picked absently at the bits, still in shock and shaking.

"Moriko," Gustav said gently, "did he hurt you?"

She looked up at her intercessor dully, saying nothing, seeming to see through him.

Gustav glanced around the tiny house and spotted a kimono that he had seen Thomas wear. He took it off the nail and folded it over his forearm. He walked over to Moriko and gently lifted her off the bed carrying her out the door down the little path to the hot bath. Setting her down on a small bench, he covered her with the towel he found hanging on its nail and rekindled the fire under the old black kettle.

"You don't worry, Gustav will stay with you. Nobody is gonna hurt you. I will take care of you till Thomas gets home."

He poked at the fire, testing the temperature of the water periodically, and when he finally decided it was okay he scooped out buckets and poured them into the molasses barrel. Then he got Moriko to her feet and began to wash away the remains clinging to her hair and skin. With the innocence of a mother bathing her newborn he washed her hair and face and then the rest of her body. Carefully and gently he sponged away the scarlet witness from her skin, and when he had finished and rinsed off the soap, he picked her up and placed her in the tub she had occupied only an hour before. He added some hot water and spoke to her once again.

"Moriko-san, I'm going to clean up the house, will you be all right?" He knew she didn't fully understand but he hoped if he kept his voice quiet and steady it would help. He filled a bucket with hot water and picked up a brush and started for the house. As he turned to leave, a strong hand gripped his forearm fiercely.

"*Domo arigato gozaimasu, Gustav-san.*" Her eyes held his for several moments then she released her grip and turned to stare at the bathwater.

When he had cleaned up in the house, he returned to the little enclosure and finding the tub water tepid again, lifted his charge from the water. She had stopped shivering and occasionally made eye contact, but still had a faraway look. He toweled her dry and placed the kimono on her shoulders putting each arm in a sleeve like dressing a child. He pulled the robe closed and tied a knot in the belt at the waist. Moriko's modesty and dignity had been restored. Damaged and battered as it was, her psyche could now begin the slow process of healing.

Gustav led Moriko back up the path intending to put her to bed, but as she neared the little house she resisted until finally she would go no farther.

He knew he couldn't leave her like this to go searching for Thomas or even the Lahaina constable, so he did the only thing he could. He went inside and brought out the two chairs and the little table and set them down in the yard near the vegetable patch. Then he and Moriko simply sat down and waited.

Maui Island Courthouse
Lahaina, Maui
Hawaii Territory, U.S.A.
November 18, 1898

On the second floor of the squat building with Doric columns where so many field laborers had first registered their entry to the island was a small courtroom. Polished oak furnishings, imported at great expense from California, sat inside the square room, their shining honey color glistening. Windows at the back of the room were covered in Venetian-style blinds, closed against the fierce morning sun. The domed ceiling had an oil lamp chandelier hanging from the center on a stout chain covered with a patina of lamp-black soot.

Opposite the windows on a raised platform the judge's bench stood commanding a view of the courtroom from its highest point. A tall, padded swivel chair covered in oxblood-colored leather sat empty behind the imposing furniture, flanked on either side against the back wall by flags of the United States and Republic of Hawaii. On the judge's right-hand side and slightly lower was an oak witness box topped with a decorative rail containing a hard chair. The jury sat along the adjacent wall on a two-tiered dais with a low divider segregating it from the rest of the room.

In front of the bench the court recorder and clerk had a desk. Two long tables for opposing counsels with four chairs at each were more or less in the center of the room. The gallery benches, arranged like church pews, sat behind a low partition wall which bifurcated the room. This arrangement separated combatants in the legal proceedings from mere watchers and reporters. A single swinging door in the center of the divider at the end of the gallery aisle granted access to the arena.

A constable acting as bailiff opened the doors from the main hallway and members of the public began streaming in, filling the benches. Word of the shooting had traveled like wildfire throughout the tiny island and residents of all descriptions wanted to see what they could see. Islanders, Chinese, Japanese, Portuguese and haole drifted into groups forming ad hoc gossip committees and staking out benches from which to watch the proceedings. As the gallery filled, the natural hushed silence engendered by all courtrooms would ebb and flow as the volume of chatter increased.

Normally, witnesses would be kept in a small room across the hall and would be called when it was their turn to testify. In this case the only eyewitness was also the victim, and since this was a coroner's inquest and not a trial, the rules were a little different anyway.

As the gallery whispers reached a crescendo a door opened and the court clerk emerged from a small anteroom. Behind him filed the players in the melodrama. A hush fell over the audience as leading the group was Jedediah Whitehead, owner of the plantation where the incident occurred and employer of the shooter. A graduate of Leland Stanford Jr. University in Palo Alto, California, with a few courses in law during his years as a student, Whitehead would act as counsel for Gustav who trailed behind him; next followed Reverend Pearson. He was there at the request of the court to act as an interpreter, being the haole on the island who spoke the most fluent Japanese. His friendship with Thomas Sakai was well known in the community, but his stature as a man of the cloth left him above reproach and best suited to this delicate role as cultural intermediary.

Dr. Charles Davidson, who had worked so diligently and successfully as the public health officer and delivered little Joshua Pearson (currently napping in the arms of his mother in the gallery of the courtroom), would serve as coroner.

Finally Moriko and Thomas entered the courtroom. A multi linguistic murmur arose in the gallery as they made their way to the tables in the center of the room and were seated. Moriko was wearing the western-style clothes she had worn upon arrival in Honolulu and Thomas had purchased a new suit—with pants—for the occasion.

Everyone was seated. Whitehead and Gustav whispered back and forth, the doctor consulted his notes while Pearson made eye contact with his wife, Marie.

Moriko sat in silence. She appeared tiny and frail with her hands in her lap, her eyes downcast, not moving or speaking. Thomas sat stiffly upright; stoic, inscrutable, staring at a small bronze figure of Blind Justice standing on the judge's bench.

A door swung open and the judge promptly stepped up to the bench and sat in the leather chair.

"All rise," the clerk said, standing. "This inquest is now in session, the Honorable Magistrate Franklin Speaks presiding."

"You may be seated," the judge stated. Before seats could be found Speaks began without preamble, "Normally I would not be here, but Dr. Davidson has asked that I be in attendance to address issues of the law. We haven't conducted many coroners' inquests and he feels more comfortable having me answer those questions. As you all know now that Hawaii is a U.S. Territory, some of the rules may be different. None of us here are experts in that regard, but if we all use common sense, everything should proceed without incident. Is the good doctor prepared to begin?"

"I am, your Honor."

"Then, pray, please do so."

"I call Gustav Meyer to the stand."

Gustav made his way from his seat at the table to the witness box where the clerk swore him in and he took his seat.

"Mr. Meyer," the Doctor began, "can you please tell us in your own words what happened four days ago at about seven-thirty a.m. at the residence of Thomas and Moriko Sakai."

"Yah, I can," he said. Gustav recounted how he had been riding along the tracks headed for the fields to check the progress of two new overseers he just hired when he heard screaming coming from the little house. He recounted galloping to the premises, taking note of the horse tied up outside. His testimony went on to describe in titillating detail the scene that presented itself to him when he flung open the door.

"Did you shout at the man to stop?" the doctor asked. Did you yell at the deceased...uhh, Pietro to stop?"

"No, sir, I did not."

"Why not?"

"There wasn't time—the man was in a carnal lust and I believed Mrs. Sakai's life was in danger."

"I see. How many shots did you fire?"

"One shot, only."

"One shot, entering the right temple and exiting the left occipital, is that correct?"

Gustav looked quizzically at Jed. Jed in turn pointed to a spot on his skull and nodded.

"Yes, sir, that is correct."

"What happened then?"

Gustav described placing the body on the horse and gave a circumspect account of helping clean up Moriko and the house. He explained how she wouldn't go back in the house, so he waited with her for Thomas to come home, eventually sending word with a passing train to recall him and pass along information on the incident to the constable and Mr. Whitehead.

"So you just sat waiting?"

"Yah, I figured the dead man wouldn't care..." A chuckle worked its way through the gallery, "...and I couldn't leave Mrs. Sakai alone."

"What was the first thing you did after Thomas returned to his home?" the doctor asked.

"I explained what had happened and told Thomas to stay with his wife. Then I ride back to Lahaina and bring back on his horse Pietro to the constable."

"Thank you. That will be all. Mr. Whitehead, do you have any questions?"

"Yes, I do, just one," Jed replied. "Gustav, after you explained what had happened to the constable, what did he tell you to do?"

"He told me to go home and wait. Someone would be along in couple of days to talk to me. Yesterday, he told me come here this morning."

"Did he place you in custody or arrest you at any time?"

"No, he just told me to be here and so I am."

"Thank you. That's all."

"You may stand down," the magistrate said and Gustav returned to the table to sit down next to his boss.

Dr. Davidson called a couple of more witnesses, including the Constable, who all testified as to the veracity of the defendant's statements in the matter.

"I call Moriko Sakai to the stand," the doctor said.

"As I mentioned in chambers, doctor," the judge interrupted, "we are on unsettled legal ground with regard to this testimony. Are you sure you wish to proceed?"

Jed Whitehead arose, "Your honor, if I may?"

"Counsel, you have something add?"

"Yes, your Honor. Since this is not a trial, the rules of evidence do not apply in a formal sense here. This is merely an inquest to determine whether or not charges should be brought and therefore any testimony, even from a woman, that sheds light on the circumstances should be welcome."

"I concur," Dr. Davidson said. "It is important that we know not only how Mr. Meyer viewed the scene upon his arrival but how Mrs. Sakai felt as well. Whether or not her testimony would be permitted in a trial is irrelevant here."

"Very well, doctor, you may proceed."

"Moriko?" Reverend Pearson said in Japanese, "it is time to tell your story."

She arose and allowed herself to be led to the witness box, staring at the floor all the way. The clerk rose to swear her in but the Reverend stopped him.

"Your Honor, Moriko is not a Christian, at least not yet, so an oath on the Bible would mean little. Perhaps an affirmation under penalty of perjury would be sufficient?"

"Point well taken, Reverend, please proceed."

Pearson approached her and told her she must tell the truth, it was like an obligation to the Emperor. She nodded distantly and he asked her to take a seat.

"Mrs. Sakai," the doctor said, trying to strike the right balance between decorum and professional detachment, "can you please recount for the inquiry exactly what happened on the day of the attack?"

Pearson made a slow translation, being careful of accuracy.

Moriko sat silently eyes fixed on the floor for a long moment. It was evident she was struggling with her emotions. Pearson waited for a few seconds longer, then repeated the question. Finally she looked up at him and whispered so only he could hear. The pastor leaned over to listen intently, pondering what she had said, then stood erect to address the bench.

"Your Honor," Pearson said, "this is most difficult for her. In the Japanese culture she is dishonored and a public airing of the circumstances is doubly difficult."

"Moriko," a suddenly animated Thomas spoke from his chair at the defense table, "we are not in Japan anymore; you must answer the question. There is no dishonor here or in our home."

Moriko started with surprise as her eyes sought out Thomas. Was he forgiving her? Was he saying there was no fault upon her?

Among the Japanese spectators, a chatter of surprise broke out with an undercurrent of disapproval. The public discussion of private shame was a strong cultural taboo and Thomas had just insisted that it be broken.

Judge Speaks, sensing control was being lost in his court, rapped his gavel on the bench "Quiet in the courtroom," he thundered. "Reverend Pearson, what is going on here?"

"Mr. Sakai has told his wife there is no dishonor in answering the question and the gallery is reacting to that. In Japan there is little precedent for such a thing."

"Hmmmph," the Judge grunted, "well, see if you can speed things along. I don't want this to take all day if we can help it."

"Thank you, your Honor. I'll do my best." Pearson looked at Moriko, "Do you want me to repeat the question?"

"No," she replied. She glanced at Thomas for reassurance. He nodded approval. "I was taking a bath..." she began.

When she had finished her story, pausing periodically to allow for translation, she stopped. Most in the courtroom realized that aside from the description of the initial attack, she probably knew less about the event than Gustav. Moriko had been attacked viciously with no warning by an unknown stranger with seemingly no provocation.

Doctor Davidson scratched his head thoughtfully, referred to his notes and finally said, "I have no further questions of this witness."

"Does Mr. Whitehead have any questions of this witness?" The Judge asked.

"No, your Honor," he replied. "I believe this young woman has relived this incident sufficiently for the court's purposes."

"Your Honor," the doctor said, "it is my belief based on the testimony presented here that there is no cause for action against Gustav Meyer. While not strictly self-defense, he was acting in the defense of the life and honor of another and in the heat of the moment made the only logical decision, given the circumstances."

"Your recommendation to the court is that no charge should be laid," Speaks said, "and that the matter be ruled as a justifiable homicide?"

"Yes, your Honor, that is correct."

"Counsel?" the Judge asked.

"There is no dispute as to the facts of the case. I concur with the good Doctor your honor," Whitehead responded.

"Let the record show it is so ordered." The gavel descended on the bench abruptly, Speaks stood and exited through the door to his chambers before the clerk could even get to his feet.

"Court dismissed," the clerk said weakly, "apparently."

The gallery was still trying to sort out what had happened, Pearson was explaining it in Japanese to Moriko. Thomas sat quietly at the defense table, and Gustav was pumping the fist of his employer in gratitude.

"Come along Moriko, let us go home," Thomas said, arising.

People filed out of the courtroom in reverse order of their entry. Thomas and Moriko walked out of the courthouse and headed for the station to catch the next sugar train to their little home. Much to the surprise and disapproval of Japanese onlookers Moriko was not the customary steps behind her husband. At his wish she was arm-in-arm at his side.

Manse, First Congregational Mission Church
Lahaina, Maui
Hawaii Territory, U.S.A.
Thanksgiving Day, 1898

"God has granted us a bountiful harvest which He has laid before us to nourish our spirits and our bodies. He has sacrificed His son that the corruption of the flesh in this life may be forgiven and the stain of sin be washed away before the faithful receive their reward." Reverend Pearson paused a moment then continued, "Let us rejoice in His graciousness and gird our loins with the sustenance here provided. We will wage battle against Satan each day until the trumpet of Gabriel calls us home to be in the glorious presence of the Lord Almighty in our eternal reward. In the name of our Savior, Jesus Christ, we pray Amen."

"We are honored by your presence with us today, Thomas," Marie Pearson said. "Thank you for coming, Moriko-san," she added in halting Japanese.

Moriko looked at her hostess from her seat at the table and bowed her head in acknowledgment. Thomas had tried to explain what 'Thanksgiving' was to the haoles and why it was an honor to be invited to dinner, but his understanding of the tradition was imperfect and incomplete.

As the Reverend took his seat at the head of the table he imagined that the Pilgrims would certainly not recognize this meal. Before him was a huge platter of banana, pineapple, mango and pa-

paya. Beyond that, a roasted pork leg was surrounded with green beans and slices of tomatoes from the garden next to the manse.

Thomas and Moriko had brought several small eggplants and a cabbage from their garden and thin noodles made from rice flour. She made an enormous bowl of soup and it stood steaming on the table next to a bowl of rice. No one had quite come to terms with poi, so in spite of indigenous status, it was missing from the table.

One concession to impulse and tradition had been made at the local store. Ambrose had spied a can of cranberries and in an uncharacteristic moment of weakness, had purchased them. They were sitting now in a small glass bowl next to the pitcher of passion fruit tea.

"Please, let's begin feasting," Pearson said.

Following the lead of their host, the Sakais took portions of each item onto their plates. Thomas over the years had become accustomed to western eating habits and was familiar with the use of knives and forks, but had never quite been able to fathom the mammoth portions. Moriko was having some difficulty but with the little experience from the time on the boat, she seemed to be catching on. She tasted small bites of what was on her plate and, surprised at the odd tartness of the cranberry, found that she enjoyed it.

"Thomas-san, Marie and I and Joshua are moving back home to the United States," Pearson said. "We will be leaving soon for home. We wanted to take this time to say goodbye."

Thomas nodded, hiding his surprise behind a bite of roast pork.

"We have wondered how you and Moriko-san have been these last few weeks," Marie said. "We hear rumors and we are worried."

"It has been difficult." Thomas admitted. He searched the faces of the only white people he had ever really considered friends. He could read genuine concern and was touched by it.

"Since the…incident, it has been difficult. We have little business from the Japanese on the island for writing and the other families shun us. They are old country and do not change their thinking easily."

"Maybe you should come with us to Seattle," Ambrose suggested.

"That is very generous, Ambrose-san, but Moriko and I are thinking about California. I read in the newspaper from San Francisco that there is much good farmland and many opportunities."

"Perhaps so," the Reverend mused, "but you won't know anyone or have any friends."

"I had no friends when I came here. How should it be different?"

"What about the friends you made on the ship that stayed in the camps with you after you arrived?"

Thomas had a sudden vision of Sammy with his wide grin lost forever to the cane fire. He shook off the painful image mentally. "We will make friends when we get to California and we will buy a farm and grow vegetables and chickens."

"Ummm, I suppose so." The Reverend lapsed into silence as he thought about the anti-Asian sentiment running high in California. He had heard reliable reports from visiting fellow ministers outward bound to the mission fields that farmers and ranchers in the Golden State were angry—even worried—about competition from non-whites, and occasionally violence erupted.

Conversation during dinner reverted to discussions about the weather, what life was like in Seattle and little Joshua's progress. When the meal was finished the ladies began clearing away the dishes and Thomas and Ambrose stepped outside to the garden where the Reverend filled a pipe with tobacco and lit it, taking periodic puffs as they strolled in the waning sunlight.

"Ambrose-san, why do you pray to this man called Jesus?"

There it was! A bolt from the blue; the big question every missionary hopes to hear, waits to hear and then worries about how well he answers.

"Because I have faith in the promise of a better life after I die."

"Why?"

"That, Thomas, is the greatest truth ever revealed, and one that I should very much like to tell you and Moriko about together. Shall we go inside?" He knocked his pipe against his boot and dislodged the dottle, which he crushed underfoot. The two friends then went inside the manse.

Pearson called the women into the parlor where he poured everyone a tall glass of passion fruit tea and invited them to sit.

For the next two hours, he gave a tour de force recitation of the story of the Christian faith. He recounted the histories, the prophecies and the genealogies. He told the story of Moses and the Exodus and the significance of Joshua's name. Pearson spoke with passion about the story of the infant born in Bethlehem who became a carpenter from Nazareth, of his miracles, the disciples and the betrayer from among the friends who followed him. He explained the trial, the brutality of the procession on the Via Dolorosa, the torturous sacrifice upon the wooden cross and finally he spoke of the witnesses to the resurrection from the dead the ascension to Heaven and the promise of life eternal seated at the right hand of God.

Neither of the guests had heard the full story, much less told with such fervor and conviction in their native language. Thomas was moved with the sincerity his friend evoked and sat in silence for a while after Pearson had finished.

"That is a wonderful story and it tells me what you believe, but it doesn't tell me why you believe it, Ambrose-san."

"I believe because I have faith in the word of the witnesses of the Bible and in the feeling in my heart about what is true and right," Pearson said.

"You have faith because your father had faith?"

"No, Thomas, I have searched for the truth about men and found it in the Good Book. I have searched my own soul and seen my weakness and the weakness of others and found strength in the promise that the next life for me will be in the land of milk and honey, free from sin. I rejoice in knowing that my failures and cowardice, my mean-spiritedness and cruelties and petty prejudices will be erased from the book of life and it shall be behind God and forgotten. I am humble that immortal God sacrificed His son to absolve me and resurrected Him as proof of this promise."

"I am not a Christian. Moriko is not a Christian," Thomas observed. "We cannot be blessed by your God, Ambrose-san. He is not *Jimmu,* the god of my ancestors."

"Thomas," Pearson began, "do you think the Emperor is immortal?"

"No," Thomas said, carefully selecting his words, "each Emperor dies in his own time, but when he dies he becomes immortal with *Jimmu.*"

"Has any Emperor ever come back to life after death?"

"No one in our tradition has ever said so."

"Do you fear the Emperor?" Ambrose paused for effect "Do you believe he is God? Do you really think he is divine and infallible?"

Moriko's eyes widened at the question and she studied her husband with intensity. Thomas sat quietly for some time mulling this over. He thought about all he had read about the Emperor, about the newspaper reports of war and atrocities attributed to Japanese soldiers in foreign lands, the intransigence of the Empire to aid in the plight of workers in the islands. He thought about his village and his family and how his father had believed what his father before him had believed. Faith unquestioned; unexamined for generations, simply because it was the duty of the son to carry on the traditions and obligations of the family for the glory of the Emperor. He thought of all these things and knew the truth.

"No, Ambrose. I think he is just a man. He has shown no loyalty to me or my family or village. I do not think he is a God."

A slight but audible gasp escaped from Moriko. She had never in her life heard anyone Japanese make such a statement, even if privately it was what they believed. When Thomas turned her way she averted her eyes and took a sip of tea.

"So, Thomas," Ambrose said gently, "what do you believe when the Emperor is no longer God for you?"

Thomas was very still. He had never considered religion deeply before. He had carried out the ceremonies and observed the traditions of the homeland but for more than a third of his life had not returned to the islands of his birth. Over the years, he had become disconnected intellectually and distanced emotionally.

"I believe in nothing. Life is hard work and unfair. I believe in nothing."

"I don't accept that, Toshio." Thomas surveyed his host curiously when he heard his Japanese name. "You are too good a man to believe in nothing."

"Yes, I am a good man," he said acidly. Toshio's lips were thin and tight with pent up anger. "And I see how well I am rewarded. Friends no longer speak to me. No white man will sell even a scrap of land for me to farm. Japanese I don't even know whisper about my wife behind my back as I pass by. Yes, I am a good man," he concluded, bitterness tinging his voice. Moriko had flushed crimson at his speech and studied her tea intensely.

The missionary sensed the critical moment was at hand and that now was the time to speak from his heart as a minister and extend the invitation to his friend.

"God promises trial and tribulation in this life. Joy and hope will be tempered with pain and suffering and in no way will your time here be fair. But He also promises that if you will just believe on Him in your heart and trust Him to be with you in times of trouble and triumph that you will be with Him in glory eternally. It is recorded in the Holy Bible that Jesus said, 'for God so loved the world that He gave His only begotten son that whosoever believeth in Him should not perish but have everlasting life.'

"How can I believe in the white man's God?" Thomas had relaxed his face but still wore a frown. "White men have only a mean place for Japanese in their hearts. How could they have room for me in their Heaven?"

"I am a white man, Toshio. I have room for you in my home, at my table and in heaven too. My God is no respecter of race, color, station or language. All who believe and follow him shall be rewarded in the hereafter. Indeed, Christ also said, 'Verily, I say unto thee, except a man be born again he cannot see the kingdom of God.'"

Moriko sneaked a peek at her husband. His face had changed as the significance of Pearson's words penetrated his thinking.

"I had forgotten you were white," Thomas confessed.

"Thank you, Thomas. I had forgotten that it mattered to some. All men are equal in the eyes of God and all are welcome at the feast. How about you, Thomas, are you ready to confess your weakness and sin and ask for forgiveness and life eternal?"

Moriko glanced sidelong at her husband and held her breath. She had listened carefully to the missionary and his story. She had thought about his questions and struggled with the strong cultural inhibitions that had been inculcated in her since childhood. Since coming to Hawaii and being with her husband, she had been repeatedly surprised by his strength of character and his willingness to question the old ways and embrace new ideas. As a dutiful wife she would follow him, but what had surprised her most was that he asked her what she thought and considered it carefully. This question, she sensed, and how Toshio answered it was very important.

Toshio looked at his wife and met her eyes with the question reflected in his own. She locked eyes with him and bowed her head ever so slightly, signaling her obedience and willingness to follow his lead. Thomas touched Moriko's hand.

"What must we do, Pastor?"

"Have faith, Thomas. Just have faith."

"Show us how we find this faith, my friend."

Pearson rose. Even with many such moments in his years in the mission field, the thrill of leading someone to salvation was always fresh. He gestured for his wife, Moriko and Thomas to rise and all joined hands.

"Let us pray," he began.

Pier 15

Port of San Francisco
December 31, 1899

It was hours before midnight and drunken revelers were already careening around the docks whooping it up. Smelling of beer and sausages, wine and garlic or whiskey and stale sweat, longshoreman lurched on and off the steamship *Golden State* exchanging freight and baggage from the hold with counterparts piled up on Pier 17. Porters from the steamship company were trying to make sense of the jumble of boxes, trunks and barrels making their way ashore. Disembarking passengers mingled with visitors and friends waiting to greet them while those waiting to board chatted with visitors and friends come to wish them *bon voyage*. Amid this ocean of churning humanity and associated flotsam, third-class passengers Thomas and Moriko Sakai moved about trying to locate their baggage.

Thomas had tried to purchase second-class tickets but had been turned away by the steamship company. "Japs and Chinks can't ride in the same area as white folks even if they can afford it," they had been told. Apparently this dictum was applied unevenly as third class had carried Irish passengers and other whites whose origins escaped Thomas.

Before leaving Maui, Thomas sold everything that wasn't essential. Except for his savings, he carried little more on this ocean voyage than when he had left Japan ten years earlier. Moriko, too, had trimmed her items to the minimum. Between the two them, all their earthly goods fit in two battered old suitcases and a round-top, tin-covered trunk.

Clutching the baggage receipts in his left hand and holding tightly to Moriko with his right, Thomas negotiated the confusing morass, stopping occasionally to compare numbers and then moving on to the next familiar-looking bags. When he finally retrieved all of their possessions, he searched for a porter with a baggage cart.

"Excuse me, please," he said to a black man wearing a worn navy blue uniform and round, short-brimmed cap with the steamship company insignia in brass on the front, "could you help me to move these things to the street outside?"

The tall, slender old man eyed Thomas carefully, calculating what this Oriental, a group notoriously cheap in his experience, would be likely to tip.

"Two bits to da street," he said.

"Two bits?" Thomas was unfamiliar with the term.

"Two bits," the old man said somewhat impatiently, "Twenny-five cent to take your bags to the street."

"Ah, twenty-five cents; one quarter dollar, hai. Okay, we go."

"In advance," the porter said, holding out his hand.

Thomas reached into his pocket and took out a worn leather coin purse. He snapped it open and extracted a dime and a nickel, which he placed in the outstretched hand.

"This now, rest when we get to street," he said.

The old man looked sharply at Thomas, studying him, then a broad gap-toothed smile broke over his face and he began loading the baggage onto his wooden cart. "You pretty smart for a Jap," he said, nodding his head "Okay, we go to the street."

The old Negro wound his way through the crowds and around the jumble of boxes and cargo, deflecting the occasional drunk, stopping once for another passenger who sought help with baggage. The old man loaded more on his cart and the procession continued down the lengthy dock through the gates and out to the waterfront road that hugged the shoreline.

East Street swarmed with activity from China Basin to the south all the way along the eastern bayshore side of the city around

Telegraph Hill. Horse-drawn trolleys clattered on their rails down the street, stopping periodically to discharge or acquire passengers, then continued clanging bells noisily to warn away pedestrians and other impediments.

Carriages arrived and departed, Baruch cabs drawn by single horses waited in long lines to pick up the recently disgorged passengers from the docked ship. Men in gaudy suits and scandalously clad women exhorted all who would listen to visit their saloons and whorehouses in the Barbary Coast to indulge in the debauchery, drunkenness and gambling for which the open city was so infamous. Fishermen stretched long nets for drying and repair several docks to the north. To the south, the port building could be seen at the foot of Market Street where it terminated into East Street.

"Here you go, boy," the person sharing the porter said. "Live it up a little; it's a new century and a new world." He flipped a twenty-dollar gold piece into the old man's hand as a gleaming black Studebaker carriage nudged into an opening in the wall of conveyances clogging the street.

The old porter's eyes bulged in surprise; he'd have to work a month to earn that kind of money.

"I cain't make no change for twenny dollar," he said.

"I didn't ask for change I said live it up a little," the stranger replied.

"Yes sir, I be thankin' you, sir. I surely will."

A bodyguard jumped down from his high perch and grabbed the polished leather luggage from the cart, tossing it into the rear boot. The passenger climbed into the carriage as his attendant re-boarded.

"Where to, Colonel?" the driver asked.

"Palace Hotel, Frank, Palace Hotel."

"Yes, sir!" the man replied smartly. He expertly backed up the horses and within seconds was swallowed up in the sea of activity as the carriage disappeared down the road.

"Well don't that put the cream on the kitten's paws!" the porter exclaimed. He turned to Thomas and Moriko, "This one's on me," he said gleefully. He pocketed the gold coin and withdrew a quarter, forgetting entirely he had only gotten fifteen cents, which he handed to his surprised impromptu employer. "Happy New Year and welcome to San Francisco." The old man took the three pieces of luggage off and shoved the cart just inside the wharf gate. "I'm gonna take the ress of the night off." He turned and with a few strides disappeared into the crowd leaving Mr. & Mrs. Sakai awash in a sea of strangers feeling very much alone.

Thomas looked at his bride, then at the quarter in his hand, and again at her.

"So, we are in America," he said, "land of the free, home of the brave."

Franklin Farm Bunkhouse
North bank of the Pajaro River
Watsonville, California
4:30 a.m., April 5, 1900

The only real activity at this hour was in the kitchen of the dilapidated old farmhouse. Already a fire was being built in the huge Monarch cast iron stove that dominated the room. Soon the aroma of frying bacon and ham would fill the air. Within an hour the battered old plank table planted squarely in the middle of the kitchen would be laden with baking soda biscuits with butter and honey, dozens of eggs scrambled in bacon fat, fried potatoes with onions, the aforementioned meats and a gallon or two each of coffee and milk.

An unlikely mix of rough-looking men redolent of sweat and pungent dirty socks would shuffle in from the various rooms, some cheerful and friendly, some belligerent and sullen, to take their places at the table.

For now though, only the familiar rumblings in the kitchen intruded upon Thomas as he leaned against the porch railing. His long standing habit of rising early had him gazing out toward the river just a couple hundred feet away. He couldn't see it of course, but he could hear it flowing by. Unencumbered by the old chores he had done so long on the islands, he found himself with nothing to do except think and fret. It was still pitch dark and shaping up to be a typical early spring day around the Monterey Bay. Overhead, he could sense the thick overcast of fog that brought a chill to the air and would bring a dawn that simply went from dark gray to light gray.

How different it was from Hawaii. Here, if the sun made an appearance at all today, it would be well after noon, and before sunset the overcast and chill wind accompanying it would begin to roll in again.

As he stood on the porch lost in his thoughts, he could see little points of yellow light punctuating the darkness as farmhouses throughout the region sprang to life. A few feet to his right a rectangle of light fell on the ground from the kitchen illuminating a tiny portion of the inceptive vegetable garden. He tried to imagine someone else on a distant porch, observing this kitchen window as a little dot in the distance.

Although he understood the necessity, Thomas questioned his own wisdom in leaving Maui. Since their arrival in California on New Year's Eve their situation had gone from bad to worse. That harrowing first night in San Francisco cast them adrift in the squalor of the Barbary Coast searching for transportation and lodging. From behind the doors of the saloons and gambling houses they could hear mediocre pianists pounding out "I'm Only a Bird in a Gilded Cage" on out-of-tune instruments.

Barkers serving as hook men prowled the sidewalks in front of their places of employment trying to lure in customers. Occasionally painted whores displaying sagging décolletage would hoot propositions down to men passing below the second-floor windows. Twice in their short passage, bordello operators had tried to buy Moriko as a sex slave for the brothels. Leering grotesquely, they offered Thomas large cash payments and a percentage of earnings for the beautiful woman by his side, secure in the knowledge local authorities would do nothing to aid an Asian woman, particularly if their cut of the money continued to flow.

After the first few days, Thomas and Moriko were alternately ignored, ridiculed and downright hated for no apparent reason other than the fact they were Japanese. This was something new for them. Both had felt the sting of the viscous slurs on the island, but their isolated living circumstances and mix of acquaintances had, for the most part, shielded them from any wholesale exposure to the raw experience with which they now coped.

Being careful with expenses, living in substandard conditions and taking the occasional odd job to make money, Thomas had managed to avoid spending much of the fifty-two hundred dollars he had invested ten years of his life accumulating. It was a substantial sum that would have bought a fine house in a graceful neighborhood, but Thomas wanted a farm of his own. Since he spoke and read English better than most Japanese in the City, he discovered he could glean quite a bit by just staying silent. White men talked freely, even carelessly, around most far eastern people, assuming that none would understand. By keeping quiet and listening carefully Thomas learned of the great hatred and fear many white Americans had of the Asiatic races.

"Damn filthy Chinks," one shop owner had said to a customer while Thomas swept out a store where he had secured temporary employment. "They live like rats in a cesspool. You ever see one a them houses they stay in? Sometimes twenty or thirty of 'em in one tiny little place."

The customer grunted and nodded in sympathy.

"Cheap bastards, too. Wouldn't let loose of the first nickel they ever made if the life of their first born depended on it," he concluded.

"I hear they'd as soon as kill you as look at you," the customer had egged on. "They don't eat proper food either," he whispered conspiratorially. "They eat dogs! Dogs, can you imagine that? Besides, they smell funny." He paused thoughtfully, then added, "An' heathens, too, I hear."

"The Japs ain't any better," the shopkeeper said, throwing a sidelong glance at Thomas. "Look at him. He never complains, always shows up on time and disappears at quitting time into that nest of 'em west of Broadway. You watch," he continued, "we let 'em get a toehold and pretty soon all their relatives will be comin' over by the boatload, eatin' raw fish and rice and takin' all the jobs."

"We oughta turn the boats around and put the ones already here on board and send them home," the customer offered. "That or teach them their proper place."

"Proper place!" the shopkeeper huffed. "Their proper place is six feet under—just like the injuns we run outta here."

The conversation had been enlightening, if troubling, to Thomas and he learned as the weeks passed that it was just one variant on a theme he heard repeatedly.

He longed to return to the earth and the countryside, to escape the city and its noise and crowding. Always alert to opportunity, he overheard a conversation between his employer and a wholesale merchant discussing the price of sugar. Naturally that piqued his interest and he inferred that someone named Claus Spreckels, who began with a plantation on Maui, had built a town and refinery south of a little farm village called Salinas. Claus indulged his ego by calling the company town Spreckels and constructing the largest sugar refinery on earth there. In another little community somewhere south of San Francisco called Watsonville, sugar beets were being grown, then transported to the refinery on a train line laid for the purpose by the Sugar King.

With a few discreet inquiries, the whereabouts of Watsonville was ascertained, and after a long discussion with Moriko, the decision to look for field work was made. That same evening, his bride announced to Thomas she was expecting their first child.

The decision was a month behind them now, and the move to their present location was two weeks past. Upon arrival in Watsonville, Thomas had inquired politely regarding employment in the sugar beet fields and had secured same almost immediately. His new employer owned sixty-three acres of land, all given over to sugar beets, and was anxious for field hands he could afford.

"Buck a day with two meals and a room in the bunkhouse. Your wife can help the bunkhouse cook and the laundress for fifty cents a day," the farmer had said.

"Okey dokey," Thomas had replied. It would do until he got some land of his own.

Their degradation continued right through to this morning. Among the dozen men occupying this bunkhouse, only one was white, One-Eye Bill. None of the other white workers would stay here among the Indians, Mexicans, Chinese and Japanese laborers, and for reasons unclear to Thomas, Bill wouldn't stay among the whites.

Who could blame them, Thomas thought as he peered into the darkness, *they fight among us and then they fight each other.*

Unlike Maui, there was no common language of communication. However imperfect, the unusual pidgin of the islands at least made misunderstandings less frequent. Also unlike Hawaii, the farmers here made no effort to segregate their non-white workers by race, so clashes of culture were inevitable.

The screen door squeaked open behind him and One-Eye Bill stepped out onto the porch tugging a strap of his suspenders up over his left shoulder.

"Whatcha lookin' at, Tom?" he inquired amiably.

"Another cold day, Bill-san," Thomas replied.

"Yeah, mebbe so, but you wait'll August Tom, it'll be hotter'n blazes by then and you'll be wishin' you lived with all them Methodists in the fog over in Pacific Grove."

"Maybe I own my own farm by then," Thomas said in an unguarded moment.

With his one good eye, old Bill regarded Thomas curiously.

"What makes you think anybody's gonna sell you any land?" he asked. "Don't you know them whites hate your guts just 'cuz you got slanty eyes?"

"What about you, Bill?" Thomas asked, ignoring Bill's question, still staring into the darkness, "you are white, do you hate me because I am Japanese?"

"Half-white," the old laborer corrected. "My mother was Creole so I got a little bit a nigger in me. Some Seminole injun, too. May as well be all nigger so far as white folks is concerned. Naw, I don't hate you. Hell, you work harder then anyone else in the field."

"Nigger, what is nigger?"

"Negro, uh, black man," Bill explained. "Like from Africa."

"Ah, yes, I have seen such persons. That is why you stay with us in this bunkhouse?" Thomas asked. "Whites will not let you stay with them?"

"Naw, I pass for white when I wanna. I just don't wanna be associated with them high-falutin' bastards for the most part. Who knows, mebbe you'll get yourself a farm anyway. Mebbe I'll come work for you!" Bill laughed heartily at the thought.

Thomas started to reply but was interrupted by the harsh clang of the meal bell signaling the start of breakfast. The two men went back into the bunkhouse to gather around the table and start the workday just as the first gray light began to silhouette Mount Madonna and the other foothills to the east.

The Kremlin

Moscow, Russia
Early June 1900

Tsar Nicholas II was not a happy monarch. He wanted to be at the Summer Palace with Alexandra and his children. Instead, he was listening to his generals, admirals and ministers drone on endlessly about the situation in the Asian Pacific. Before assuming the throne he had made a grand tour of the East both Near and Far. Like all young Victorian era royalty, as prince, he was exposed to the many cultures represented in the political neighborhood, and the neighborhood for Russia was vast indeed. A tour of the kingdom exhibited proper interest in his subjects. It was also an excellent opportunity to indulge in hunting safaris, exotic entertainment and indulgent shopping sprees.

As his advisors droned on he found himself daydreaming of his carefree pre-Tsar days nearly twenty years ago and his pleasant incognito forays into Nagasaki for shopping. Relations at the time were cordial and the Russian fleet maintained its base of operations there.

He ignored the sea of functionaries here in the Kremlin and spied a souvenir he had bought in Kyoto. Painstakingly carved in exquisite detail from a single ivory walrus tusk, the keepsake depicted a Japanese village complete with gardens, roads, homes, people, bridges and animals. To most observers it was merely a curiosity—brilliantly executed to be sure—but not particularly meaningful. To the Tsar, it brought a warm remembrance of places visited but also reminded him of his impression that all those foreign faces seemed so similar.

"Your father was very determined to have a united Motherland stretching from the Black Sea to the Pacific Ocean, Your Highness." Sergei Witte said, breaking the Tsar's reverie. "That is why he started the railroad, and why you are finishing it."

"I hardly need reminding by my Finance Minister what my intentions are," Nicholas replied testily, "or those of my father, for that matter."

"No offense was intended Your Highness, my apologies."

"Yes, yes, no offense intended and none taken, now get on with it." Imperial nerves were beginning to fray and the more astute observers in the room kept their own counsel as the debate re-engaged once more.

Almost immediately, the Tsar disappeared into the mists of his memory, once again picking up his recollection of the enchanting geishas he danced with in a tearoom in Kyoto. Absently rubbing at a scar on his forehead he was reminded of the incident in the small town of Otsu where he had traveled for a day. As crowds lined the streets to cheer the Russian Prince one of the policemen along the route had suddenly drawn his sword and lunged at the visitor, striking a glancing blow that drew blood in an assassination attempt. He recalled that little real physical damage was done and the actions were quickly attributed to the work of a fanatic xenophobe.

Nonetheless, upon learning of the event, his father—Tsar Alexander II—cut short the visit and had Nicholas rushed back to Pacific Russia to the new town carved out of the wilderness named Vladivostok.

In any event, despite his fascination with all things Asian and his near obsession with creating a Euro-Asian empire, *today* he didn't much want to hear about a few islands six thousand miles away inhabited mostly by peasant fishermen and sea lions. He shook himself back to the present. This discussion was particularly galling given the ruinous expense in the last decade for the Trans-Siberian Railroad. His father had arranged for him to break ground on the eastern terminus of the railroad, principally to show critics in the royal court of his serious intention see the massive project completed. Now, with internal dissension and public criticism of the Pacific strategy becoming increasingly strident, he would have to push the construction through to justify what had already been done. To stop now would be to admit defeat. *We simply have to find a way!*

"Have we not been granted a concession and lease in our treaty with the Chinese for the railway to Port Arthur?" the Tsar asked impatiently. "Have we not secured with our Pacific fleet the harbor there? Do we not have Russian soldiers in garrison along the Liantung Peninsula?"

"Your Highness, all those things are true, but it is also true that the Japanese have annexed by force huge tracts in China. They resent our presence in Korea and China, particularly since it was the Motherland and our European allies that forced them to vacate much of the territory we now occupy. It must be very bitter for them. Whatever goodwill that once existed between our countries is now surely gone." He continued, "I believe they intend to try for all of Sakhalin Island and perhaps Vladivostok as well."

The Tsar was trying to remember which Admiral this was—without success.

"We must resist vigorously," the admiral concluded, "should we lose control of the region, our only year-round Pacific port would be gone and the Japanese would be free to overrun Manchuria and Korea with impunity."

This fool thinks I do not know or understand this? Perhaps his retirement is overdue, the Tsar thought.

"Let us not forget, Nicholas, that there is money to be made out there," Finance Minister Witte said. "We built the railroad to increase our trading connection with the Pacific, and we are not the only country with colonial ambitions in the area. There are vast resources within the region. If we don't control them, our enemies will."

Slightly annoyed by his ministers' familiarity in the presence of the military officers and his imperial forbearance worn thin, the Tsar abruptly arose. A gaggle of senior officers leapt to their feet sending maps and papers flying.

"There are vast resources available in the Motherland which we cannot even begin to use now," he stormed. "What value is it to spend huge sums to control more resources we cannot use?"

"To deny those resources to those who would use them against us," the Foreign Minister responded smoothly. Several of the senior officers in the gathering nodded their approval of the assessment.

"Very well," the Tsar said irritably. "Admiral, prepare the fleet in whatever manner you deem proper and proceed with the defense." Turning to the Foreign Minister he said, "Try to negotiate something with the Japanese, or failing that, at least tell them our intentions are benign." He turned on his heels and left the room. This time he was going to the Summer Palace.

Alki Point
West Seattle
Washington State
November 30, 1900

The heroic appearance of late autumn sunshine had attracted a few hardy souls to the water's edge for a last glimpse of brightness before the typical rain, wind and cloud cover of the Pacific Northwest winter settled in for the next five months. Among the small cluster of people enjoying the moment was the Reverend Pearson, his wife and two children. He and Marie each sat on a rock cuddling a child against the chill breeze that blew in spite of the sunshine. Across a few miles of water, Bainbridge Island glistened like a polished emerald floating in a sapphire sea, as a shaft of light illuminated the water and trees dotting the hills of the island. Tugboats, log tenders and ferries from the Mosquito Fleet chugged purposefully through the waters on appointed rounds.

"We received a letter from Thomas Sakai today," the Pastor said to his wife.

"Really? That's wonderful! I've been wondering how they have been. Will you read it to me?" Marie asked.

"I've been thinking perhaps we should renew our invitation for a move up here," he said. "Tell me what you think after you hear this:

"*Honorable Ambrose and Marie,*

Moriko and I are hoping this letter finds you and your son well. We are living in Calif. now in a bunkhouse on a farm near Watsonville. It is between Monterey and Santa Cruz. I work for a farmer growing sugar beets for a big refinery. It is much different than Hawaii. The work is very difficult, but no more than on Maui.

"It please to tell of my new child. Moriko brought forth a son just two weeks ago. Almost the same birthday as Joshua! He is pink and hairy and cried loudly when he was born, just like a Samurai! His birth was recorded at the county courthouse in Santa Cruz so my son is citizen of United States. I think now I can buy land somewhere if I can find farmer willing to sell.

'Each day in our room we read the bible you gave me and we pray. We pray for you and our other friends and we pray for those who hate us and fear us but we don't understand...'"

"Good Heavens, Ambrose. It sounds dreadful in California. What is the world coming to when a small family is the object of such bitterness?"

"Unfortunately my darling," the missionary replied, "we are barely more than a generation removed from a time when white men traded in human flesh as property. Humankind since the fall from grace seems to have a peculiar gift for cruelty, injustice and hate. Some people look for excuses for their own shortcomings and failures and find easy targets among the colored races."

"Well, I find it despicable." Marie adjusted her infant daughter under her shawl, offering her breast to the hungry newborn. "Pray, continue reading, my dear."

"Yes, of course... Uhmm," he fumbled with the paper and continued:

"'...and we pray for those who hate us and fear us, but we don't understand why anyone should. All I want is a small farm of my own and the freedom to be my own Luna. Why should anyone fear me for that?

'I have named my son Franklin. I have read about the Founding Fathers of the United States and Benjamin Franklin. This year I read his Almanack and found many useful informations in it. Benjamin is a good name too, but one of the men I work with is Benjamin and he is not a good man.

'The owner of the farm where we are living says that there is no work for me or Moriko in the winter and he will not pay us again until March or April. I was going to move to another place in California where winter is more like Maui but I read in newspaper that

Chinese and Japanese men are sometimes hanged or beaten. Maybe I will go back to Hawaii to a different island.

'Moriko wishes me to remind you of how much we miss you. You have been good friend and helped us find God to whom we pray daily.

'Your faithful friends in Christ,

'Thomas and Moriko Sakai and Baby Franklin'"

The wind had picked up and gray clouds had scudded across the sky obscuring the sun. Around the point a squall line could be seen approaching from the northeast. It would only be a few moments before a cold November shower would shroud the area.

"Come along, dear, little Rachel can finish her supper later. Let's get back to the buggy and head for home. I'll write to Thomas and invite him to come here."

Japanese Imperial Palace
Tokyo, Japan
April 15, 1901

"The Tsar goes too far. He asks too much. I cannot present such a message to the Emperor." The words spoken by the minister were formal and in the carefully modulated tones peculiar to diplomatic exchanges.

The Russian ambassador to Japan observed his counterpart blandly, betraying nothing in his own countenance and discerning nothing from his study. After a slightly longer-than-polite pause he made his response.

"I am instructed by my government to reassure the Emperor that our intentions in Port Arthur and on the Liantung Peninsula are benign. We wish only to continue to service our rail link with Vladivostok to facilitate the transportation of mercantile and farm and trade goods to and from the Motherland."

"And to resupply troops stationed along the rail line and sailors of the Russian Imperial Fleet at anchor in Port Arthur," the Japanese diplomat said mildly, not really a question, not quite an accusation, just an assertion of fact.

"Their presence is merely to defend the line from saboteurs among the Chinese who do not honor their country's treaty and lease with us," Sergei Ivanovich continued. "Surely His Highness cannot object to a few men serving as policemen along our rail line."

Oishi Akagi was about to spring the trap but knew he must proceed cautiously and not scare away the quarry.

"And just as surely," Akagi said with calculated offhandedness, "the Tsar and his European allies could not object to our continued exploration for the resources Japan needs for growth and self-defense...in non-treaty areas, of course."

Tiny hairs on the back of Sergei's neck bristled a warning and his mind raced. *Be very careful here, Ivanovich,* he thought. *The Japanese were very upset by the pressure of our allies that forced them from the mainland. This devil is up to something!*

"The Tsar and his allies understand the dilemma the search for resources and the requirements for defense pose for all nations. We too, search for resources and new markets for our products." Sergei paused for a moment, then continued with a firm but polite edge to his voice. "We honor and defend our treaties and leases and rely on our neighbors and friends to respect them. Tsar Nicholas expects his friend the Emperor would do no less for Japan."

"Certainly not," Akagi said responding with corresponding firmness. "The Imperial Army and Navy will do what is necessary to defend the home islands and seek out prosperity in a modern world for our citizens and the citizens of nations historically bound to us through language and culture."

There it is! They want to break our Chinese treaty and claim 'historical' ties of culture and language forced them to act. Ivanovich sat very still, saying nothing, waiting for the other shoe to drop.

"Naturally, if neighbors and friends should ask for help from the Emperor in a matter of mutual interest, he would feel obligated to lend a hand," the Japanese Foreign Minister concluded.

"Of course, Oishi-san." Ivanovich hoped a little familiarity would put his counterpart off guard. "And of course, Russia, too, would hold out the hand of charity and assistance to an ailing ally. So you see my friend, our two countries are not so different after all."

"Not so different after all," Akagi echoed reassuringly. In his mind he thought, *We are very different, and soon you will know firsthand just how different.*

Warnings issued by both sides, the Russian thought. *Both sides understand the limits of the other. This is good. I must report to the Tsar.*

The Russians are weak and overextended. They will rely on distant allies with little stomach for battle, Akagi mused, *I must convey this right away.*

Oishi arose as did the Russian diplomat. Akagi bowed slightly from the waist and extended his right hand. Ivanovich mimicked the bow and grasped his host's hand warmly. Both men left the room and reported to their respective monarchs. Neither recognized the subtle differences in the nature of their mutual warning, and thus repeated entirely incorrectly the intent of the other. Trouble was just out of sight over the horizon and neither government had understood the other.

Headquarters, Japanese Imperial Fleet
Tokyo City
Tokyo Prefecture, Japan
July 6, 1901

"The army can't even manage its field officers half the time. Junior officers wander off on adventures Tokyo can't control and now they get the biggest portion of the budget." The Admiral of the Fleet was raging to several other admirals and Minister Akagi in his office. "How can it be that a nation comprised of islands in the Pacific Ocean whose very lifeblood depends on shipping and naval vessels of all shapes and description spends more on its army than it does its navy?"

This was not merely a rhetorical question on the Admiral's part. After seeing the preliminary figures for the next budget he had been astounded by the disparity and was determined to do something about it. Akagi had been sent by the Emperor to cushion the blow for the Admiral, but truthfully he believed the old sailor was right and had told the Emperor so on several occasions. Finally, after heated rhetoric from the Imperial Army General Staff, Akagi and the Emperor, at some personal risk, had won the day. He was here to deliver good news to the Admiralty. But first he would let the warrior blow off some steam.

"We hear almost daily," the Chief of Staff continued, "about the threat of the Russian Fleet at Port Arthur and how the Baltic Fleet may be sent to reinforce them. How do I respond? Should I commandeer a few Chinese junks from fishermen and put sailors with peashooters in the bow?"

A chuckle circulated among the assembled admirals and commanders but was snuffed quickly with a stern look from the speaker.

"You find that humorous now, but you will feel differently if you find yourself aboard a light cruiser with five-inch guns facing a Russian battleship with ten-inch guns, armor plating and twice the firing range." Spent, he sagged back into his chair behind his desk. Oishi now took the opportunity to deliver his news.

"The Emperor has reviewed the budget..." Akagi began. The Admiral shifted to a more upright position in his chair. "...and believes it was poorly conceived for the next year. He has instructed the Finance Minister to resubmit, within ten days, a budget that increases the portion for the Imperial Navy by fourteen percent."

An audible murmur of surprise went up. It was uncommon for the throne to comment on the budget of the military. An actual intervention was unprecedented.

"As you might imagine," Akagi continued, "the army was not pleased with the news and has made known its displeasure on several occasions."

The admiral could very well imagine the reaction of his land-based counterpart and understood that defying the army was risky indeed, even for the Emperor. The challenge had been laid before him and it was time for the navy to pick up the gauntlet.

"The army can't do a damn thing without the navy to carry them and all their guns and horses around," the admiral said. "I will have a conversation with the general and explain how much better cooperation will be for everyone. The Emperor can count on the navy," the old salt said eying his subordinates fiercely, "can't he, gentlemen?"

"The Emperor will be pleased and reassured by this information," Oishi said as he watched the assembled sailors nod compliantly. "And he will remember the loyalty of the navy." He arose and bowed to the gathering and left the room, heading down the hall and out of the building. *Managing the army is becoming a full time job,* he thought, *and a dangerous one, too.*

Back in the Admiral's office, all the attendees had dispersed after the meeting and the senior officer was alone with his deputy.

"What do you think?" he asked.

"I think the Emperor is on a long limb carrying a heavy stone."

"So do I," the Admiral said, "we must make certain that no one tries to chop it off."

Japanese Naval Academy
Tokyo, Japan
July 10, 1901

Isoruku, along with dozens of other fresh-faced cadets, sat at attention in his seat at the Academy. The instructor was a commander droning along about shipboard discipline, chain of command and managing subordinates. Iso had already perfected the technique of appearing attentive and engaged while his mind wandered elsewhere. It wasn't that he didn't care what the instructor had to say, it was simply that the topic at hand didn't require his full intellectual attention. While many young cadets were rapt and diligent, Yamamoto was alternating between erotic visions of beautiful young women and serene expressions of his calligraphy. Most students envisioned heroic sea battles in which they figured prominently in victories for the Emperor and glory for themselves.

Instead, Isoruku watched several flies hovering in endless circles in the classroom. Idly, he thought how wonderful it would be to view the world from high above like a bird—or a fly. It would be many years before his fledgling academic daydreams would become the basis for a new theory of naval warfare.

Alisal Land & Title Office

Salinas

Monterey County

California

July 10, 1901

Thomas sat patiently in an oak chair in the waiting area of the office. Sitting erect and displaying no emotion, he would occasionally sneak a peek to his right into the glass-enclosed office where two men were conducting a heated discussion. Most of the time he couldn't make out the words, but the emotions displayed were clear. One was a raw-boned man in Levi's and a plaid shirt. His face was red below the white line where his hat protected him. It was hard to tell if the red was from the sunburn he sported from long hours spent farming in the sun, or from the anger evident in his face. The other man, wearing a dark suit and a string bow tie, was sitting in a swivel office chair behind a desk stacked with papers. He was cool and collected and appeared to be trying to calm the overwrought man across from him.

"Damn it, Sam, I don't wanna sell to no damn Jap. I got enough trouble with my neighbors as it is over water rights from the river. Hell, if I sell to this guy, I'll get run outta the county for sure. I'm gettin' too damn old to be startin' over again somewheres else."

"Billy," Sam replied, "with the money he's offering for your spread, you could start up a store or something. You and Hilda wouldn't have to work so hard anymore. Like you say, you're getting a little long in the tooth to be working fields alongside the Mexicans, even if you do own the land. So what if this guy's a Jap? Hell, if you can't make a go of it, he won't be able to either. In two or three years he'll have to sell anyway and the neighbors will forget he was ever there."

"Well, I ain't gonna do it. I ain't gonna sell out to no Jap. I got six more weeks till the bank note is due, so I'll wait."

The land broker scrutinized the face across the desk and saw the stubborn set of Billy's jaw. He realized any further discussion would be fruitless. "You're afraid, aren't you, Billy?"

"Afraid of what?" he asked.

"Afraid that little man sitting out there in the waiting room might be able to make a go of it when you couldn't. That'd be really hard to swallow, wouldn't it?"

Billy jumped to his feet, his face surging red as a beet with anger, the veins in his neck bulged as he pointed right at Sam's nose "You go to hell, you son of a bitch! I ain't afraid of nothin' of the sort! You just find me a proper buyer, a white man. Don't be bringing me anymore Japs. Or chinks or niggers or spics neither. Now you do that or I'll look for an agent that will!" He picked up his hat, shoved it down on his head and stormed out of the office. He slammed the door so hard that Sam thought surely the windows would break.

Thomas followed the man with his eyes as he strode purposefully out of the office, past the chair in which he was sitting and out the door, pointedly not looking at him.

"I'm sorry, Thomas," Sam said. He had followed Billy out the door and was standing next to the frustrated buyer. "He says he won't sell to you at any price."

"Because I am Japanese?" He looked at Sam, already knowing the answer.

A Letter
July 14, 1901

Dear Ambrose and Marie,

Thank you for your kind invitation to come to your home. It is most generous and welcome. Moriko is feeling well and Franklin grows bigger and stronger with each passing week. Already he crawls about on the floors so fast we sometimes cannot catch him!

I try many times to buy land for a small farm but can find no haole willing to sell to me. I work in the fields now again but can think only of my own farm. Are there farmers in your Seattle? If we come there will we be able to buy a farm?

Each day I pray to God for His will to be done, but I don't think I understand what is His will. Maybe you can explain this to me when we visit.

I have saved money for many years now and we will come to your home next month. I will buy tickets for a ship's passage from San Francisco to Seattle. When I get them I will send a telegram to you so you may plan upon our arrival. Please to find us a suitable hotel in Nippon area of Seattle to stay.

Your friend in Jesus,

Thomas

Pearson Family Residence
West Seattle
Washington State
August 18th, 1901

"Joshua Pearson, you come here this minute!" The two-year old toddler peered at his mother between the slats in the dining chairs. With a shriek of laughter he suddenly darted left and ran as fast as his short wobbly legs would carry him down the hall toward the nursery. Seeing her opportunity, Marie raced down the hall and snatched the child swinging him into her arms. Peals of delighted laughter cascaded from the child as Marie headed back into the main parlor and handed the squirming child to his father.

"Reverend Pearson, if you would please hold this wiggle-worm while I fetch his sister, we can be on our way."

"I would be delighted, my dear." The child settled down quickly and submitted to being bundled into a tiny shirt.

With the children gathered, the family stepped out of their modest home to the carriage awaiting them outside. Swinging his son up and then helping his wife, the reverend called up to the driver, "To the Black Ball Terminal at Alki Point." The driver tipped his hat and the group lurched into the morning.

The Mosquito Fleet ferry chugged along the peninsula jutting into the Puget Sound, finally rounding the last point to reveal the city of the clergyman's birth. It clung tenaciously to the hills, rising from the shore's edge. Seattle had been a backwater timber-and-fur trading port with a booming fishing industry when he was born, but now it was a wiry upstart of a metropolitan center rebuilding after a devastating fire had leveled huge portions. Like San Francisco a half-century earlier, Seattle had experienced explosive growth, the result of discovery of Canadian gold. Even the mayor of Seattle was smitten with 'that damned yellow fever', abandoning his elective post to seek a bonanza.

Seattle served as a jumping off point for fortune hunters headed to the Klondike. As in California, most of the real riches were found in providing outfitting and supply. The provincial government required six months of victuals and tools—per person—before gold-fevered adventurers could begin the perilous trek to the panning fields. Bordellos, saloons and gambling houses abounded as did thieves, murderers and unscrupulous merchants. It was to this sinful city the Reverend Ambrose Pearson brought his wife and two children this morning to find their old friends.

After the short passage, the ferry tied up at the dock at the foot of Coleman Avenue. The Pearson family fell into line with the motley assortment of disembarking passengers and picked their way through the crowds swarming the wharf near the pier entrance.

Thomas and his family would be arriving sometime that afternoon at another pier, so Pearson engaged the services of a porter—in advance of the ship's arrival—to ensure timely help with the luggage. While steamships had made passages more reliably accurate —measured in hours rather than days or weeks—they had also made arrivals and departures insufferably more chaotic. Hordes of well-wishers for those embarking for points elsewhere would be dueling for precious dock space with throngs of cabbies, porters, sailors and folks just like the Pearson family awaiting arrivals. All would have their own agendas and disarray would be the order of the day.

The sun shone down on the protected waters of Elliott Bay and the warmth was lulling the entire area into lethargy. Longtime residents of the area knew such a day was to be lingered over and enjoyed. Savored and remembered, to be recalled during the long, cold nights of rain and wind that would be upon them in just a few short weeks. The family ambled down the embarcadero among the screeching fishmongers and steam-belching factories populated with eternally weary salmon cannery workers, past the bull-necked, bustling longshoremen, weaving among the multitude of horse-drawn drayage wagons. The reverend observed to his wife how waterfronts throughout the world resemble each other even to the languages heard in every port. It was a glorious morning to be alive strolling with your spouse and children along the waterfront.

After a while with the children beginning to fuss, and the smell of fish, manure and rotting seaweed beginning to lose its piquant allure, Ambrose hailed a hansom cab and instructed the driver to take them to the shopping district. The two-wheeled carriage nimbly snaked through the area, dodging stacks of shipping containers and occasionally eliciting an angry shout and clenched fist from pedestrians forced to flee its path. Mrs. Pearson desired a visit to a millinery shop and a dry goods store on Denny Avenue. There were some specialty items needed at the hardware and a suitable lunch to be found as well. It was expected they would return to the docks in a few hours, gather their friends and be on their way home by evening.

What had started as a beautiful day had evolved into a rare event in the Puget Sound area, a scorcher. The mercury had risen dramatically in four hours to eighty two degrees—a record it was said—without a whisper of breeze from any direction. Even the reverend was in rolled-up shirtsleeves as his entourage awaited the final docking of the giant ship. Ponderously pushed into position dockside by a swarm of tiny tugboats, the *Klondike Princess* finally began to disgorge passengers when the gangways were secure.

The minister surveyed the scene; as expected first-class was debarked first, met either by liveried servants, or politely snooty relatives. Second-class and steerage was a mix of businessmen, looking harried for the most part, and individuals and families of every stripe. Tempers had risen with the thermometer, so shoving matches and coarse language surrounded some of the luggage carts. Marie gasped as she saw one particularly salty-tongued woman pull a hat pin from her coiffure, and shove it to its pearl hilt into the buttocks of a fat, sweaty man blocking her way. Colorful parasols, initially used to fend off the sun had been pressed into service as lances—or even swords—either as self-defense or to mount an assault on a particular bag being held hostage by the impenetrable sea of people.

It was Ambrose who finally spotted Thomas and Moriko treading about halfway down the ramp. Pearson summoned the porter he had engaged, pointing out his target. When he was certain the man had identified the object of his employment he carefully instructed him and retreated with his household to the relative safety of the wharf entrance.

The reunion of the friends so long apart was a joyous event. Wide smiles, earnest handshakes and unselfconscious hugs were exchanged, and tears of joy mixed with rivulets of perspiration were mopped away. More than one eyebrow had been raised among onlookers as the unlikely group jabbered away in an odd amalgam of English, Japanese and Hawaiian Pidgin.

The porter had carried the trunks and luggage and stowed them with the boxes of new purchases from the Pearson's shopping excursion. The group found seats in the wagon for the short ride back to the ferry, thence to Alki and home.

"Thomas-san," the reverend enthused, "it is so good to see you and your family once again."

"You honor me and my humble family with your words," Sakai replied earnestly. "It is good once again to be in the presence of friends."

Upon docking in West Seattle, Minister Pearson hailed one of the many carriages for hire that always met the little boat when it arrived; the goods and passengers were loaded and began the ride back to the house the Pearsons had occupied for over a year.

The two friends lapsed into the easy silence allowed men of long acquaintance and listened to the womenfolk chatter and the carriage clatter over the rocky road that carried them home.

Forward Gun Turret
Heavy Cruiser *Nisshin*
Waters between Iki and Tsushima islands
Sea of Japan
15:17 hours local time, May 25, 1905

Ensign Isoroku Yamamoto scrutinized the papers in front of him. A clipboard, holding the inventory sheets he was managing, swung freely from a chain around his neck allowing his hands to remain free. A warning rang out from the loader and the young Ensign dropped the board and clapped his hands over his ears. Seconds later the deck shook violently beneath his feet and a tremendous report was heard as the eight-inch guns belched another fusillade of high-explosive shells toward the Russian warship *Zhemchug* several miles away.

Calmly he retrieved the paperwork and made a notation of the number of shells fired. It was critical to know how much ammunition had been expended so the captain could make the proper decision about whether to press an attack or withdraw for re-supply. Iso listened to the whine of the steam-driven elevator lifting new shells from the magazine deep within the bowels of the British-made warship. He could hear the hydraulic ramrod pushing the shells into the barrels and thought he could also make out the whisper of the silk bag of gunpowder loading into the gun breech as well. The breech block rotated into locking position and again the loader sounded the firing alarm.

In that moment Hell's fury seemed suddenly unleashed. The deck plate below his feet heaved wildly as an enormous explosion rocked the ship. Suddenly engulfed in smoke and flames, the stunned young seaman tried to regain his feet only to fall again onto the buckled deck. Dazed, he looked around. Some sailors were scrambling to douse fires, others were helping shipmates wounded in the explosion; others still had the haunted eyes of wild panic that overwhelms many recruits at the first exposure to combat.

As he staggered to his feet he reached to pull his uniform tunic down but could not grip the bottom. Staring at his left hand he observed remotely that his index and middle finger were severed, hanging only by thin flaps of skin. He seemed to be covered in blood as well. He pawed at the stains ineffectually, but they stubbornly refused to disappear. This distressed him. His uniform was not in proper order. The captain would be displeased. He must return to his quarters for a clean uniform.

The Ensign's first deployment, as was his role in this war, was over. It was quite some time later, in the hospital, when he learned of the outcome of the engagement. Upon their detection, his admiral had shadowed the combined Russian Baltic and Pacific fleets and had launched an attack. The rout had been complete; the victory crushing the Russian Fleet and securing the victory won in Port Arthur the previous year. The way was clear to retake Korea and capture key ports in the Philippines without meddlesome interference from Moscow.

Russian Admiralty Headquarters
The Kremlin
Moscow, Russia
June 7, 1905

The magnitude of the disaster of the Battle of Tsushima was just beginning to sink in as threadbare reports filtered in from survivors and the few ships that had managed to escape destruction by fleeing under cover of smoke and darkness to neutral ports. Thousands of Russian sailors were dead, carried to the bottom of the sea with the loss of twenty or more capital ships and possibly another two score of miscellaneous tenders and cargo ships.

The combined Russian fleets had been eviscerated by an Imperial Japanese fleet of stronger vessels with better commanders, tactics and training. The humiliation of the Port Arthur debacle the previous year was now but a pinprick, comparatively speaking. The Japanese now commanded the Sea of Japan. Indeed, the whole of the western Pacific was theirs to roam unchallenged by any, except perhaps the Americans. Withdrawal from the Korean Peninsula and the abandonment of the Chinese portion of the railroad was likely in the near future simply because there was now no way to defend it. Someone was going to pay dearly for this, although at the moment, there were lots of candidates but no clear front runner.

"How is so complete a disaster even possible, admiral?" The Tsar was tight lipped and grim as his eyes bored in on the Chief of Naval Operations. "How is it possible to lose nearly every ship in the fleet without sinking even one vessel of the opposing forces?"

The uncomfortable admiral squirmed nervously standing at attention. Beads of flop sweat popped out on his forehead and upper lip. He tugged at his tunic collar trying to catch his breath as he glanced at some of the reports that lay in front of him.

"Truthfully, Your Highness, I cannot yet say," he equivocated. "I will need to study these reports and others as they come in before I can answer your question competently."

"Competently!" the Tsar exploded out of his chair and began frenetic pacing the length of the room. "Competently!" he blazed. "The entire Baltic and Asiatic fleets are at the bottom of the Sea of Japan in only two days and you have the audacity to even speak that word!"

"Well, naturally the admiral commanding the fleet must certainly bear ultimate responsibility for its loss," the chief of staff said reasonably.

"Yes, I can imagine that your plan for this grand escapade was flawless and the staff here in Moscow most diligent in perfect organization." The sarcasm and irritation were clear in Nicholas' voice. "And I expect you will deduct the cost of the fleet from his pension."

"I will personally take charge and conduct a thorough investigation of this incident, Your Highness. The guilty parties will be brought to account."

"Don't forget to wash your hands carefully," the Tsar said sourly.

"I don't understand, Your Highness."

The Russian ruler stared out the window at the soft breeze riffling through the spring growth on the trees below the window. "The blood of six thousand sons of the Motherland is on your hands; and on mine, Admiral, and on mine."

Bainbridge Island

Lower Puget Sound
Washington State, USA
June 17, 1910

"Well, Thomas, the time has finally come!" the reverend exulted. "I am most pleased to hand you the deed to your property. And a fine parcel it is, too."

"Thank you Ambrose," was all his emotionally overcome friend could choke out as he took the papers. "Thank you so much."

"You're more welcome than you imagine." Pearson draped his arm around his friend. "But this is your victory, your struggle and reward. You and Moriko earned this. I am only the delivery boy."

"But you bought the land for me. You made the arrangements. Without you, Moriko and I would still be servants." Thomas looked at his wife and their second and third child playing with the young children of their friends.

"Poppycock! McGonical was an immigrant, too. The Irish are despised and hated in the east almost as much or more than the Japanese are here in the west. He knew the pain you've endured and how much you wanted your own place."

Thomas saw Joshua and Frank laughing and tottering at the end of the plot by the survey stakes. His eyes welled up again as he glanced at his friend then gazed out at the five little acres overlooking the Sound.

Five acres of timber stumps, rocks and Russian blackberries; five acres of back-breaking labor: No house, no water and no equipment. Five acres of land on a little island with few roads and fewer neighbors; Five acres of potential.

Finally, the dream was *his*.

Part Two

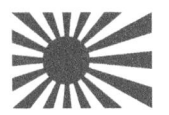

Pike Place Market
Seattle, Washington
6:15 a.m., June 23, 1938

"These are the last of the strawberries, Dad," Frank Sakai said to the old man in the produce stall. "Everything else is spinach, lettuce, green beans and radishes."

"It will be enough for now. Grocers will come first, then the cooks. Maybe we will be on our way home before noon today."

"I'll finish unloading and move the truck," Frank agreed.

Thomas Sakai went about the work of setting up the little market space as he and his son had done every weekend of the growing season for years. His routine, as well as those of many other *Issei* growers and fishers that had shops in the Pike Place Market, was well rehearsed, and he daydreamed as he shuffled boxes. Gazing west through the windows of the idiosyncratic building clinging precariously to one of the many hillsides of Seattle, he could see his island home across Elliott Bay and marvel at all the changes the years had brought.

Thomas thought about the news of his father's death years ago. A letter from his sister told of the event and a recent one said his brother had joined the army and was a major now, stationed somewhere in China. His sister had given birth to four children, all sons. She worked in a bullet factory and her husband, Ichiro, worked in the Mitsubishi shipyards of Kobe building warships for the Imperial Navy. All the nieces and nephews were also in the military. This worried Thomas but he said nothing of it in letters. He could not change things and didn't wish to unduly upset his sister.

His own family was prospering and he told his sister of his own grandchildren. His oldest son Frank and his wife Eleanor had three children. Steven was twenty, Mary was eighteen and Benjamin, who was a surprise, was eleven. They still lived with Thomas and Moriko in the family home built over thirty years ago on the island. Some modernization and expansion had been required of course, but the old man remembered every nail driven and brush full of paint applied, for he had carefully accounted for each in tidy ledger books.

His daughter Sarah had married a Merchant Marine and lived in nearby Bremerton with two children of her own.

The family had prospered in spite of the country's daunting economic circumstances, because people still needed to eat. His farm was tolerably isolated and plunder by strangers was rarely a problem. Frugality had always been a way of life for his family. Everyone contributed to success even the children in his or her small way.

"Hey Gramps, you forgot this!"

Startled from his reverie, Thomas looked up at his oldest grandson holding out a cedar cigar box, worn with age and often repaired.

"Quietly, my child," he chided, gently taking what served as a cash depository and secreting it among the clutter of farm crates. "This is still a depression and it is not wise to display your wealth, even modestly, to desperate people."

"Oh Gramps, you worry too much," the young man said with a broad grin.

"Better to plan for prevention than worry about a cure." Sometimes he imagined the reckless smiles of his long-dead friend Sammy in the face of his grandson.

"Your grandfather is a wise man, Steven. I would pay him great heed."

Thomas and Steven turned to greet the owner of the rich baritone voice. The Reverend Ambrose Pearson was still a striking presence even though his remaining hair was a great shock of white and his gaunt figure slightly stooped.

"My dear friend," Thomas said, "Still the first customer of every week after all these years."

"It's because you still grow the best strawberries and vegetables in all of Washington. The rich soil produces the greater harvest than the barren rock. I come to you because you cast your seeds upon the rich soil."

"And the tree stumps, too," Thomas laughed.

"May the Lord have mercy, there were plenty of those, weren't there!"

The two old friends shared a quiet moment of recollection of the blasting and hauling and burning and chopping and digging it had taken to clear not just the land Thomas had, but that of all his neighbors who pitched in to help him. In ten years more than a thousand acres of timberland on the island had been changed into lush acreage – mostly operated by Japanese farmers. Providing much of the produce used in Seattle. Its success was also creating a worrisome backlash of jealousy among white farmers with less efficient operations.

"Will it be the usual, Reverend?" Frank had returned from parking the truck.

"No actually, Joshua and Josephine are visiting from Oak Harbor this weekend. I'll need twice as much as usual."

"Will my namesake be along as well?" Frank asked.

"Richard Franklin? Certainly, and precocious as ever. his eleventh birthday has already long since passed. Can you imagine that?" The retired preacher returned his attention to the old man in the stall. "Toshio we are becoming old men!" he said in mock astonishment. "What are we to make of it?"

Thomas laughed heartily. Ambrose was the only person besides his wife who still called him by his Japanese name. "*Becoming* old men," he retorted, "we've been old men a long time already. My son is *becoming* an old man." His humor subsided as he locked eyes with his dearest friend.

"What are we to make of it? It has been a strange journey through life, Ambrose," he replied. "But I am a satisfied man. I have my farm and my family and my friends. It is a good life I have. More than I could have imagined when I was cutting cane in Maui."

Returning his gaze, the cleric studied his friend pensively for a long moment then spoke. "Yes, it has been an interesting journey, but I must admit that while I don't seek to end this path prematurely, sometimes I yearn for Gideon's trumpet to call me home. I sorely miss my dearest Marie and wish to be reunited in eternity."

"How many times have you told me, Ambrose," the elder Sakai said, "that the God, who knows even the sparrow's fall knows also your pain and will reward you with eternal glory in His presence?"

The pastor accepted the groceries from Frank who politely refused payment as he did each week. "And so it is that the pupil shall become the teacher."

In the Imperial Valley
California
Mid-July 1938

Goro Akagi studied the document before him carefully. The skillfully drawn *kanji* informed him he was being recalled from his long posting as an agricultural attaché in the United States. He was to book passage on the next vessel departing San Francisco bound for Honolulu there to await further instructions. The very blandness of the document served as a warning from his father.

He had first been sent to California as a spy by his father in 1920, posing as an agricultural specialist. His wife had given birth to their first child, Arimoto, in a small central California farm town called Salinas. Dutifully, he remained in the United States for seven long years, trekking up and down the West Coast studying potatoes, sugar beets, carrots, grain, hops and fruit trees. All the while he carefully coded more important information in the routine reports about crop-raising he sent back home. By virtue of exposure he had actually become expert in agriculture as well. By now even his regular cover reports had real value. When first called home briefly several years earlier, there was some embarrassment and loss of face when it was revealed that his son actually spoke English —and even farm worker Spanish—far better than Japanese. All totaled Goro and his family had live in the U.S. for sixteen of the last twenty years,

Goro and his father Oishi, still powerful as the interlocutor in the Imperial Court and the *zaibatsu*, had arranged for private instruction for the child when they were in the home islands. Slowly his native language skills improved, although he never quite lost his odd American accent.

Now Goro was being recalled from his second lengthy posting. His wife still spoke almost no English and his son had nearly finished in an American high school in San Jose, California. His son Arimoto had studied United States history and recited the Pledge of Allegiance along with his friends and fellow students. He wore Levis and preferred Coke and meatloaf over tea and sushi.

Goro had wanted to send his son back to Japan to live with his grandfather, but his wife had implored him not to take her only child from her and to his current regret he had relented. *So, the time is near and I must be most careful!*

Akagi quietly began arranging to return to Hokkaido and one day the following week, after a bothersome quarrel with his recalcitrant boy, he and his small family boarded a Japanese freighter and vanished from the California landscape like fog fleeing the sun. Some of the Nisei field hands he had come to know wondered briefly what had become of their acquaintance. His son's final year of high school was nearly a month passed and his son's friends were accustomed to sudden departures for days or even weeks. The growing season was in full swing so not a single busy farmer noticed he was gone.

Hokai Residence
Honolulu, Hawaii Territory
August 7, 1938

"I welcome the honorable Akagi-san to this miserable house and I apologize for the poor meal that will be served." Hokai spoke as Akagi entered the spacious Honolulu residence. Hokai was a slightly built, slightly stooped, frail elderly man with a drooping mustache, a quiet voice and a commanding presence.

Goro bowed deeply and replied, "I am your humble servant unworthy of such a feast." With that the two men walked from the foyer into the room that served as a shadow embassy, office and clearing house for information and intelligence making its way from the islands back to the homeland.

Set amid a forest of ancient bonsai was the polished walnut cabinet of a Victrola record player. Hokai selected a platter from a small collection stacked nearby and carefully placed the cactus needle into the groove of the spinning disk. For a moment he indulged his idiosyncrasy for aloha music, listening to a raspy recording of the MacDowell Sisters—The Sweethearts of the Air—worn with use. As he turned his attention back to Akagi, he motioned for the younger man to come closer.

"You have new instructions from Tokyo," he said.

In the seven days since leaving San Francisco, the plan apparently had changed. Instead of returning to Hokkaido, he was now to take up residence here in Oahu, learn what he could about the United States Naval Station at Pearl Harbor and send the information to the War Ministry. Clearly distressed, he looked up at the old man.

"Is this message from my father?"

"Your father is aware of the new assignment."

The Consul had chosen his words carefully. Both men knew the political situation at home was highly volatile at the moment, and in some respects being four thousand miles away was probably a good thing. But having his wife and teenage son here for this new task was worrisome.

"I will respect the wishes of my father," he said.

Within two weeks Goro Akagi had secured employment for himself at the U.S. Naval Headquarters at Pearl Harbor and for his own safety his reluctant son Arimoto had been sent back to the homeland.

After his basic training, Arimoto was assigned to the Kasumigaura Aviation Corps. Navy Vice Admiral Yamamoto had once been second in command as a captain. Now Akagi was learning to fly with the sons of officers of the Imperial Japanese Navy.

A Public Bathhouse
Nagaoka, Japan
April 12, 1939

The scalding water of the bath was soothing to Isoroku. In the years since the explosion aboard *Nisshin* his left hip and knee ached whenever the weather changed. He never mentioned it to anyone, for what could be done except the luxury of the bath now and then and where better than in his favorite bathhouse in his beloved hometown?

The hot water soothed his mind as well. He allowed the steaming liquid to dissolve away the tensions of being Vice-Admiral of the Fleet. It was a time when his principal occupation seemed to be carefully but vigorously, resisting the lunacy of building a war machine his country could neither fuel nor man. It was all the more galling that it was being built to fight an enemy it could not defeat.

Yamamoto's mind focused on his days in Washington D.C. attached to the Japanese Embassy. He had traveled extensively across America, taking in with respect the immense vitality and self-confidence of the citizens. In Bethlehem, Pennsylvania his tour of a steel factory was most notable for the endless procession of railroad cars loaded with ore and coal destined to become coke fuel to feed the insatiable appetite of the blast furnaces. In Texas he watched armies of roughnecks manhandle drilling rigs amid a forest of oil derricks and pipelines that reminded him of a bowl of udon noodles.

Overall his impression of the United States was one of an overwhelming exuberance of energy and determination. He had long counseled to deaf ears in Tokyo to try to cultivate the U.S. as an ally rather than a foe. Instead, even now as the bath drained his tensions away, there was bickering between the government, the Emperor, and the military about how—or even if—they should conclude the Tripartite Pact with Germany and Italy. This was more folly in his view. Trying to adopt the agreement was impossible. The fools were trying to dance around being obligated without actually committing the scarce resources of Japan or naming the foe. *War with German and Italian allies against the British bulldog and the American cowboy. Ridiculous!* He thought. *This will end disastrously for Japan.*

He shook off the thoughts and returned to the simple pleasures of his bath. Stepping from the tub he sprawled naked on the adjacent wooden bench to cool for a moment. As if by magic his mistress of many years, Kawai Chioko, appeared from the mists of steam and began massaging his back with expert hands. The Vice-Admiral, resting on his elbows, drank down a large glass of sake then sank back down to the bench. As he drifted in a twilight of semi-consciousness random images of his past flashed through his mind; standing on the Shinano River Bridge overlooking Niigata as a child, graduating from the naval academy and later accepting the congratulations of his adoptive father, the elder Yamamoto, upon a promotion. He lingered on a recollection of the red-feathered *torii* flitting among the cherry trees as his mother often dragged him by Hakusan Park to the marketplace in spring.

Kawai's ministrations stirring something other than old memories in the sailor and he rolled over on his back and gazed up at the woman. As they began the comfortable eroticism of an embrace shared by long time lovers Isoroku thought, *Tomorrow I will return to Tokyo and sit behind my desk. There won't be a war tonight, so I will make love and drink too much sake. Perhaps I will gamble and win some money for her.*

Isoroku Yamamoto did just that for he had long been a high stakes gambler and had always been exceedingly lucky.

Mitsubishi Shipbuilding Yard
Kobe, Japan
August, 1939

Ichiro Kamagusa sat on a steel beam in the Mitsubishi Shipyards in Kobe. He was a heavily muscled man with tufts of unkempt hair poking out randomly from under his welder's cap. His face had an odd look. Years of arc welding glare had burned his skin to a dark mahogany except around his eyes where goggles had protected them. The effect was rather the reverse of a raccoon. As he looked around him at the swarm of workers crawling over the hulking skeleton of the newest Imperial Navy submarine, they reminded him of ants tugging against each other over a scrap of fish. Next to him on the beam was his friend and co-worker of many years, Kaiji.

Between huge bites of lukewarm rice and raw mackerel Kaiji said, "Another Imperial submarine we are building, and so big!" Bits of rice and fish went flying as he spoke. "Surely we are a great empire, feared and respected in the world."

Ichiro was not so sure but did not say so. His wife's father, living in America, had been silent on the matter in his letters. Instead he replied, "The work is hard and honorable for the glory of the Emperor, but the boat is unlucky without a name."

Kaiji grunted. It was hard to understand the navy. Every surface vessel had a name. Aircraft carriers were named after dragons and battleships after provinces. Even torpedo boats (named after birds) and light cruisers (rivers) had a name. But submarines only had numbers. Ichiro was right, it was unlucky. The two friends ate their lunch and lapsed into thoughtful silence for a few moments. Then Kaiji brightened considerably and exclaimed, "So my friend, let us give this one a name!"

Yamagusa peered around the shipyard again. Years of exposure had inured him to the pungent ozone smell of the welding, but the resulting smoke hung motionless, creating a pall in the huge dry dock. Not a breeze was stirring and the sun beat mercilessly upon their backs through the haze. Even the most distant of other shipbuilders could be seen glistening with sweat mixed with dust and smoke. Hundreds just like him were sitting anywhere even a square foot of shade was available, finishing their lunches and reluctantly putting on heavy leather gloves and dark welding goggles. Slowly he picked up his welding crayon then carefully wrote '*Pufferfish*' in kanji on the beam in the space between them. Ichiro then poured some of his sake on the beam as well. "In the spirit of bonsai and for the glory of the Emperor, I name you *Pufferfish*. Be as prickly and as deadly as your namesake." The two friends pulled on their heavy gloves, picked up their tools and went back to work on Imperial Navy submarine *I-28* (Experimental).

Oval Office

The White House
Sometime in May, 1940

Captain Richard Jones was sitting in a genuine Federalist side chair. He was one of several barely visible functionaries gathered in the Oval Office at the behest of their masters. Jones' particular master was Admiral Raymond Spruance. Spruance was presently awaiting an opportunity to interject what Jones hoped was Spru's vision of How Things Were In The Pacific. As he sat, other equally invisible functionaries trundled in and out of the room, rummaged through briefcases for papers, and otherwise tended to the gathered Big Shots like workers swarming over queen bees. The current big-wig holding forth was the President of the United States. With his cigarette holder clamped firmly in his tobacco stained teeth and his patrician air permeating the space, he was without doubt the Biggest Big Shot in the joint.

"...and that is why the United States needs to support the war against Germany without actually being at war. Guns for Churchill —and Stalin if we must—but butter for the home front," he concluded.

"I agree," Spruance said seizing the moment, "but if we focus only on the Atlantic and European situation there might be real trouble in the Pacific."

"Come, come, Ray," Roosevelt said, "How far could the Japanese reasonably extend themselves? Their supply lines are much longer in the Pacific than ours in the Atlantic."

"Everything hinges on Hawaii, Mr. President. The Emperor has sent his fleet well into the Philippines to extend oil supplies. Begging your pardon, Sir, but Hirohito and Tojo resent the hell out of this embargo you've put in place. They see it as a direct threat to their national security."

"So what?" the new speaker was Secretary of State Cordell Hull. "We have every advantage in distance, resources, manpower and military strength. We wouldn't have imposed an embargo if the Japs weren't so hell-bent for belligerence in China and Indonesia."

"That assumption isn't really true, Mr. Secretary," Spruance said. "We can't currently defend Midway or Guam in substance and even if we send the fleet from San Diego to Pearl we would still be perilously outnumbered, and frankly, under-trained. Not to mention outgunned by their battleships."

"Well, what would you propose?" The President asked.

"More ships, more planes, more fuel, more training. But most of all, more time. Negotiate with more urgency and try to get a real resolution," the Admiral was warming to the subject. "Australia is practically catatonic with worry. They have nothing to match the size and competency of Yamamoto's fleet, and we probably couldn't defend the Aleutians right now, much less do more than send a token force to the Aussies. The truth is, sir, if Yamamoto sailed into Honolulu right now we couldn't do a damn thing about it."

"More ships, more planes, more fuel," the President echoed wearily. "Ray, you must think all we do is snap our fingers and they magically appear."

"No, sir," he protested, "I understand the complications..."

"Relax, Ray, I know you do." Roosevelt sighed heavily exhaling a cloud of smoke. "So what is your proposal?"

"Move the fleet from San Diego to Honolulu. Kimmel is a good commander and we must insure that the Japanese cannot establish a forward resupply base."

"What do you think, Admiral Stark?" the President asked his Chief of Naval Operations. "Doesn't that leave the entire West Coast essentially undefended?"

"Technically yes, but Yamamoto cannot prosecute, or probably even mount a useful attack such a distance from resupply. He would have to hit five major regions separated by more than fifteen hundred miles by dividing his fleet and have a coordinated attack. Over those distances and so far from any help such an attack would be unthinkable. It's a small but calculated risk." The Chief replied. "We are also counting on a deterrent effect as well when Japan discovers the move," he added.

"We are walking a tightrope, gentlemen," Roosevelt said. "Japan is about to sign a treaty with Germany and Italy. Germany has a non-aggression pact with Russia, and England is hanging on by her fingernails. I would like to rein in Hirohito some and if you all think this is the best way then it shall be so. Well, Knox you're the last man standing, how say you?"

"Move the fleet, Mr. President," the Naval Secretary agreed. "With the navy in Pearl Harbor, Japan would be crazy to try anything big."

"Very well then, send them," he said smiling, "and pray that God truly does favor the foolish."

Imperial Fleet Headquarters
Tokyo, Japan
November 8, 1940

"Iso-san, you must be completely crazy!" Shimada Shigetaro warned. He was a classmate from the Academy and along with Yamamoto and another fellow student—Yoshido Zengo—he had been promoted to full Admiral only 3 days earlier.

"Yes, quite probably you are right. But hear me out first." Yamamoto paced the length of the room forming his thoughts.

"Despite all our warnings, negotiations with the Americans are failing and we are likely to find ourselves at war with them sometime soon. Do you not agree?"

"Reluctantly yes," Shimada said, "I fear it is inevitable."

"We cannot hope to win such a conflict in spite of the rhetoric coming from the Army. I have told the Emperor himself that at most we could hold them off for a year and a half." The CINC of the Imperial Fleet continued. "The best possible outcome would be a short conflict where we consolidate strategic positions in the Pacific, then sue for peace while Marshall and Roosevelt are still preoccupied with Europe."

"How does your plan accomplish such a thing? It is a huge risk with no guarantee of success."

"On the contrary, war at all is the huge risk with no hope of success. My plan at least might work.

"Perhaps, Iso-san, but how would you propose to carry out a coordinated surprise attack against multiple target on the mainland of the United States? We certainly couldn't occupy any territory, especially in the west. It is well known that every American owns a gun and would fight, as we would, to the death."

"That is the beauty of the idea. We do not need to hold any territory on the coast. We don't even need to engage their fleet first. All we need is to strike fear into their hearts and inflict damage on their capacity to operate ports and factories," Yamamoto paused.

"I still don't see how that secures the Pacific for Japan," Shimada wondered aloud.

"If we can render the coastal ports useless for just a few weeks we can take Pearl Harbor at our leisure. Their Pacific fleet is outmanned, outtrained and outgunned by just your Second Fleet Command. When Hawaii is secure, along with denying Midway and Guam, it will take more than a year for the U.S. Navy to have any plan to counterattack." Iso stopped pacing and looked directly at his school chum. "Then *we* must force the politicians to craft a peace agreement that consolidates our position."

"You must be absolutely crazy, Iso." Shimada shook his head. "No one will agree to such a plan, no one."

"I am sending submarines to scout targets in Seattle, Portland, San Francisco, Long Beach and San Diego. When they return with the pictures and information I need, I will be able to prove my idea to the Emperor. We may yet avoid annihilation at the hands of the Americans, Shimada."

"What if you cannot make this plan work?"

Yamamoto replied simply. "Then I will make another."

Kobe Harbor
Japan
February 5, 1941

Captain Hidashi Komatsu was of small stature even among the Japanese, but his stern countenance and legendary discipline more than compensated. His native *Ainu* features revealed his Hokkaido Island origins and it was rumored that as a youth living on the rugged banks of the Ishikari river, he had conquered discrimination against his tribe by being the fiercest member of the *Ketsumeidan*, the feared League of Blood. As if to support the legend, the Captain sported a long scar running from a missing left earlobe along the jawline and then back up to the corner of his mouth. The pale line of the scar contrasted sharply with the sunburned leathery skin of his face and neck.

When Komatsu was stressed he would grind his teeth and the scar would writhe as though alive and with his new command and untested crew he was grinding audibly. Though no one had the courage to say so to his face this quirk had earned the Captain the nickname "Sea Snake" among his crew.

"Commander Katsu," barked the Captain, "why are we not submerged to periscope depth as I commanded?"

The junior officer noted the scar was writhing ominously; even so, it was hard to concentrate as he towered over his Captain by nearly a foot. "The port side ballast valve failed to open, sir. The Chief Engineer is working to correct the problem now," the second in command reported.

Komatsu's scowl deepened as he studied his Executive Officer. Newly promoted, Commander Katsu had come to the submarine service highly recommended by his superiors. He was taller than most in the sub service making the contrast in height seem all the greater. His hair was jet black as with most of his race and his black eyes revealed a little uncertainty just now about his new superior. *He is still soft from the easy life aboard a battleship,* Hidashi thought, *but he has potential.*

"I did not see an order for repair." the Captain growled. "Your job is to report all repair orders, only then can I make informed decisions. Is that clear?"

"*Hai* Captain, it shall be as you command. Shall I order the Chief to stop?"

The Sea Snake sighed inwardly. *I hate sea trials,* he thought, *especially with new crews.* In a softer voice and a more relaxed posture he replied, "No Commander, he may continue. But you must follow the chain of command and report problems to me as soon as you issue orders. Only in discipline will we find success and glory for the Emperor. When the repairs are complete take the boat to periscope depth and call me in my quarters."

As the Captain left the bridge, no one looked him directly in the face. *So, they are afraid of me. It is a good beginning.*

Admiral's Suite, Kobe Imperial Hotel
Kobe, Japan
1 p.m. February 9, 1941

Sea Snake wasn't afraid of many people but Admiral Isoroku Yamamoto was on that short list. Komatsu stood absolutely erect and rigid and was barely breathing as the Admiral sat behind a desk in his hotel room.

After a few moments Yamamoto looked up and said mildly, "Please Captain, sit down. May I offer you some tea?" The admiral waved away a steward who left the two men alone as the Admiral poured tea for Komatsu.

"*Sumimasen Tai Sho Yamamoto,*" the Captain said taking the tea. He tried not to stare at the fingers missing on the Admiral's left hand while he perched rigidly on the edge of the proffered seat. *I'm having tea with Yamamoto!* He thought. *"What's next,* shokuji *with the Emperor?*

"Captain Komatsu, you are a highly regarded commander among the officers in the fleet. For that reason you have been chosen for a special mission known at this moment only to myself, my Chief of Staff and now you. As you know, both your submarine and the aircraft it is carrying in its hangar are experimental. This mission is to test the performance of both the submarine and the aircraft. While potentially very dangerous, it is also of vital importance to the Empire." The notion of asking for a volunteer would never have occurred to the Admiral.

"*Hai*, Admiral, as you command." Sea Snake shifted uncomfortably in the seat, carefully holding but not drinking from the teacup in his hand. The notion of questioning the mission would never have occurred to Komatsu.

The Admiral arose and walked over to look out the window. He paused then said, "The mission is highly sensitive and most secret," Yamamoto continued gazing out across the Kobe harbor sipping his tea. "You and your crew will rendezvous at sea to pick up a specially trained pilot and proceed to the United States."

The United States! Komatsu could not imagine what the Admiral had in mind for a single submarine in the waters of United States. *What arrogance Hidashi, yours might not be the only boat!*

"Your submarine alone will undertake this mission," the Admiral lied. He returned to his desk where he handed Komatsu a sealed envelope and said "No one outside this room is to know of the true nature of your sailing. Open these orders privately after you have put out to sea. They will direct you to coordinates where the nature and importance of this assignment will be made known to you. In this mission I speak for the Emperor. Thank you for coming by, Captain."

Magically on cue, the door to the Admiral's room swung open as Yamamoto finished. The steward came forward, bowed slightly first to the Admiral then to the Captain who was by now also standing. Captain Komatsu of *I-28* (Experimental) bowed to Imperial Naval Fleet Commander-in-Chief Admiral Yamamoto, turned on his heels and marched smartly out handing his untouched tea to the steward. Outside the door he was nearly overwhelmed. Yamamoto was his *on jin* and had just imposed a *gimu chu* of staggering proportion.

The Admiral sank back into his chair and rested his chin on his clasped hands contemplating the assignment he had just given. *This coming war is a fool's errand. It will be a waste of resources, equipment, and good citizens. It will bring dishonor to the homeland,* he mused. *And the weather alone will probably doom this recon mission to failure. But it must be tried for the honor and glory of the Emperor,* he thought bitterly. He turned his attention back to his desk and began calligraphy on a ceremonial scroll, promptly excluding this line of thinking.

Pier 41

Kobe Harbor, Japan
February 12, 1941

Every imaginable location inside the submarine carried provisions. Under the deck plates, stacked in the aisles, in the torpedo tubes, under bunks, hanging from valves and between torpedoes. Each item was carefully secured.

Last to come aboard were the fresh fruits, vegetables and fish. They made their way both fore and aft into the torpedo tubes, the coldest locations on board, to be stowed. These would be gone within a week anyway and could be easily ejected in an emergency. Indeed, more than one submarine had cheated certain death by jettisoning the stored contents of the torpedo tubes in an effort to fool a destroyer overhead.

Captain Hidashi Komatsu walked briskly down the wharf headed for *I-28* (Experimental) taking note of the activity, spotting his second in command on the dock. '*Pufferfish* was moored in Kobe taking on provisions preparing for its first assignment at sea. A brisk March wind sent dark clouds scudding through the skies, alternately threatening rain or glimpsing bright sunshine. The Commander had the collar up on his jacket and was looking over the manifest while his crew and dock laborers hauled provisions over the side to disappear into the bowels of the submarine. Sacks of rice, wooden boxes filled with dried fish and stacks of *nori* bound together like reams of paper were covered with canvas as protection against intermittent raindrops. Ten cases of tea disappeared down a hatch headed for the seaman's mess and ten cases of *sake* for the officer's wardroom.

Commander Katsu came to attention and saluted.

Sea Snake returned the salute. "Stand easy Kasahiro, we have sailing orders. What is the status of our supply?"

Kasahiro looked down at the clipboard he was carrying then looked around the dock. Most of the pallets of provisions had been loaded. The last of the diesel fuel trucks was already gone and the docking water supply had been disconnected.

"We should be secure in about thirty minutes, Captain. What are your orders?"

"It will be a long mission, Commander. Ask the officer in charge of the pier to post armed guards here overnight. Release the crew not on night watch to go ashore, but they must return by ten a.m. tomorrow. We will cast off by noon."

"Yes Captain, I shall see to it." Katsu was surprised. It was common to grant shore leave *after* a long sailing, but rarely the day before. As the Captain walked up the gangplank onto the sub the Commander motioned to a junior officer and relayed the orders with additional instructions. Katsu looked back at the sub just in time to see Komatsu disappear climbing down to the bridge. *I will never understand this Captain,* he thought, *but I am not afraid anymore.*

The final crewman came aboard in a driving rainstorm at 9:45 a.m. much to the satisfaction of Kasahiro Katsu. By eleven every checklist item was finished and the Captain cast off an hour early. There were no throngs of people pier side waving goodbye, just a few dock hands ignoring the Imperial Navy's largest class of submarine. *I-28* (Experimental) spooled up its twin 12,400 horsepower Mitsubishi diesel engines making turns for dead slow on the propellers and drifted the 2,584 ton, 356 foot long vessel into the shipping channel and slowly out to sea.

The last glimpse of the sacred home islands belonged to Sub-Lieutenant Takami standing watch in the conning tower. As the *Pufferfish* made her way along the *Kii-Suido* the lights from the fishing village Anan on the island of Shikoku winked feebly through the gloomy storm. The island itself was more a suggested shape as the gray hills of Tokushima seemed to merge with the sky.

Takami was swaddled in foul weather gear against the rain and wind, but his ship was making about fifteen knots with an equal following wind. The effect was that of little apparent wind and he was actually getting too warm. He opened the jacket and from time to time he would scan the horizon with his binoculars looking for other vessels whose course and speed might offer a conflict with his own. Seeing none he would lower them and replace the covers on the lenses. The young officer actually looked forward to standing watch in the sail. It replaced the tedium of drills below decks with the tedium of an endless expanse of empty ocean. It also provided two other benefits in short supply aboard a submarine, some time alone and fresh air.

While Sub-Lieutenant Takami was mulling the virtues of fresh air, the Captain of *I-28* (Experimental) was in his quarters opening the sealed orders he had received from Yamamoto.

From: Admiral Yamamoto
Chief of Naval Operations HIJN
To: Captain Hidashi Komatsu
Commanding Officer HIJN I-28 (Experimental)
Subject: Mission orders
Date: March 6, 1941

Upon receiving these orders you are to set course for twenty degrees north latitude 158 degrees west longitude. Upon reaching coordinates you shall await the Kobiashi Maru and take aboard Lieutenant Arimoto Akagi who will hand you additional orders under my seal. Such additional supplies as he may require will be available on the Kobiashi. This order is not to be shown or transmitted to any member of the crew. Destroy after reading.

ss/ Yamamoto

Komatsu placed the document in the sink and touched a match to one corner. He watched absently as it burned, then crushed the remains and rinsed them down the sink.

"Captain on the Bridge" the first officer barked as *Sea Snake* made his way onto the deck.

"Commander Katsu" Komatsu said rather more sternly than he intended, "lay in a course for 20 degrees north latitude, 158 degrees west longitude and make turns for twenty knots. Instruct all crewmen standing watch in the sail to sing out immediately upon any visual contact regardless of flag." He turned to leave the bridge and then as an afterthought he added, "Maintain radio silence."

Hawaii! Katsu looked around the bridge. Other crew members were exchanging glances as they mentally calculated where in the world the coordinates would place them and then tried to imagine what their mission might be.

The further south they traveled the milder the weather became and the crew settled into a routine. In fair weather all the hatches would be open to allow fresh air to circulate. Once this week, crewmen not standing watch were allowed a cold seawater shower on deck, and even a precious quick freshwater rinse. The Captain imagined this was probably better for morale than six weeks of shore leave. Long ago Komatsu had learned the virtues of tempering the strict discipline of command with compassion for the plight of the ordinary sailor.

He had seen and dismissed the brutality, even torture, of trainees meted out at the hands of his Army brethren. It was such soldiers, terrorized and stripped of their cultural values that had stained the reputation of Japan with the Rape of Nanking and the Manchurian incident earlier. As a Japanese naval officer he believed such behavior trickling down the ranks hurt the efficiency of the troops. Army soldiers may perform out of their sense of obligation to the Emperor, or more likely out of fear of reprisal by senior officers, but the result was little better than a mob with a mission. The proud tradition of the Imperial Navy needed seamen who performed with precision and accuracy. So instead of demeaning and torturing his crew, on a daily basis he ran the boat through exacting torpedo drills, fire and damage control rehearsals, plane launches and emergency dive exercises. This was a good source of discipline for the crew and overall *Sea Snake* was pleased. The crew seemed to be adjusting well.

The dives however, were giving the Chief Engineer fits. In the engine room the Chief pored over blueprints of the *Pufferfish* looking for a clue to the reason the port side ballast valve operated only intermittently. He had replaced the valve after sea trials and everything seemed to work well, but since putting out to sea, balky was the only description for it. His crew had checked the switches in the circuit and now they were engaged in the tedious chore of checking each wire for continuity. *This is a big boat,* he thought, *this could take a long time.*

Somewhere in the Pacific Ocean
Mid-day, March 17, 1941

"Sound general quarters, bow planes down full, emergency dive," Commander Katsu screamed. The klaxon sounded as the sailor standing watch topside slid down the ladder securing the hatch behind him in seconds. The dive officer repeated the command and watched as the dive angle indicator showed a fast dive. As they passed through fifty feet the sub began to heel to the right as the starboard tank filled with seawater.

The boat struggled through one hundred feet listing so far to the right that crewmen now had to hang on to keep from sliding into bulkheads. Just as the Captain was about to cancel the drill, the sound of escaping air from the port ballast tank signaled a working valve, and the sub began to right itself. Amidships port side the Chief Engineer stood with a wrench in hand, having manually opened the valve.

"Level off at two hundred feet," Hidashi said. "Secure from general quarters. Run a zigzag pattern for twenty minutes then come to periscope depth."

Kobiashi Maru came into view as a tiny dot on the horizon but within a few hours had come alongside *I-28* (Experimental), its massive bulk looming above. Under the best of circumstances a transfer from one vessel to another at sea was challenging. These were not the best of circumstances. The seas were running about twelve feet with a stiff wind blowing spray all the way across the top of the sail.

The process was further complicated by the lack of commonality between a civilian cargo vessel and a submarine. Initially a line with a bosun's chair was tried and rejected after the line parted four times as the seas alternately brought the vessels perilously close then sent them drifting apart. Finally it became apparent the only solution was to put a lifeboat in the water with the new officer aboard.

As a boat with three men aboard drew alongside *I-28* (Experimental) a large swell heaved it into the deck, slamming it against the topside 5.5 inch cannon forward of the conning tower, dumping its occupants onto the rolling deck of the submarine. Scrambling to their feet the three sailors made a run for the sail ladder just as a second blast of seawater broke over the decks. The wave knocked a seaman hard to the deck and swept the other off the boat into the churning seas. One man reached the ladder and clung like a barnacle, barely resisting being peeled off and dragged into the sea. As the wave washed past, he looked back to see the deck awash with blood spilling from a jagged head wound on an inert sailor. There was no sign of the missing third man. Moments later another wave lifted the body and the shattered lifeboat from the deck and deposited them in the water on the port side. The survivor climbed the ladder and into the conning tower. By now the lifeboat and bodies had sunk taking any evidence of their existence toward the bottom of the sea.

"Lieutenant Arimoto Akagi" reporting as ordered sir." He stood breathlessly on the bridge trying to maintain his balance at attention as the deck pitched beneath him. Seawater dripped off his uniform and could be heard squishing in his shoes.

Komatsu regarded the young officer for a moment. He was no more than in his early twenties yet two ranks higher than would be expected by now, but there was *something* about this man the Captain couldn't quite put a finger on. Even at attention in the presence of a higher-ranking officer there was a kind of arrogance, or maybe an air of superiority, as if he knew something important no one else did.

"At ease, Lieutenant," the Captain said. "Commander Katsu, show Lieutenant Akagi to his bunk and arrange for a dry uniform. Lieutenant, report to me here when you have changed."

"With your humble pardon, sir, I was commanded by Admiral Yamamoto to transmit orders to you immediately upon arrival. May I respectfully request we retire to the Captain's quarters?"

Yamamoto himself gave orders directly to a Lieutenant? Sea Snake wondered. *This man and his mission are very unique indeed.* "Very well then, follow me. Commander, you have the bridge."

Once in his quarters the Captain turned to Akagi and said "Well, let's have those orders that couldn't wait another moment." The young officer reached into an inner pocket and gingerly removed a sodden envelope, which he handed to the Captain.

From: Admiral Yamamoto
  Chief of Naval Operations HIJN
To: Captain Hidashi Komatsu
  Commanding Officer HIJN I-28 (Experimental)
Subject: Mission orders
Date: March 7, 1941

Your mission is to covertly penetrate the Lower Columbia River Basin and the Puget Sound of Washington State USA, assemble and deploy your seaplane with Lieutenant Arimoto Akagi as pilot and to the extent possible photograph from the air strategic sites in and around Seattle and Portland. Such sites should include aircraft and other manufacturing facilities, airports, port facilities, dams, power plants, foundries, military installations and key transportation sites.

Lieutenant Akagi has been briefed separately and may wish to make modifications to the airplane before undertaking his portion of the mission. Any such modifications are approved.

These orders may be shown to senior staff officers after March 19. Under no circumstance is your vessel or any member of your crew to be captured. You are not to engage any vessel after contact with Kobiashi Maru and will maintain radio silence for the duration of your mission.

Upon completion of the mission you are to return to the previously ordered coordinates and await coded transmission of addi-

tional orders on April 15 at 14:00 hours. Coded message will be repeated daily through April 20.

In the event you cannot receive transmission of orders you are to proceed to Tokyo Naval Base and report directly to me or my Chief of Staff. Crew members are not to leave the ship without orders directly from me.

Bushido, Hidashi-san.

ss//Yamamoto

Komatsu blinked at the document. *Bushido, the Samurai honor code of victory or death!* Still, the Admiral had made it clear this was an obligation to the Emperor, which no Japanese could refuse. To do so would bring dishonor to his household, and a burden which a thousand generations could not repay.

"Have you seen these orders, Lieutenant?"

"Yes sir, they were attached to my own orders."

"Are there any supplies aboard the *Kobiashi* which you need?"

"Yes sir, I am hoping the swells subside enough to make the task a little easier."

"Very well then, report to the Commander for dry clothes and meet me in the con in twenty minutes, dismissed." *He has an odd accent,* the Captain thought.

They waited four hours until the winds had diminished enough to make the transfer of equipment a safer project, but a buzz was circulating among the crew about what had come aboard. Imaginations ran wild about what would be done with two gallons of orange paint, two rubber boats with small outboard motors, six boxes of camera equipment and two empty cylindrical metal tubes about eight feet long. While the cargo was being loaded the Captain asked the navigator about charts for the coastal waterways for British Columbia, Canada, and Washington and Oregon, U.S.A.

"Our charts of the region" the navigator reported, "are a scale too large for close navigation." The navigator knew very well that secretly entering territorial waters covertly in a warship was an act of precipitous aggression against the United States. The Captain's response would likely reveal much about the mission.

"Thank you *ko ka cho* that will be all."

The disappointed navigator shrugged inwardly and returned to his duty station, not the least bit enlightened.

Hidashi climbed into the conning tower. Lieutenant Akagi was supervising the transfer of the remaining items and the Commander was speaking on the ship's phone with someone below.

"Katsu, please report to the bridge and take the con," the Captain said. After he had disappeared down the hatch *Sea Snake* turned to Akagi; "My navigator informs me we do not have adequate charts for this mission. Did the Admiral mention this in his orders for you?"

"Yes sir, it is most unfortunate they were lost during the transfer when the lifeboat sank."

"Most unfortunate indeed, perhaps you should return to the *Kobiashi* and commandeer their charts. This time try not to drop them into the ocean."

Pufferfish had been resupplied and refueled with provisions stowed on the freighter for that purpose. Now fully loaded she was running toward her mission destination. During daylight the Captain kept two men on the conning tower as *I-28* (Experimental) ran northeast first and then turned east. One searched the skies looking for U.S. Navy patrol planes, the other scanned the horizon for any ships that might appear. Both were listening carefully for telltale engine sounds, which might betray an aircraft not otherwise visible.

At night, with the ship running dark and near full speed, one sailor manned the conning tower concentrating on searching the horizon in front of the sub for any traffic. After forty-eight hours of this pattern the Captain was sufficiently convinced that *Pufferfish* was well and truly hidden outside the shipping channels in the vast expanse of the eastern Pacific. He ordered the vessel to reduce speed to slow two hours after local sunrise. There were details for clandestine refueling stops along the way but this new sub had extensive range and maintaining radio silence would be paramount If need be he could complete the mission with the fuel onboard and still return to home waters. It required pinpoint navigation skills not only from his men, but the sailors aboard the fuel tender as well to meet for a transfer. It was a worry. Being adrift at sea on a submarine without fuel could be catastrophic but he judged the risk to be acceptable.

Shortly after changing the watch, when most of the crew would be awake, Komatsu lifted the ship's phone to his ear and read his orders from Yamamoto. Technically it was a violation of those orders, but as a practical matter it would be impossible to keep the general intent of the orders secret and this forestalled idle speculation among the crew. It also made clear to everyone aboard his solemn duty. If they may die for the glory of Emperor and empire they would at least know why.

The seas were mild and smooth as Lieutenant Akagi opened the forward hatch. Along the deck the other hatches were opening as well and sailors emerged blinking back tears created by the sudden glare of the sub-tropical sun.

"Let's bring it out so we can work on it," he said. The hangar was built as part of the after side of the conning tower and as the hatches were opened an unlikely piece of standard equipment aboard this submarine began rolling out toward the launch catapult on deck.

Three sailors, stripped to the waist, wrestled the seaplane into position on deck then secured it against slipping into the sea. One man opened a can and all three began painting the wings bright orange. Two and a half hours later all the appropriate visible exterior portions had been coated and were drying on the deck.

"So, Lieutenant, what is your plan for this highly secret, clandestine mission to the mainland of the United States?" The Captain surveyed the deck shaking his head in wonderment.

"I plan to hide in plain sight," he replied. "A Japanese seaplane would obviously attract unwanted attention even among the lazy officers of the American military. Everyone will ignore a bright orange crop duster. The two tanks I brought aboard will appear to contain insecticide, but they are really fuel tanks to extend my range. I could probably land on Lake Washington and refuel at the seaplane dock if I had to."

Despite himself the Captain thought *this is so insane it might actually work!* "Very well, carry on. Inform Commander Katsu when your modifications have been concluded. I will have him run the crew through deployment drills before we get underway again."

Sakai Residence
Bainbridge Island
March 21, 1941

Thomas had built his red two-story clapboard home on the island with a broad front porch. It had a low, open railing with a bead board ceiling and was situated on the land to take advantage of the breathtaking view of the Puget Sound and Seattle in the distance. In fair weather he would sit on the porch watching the ships and ferries plying the waters. When it was cold he would sit in an old rocker inside next to the front window and take in the same vista while he sipped tea and nibbled ginger snap cookies. It was a taste acquired when Marie Pearson had brought them along as a bread and butter gift while she and the Reverend visited their old friends.

Today Thomas was sitting inside in his rocker gazing at his wife out on the porch. He drifted into a reverie of treasured memories of the life they had shared for so long; of the heartache and triumph and simple pleasures of just being together. *I'm a sentimental old fool!* He thought. Moriko shifted in her seat on the porch and her shawl slipped down. As he saw his granddaughter reach over from her seat and tenderly replace it around her shoulders he was struck by how much his granddaughter resembled his wife as a young woman. *So beautiful and so smart! God blesses me bountifully.*

Mary Sakai, for her part, sat shivering on the porch with Grandmother Moriko. She had no idea why she insisted on sitting out here in the cold, staring at the fields of the farm. As she followed her gaze, all she saw were squares of gray-brown mud with the occasional fuzzy ground cover of weedlings and early season blackberries sticking up forlornly. Here and there the tulip bulbs planted last fall could be seen poking their shoots out of the chilled ground. Soon the weather would begin to warm and the early flowers would bloom, but now only the small patch of lawn in front of the house showed signs of life. The early willows along the ditch bank by the road and the vine maples were beginning to show the hint of bright green leaves too, but mostly it just looked dead to Mary. The Aeromotor windmill, which lifted water from the well in the summer, stood at the high end of the fields, its rusty blades spinning lazily in the breeze. Beyond the fields the land sloped gently toward the Puget Sound and on nice days Seattle could be seen from the vantage point of the porch on Bainbridge Island.

"I planted that maple tree near the barn before you were born," Grandmother said pointing a gnarled finger vaguely in a northerly direction. Mary was brought back to the moment by the sudden animation from the old woman.

"Was it the first thing you planted, Grandmother?" Mary asked. Occasionally the elder would slip into the language of the homeland. Mary's Japanese was fair but not perfect and sometimes she had trouble understanding.

"No child, we planted cabbages and carrots and green beans. Your grandfather and I needed to have something to eat first," she explained. "When we came here this land was filled with stumps from the old cedar trees cut down by the lumbermen. There were only four other *Issei* families on the island. We shared two mules and helped clear each other's land. Your grandfather worked very hard in the fields. He is a good man and a good husband." She struggled to her feet balancing on a twisted madrona cane and held out her hand for her granddaughter. "I have prattled on too long now. Come, it is time for an old woman to sit quietly by the fire and dream about the past."

Mary arose and took her grandmother's hand gently, guiding her toward the door. From Eagledale dock the whistle of the *Kehleken* sounded the last boarding call for the ferry. *Darn,* she thought, *I won't get to Seattle to see Clark Gable tonight. Oh well, maybe tomorrow.*

Aboard *I-28* (Experimental)
East of Hawaii
March 22, 1941

The problem the Chief Engineer was struggling with began in the Kobe shipyards. A couple of wires being pulled through watertight conduit happened to slide over a burr, stripping away insulation and abrading one wire to less than half the diameter specified to carry the load for the port side ballast valve. It severed the battery compartment exhaust fan line completely. About half the time the valve worked fine. Each time it overheated though, it further degraded its surrounding insulation. The battery compartment was where this conjunction of wires and tubes met and so far the inoperative explosion proof vent blower had gone undetected. This wouldn't have been a problem if the exposed wire sections weren't in the middle of an ell. It probably wouldn't have been a problem on a battleship, but submarines are closed systems. Charging batteries creates odorless, explosive hydrogen gas, which must be vented regularly for safety.

Slightly built and rather bookish, the navigator spread the charts taken from the *Kobiashi Maru* on the plotting table in the bridge, cleaned and adjusted his glasses, then leaned over to study what he saw. One problem became apparent immediately; the charts were in English. The soundings and headings wouldn't be a problem, but any special notations would have to be translated. Inwardly he sighed then turned to seek out the watch commander who would in turn seek out the Executive Officer who would find the Captain and repeat the issue. In similar manner most problems aboard the *Pufferfish* rose to the top of the command chain remaining unresolved until personally dealt with by the Commanding Officer of *I-28*. It was old fashioned and inefficient, but to ask a second time would imply that the officer had failed or was inadequate for the job. This loss of face could not be tolerated in *giri* to the name of the officer and thus the truth was some items just got lost in the shuffle.

None of this was currently an issue. The Captain had ordered a course to be plotted that would put *I-28* about sixty miles south of the Columbia River and forty miles east of Cape Meares, Oregon. Little had changed in the practice of navigation since the British Admiralty had commissioned a contest to secure a working chronometer sufficiently accurate to plot longitude. That was achieved over a century ago. For now course heading, speed, local time and daily sextant readings combined with reasonable math skills and good charts were all that were necessary to closely fix their location on the planet.

Fifteen hundred miles north in the interior of British Columbia, and wholly unknowable to the crew of the *Pufferfish,* frigid Arctic air had begun rotating counterclockwise and was being drawn into a vortex created by high-speed winds in the upper atmosphere. Warm moisture laden tropical air began a similar journey from the southwest. Most of the wind and rain from the resulting collision of the two would fall harmlessly into the Pacific Ocean. Some would not.

When conditions are perfect aboard a submarine life is only miserable. Any deviation from perfect and all the elements of a living hell are close at hand. As an ocean going vessel a submarine is an uneasy design alliance. On the surface it has the keel configuration to run truly well. The objective underwater is to be sleek and quiet. But running on batteries is a slow, short-term affair, lasting a few hours perhaps before she must surface and run the engines to recharge. Like the submarines of all navies this one ran on the surface most of the time. *Pufferfish* was like a duck pretending to be a fish. It wallowed through heavy weather despite being faster than most surface warships.

Unfortunately for the crew, as *I-28* (Experimental) made its way northeast through the Pacific it began to encounter the outermost bands of a storm still to the north.

The navigator was first on the bridge descending from above. He had made the best reading of position he could considering the partial cloud cover. He took his instruments and figures to the chart table and began making notations. The Captain climbed down from the conning tower after checking the gathering weather for himself. "Commander Katsu, reduce the watch, order all hatches except the con to be closed and rig for heavy weather."

In the engine room, part of the challenge was keeping the engines oiled. The movement of the ship required using one hand to maintain balance and the other to squirt oil into lubrication ports. The action of the engines created an aerosol of lubricating oil and diesel fuel, which the ventilation system dutifully distributed to every corner of the ship.

When combined with the stench of poorly functioning toilets along with twenty-four officers and fifty unwashed seamen, it created an aroma certain to turn the stomach of the most seasoned submariner. Having done so, the putrid smell of vomit was added to the misery index.

The best estimate the navigator could give the Captain as to their location was about four hundred miles southwest of Cape Disappointment at the mouth of the Columbia. For three interminable days the sub had waddled through high seas and gale force winds as the last gasp of winter 1940 to '41 pummeled the Oregon and Washington coastlines. The Captain kept the wind direction to the aft port quarter of boat; the wrong quarter to be sure, but that had far less effect on his sleek vessel than it would on a surface ship with a much larger wind profile. Even so it was still likely that they were miles off course, and probably one more day until a decent reading could be taken.

Pufferfish had performed well. On six occasions Komatsu ordered a dive to run slowly under the storm for a few hours. This gave the crew an opportunity to eat with a chance the food might stay down. In the galley the cook had been making sushi by rolling sticky rice and pickled cucumber into cylinders wrapped in *nori*. These were sliced into bite-sized pieces and distributed among the crew, officers and enlisted alike. They were fast, easy and filling. They were just what were needed. Those not currently standing watch washed down a few pieces of sushi with lukewarm tea and hit the bunks.

The fourth night the storm blew itself out and at precisely 21:36:42 hours, the navigator took a reading. It had been eighty-seven hours since his last full reading and he was anxious to plot their position. His anxiety was partially professional, partly personal. His work was a matter of some pride and he wished to be accurate, but he was also concerned that a significant discrepancy in his estimate and their true position might jeopardize the success of the mission. Carefully he stowed his instruments then removed his glasses for cleaning. When he had concluded this ritual he took his ruler and dividers and began his plot. After a few minutes a broad smile broke across his oval face. *Two hundred miles! Only two hundred miles from my estimate after four days of storms!* For today his pride was justified.

"Up periscope," the Captain said. "Make your speed ahead slow." Komatsu peered through the Nikon optics installed in the hydraulic tube and scanned the horizon surrounding the sub. In every direction the empty sea filled his field of vision. "Down scope, all stop. Make your depth twenty feet." His order repeated itself through subordinate officers to enlisted sailors, who acknowledged and executed them.

At twenty feet, only the sail of the ship would be visible above the water. The entire vessel would, of course, be visible from the air but it was a chance he must take. Climbing the ladder to the conning tower he cracked the hatch and was rewarded with seawater dribbling onto his face. He climbed onto the deck of the tower and began a more thorough examination of his situation. As he stood surveying the area, the navigator clambered up the ladder into the conn intent on getting readings.

"So, Lieutenant Chosiro, you have brought us to within forty miles of the United States. Can you bring us to within 4 miles of Portland?"

"Yes Captain, if the river is deep enough to allow us to swim upstream.

KEX Radio Portland filled the claustrophobic confines of the radio room as Arimoto listened along with the signals Ensign. Currently a tinny sounding Duke Ellington was filling the speaker. He was waiting to hear the weather and 100 miles to the east an audio engineer struck three steel bars tuned to create the NBC radio network sounder.

"Good morning, this is your Portland and vicinity weather forecast. Mostly sunny today; winds from the west at ten to twenty miles per hour. High temperature today is expected to be 52 degrees, overnight low 40 degrees. Barometric pressure is 29.95 inches and rising. The time is exactly 8:00 A.M. 1190 kilocycles KEX Portland, Oregon, this is Edward James speaking."

Moments later network programming began and Lieutenant Akagi rose and headed for the bridge.

"Sailing up the river in daylight would be suicide!" a junior Sub-Lieutenant exclaimed. The Captain noted with disapproval that he was a little excitable, but probably correct in his assessment. He looked around the wardroom at his other officers waiting for someone to contradict the excitable Sub-Lieutenant. No one did.

"I am open to suggestions," he said. "Let's hear from the navigator first."

"*Hai, tai so* Komatsu-san." The navigator unconsciously removed and cleaned his glasses then replaced them on his face. He leaned over the chart on the wardroom table and pointed to a spot. "This is the lighthouse at Cape Disappointment. There is a United States Coast Guard station there which actively patrols the river. If we come in at high tide there should be enough water to hide our passage."

"Where would we be able to surface and assemble the plane?" Commander Katsu queried.

"According to the chart there are several unpopulated small islands about twenty miles upriver. We should be able to hide among those," the navigator responded. The officers nodded their heads and murmured approbation.

"Very well then," the Captain broke in, "we shall enter tonight just before the slack tide. Dive officers remember to calculate our buoyancy in freshwater and make adjustments accordingly. Prepare your stations well for this mission. Dismissed."

As the officers filed out and returned to their duty stations Akagi lingered, awaiting a private moment with the Captain.

"Yes, Lieutenant, you have a question?"

"Not a question sir, a concern. The crew has never launched the seaplane in the dark."

"Nor will they this time. From the shore this will look like the U.S. Navy conducting exercises." The Captain sounded much more reassuring than he felt Lieutenant Akagi thought to himself, *I doubt if the U.S. Navy uses orange crop dusters on their subs.*

"Unless you enter the lion's den, you cannot take the cubs"
Japanese Proverb

When the snows melt on the eastern slope of the Monashee Mountains and the northwestern slope of the Rocky Mountains they make their way to Columbia Lake, headwaters of the Columbia River two hundred miles north of the U.S-Canadian border in British Columbia. As the crow flies it is nearly six hundred miles from the mouth of the Columbia but in its meander the river is twelve hundred seventy miles long.

The first trickle of snowmelt began two weeks earlier into the marshes scattered among the sage and scrub pine dotted Ruby Mountains of northern Nevada and headed for the Owyhee River just north of Elko. From there it was coursing through the black basalt lava flows into the Snake River near Ontario, Oregon.

Eight hundred fifty miles east-northeast of Astoria, the Snake River begins its journey from Teton Lake near the northwest corner of Yellowstone National Park. It carves a huge mirror-image horizontal S from eastern Idaho across southern and western Idaho and eastern Oregon on the way to a confluence near Richland, Washington. All totaled the Columbia River watershed drains 258,000 square miles of land, an area nearly twice the size of the Home Islands of Japan, through an opening just five miles wide at the Pacific Ocean.

While the *Pufferfish* had been making its way through the storm in the Pacific toward the coast of Oregon, rain had been falling in torrents on the western slope of the Cascade mountain range. Each raindrop sought to find the lowest point on the landscape. Those not trapped in the terrain joined with others to form trickles, rivulets and streams flowing into rivers carrying with them silt, sand, uprooted trees, dead livestock and debris, all headed for the Columbia already swollen with early snowmelt returning to the Pacific Ocean.

As it neared the conjunction of the Pacific Ocean and the Columbia River the sub began to experience the unique forces of that outflow. Even with the high tide, the sheer force of the water from the river created treacherous conditions. Cross-currents collided creating dangerous rips. Inbound ocean tides met outflowing freshwater creating colossal breaking swells and an ever shifting sandbar. Rounding Point Klatsop on the south shore the seaman on watch caught glimpses of the lighthouse at Cape Disappointment as *Pufferfish* rose to the crest of a swell then settled back into a trough. He thought he glimpsed another beacon about three miles to the aft starboard quarter. He searched a few more times in that direction but the beacon from the *Lightship Columbia* eluded him.

"Watch reports a lighthouse fifteen degrees off the port bow, Captain. Estimates about six miles," Commander Katsu reported.

"Very well, Commander," Sea Snake replied.

The bridge rolled and heaved under the feet of the officers. The occupant of each duty station with a seat had long since belted in firmly but still had to hang on to maintain balance. Throughout the vessel men were clinging to anything readily adapted as a handhold.

"Commander, recall the watch and prepare to dive."

It was a calculated risk but it must be made. Traveling upriver in the dark, underwater, using only speed and heading for navigation was safer than shaving with a broken bottle, but just barely.

"The boat is ready to dive, sir," reported the Executive officer.

"Dive to periscope depth, Commander. Sonar, begin active search." Sonar was new on subs, and part of this stolen technology was what made *I-28* experimental.

"Aye, sir," the sonar man responded.

Slowly the boat began to sink below the surface waves and the relentless buffeting began to subside. *I-28* still moved unnaturally as the currents and tidal forces whipsawed the bow one direction and the stern another but at least the up and down motion had diminished.

"Up periscope" the Captain ordered, "sonar, report."

"Sonar, aye. Impossible to make any useful readings sir, I have returns everywhere."

As Komatsu had feared, the debris, temperature, salinity differences and sheer turbulence had rendered sonar useless. He was going to have to do this visually. Komatsu looked out the periscope into the inky darkness searching for the lighthouse. They were still in the huge swells and only occasionally could he glimpse lights on the shoreline. There seemed to be no forward progress at all.

"Ahead flank speed," he said as he continued to search the night with the periscope.

At top speed the sub was slowly gaining against the river and the Captain took a moment to break from searching the horizon. He had just opened his mouth to say something when a tremendous crash and shudder reverberated through the bridge and down the length of entire vessel. Water coursed down around the periscope tube now knocked from perpendicular by three inches. *Sea Snake* had been knocked off his feet, sustaining a nasty gash in his knee and a terrific blow to the temple.

"Emergency surface, blow all tanks. Engines all ahead slow," shouted the Exec. "Damage control, report."

The Captain was struggling to his feet as the nose of the sub angled steeply up. Just as the bow was about to break the surface another wracking blow was felt and the sound of tearing metal could be heard. The Captain lost his feet again and hit the deck hard.

Back on the surface *Pufferfish* was again buffeted by the waters off Cape Disappointment. Commander Katsu ordered a sailor into the conn to take a look, but the searchlight was gone and in the dark he was unable to determine what had happened.

"Helm, make your heading two hundred seventy degrees, engine room, ahead full." It was clear to Katsu they were not going to Portland tonight.

The next morning *I-28* (Experimental) was again about forty miles west of the Oregon-Washington border bobbing peacefully on the surface. Crewmen pored over every inch of the sub, grinding, welding & winching to make repairs. The main 5.5 inch deck gun and the railing around it had been ripped right off its bolts. A section of the sail at the top was bashed in with a huge gouge. The antenna was missing and the periscope was leaning slightly aft and to starboard. One of the crew brought something over and handed it to Commander Katsu. He took the item, grunted an acknowledgment and disappeared down the deck hatch into the belly of the ship.

Even in one of the largest submarines in the Japanese Imperial Navy, sick bay was little more than a storage closet with a fold down rack. After his initial treatment an unconscious Captain Komatsu had been wrestled back to his quarters and put to bed. He was now sitting on the edge of the bed rubbing a dark purple bruise on the side of his head when his XO knocked then stepped inside.

"It is good to see you awake, Captain. We were concerned about you."

"Thank you, Commander," the *Sea Snake* replied weakly. He didn't tell him he was having trouble focusing and was fighting off a massive throbbing pain in his head. "What is your report, Katsu?

"Sir, here is a souvenir of our collision last night." Katsu handed the object to the Captain.

The Captain took it and with some difficulty focused on a branch, stripped of most of its bark with a few needles still attached. *A pine tree? A pine tree...of course! When we hit our combined closing speeds must have been thirty-five knots.*

"How bad is the damage?"

"The forward gun and railing is gone. The antenna and searchlight are missing. The sail has a big dent but the damage is only cosmetic. The periscope and tube are badly bent. The engineer says he can replace the optics and seal the leak but only by welding it in place. We cannot bring the scope down."

"Very well, Katsu, have the engineer make the repairs." Komatsu was having trouble focusing and the throbbing in his head was becoming more intense.

"Yes sir, and Captain, Lieutenant Akagi wants to fly his mission from here. He thinks his extra fuel tanks give him the range. What should I tell him?"

Sea Snake lay back in his rack, took a deep breath and said, "Use your best judgment, Commander, dismissed." The second in command headed for the deck as eternal darkness carried the Captain to his ancestors and far away from the cares of this world forever.

Astoria Column
Astoria, Oregon
Monday morning, March 24, 1941

Corporal Fred Barnes, U.S.M.C (Ret.), late of the Allied Expeditionary Force under the command of General 'Blackjack' Pershing was panting heavily as he took the one hundred sixty fourth —and final—step into the observation tower of the Astoria Column. Perched on the highest most western hill of Astoria, its one hundred twenty five foot height offered a commanding view from Tillamook Head twenty miles south to the North Head Lighthouse across the river in Washington. He had carefully studied the friezes in the reinforced concrete depicting the European discovery of the river by Captain Robert Gray in 1792, the American claim on the Northwest Territories, the westward expansion and finally the arrival of the Great Northwest Railroad. It conveniently ignored that the native populations had been decimated following the 'discovery' and subsequent settling.

Walking around the small landing he thought he detected an airplane engine far in the distance. It is difficult to determine the direction of a distant aircraft by sound because it seems to come from no particular direction. Fred however, was aided by the Column. As he went around the east side the sound would diminish then strengthen on the west. Idly curious he began searching the horizon with his binoculars, finally bringing into focus a tiny orange dot probably five or ten miles west over the open ocean.

"Now that's damn peculiar," he said. Since the War to End All Wars, Barnes often spoke only to himself excluding most everyone around him. It was a peccadillo that caused some consternation among his family and eventually had cost him most of his pre-war friends. As the orange dot grew larger in his lenses he began to make out the aircraft type. This perplexed him even more. "What in the hell is a crop duster doing coming in off the damned Pacific Ocean?" It was a rhetorical question he would never have answered.

Arimoto was soaring above the river in his orange 'crop duster' having already taken pictures of the Longview and Columbia River Bridges. A low detour south along the Willamette River at Portland had netted aerial photos of seven other bridges including the newest, the St. John's suspension bridge and shipping terminals throughout the region. The weather was still perfect and he had plenty of fuel so he brought the plane around and headed back toward the Columbia. A few miles upstream he snapped a dozen more pictures from various angles of the Bonneville Dam and power plant. Akagi checked his map briefly then took a heading northwest for the Grand Coulee Dam. Before he reached it he would pass the point of no return and that would require a stop for refueling, but right now that wasn't a problem he wanted to think about.

"I don't give a good god damn who's in charge, Chief, I just wanna see him." Fred hadn't spoken that many words to a stranger in twenty years, but this might be important. He hadn't come all the way to the Coast Guard station to be patted on the ass and sent on his way.

"I'm sorry sir, the Captain isn't available now," Master Chief Petty Officer Stan Harvey explained. "He is in Portland and won't be back today."

Barnes mumbled under his breath for a moment then asked, "Well, who is in charge today?"

"That would be Ensign Gordon, sir. Shall I call him?"

"Ensign!" He exclaimed. "That's the best you can do? A goddamned Ensign! Shit, Chief, you've got more chops than a pimple-assed Ensign!

"That may be true sir," Harvey replied, "but he is still the officer in charge. What would you like me to do?"

Barnes fumed. He stared at his feet then at the Chief, finally he blurted, "Look, Chief, I'm gonna tell this to you. You decide what you're gonna do with it." He recounted in explicit detail his trip to Astoria Column, including historical data, concluding with the orange airplane. "It kinda looked like a crop duster, 'cept it had sponsons and floats with wheels underneath. I just thought it was pretty damn peculiar comin' in off the ocean like that."

"Thank you sir, I'll see to it this report gets to the proper location right away. Thank you from the Coast Guard for your concern." The Chief had been taking notes on an official report form. He completed it and signed it with a flourish. "If you would just read this and sign on this line we'll be all finished."

Fred glanced at the report, added his initials while mumbling to himself, then turned without another word and left the station. It would be ten years more before he spoke directly to another human being.

'Who was that, Chief?" the Ensign asked as he walked by the desk.

"Just a crank sir, nothing to worry about." Master Chief Petty Officer Stan Harvey made a deposit in his deskside circular file and returned to the work before him.

Pacific Ocean
40 miles west of the mouth of the Columbia
March 24, 1941

It was the Chief Engineer that discovered the body of Captain Komatsu about the same time Akagi was piloting his plane over Yakima. He had come to report the completion of emergency repairs but instead found an unresponsive body. The medic was called and the pronouncement made. Shortly thereafter Commander—now Captain—Katsu convened an urgent meeting of the officers in the wardroom.

"We will log the time of death of the Captain and make a note that I am assuming command of *I-28* at this time," Katsu said. "I am also assuming the temporary rank of Captain, and elevating the next most senior officer, Lieutenant Chosiro, to temporary rank of *Sho-sa*. Chosiro is now second in command." Katsu had already pinned new rank insignia on his collar and handed the navigator his new fittings as well.

The new executive officer removed his glasses and cleaned them vigorously then removed the old pins, took the new ratings and clipped them to his collar. He smiled nervously at the assembled group before replacing his glasses. "Thank you, Captain. What are your orders?"

Captain Katsu surveyed his officers. The excitable young Lieutenant was very still and somber. A more senior officer had advised him of his station in stern terms. He would offer no further observations unless asked directly. Most had an expectant look. *This is my command, my boat now. I must do honor to my giri.* "Commander Chosiro will arrange a sea burial detail for Komatsu. I will review our mission once again to determine if we should continue. Meantime each of you shall inform your crewmen of the changes in command. When Lieutenant Akagi returns, stow his plane immediately and dive. Then have him report to me in the Captain's quarters, dismissed."

Recon Aircraft
Over Washington State
March 24, 1941

Akagi had been airborne flying leisurely for hours. He had flown up the river through the pass it created in the Cascades then skirted the eastern foothills on a northerly heading. He was flying over a patchwork of small fields and dormant orchards surrounding what he figured must be Yakima when he ate his sushi rolls and drank some cold tea. As he looked toward the hills to his left he could see shadows already lengthening, the early spring sun having passed its apogee two hours before. It suddenly occurred to him that fuel wasn't going to be his only problem.

Quickly he mentally calculated his fuel, airspeed and remaining range. Allowing forty minutes to refuel—assuming he had no problems—if he turned back now he could reach the sub by dusk. *Approaching with the sun in my eyes, dark on the water looking for a tiny dot on the ocean; I would have to fly beyond the sub, then try to find it flying east again. If I miss it I spend the night on the open ocean in my plane or try to race back for a forced landing on shore, in the dark.* The decision was an easy one. He consulted his map once more and continued north northeastward.

Fuel was now becoming something he could no longer ignore. Arimoto had about one hour of flight time left, but even more urgently the call to nature was making itself felt. He calculated he was about twenty miles from Wenatchee as he scanned the ground for signs of a landing strip. Every so often a farmhouse was visible near a road and it seemed every one had towering Lombardy poplars planted in a neat row along a nearby ditch bank forming a windbreak. A few minutes later he saw a wind sock hanging limply from a pole next to a tin building with 'W'nchee' painted in huge letters on the roof. A tank truck sat motionless by the runway next to a smaller building. The Lieutenant carefully secreted all his Japanese language documents in a small compartment under the instrument panel and began circling to land.

"What in the blue blazes is this?" Hank asked aloud looking out the grimy window of the hangar's tiny office building. Joe Strand put all four legs of the chair in which he was leaning back on the floor, got up and peered down the runway past the lengthening shadows.

"Looks like a orange crop duster, sorta," Joe replied. The two men watched as the plane landed then taxied toward the hangar. They left the building and headed for the plane, catching up with it just as the pilot shut down the engine.

"Howdy, friend," Hank called out. "Don't reckon I've ever seen this plane, whereabouts you from?"

The cockpit door was already folded back and the pilot stepped down to, then off of the float. He took off his helmet and gloves tossing them back in the cockpit and in perfect English without a trace of an accent said, "Man, I need an outhouse bad. Have you got one?"

Hank looked at Joe who returned his stare of incredulity then looked back at the pilot. Joe spoke first, pointing to his right, "Uh, sure, it's over there behind the office."

"Thanks," Lieutenant Akagi replied as he dashed off toward the privy.

"He's Chinese or somethin'," Hank said as he circled the plane slowly.

"No kidding, Sherlock. What in the hell is he doin' way the hell out here?"

"Dustin' crops it looks like." He peered at the opening in the underbelly of the plane.

"In March," Joe wondered aloud, "in a seaplane?" he concluded.

"Well, let's ask him, here he comes." Hank responded.

The Imperial Japanese Navy Lieutenant, back on U.S. soil for the first time since his father had been recalled by Tokyo, came back toward the plane stuffing his red plaid shirt into the waist of his worn Levi's. He was carrying a battered leather flight jacket over one arm, and was clearly much relieved. "Thanks," he said to the two men, "I feel much better now."

"What kinda rig is this?" Hank asked. "I ain't ever seen a crop duster like this. 'Specially one with fold up wings."

"No, I imagine not. Actually it's a seaplane I bought in Tacoma, they told me it was surplus from the War Department. I'm headed for Omak. My family is leasing a farm there. We're going to plant some cherry trees." I'm going to try to convert it to a crop duster."

"You come over Stampede Pass?" Joe asked."

"No, I had to go to Portland first for some parts." Arimoto responded. "I just ran out of fuel and daylight, so I put in here. Can I buy fuel here?"

"Sure can," Joe replied. "You wanna to do it now or in the mornin'?"

"Now suits me fine if it's convenient for you.' He noted Hank's ongoing interest in the camera and added, "She used to be used by a navy photographer, and they had extra tanks put on, so it takes a lot of fuel to fill it. I want to change them to insecticide."

Hank drove the fuel truck over and the three men chatted amiably about the weather, the war in Europe and the fishing in the Wenatchee River.

"I've never fished the Wenatchee," Akagi admitted, "but the Okanogan is pretty good later in the spring."

'We don't see many Chinese out in these parts." Hank said, doing a little fishing of his own.

Akagi had to catch himself before he automatically corrected the local. Thinking he was Chinese was a stroke of luck, and right now luck was a good thing.

"No, there aren't many of us here," he replied.

"Boy, the Japs are kicking your butt back home. Or so I read in the paper," Joe said.

"Well, I'm an American so it doesn't affect me much, but my grandfather is very distressed." Arimoto was getting a little nervous with this line of conversation so he changed the subject. "Say," he asked, "is there anywhere I could buy a little food. I ran out somewhere over Yakima."

"Nope," Hank replied, "closest place is near four miles. But I can call the missus and have her bring along something when she comes to pick me up. She had to go to the doctor as she's expecting in June. What do you want her to bring?"

"Any kind of fruit and a loaf of bread would be fine. Maybe some fried chicken from a diner, only if it's not a bother. Maybe a soda, too."

Hank turned and retreated to the office to make the call. Joe was winding up the hose from the tanker and checking the meter.

"How much do I owe you?" the pilot asked.

"Lemme see; one hunnert an eighty seven gallons at twenty nine cents a gallon..." Joe had taken out a pad and pencil and was ciphering on it, "...comes to fifty four dollars and twenty three cents."

"Wow!" Akagi whistled. "Flying sure is more expensive than taking the bus!" He removed a well-worn wallet and removed fifty-five dollars in old bills, none larger than a ten, and handed them to Joe who in turn fumbled for some change in his pocket handing it back to the pilot. He signed the paper he had calculated on and handed it back as well.

"This is your receipt, sorry it don't look real official. Are you gonna fly out tonight?

"No, I thought I'd just sleep under the wing till morning."

Joe thought about this for a moment then said, "well, hell, it'll be damned cold by mornin'. I gotta bunk in the hangar you're welcome to use." Joe wasn't so sure about a Chink sleeping in his bunk, but he *had* spent fifty bucks after all, and he could always have his wife wash everything when the guy left.

"That's mighty neighborly of you, I appreciate it." Frankly Akagi had expected a lot more hostility and trouble. This was turning into a pleasant surprise.

Hank returned with news he had reached his wife by phone and she would bring the requested items. Three hours later, his hunger satiated, the young Lieutenant hit the bunk in the hangar and within minutes was soundly and peacefully asleep

By the time Joe and Hank returned to the airport the next morning the orange plane had been airborne for over an hour. Joe found the bunk neatly made up with a brief thank you note placed on top. He thought about it for a while then decided there wasn't any particular need to have things washed. Hank found a similar note, with a few dollars tucked in, stuck in the door jamb of the office thanking him for the food. The two of them decided after some discussion that the Chinese guy was okay by them.

Fore deck of *I-28* (Experimental)
Pacific Ocean off Oregon Coast
March 24, 1941

No one aboard *Pufferfish* actually knew what religion the late Captain might practice so it was decided that a Shinto rite should be performed. The cook made small cakes for each officer to present acting in behalf of the deceased man's family. A crewman from the torpedo room brought a dried chrysanthemum flower he had carried for luck and placed it on the small table under a portable shrine. Acting Captain Komatsu sprinkled some salt from the galley in the purifying ritual then chanted a prayer to *Kami*. A song of grief was sung and the shroud-covered corrupted body of the *Sea Snake* slid off a plank into the western sunset of the Pacific Ocean.

"Commander," Chosiro said, "Lieutenant Akagi is overdue and darkness will be here soon. Should I post a lookout with a beacon?"

"Captain," Komatsu corrected. "You are the Commander now."

"Just so, Captain. Please forgive me, I misspoke."

"As we all will for a while. It is a difficult adjustment for us all." The new Captain thought about his reply for some time. "Post a lookout, yes, but not with a beacon. Akagi will not try to find us this late."

Chosiro saluted and turned on his heels leaving the newest submarine Captain in the fleet to ponder what to do next.

It is possible he has been shot down. He considered this unlikely, as the U.S. military was probably not in the habit of shooting down crop dusters. *It is possible he has crashed.* Certainly a possibility given the fact it was an experimental airplane flying in mountainous terrain, but the weather was perfect and the Lieutenant was a superior pilot according to his record. *He may have been forced to land and been captured.* This was the most unsettling prospect because he might have been forced to disclose the submarines existence, mission and location. *He probably realized it would be dark before he could return and decided to wait until tomorrow.* There was no particular urgency to relocate the submarine, it was in international waters, and no formal hostilities existed between the U.S. and Japan. For now, he concluded, patience was a virtue. He would wait up to twenty-four hours before he aborted the mission and headed back toward Hawaii.

By now Chief Engineer Ozawa had been reduced to having his crew trace each individual wire and visually inspect it. This was tedious, time-consuming and in some places impossible. Wires were alternately in conduit or exposed depending on where they were in the ship. Wherever they were exposed they had been painted gray in the shipyard so paint had to be scraped away from each wire to reveal its color combination. He was doing this a little at a time as he could move people from collision damage repair and regular maintenance. In the meantime he would operate the ballast valve by hand as he had since *I-28* (Experimental) left Japan.

Pacific Northwest Region
March 25, 1941

The young Lieutenant wasn't meandering today. He was making a beeline toward Grand Coulee Dam to take some pictures and then head right back for the sub. His return would have to be soon enough that the plane could be broken down and stowed before dark. That took at least half an hour and he knew he would have to stop for fuel one more time as well. He hoped it would go as smoothly as yesterday's stop. Briefly he considered returning to Wenatchee to refuel but rejected that as likely to elevate idle curiosity to real suspicion.

As the sagebrush covered countryside slid by beneath his wings he noted a few scrub pines here and there. Young grasses and budding willows added a faint green swath along either side of McCarteney Creek. Jameson and Grimes lakes glittered like sapphires in the morning sun of the desert plateau. According to his map it wouldn't be long before the dam came into view. He adjusted himself in the pilot's seat then pulled an apple out of the sack Hank's wife had brought and took a big bite.

Approaching from the southwest, Akagi saw the lake behind the dam first. Only recently completed, the river had not yet filled the inside of the dam. As he banked his plane and came around for a photo run he was stunned at its immensity. Nearly a mile across at the top and five hundred fifty feet tall, the concrete and polished granite structure was anchored at either end into notches in the black volcanic basalt, which had formed an enormous plateau flowing from a long dormant volcano untold eons ago. It was incongruous to see all that water accumulating there surrounded by hundreds of thousands of acres of arid desert. Viewed from the air the dam had an asymmetrical geometry. The top reminded him of a hockey stick. As a child he had seen the game played in Seattle. He remembered that it seemed utterly incomprehensible. *This is no time for daydreaming. Take your pictures and head back.* The flier, heeding his own advice, banked for one more pass then turned and headed straight back southwest, all the while looking for an inconspicuous place he might refuel.

The closer he got to Yakima the more into the eastern foothills of the Cascade Range he flew. Arimoto didn't want to stop at the Yakima airport if he could avoid it because he would be too conspicuous. What he was searching for was a little rural strip, maybe even a private one to set down on. Just north of the larger town was what he was looking for. Outside what his map told him was Gleed, Wash. pop. 31, he spied a small grass airstrip with an open-air hangar and two gravity-feed fuel tanks perched atop spindly metal legs. The windsock showed a slight quartering breeze as he came around to land. As he approached he reached down and turned his fuel supply petcock nearly off. Just before touching down the engine began to sputter and misfire from fuel starvation. The plane shuddered down the runway as he taxied toward the fuel tanks finally expiring altogether about thirty feet away.

Before the plane had even stopped rolling the back door of the nearby house had opened and a huge man stepped out wearing overhauls and carrying a Model 21 Winchester shotgun. A checkered walnut stock, blue steel, side by side double barreled, twelve gauge, middle break affair. He did not appear to be pleased to see this intruder and was crossing the distance between them with long purposeful strides.

"Well now, you can just turn this crate around and fly right on outta here. This is private property and I aim to keep it that way." The man's 6'10" heavily muscled frame coupled with a fierce demeanor brooked no opposition.

"I would like to do just that," Akagi said, "but I'm out of fuel. I must have forgotten to fill one tank." The flier stayed in the cockpit, helmet and goggles in place.

"I'll sell you enough fuel to get to Yakima, that's all," the red-haired giant said. The shotgun rested comfortably in the crook of his right arm, barrels pointed toward the ground.

"Fair enough, but I'm willing to pay sixty five cents a gallon for a fill up." It was risky to offer that much more than the market. It would make him more memorable to the man. *As if an orange seaplane is routine for this guy,* he thought.

That caught the big man's attention. Here was a chance to make some money and he could sure use extra cash. At that price he could make two weeks wage. "Lemme me see your money," he called up suspiciously to the pilot.

The Lieutenant wasn't sure that was a great idea either. He didn't have the shotgun. He reached into his back pocket and took five twenty-dollar bills from his wallet and held them aloft. "People are expecting me in Seattle in a few hours," he said, hoping the announcement would deter any murderous thoughts his inquisitor might be harboring. "I just don't have time to get back to the airport in town."

The man with the shotgun mulled his options for a moment then cracked the gun open and rather pointedly checked the shells. Satisfied he snapped the action shut and resumed his former position. "How much gas this thing hold?" he asked.

Akagi thought about it a moment. *I've got about twenty gallons left. Capacity is two hundred gallons.* "About a hundred and fifty, or so."

"I got no meter on these tanks but each one is two hundred gallons. The one on the right is full. You give me the money, you can fill up and then git." He stood expectantly next to the plane.

The pilot climbed down from the cockpit leaving on his helmet, tinted goggles and gloves. He hoped the grime from flying obscured what skin was still exposed. Once on the ground he handed the money over. It disappeared into man's massive paw and thence to his left front pocket. He immediately turned from the Japanese officer and walked into the house. He didn't even look back.

Twenty minutes later, after filling every tank to the limit and answering the call of nature in a nearby outhouse the airborne spy was taxiing down the runway preparing to return to the skies. Once airborne Akagi began to notice weather was making a change and wind started buffeting his craft. Nothing serious, just uncomfortable.

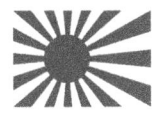

Aboard the *Pufferfish* Captain Katsu had submerged twice to avoid possible detection when the conn lookout spotted vessels likely to get close enough to take note of the submarine. Once underwater he would run on one random heading for half an hour, then retrace his path. The navigator would take a reading and whatever adjustment to their position was required would be made. Chief Osaka was trying to figure out a way to view through the damage periscope. When the trees knocked the scope off perpendicular it created a real problem.

The problem was that except for a skewed view from port & starboard it was impossible to see the horizon. Toward the bow the viewer looked into the sky, to the stern onto the deck just aft of the catapult. This made firing torpedoes accurately nearly impossible; the best you could hope for was a lucky shot blindly fired in the general direction of a target. After some discussion and experimentation the upper and lower mirror angles were adjusted to correct for the offset caused by the damage. It was a marginal solution that gave the Captain about a sixty-degree arc of vision off the bow. At periscope depth they were completely blind to the rear and either side.

Sitting on station forty miles out to sea in choppy waters just waiting was *I-28* (Experimental). Her new Captain had run a few drills and after that the seamen on duty had whiled away the time cleaning & inspecting their duty stations. The Executive Officer had granted permission to inflate the two rafts & attach the outboard motors. This was done ostensibly to ensure everything was in proper working order; what it really did was give the cooks a chance to do some fishing hoping to have some fresh food. Below decks the engineering crew was still searching for the bad actor among the wiring, still unable to isolate the problem.

"Good mornin' Cap. How was Portland?" MCPO Stan Harvey handed a cup of coffee to his C.O. then poured himself one.

"Fine. Great, actually. The weather was beautiful. The admiral was pleasant and the new boat looks great," the Captain responded. "It must have been a beautiful day for flying too, we got buzzed down on the docks by an orange seaplane."

The Chief nearly choked as his coffee went spewing in every direction.

After apologizing to the Captain, whose dress whites he had sprayed with coffee, MCPO Stan Harvey recounted the story the WWI veteran had told him yesterday. Captain Jackson allowed as how it did seem unusual. He directed the Chief to make some phone calls while he went home to change his clothes.

If the Army is run by Sergeants then the Navy and Coast Guard are run by Petty Officers. Stan Harvey had called, among others, the top kick for the Army Air Corps in the region, Theodore Kowalski. The two of them had been punching each other in bar fights up and down the west coast since they were recruits, but when they were on duty it was all business.

"Ski, this is Stan over in Astoria. How's your sister since the last time I screwed her?" He really enjoyed needling Army guys.

"Pining away waiting for somebody with a dick bigger than a pencil, you asshole! What's up that you would deign to call a lowly Army grunt?" the Sergeant asked.

"I took an odd report yesterday morning about an orange seaplane, or maybe seagoing crop duster coming in directly off the Pacific. It came around and buzzed the docks on the Willamette in Portland as well. You guys have any secret weapons painted orange over there?"

"Hey, there's a great idea," Kowalski said sarcastically, "we'll send Churchill some ag planes so they can crop dust the Huns back across the Rhine. Tell me you're not serious."

"Actually, I am. It just doesn't feel right. It's too early to be dusting and we've heard rumors that some of those Jap subs, the big new ones, carry planes on board. Anyway you're probably right, it's probably nothing, but my boss wanted me to call it around some."

One thing every non-com learned early was to trust his gut feelings so this was probably the real thing. Chief Master Sergeant Kowalski said, "Hey listen Stan, if this is serious shit I can have a couple of Corporals call around to see if somebody else saw this guy. He's gonna have to get some fuel somewhere and I can't imagine anybody would miss an airship like that. But jeez, the Japs? What in the hell would they want way over here?"

"Beats me Ted, that's above my pay grade. You and me, we work for a living. Thanks Ski, I appreciate your lookin' into it," Harvey said. "Give me a call if you turn anything up and tell your sister ol' pencil dick misses her terribly and thinks of her often."

"Fuck off, asshole." Sergeant Kowalski hung up the phone with a smile.

About the time the overdue flyboy was halfway to Grand Coulee from Wenatchee an Army Corporal was making his eleventh telephone call to an airport. He had already called Sand Point Naval Air Station and Boeing in Seattle, the airports in Portland, Salem, Yakima, Kennewick and Spokane and smaller fields as well, all to no avail. Now he was moving to the list of small outlying rural airports. "Maggie, is that you? This is Bill again, can we try another one?" He was on a first name basis with the long distance operator by now. He gave her the new number and waited as the phone began ringing.

"Wenatchee Airfield, this is Joe," the voice on the phone said.

"Hello Joe, this is Corporal Bill Renner with the Army Air Corps calling."

"What can I do for ya' Corporal?" Joe queried.

"We are investigating a report of an orange seaplane, or maybe a crop duster having some trouble. We are wondering if you or someone else there might have seen such a plane."

"Sure have. Me and Hank. Hank's my pilot you see, he flew in the Great War you know. Got himself a Frog medal he did, the Crux dee Gear, Ol' Hank was an ace fighter..."

"I'm sure Hank is a great pilot," the Corporal interrupted, "and I'd be glad to hear all about his flying experiences over a beer sometime, but right now my Sergeant is breathing down my neck to find out about the orange crop duster. What can you tell me about it?'

"Say no more, I had a sarge just like that in Belgium. He used to yell at us too. Seemed like every time he'd talk to the Lieutenant or the Cap'n he come back cussin' in eye-talian under his breath and start bitin' heads off like a circus geek. One time he..."

"Excuse me, Joe," Bill broke in again sounding a little exasperated, "what about the *plane*?'

"Oh, right, that's what you called about ain't it. Well, he flew in here yesterday evenin' runnin' low on fuel. He tanked up last night, took a hunnert an' eighty-seven gallons with the extra tanks, and was gone when we got here this mornin' at nine. Slept on a cot in the hangar last night," Joe paused thoughtfully, "I was gonna have the wife wash all the sheets after he left, but he seemed like a pretty clean fella so I changed my mind. You ever do that? Change your mind about somebody, I mean. Well, he didn't seem to be havin' any trouble to speak of, 'cept of course bein' low on gas."

Finally, I'm getting something useful! Renner thought. "I see, did you happen to catch his name or anything that might help us locate next of kin if we need to?" He had been instructed to be circumspect and fairly casual about his questioning. Make it sound routine, the Sergeant had instructed.

"No, I'm sorry I didn't. But he did say his family was leasin' a farm in Omak. Gonna plant cherries, he said. I like cherries pretty good, but peaches are my favorite. There's nothing like a ripe peach picked right off the tree. You take a bite an' the juice runs down your chin, mighty good eatin'. Now Hank, he likes raspberries real good, but the seeds get stuck in my teeth."

"Can you tell me anything else about the plane?" the Corporal interrupted again. "What about those extra tanks?" He scribbled notes on a pad in front of him. Sighing inwardly he crossed out the note regarding seeds in Joe's teeth.

"Well," Joe thought for a moment, "it *was* kinda unusual like. It was a fold up wing-under with floats. Had wheels underneath and sponsons too. Had a couple extra tanks attached under the plane between the floats. He said he bought it in Tacoma from surplus. It still had the camera in the belly. I had a camera once, a box Brownie. I carried it with me all durin' the war till it got a hole shot in it. You ever take any pictures?"

Bingo! The Corporal's heart was racing now, "Uh, snapshots occasionally. Hey Joe, is there anything else?"

"He spoke mighty fine English for a Chinaman, better'n me for sure."

"Chinese did you say?"

"Well, I reckon he never did say, but he looked Chinese or somethin' like that."

"Thanks Joe, you've been a great help, say hello to Hank for me. I've got to go now, 'bye." The Corporal slammed down the phone and turned to the Sergeant. "Pay dirt, Sarge!"

Recon Plane

Airborne near east face of Cascade Mountains
Washington State

It was after noon and the pilot of the seaplane made a daring decision. If he went back down to follow the Columbia he would likely still be trying to find the sub in the waning sun. If he took a path through the Cascade Mountains he could save at least an hour of flight time. Part of that time he would be at ten thousand feet or higher. At that altitude on the last day of March the air temperature was probably near zero, with the wind chill it would be thirty below. That was the easy part. If he didn't freeze to death in the unheated cockpit the wind coming through the pass might toss him around like a kite. The engine could freeze and stall or he could just crash right into a mountain. But he could save an hour. He took the chance.

Initially he pointed the plane northwest flying along the western edge of the Upper Naches Valley then came around to west southwest as he began following what appeared to be a gravel road next to a river his map identified as the Tieton. This wound steadily upward past Goose Egg Mountain on his left then Clear Lake straight west. The first wind began to push the plane around as he skirted north past Round Mountain. He gained some elevation to reduce the ground effect of the wind. Akagi couldn't decide if the controls were sluggish or he was losing his touch. His fingers on the stick were icy cold and numb. He could barely move the foot pedals and couldn't feel his feet at all. His breath had frozen solid to the scarf around his mouth and nose and he could feel uncontrollable shivers beginning to set in.

It took all his concentration to maintain level flight as the gusting winds of the flatlands began rising to be compressed against the west side of the Cascades sometimes reaching gale force as they accelerated upward. As he flew over White Pass and began down the western slope a sudden gust threw the aircraft sideways sending it into a steep dive toward Cortright Point. Struggling with the controls he recovered just yards above the treetops. As his heart struggled to recover a normal rhythm he picked up the course of the clear fork of the Cowlitz River. He followed this northwesterly heading directly toward the snow-covered south face of Mount Rainier looming eight thousand feet higher than his current altitude until the river mercifully turned southwest again. Within minutes the altitude began dropping and he brought the plane as low as he dared in the valley. He had survived and gained his hour, but he wasn't sure he would ever be warm again.

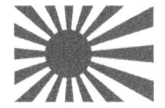

What had begun as an idle observation by a curmudgeonly World War I veteran followed by a routine morning conversation in the office was now poised to become a full-scale search. It would involve forces from the Army Air Corps, the U.S. Navy and the Coast Guard with assorted civilian agencies prepared to contribute land, sea and air assets. Guessing at a capacity of two hundred gallons of fuel, a five hour head start and factoring in what he expected was the airspeed of the craft, the Sergeant scribed a circle on a map of the Pacific Northwest. With Wenatchee as the center point he encompassed the area within which the suspect plane could have likely traveled.

"Whew," the Corporal whistled softly, "those are mighty big search parameters!"

The Sergeant and the Light Colonel who commanded the air wing at the base peered at the circle. Within its confines were

Washington State, the panhandle of Idaho and as far into southwest Idaho as Bliss, all of Oregon and nearly a hundred miles into British Columbia. Probably half a million square miles, maybe more counting the little parts of Montana, California and Nevada captured by the circle.

"We are certainly not going to search, or even begin a search of an area this large," the Colonel said unnecessarily. "Let's think about this. Where did he come from, where was he seen, what is his destination?" He paused then continued, "and what is his mission?"

"Except for the sighting in Astoria, the flight path the contact in Wenatchee recalled jibes with the story he got." The Sergeant continued, "It's that coming in off the ocean that doesn't fit. If he had to go to Portland from Tacoma, why wander all the way out past Astoria?"

"New plane, beautiful day?" Corporal Renner speculated. "Maybe he was just whale watching or giving it a shakedown."

"Would you take an unfamiliar airplane miles out over open ocean for a shakedown flight?" While the Colonel had long encouraged his non-commissioned officers, even Corporals, to share their thoughts, he wanted them to think as well.

"No, probably not, sir," conceded the Corporal, "but then why the roundabout route?

"What would the military reconnaissance targets be along the flight path?" the Colonel wondered aloud.

"The obvious is bridges, shipyards, airports, rail yards, maybe manufacturing sites. What else?" Sarge wondered aloud.

"Dams!" Corporal Bill Renner blurted, "Grand Coulee Dam to be specific, sir. Look," he said, pointing to the map, "probably less than three hours by air from where he stayed last night. He may have taken pictures of Bonneville yesterday."

"Sergeant," the Colonel was now urgently all business, "start calling the civilian agencies along the flight path. Make the following assumptions: Japanese plane and pilot disguised and well trained. Photo surveillance along the Columbia Basin for sure, probably the Puget Sound as well. Destination is possibly a submarine or perhaps a cruiser adapted for small planes off the coast or hidden in the islands in the Sound. Ask for an APB to look out for the plane and advise but do not approach if located. By the way, good thinking Corporal."

"Thank you, sir. Come on Sarge, let's start making those calls."

"On second thought, let's not mention a submarine just yet, especially to civilians. They tend to get a little excited. I'm going to kick this up to the General and see if we can get some real horsepower behind us." As he walked down the hall toward his office the Colonel thought *that boy is about ready for another stripe.* He would have to see to that.

As the ponderous machinery of the combined authorities of the United and various individual States swung slowly into action, the object of that effort was flying over Toledo, about fifty miles straight south of Olympia. The long hours of flight over two days were taking their toll. Even for someone young and in great physical condition, twenty out of the last thirty-six hours spent in a cockpit was debilitating. He was hungry, thirsty, tired and cold. His extremities throbbed as warm blood forced its way back in. He convinced himself this was a good sign; probably no frostbite. Arimoto tried to read his map but was having trouble focusing. He removed his darkened goggles and rubbed his eyes then tried again. *Probably no more than a couple of hours, I can hang on that long.* He put his goggles back on and continued westward.

It was purely coincidental that Major Michael Francis Harris, USMC and his seven crewmen happened to be in Astoria. They had taken possession of a brand new Consolidated PBY-5A Catalina only days before and had been given orders to fly out and conduct search and rescue drills with a loosely organized task fleet of navy vessels needing modifications currently headed north to the Puget Sound Naval Shipyards. They were sixteen hours ahead of the ships and had tied up at the Astoria Coast Guard pier, their liaison station.

Harris was from Decatur, Illinois and had a midwestern accent, which really meant no accent at all. He had taken to chewing bubble gum in an effort to stop smoking and from time to time he would blow a big pink bubble. Occasionally it would pop unexpectedly and stick to his bristling brown mustache. He had been chewing the fat with the Master Chief when a call came in from the Admiral's headquarters in San Francisco.

"Good afternoon, this is Captain Ashley at fleet headquarters. To whom am I speaking?"

"Good afternoon, Captain, this is Master Chief Stan Harvey. How may I help you today?"

"Chief, is your C.O. there? I have an urgent from CINCPAC Fleet."

"I'm sorry sir he has stepped away from his desk for a moment. Is there something I can do for you?" In actuality the C.O. was playing golf with the mayor, burnishing the public relations lamp.

"Maybe so, Chief. We have a report from the Army Air Corps of some type of Japanese military aircraft disguised as an orange seaplane or crop duster."

"Yes sir, I generated the initial report this morning. It came in from a civilian." He didn't mention it came in the day before.

"Great, so you know the story then?"

"Only the initial report sir, not any subsequent details," *Damn that Ski, he didn't call me back, and now my station is looking stupid to the navy brass hats.*

The Captain filled in the details for Harvey who was taking quick notes and then asked, "Is the PBY we sent out on station yet?"

"Major Harris is standing here with me right now," the Chief responded.

"Put him on the line, Chief."

He handed the phone to the Major who gave him a quizzical look, "Major Harris speaking."

Stan stood by as the Major listened to the voice on the end of the telephone line. He grunted occasionally, punctuating the monologue with a periodic yes sir, no sir and I understand sir. After a couple of minutes of this he straightened and said, "Aye-aye sir, goodbye."

"Chief, get on the intercom, round up my guys and tell them to meet me at the PBY in five minutes. I want to be airborne in fifteen."

"Aye, Major, will do and good hunting."

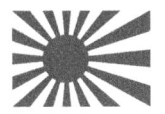

Akagi's eyes were burning and his head was pounding with pain in rhythm to his heartbeat as he continued his westward flight. He was only about twenty minutes from the coast upriver on the Columbia so he had to begin lining up his landmarks and get his heading correct. It was a vast ocean and even a near miss could be disastrous.

Major Harris throttled up and the twin Pratt & Whitney R-1830-92 Wasp Radial Engines sprang to life and pulled the plane eastward through the waters of the Columbia River and into the air. With a one-hundred-four-foot wingspan and a sixty-four foot fuselage his new craft was proving to be an agile airframe and he relished the opportunity to do some real work with it.

"Okay boys, let's go fishing." He banked the plane to the right until he was 180 degrees about from his takeoff and headed due west toward the open ocean beyond the mouth of the river.

The *Pufferfish* was expecting an aircraft, which made being a lookout particularly difficult. By the time you could identify an inbound craft it would be too late to escape detection with a dive, but if you stayed submerged the plane coming home couldn't find you. The new Captain, after much discussion among the officers had decided to stay on the surface. The consensus had finally been that unless they were caught together with the plane alongside or on deck, their mere presence, while embarrassing, probably wasn't fatal to the homeland. *Besides, if the flier isn't back by dark I'll abort the mission and head home.*

Unknown to either, the pilot of the orange spy plane was a mere three miles behind and two thousand feet below the PBY on the same heading. Members of the crew in the Catalina were peering out of the observation bubbles just behind the wings on the fuselage scouring the sea below them in search of the Japanese vessel thought to be lurking in the waters. The sun was low on the horizon and reflecting mercilessly off the water and clouds had begun forming below them. As diligent as they were they flew right over the sub and missed it completely.

The lookout in the conn of *I-28* (Experimental) mistakenly thought the PBY was the overdue Lieutenant's plane, despite the obvious difference in the engine sounds, and fired the green flare that was the prearranged signal between Akagi and Katsu.

From behind and below the U.S. Navy plane, Arimoto spotted the flare and homed in on the smoke trail. Within thirty minutes *Pufferfish* was safely a hundred feet underwater, its plane stowed in the deck hangar; its pilot safely stowed in a bunk.

Major Harris and his crew had flown a search pattern over the Pacific for two hours, crisscrossing back and forth over a seventy-five mile square grid, dropping altitude each time as clouds dropped the ceiling. Finally defeated by darkness and worsening weather he headed back to the Coast Guard station. He would report seeing commercial traffic in the sea lanes, a cutter attempting to rescue a distressed vessel trapped while trying to cross the sand bar and a pod of California Gray whales heading for Baja. His report would not include a submarine or an orange airplane.

Northeastern Pacific Ocean
Near U.S. Territory
Late night, March 25, 1941

Making four knots underwater *I-28* (Experimental) stayed submerged for four hours until Captain Katsu was certain that deep darkness had overtaken the open skies above them. Commander Chosiro, in addition to his new duties as second-in-command, was still the principal navigator so the overcast and rain they both discovered upon surfacing was bad news for him.

"Captain, for now we can continue north on this heading for fifteen hours at 12 knots. That will put us about fifty miles west of Cape Flattery at 1100 hours tomorrow morning. If there is no break in the cloud cover it will be difficult to fix our position as we head into the Strait of Juan de Fuca."

"Hmmph," Katsu grunted. When he spoke he was thinking out loud. "I can't sail through the strait in the middle of the afternoon." He would no longer be in international waters he knew. "Maintain this heading and speed. In the morning we will decide what to do. Let us get some rest, Chosiro, tomorrow the Rising Sun shall shine on the American Eagle."

Along with the task force steaming northward, all the Coast Guard stations in Oregon and Washington, all the military airfields and selected public ones, Private First Class Wilson Monroe had just received orders to be on the lookout for a submarine coming into Admiralty Inlet. Private Monroe was sequestered in a cold, dank, reinforced concrete lookout tower with only a stool, a phone to the M.P. station and huge naval binoculars permanently bolted to a rotating tripod head. The tower and several others exactly like it stood abandoned in a row stretching two hundred yards on either side of him guarded behind the sandy bluffs of Fort Casey.

His perch overlooked the entrance to south Puget Sound, from Admiralty Head on Whidbey Island. Along with Fort Flagler almost directly south on Marrowstone Island and Fort Worden at the northeast tip of the Quimper Peninsula, Fort Casey formed one point in a triangle of forts established when ships were still driven by wind.

This triangle had created an unrestricted field of fire in defense of shipyards and cities to the south. Combined, they could lay down a withering volley of shells in the killing zone it encompassed. However, since the invention of battleships that could lob a shell twice as big and twice as far as the cannons of the forts, they had become anachronisms. Converted to a toothless training facility, its cannons already removed for scrap, Fort Casey was nonetheless, a military outpost. As such, someone had to stand watch. The short straw had gone to Monroe this time.

The lunacy of searching for a foreign submarine crossing his field of vision in the dark was not lost upon the private and served to confirm his low appraisal of officers in general and senior officers in particular.

Whidbey Island
Puget Sound
March 26, 1941

Useless Bay, despite its moniker, wasn't useless at all to a fifteen year old boy just home from school. The distance from Double Bluff Point to Indian Point on the southwest shore of Whidbey Island is just shy of five nautical miles. Overall the long, slender island forms the eastern shore of Admiralty Inlet, a strait that is the gateway to the southern reaches of the Puget Sound. On days when a steady wind was blowing, Ritchey Pearson could race his father's battered little yellow sailboat from one point to the other in as little as an hour.

Today he was hunkered down in the stern clinging to the tiller racing northward toward Double Bluff. Every now and then his blue eyes would shift from scanning the waters in front of him to peeking to the top of the mast from beneath the well-worn yellow rain cap that was part of his foul weather gear. A rag tied to the top revealed the wind direction and Ritchey would adjust the heading to capture the most energy. The billowing triangular canvas sail was gray with age and sported a multicolor patchwork of repairs. His father said it reminded him of Joseph's coat. The wooden mast was well worn with years of hoisting and lowering of the sail rings. It bent ominously against the strain of the close-hauled sail.

Today was a typical late March day in the Puget Sound. A windy, gloomy, gray overcast alternately promised sunshine but then fulfilled the threat of rain. Stormy winds were often created when warm moisture laden sub-tropical air streaming in from the southwest slid through the Chehalis gap between the Coast Range in northern Oregon and the southern reach of the Olympics then collided with cool north-westerlies coming through the Strait of Juan De Fuca from the Gulf of Alaska. Most of the moisture is squeezed out against the western and southern slopes as the wind compresses against the mountains. It's race creates a sort of venturi effect in a convergence zone roughly encompassing an area west to east from Port Townsend to Arlington and north to south from Mount Vernon to Edmonds. This curious geographical quirk produces a dense conifer rain forest on the windward side of the Olympics and a rain shadow on the lee from Port Angeles around the peninsula to Quilcene. Within the confines of the zone it frequently creates strong unpredictable winds, drenching rainfall and from time to time powerful thunderstorms.

Young Pearson was a veteran sailor of these waters. Before the previous spring he and his father had sailed around Useless Bay for hours. He would listen carefully to the lessons given him about the waters and weather. Father would point out the gaudy Harlequin duck or the tall Great Blue Heron with its stick-like legs. Sometimes they would watch a heron as it walked about Deer Lagoon on its stilts, stopping occasionally to thrust its rapier beak into the brackish water. Having impaled a hapless fish or frog, it would fling it into the air and gracefully catch it in mid-flight and slide it silently down its gullet.

They would dangle hooks covered with globs of borax and brown sugar cured orange salmon eggs to tempt sockeyes returning to local streams, or throw a crab pot with a piece of liver securely wired inside to the bottom hoping for a few succulent Dungeness crabs for the dinner table. Sometimes Father suggested conspiratorially that he had heard certain rumors from other local fishermen. They would set shrimp traps in the cold waters. After such a day the pair would bring the catch up to the house and Mother would prepare it for supper. After prayers of thanksgiving for God's bountiful grace, the home would be filled with laughter as father and son told stories on one another. After dinner the dishes would be washed and put on the wooden rack to dry, Bible verses would be studied, hymns sung and Ritchey would be scurried off to bed with hugs and kisses.

Some days, their venturing took them just north to Mutiny Bay. The two of them would gently ground the boat on the sandy beach running the length of the bay at the waterline. At low tide they would use rakes and shovels to dig furiously for the plentiful littleneck, butter, razor and Manila clams.

Once a year on the Fourth of July, if the weather was fair, Mother would come along with a picnic basket. Mother remained stoic during the trip but she was terrified of the sea. While these were not exactly the raging waters of the open ocean, the Puget Sound still demanded respect. Father was always especially careful around the point as it was shallow with hidden rocks near the shore but quickly dropped off to fifty fathoms in the ship lanes. Outbound commercial freighter traffic from Elliott Bay in Seattle and the Port of Tacoma further south, passed as close as half a mile from Double Bluff Point, and the wake from those ponderous leviathans when it pounded the shallow shores could easily swamp their little vessel.

Father would ground the little boat at the beach and Grandfather Ambrose and Grandmamma Marie would already be there, bringing food and utensils for the celebration that was to follow.

"Joshua," Grandfather would call out, "help your bride out of that frightful little boat and get her ashore."

A huge bonfire was laid in for the evening and a blackened old iron pot that everyone left on the beach for communal use would be filled with a little seaweed, corn, potatoes, onions and carrots from the garden. Some water along with the catch of the day was added and the contents then steamed. After the feasting Grandfather and Grandmamma would converse with Joshua and Josephine, then strike up conversations with other families that had made their way to the beach for a celebratory picnic. They always left early as Grandfather Ambrose didn't like to drive in the dark. Father would stoke the fire against a cool breeze which would come in from the southwest and then ignore it, allowing the fire to slowly burn itself to coals.

The Olympic Mountains were silhouetted black against the lingering sunset while the skyline blazed in crimson fading to salmon pink then cerulean and finally cobalt blue, revealing the stars as brilliant points of blue-white light. The marsh wrens that had been flitting and chirping through the thimbleberries would find a place to sleep for the night, and the great horned owl that lived in the snag partway up the hill would swoosh silently by, searching the grasses behind the beach for an evening meal. When the last faggots of fire were barely glowing, Father and Mother would walk hand in hand from the beach to the Ford Model T truck he had secreted the day before. Ritchey trailed at a respectful distance bringing the basket and blankets. He would wrap himself in the blankets and climb into the pickup bed for the short ride back home; trying to remember the names of the constellations he spied. The next day he would return with his parents, Mother driving this time, and he and Father would sail the little wooden boat home.

Father didn't go sailing much since Mother had died last autumn. He just went to work and came home. The garden was left mostly untended, only occasionally worked by sympathetic neighbors. Prayers weren't spoken much, hymns weren't sung and the sparkle was fading from his eyes now. When he thought about it, it made Ritchey sad.

In his storm driven daydreams while gliding through the choppy waters, Ritchey concluded he would become a battleship Captain. This would distress his pacifist Presbyterian father no end, which, of course, was the notion's principal attraction. It was not the least incongruous in his mind that he commanded a great naval dreadnought fleet dressed in pirate garb with a cutlass held fast to his waist by a scarlet sash. He was issuing battle orders to similarly clad sailors who smartly saluted, then snapped into action to carry out his commands. The ensuing engagement was broken up by the racket of a few Glaucous gulls screaming overhead as they followed behind the tiny sailboat begging for scraps of fish. The seagulls, of course, had no idea their interruption had saved the enemy fleet from certain annihilation.

Ritchey searched the horizon and detected heavier weather coming in so he reluctantly came about and set a new course toward the small dock just south of the notch in the island between the bluffs near his home. The fleet was coming back to port to refuel and resupply, but if the weather was nice and Father approved, they would put out to sea tomorrow after lunch when the chores were finished.

By the time Ritchey got back to the little dock the heavier weather was upon him. The wind was whipping the old sail making it difficult to handle as he lowered the rings from the mast. In the cold rain he secured the sail, then took a ragged canvas and covered the cockpit of the boat. When he was certain everything was ship shape and in Bristol fashion, and was equally confident the storm would do no damage, he turned and ran up the hill to his house.

Pacific Northwest Waters
March 26, 1941

Commander Edouard Giseaux clasped his hands and rubbed them gleefully. Resting easily alongside the dock in Vancouver, British Columbia was a submarine. It was the latest addition to the modest Canadian naval forces. Built in 1934 by the U.S., it was the newest, most advanced underwater vessel owned by Canada for patrolling coastal waters. The diesel/electric boat was one of only four submarines in the fleet, it was *the* elite command, and it was his. Giseaux and a few junior officers and sailors had finished their six weeks of temporary duty aboard an American sub and now it was time to take his vessel and its rookie crew out for training exercises. He would start with something safe and simple. The Strait of Juan de Fuca had lots of commercial traffic; it would be the perfect place to conduct dry torpedo ranging drills. At Giseaux's command, the newly re-christened *Newfoundland* slipped away from its mooring and headed for a new set of patrol maneuvers.

Captain Harry Tonto was not a man to miss an opportunity, so when the submarine warning was issued to the little fleet he was commanding, he seized it. Immediately he ordered the group to reconfigure, putting his largest warships, two destroyers and a heavy cruiser, in front all ahead full. They were further instructed to begin using active sonar search. The rest of his ragtag fleet fell in behind and began random zigzag patterns. It was of some concern to him that he carried almost no ammunition on board. Most had been removed in Long Beach before he began shepherding the ships north for the sundry repairs and refits scheduled for the shipyards in Bremerton. Except for small arms ammo, he had in his command only ten depth charges on two vessels and a few dozen rounds for the deck guns and anti-aircraft weapons.

He looked like what Hollywood would cast as a battleship Captain. He was tall at six foot five, muscular and blond with just the right amount of gray at the temples, blue-eyed with broadly chiseled, even features on a square-jawed, hell-bent-for-duty face. Today maybe he would get to act the part. The U.S. Navy, his navy, was at peace officially and even with the war in Europe and significant friction with the Japanese in the Pacific, advancement in a peacetime navy was maddeningly slow for one so ambitious. It also explained why someone of his rank was reduced to such a menial chore as babysitting a few ships heading for dry dock. Unless something spectacular occurred, he was probably not on the list to make his first star. Now, however, the navy had handed him that chance on a silver platter. All he had to do was find the sub and that star would likely be his.

Overnight, as they steamed northward, the rain had grown increasingly persistent and the ceiling lower. The wind wasn't particularly strong, but more than sufficient to make the water choppy with six foot swells. Katsu and Chosiro stood together in the conn viewing the gray expanse stretched before them, each lost in their own thoughts. They remained this way for several minutes until Lieutenant Akagi shouted up the ladder, "Captain, I think you should hear this."

The spell broken, the two top officers climbed down the ladder onto the bridge where the pilot had directed the radio operator to pipe incoming traffic to the speakers.

"...looking for Japanese submarines? What do we do if we find one, throw Coke bottles at it?" The question hung in the static for a moment then a different voice "...No Commander, we have some depth charges available if need be. But I would like to force it to the surface instead of sink it. And I want to start using coded messages instead of open air. It's too difficult for ship-to-ship light signals while we're running a zigzag, so switch to coded radio effective immediately, out."

Akagi had been translating for all on the bridge to hear. All eyes were figuratively if not actually focused on the Captain at the moment. "So, we are discovered then, Lieutenant?" he asked.

"No sir, we are suspected. None of their radio traffic suggests they have actually seen anything. Apparently many believe it to be a training exercise."

"And the airplane," Katsu continued, "any word on that?"

"Not on my plane. There was mention of a PBY, apparently a new seaplane they have for reconnaissance, but the weather seems to have grounded it for now."

"Are we to suppose they would send unarmed vessels against us? This must be a ruse of some sort," Chosiro broke in.

"I don't think so Commander," Akagi responded. "The radio chatter among vessels reveals Bremerton as the destination. Bremerton is where the new shipyards are located. I think it is a convoy of vessels headed for repair or refit. That would explain a lack of ammunition and why so many think it is an exercise."

"Then this convoy is coming from the south of us?" the Captain asked.

"Yes sir, Probably San Francisco or possibly Long Beach or San Diego."

"How far away?"

"It's impossible to know for sure, but the radioman thinks probably no further than fifty nautical miles based on their signal strength."

"So," Katsu mused, "this is where we test our mettle. Do we go forward with the mission or tuck our tail between our legs and run for home?"

"May I remind the Captain," Chosiro offered, "that right now we aren't even sure where we are, and until we either see a landmark or take a reading we are only guessing."

"That means our fate is in your hands, Commander," Katsu said breezily. "Make your guess the best possible." The Captain had reached a decision. "Make your best estimate for a heading for Vancouver Island, have the helm lay in that course all ahead full. We shall enter the strait in Canadian waters about 3 miles offshore. That will allow the Americans to run by our position. We will follow behind them hiding in the cavitation noise of all those propellers. Then we will wait for the weather to clear and for them to forget about us."

Newfoundland sailed across Georgia Strait then passed between Valdes Island and Dionisio Point on Galiano Island. They are but two of dozens in a chain of islands running through the area alternately called the San Juan Islands in the U.S. and the Southern Gulf Islands in Canada. Essentially tree covered rocks of widely varying sizes, these islands rise above the deep, swift-flowing tidal waters of the cold Pacific. Most are guarded by rocky outcroppings lurking just below the waterline. Giseaux was being careful threading his way through these islands and it wasn't until he cleared the easternmost point of Saltspring Island and headed south that he felt more comfortable. In about two and half hours he would round the southeast tip of Vancouver Island past the provincial capital of Victoria, then Rocky Point forty minutes later headed for the strait and out to sea.

Anticipating a possible ambush, Captain Tonto opted to bring most of his ersatz fleet west of Tatoosh Island rather than between it and Cape Flattery, the southern entrance to the strait. Instead, he sent one cruiser and two tenders through with instructions to be as noisy with sonar as possible hoping to drive any sub northward. With luck if there were a sub, it would make a break for open ocean where his ships could intercept and cut off its escape route.

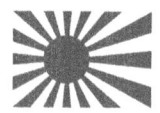

Pufferfish was making way on the surface along the southern coast of Vancouver Island well out of the shipping lanes and with little chance of being identified from the rugged isolated timberland that was the coastline. Even if the Americans caught sight of her, they would not cross into Canadian waters to pursue. The Canadian navy was no threat at all.

Sooke Bay was behind Giseaux now and it was time to begin some real training exercises in the Strait of Juan de Fuca. He positioned his boat in the middle of the strait just inside Canada at the watery border. He fixed his position on the chart, made his course known to the Exec and ordered the vessel to dive. His intent was to sink, figuratively speaking, as many targets as he could lay a scope on.

Aboard the *Northwest Passage* the Master of the timber-hauling freighter bound for San Francisco was leaving the bridge. Wearing a pea coat and blue cap, he was a grizzled old salt in his late fifties, sun burnt with watery green eyes, rough gnarled hands with coarse gray hair and a beard. He lit a cigarette, dragging deeply as he headed down the companionway for the officer's mess. With a plume of smoke trailing behind him; as he walked he had no idea he was about to be sunk by the Canadian navy, figuratively speaking of course.

As he sailed down the strait with his convoy, Harry Tonto could feel his star slipping away. No submarine had been detected, and now he himself was beginning to wonder if perhaps this was an exercise of some sort dreamed up by fleet headquarters. With only six nautical miles of U.S. waters to maneuver in, he had called a halt to the zigzag patterns, suspended active sonar sweeps and had slowed the fleet to normal speed. Dejected, he resumed his course toward Bremerton, his little command lining up dutifully behind him. Standing on the bridge he absently scanned the waters around him noting with no interest whatsoever a timber freighter slowly making a northwestward transit.

"Up periscope," Commander Giseaux ordered. The hydraulic tube slid up into position and he began turning to scan the waters above. He stopped when he saw the *Northwest Passage* plodding along. *Perfect!* He thought. *Slow, steady, big, she's just right for our first targeting exercise.* "This is a drill. Repeat, this is a drill. Mark bearings," he said. "Identify target as EX 1."

"Target is so marked and identified. Bearing is 279 degrees, sir." The Executive Officer called out.

"Very well. Sonar, report range."

The sonar man sent active pings from the sub then waited for the echo to return. The vacuum tube equipment measured elapsed time electronically far faster than humans could. It would give him a solid fix on the distance to the target. "Sonar reports range at four thousand meters, Sir."

"Helm, come to heading 279, engine room make turns for six knots" the Captain ordered. "Torpedo room, ready tubes one and two and stand by to open outer doors."

"Engine room, aye sir, making turns for six knots."

The fire control officer reported, "Tubes ready, sir."

"Helm reports heading of 279 degrees, sir."

"Very well, open outer doors. Down scope, sonar report range."

"Sonar reports three thousand four hundred meters and closing, sir."

Holy shit! The sonar man aboard the destroyer nearly broke his skull on the bulkhead as he jumped up. "Sir, sonar reports positive underwater contact bearing eighty seven degrees, range nine thousand yards! Target has gone sonar active and is closing on a surface target."

The report electrified the bridge and Tonto's mind instantly went from distantly disengaged to fully alert. "Sonar, verify that contact, now!"

"Contact verified, sir. I think they're targeting a freighter."

"Sound general quarters, man battle stations. Radio room, contact the fleet; advise them of my order to come to battle ready condition. Acknowledge."

"Aye, Aye, sir. Transmitting order now," Sparks responded.

"Helm, come to bearing eighty seven degrees," the Commander ordered, "Engine room, all ahead, flank." He turned to his executive officer and said, "Well, Bill, I may get that star after all! Have the firing crew set the depth charges for seventy five feet."

"Captain Katsu, the radio room reports sudden unusual traffic among the ships of the U.S. naval group." Commander Chosiro was out of his element, really. He was a navigator, unaccustomed to making strategic or tactical analysis. As he thought about it, in fact, he had never made battle situation decisions.

Katsu turned to speak but was interrupted by the sonar man: "Sonar reporting multiple active sonar targets. They all seem to be converging at top speed on a freighter bearing one hundred seventy seven degrees range seventeen thousand five hundred meters."

The Captain thought about this for a moment. "Sonar, are any vessels on an intercept course with us?"

"None detected, sir."

"Chosiro," Katsu said quietly, "sound general quarters, maintain current heading, all ahead flank."

On the bridge of the *Northwest Passage* the first mate had at first viewed casually the U.S. Navy frigate as it had changed its heading for an intercept course. She was three miles away and would miss by a wide margin. His demeanor changed to one of alarm as he saw the smokestacks begin belching dense black smoke as the navy ship's engines reached maximum speed. The safety margin was disappearing rapidly. He picked up the ship's phone and said, "Captain to the bridge immediately." Then he called to the radio room, "Warn that navy ship away!"

The crew aboard the *Newfoundland* was concentrating on sinking their first target so the sonar man didn't pause to think much about the other targets on the surface. This was a busy strait with lots of vessels. Nothing unusual, besides, this was an exercise, so he didn't bother the Captain with it.

"Fire one," Giseaux ordered.

A bolus of compressed air was released from the torpedo tube simulating an actual shot. "One fired, sir," the firing officer reported, "simulation running straight and true."

"Fire two," he commanded. He got the same response, "Time to impact?"

"Forty-five seconds, sir."

"Very well, up periscope." He wanted to view his hypothetical torpedoes sink his first target.

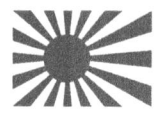

An Ensign on the bridge of Captain Harry Tonto's flagship was the first to spot it and call out excitedly, "Periscope five degrees off

the port bow about fifteen hundred yards." Six pair of binoculars swung in that direction to confirm the sighting.

"Helm, fifteen degrees starboard, engines ahead standard." Tonto was giddy; "we've got him by the balls now, Bill! Reset depth charges to fifty feet. Sparks, warn that freighter off."

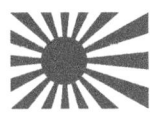

Giseaux peered into the ocular of the periscope looking at the hypothetically doomed freighter then casually rotated the viewing head to scan the horizon. *Sweet Jesus and Holy Mother!* Nearly on top of him was a frigate bearing down hard. It was so close he couldn't even see the flag. "Emergency dive," he shouted, "rig for collision!"

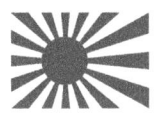

Master of the *Northwest Passage* came on the bridge just in time to hear the first officer's order.

"Helm, hard over to starboard, engine room all ahead emergency power."

The radio operator looked up, "the navy is warning us to starboard, sir."

The Master blinked at his first mate his eyes wide as saucers. "Damn considerate of them, isn't it!" He reached into his pocket for his cigarettes and moments later, was wreathed in dense blue-gray smoke.

"Commence depth charge run." Tonto ordered.

"Sir," the navigator spoke up, "we are in Canadian waters right now."

"I'm not gonna let this guy escape because he's ten feet over the border, fire when ready." *Besides,* he reasoned, *they'll probably give me a medal for this.*

"Sir, I must protest," the XO exclaimed. "We have no authorization to engage an unidentified target in foreign waters."

"I have reason to believe I may interpret my orders to include engaging an enemy vessel located in friendly waters," the Captain said. He looked at his Exec hard and said, "Do you have a further comment, Commander?"

"No, Sir. I'm just doing my job, Sir," he responded.

"So am I, Joe," he turned to an Ensign pressed into duty as a fire-control officer. "Carry out my order, son."

"Aye, aye, sir." A slight shudder ran through the ship as each of five depth charges was launched at the Ensign's direction. About ten seconds after hitting the water an enormous plume would erupt on the surface like a huge belch from Neptune.

The first charge caught everyone on the sub by surprise. The violent buffeting it caused threw personnel and equipment all around. Leaks sprang out from pipes, valves, foreheads and knees. By the third explosion, panic had been replaced with training and the crew was racing to repair damage.

"Emergency surface, blow all tanks. Let's get upstairs before he can make another pass at us." Giseaux was livid; whoever was responsible for this was going to have hell to pay.

"Helm, come about, engine room to dead slow," Harry Tonto said. He had exhausted his depth charges and would be a sitting duck if he had missed. "Let's see what happens." The vessel made the turn and slowed. Crewmen were scanning the ocean surface for debris or an oil slick that might indicate a sunken submarine that would never return. Two thousand yards off the starboard bow a submarine popped up from an emergency surfacing order.

On the bridge of the frigate the Executive Officer saw the sub come up. When it had settled on the surface he viewed it with his binoculars and saw the crimson flag with the Union Jack in the upper left and a seal in the field stenciled on the sail.

"Congratulations, Admiral," he smirked at Tonto, savoring the words saying them slowly—just short of insubordination. "You just saved us from the Canadian Navy."

Ferryboat *Kalakala*
Seattle
8:00 p.m. March 26, 1941

Tied up to the Coleman Dock at the foot of First Avenue in Seattle, the art deco masterpiece of maritime ferry architecture *Kalakala* was preparing for its evening dance excursion. Looking nothing at all like the bird from which she had derived her Chinook pidgin name, she more closely resembled a monstrous streamlined covered butter dish. The porthole dotted silver silhouette could be seen criss-crossing between Seattle and Bremerton each day. It made six round trips daily carrying up to one hundred cars and two thousand foot passengers.

Kalakala was certainly a beautiful expression of the art deco style so popular now, but her bridge was perched high atop the butter dish and set back just far enough to make it impossible to see the bow of the boat as it approached docks and smaller vessels. More than once even a diligent crew had collided with other objects, much to the embarrassment of the Captain and the expense of her owners. But none of that mattered right now as Joe Bowen and his "Flying Bird Orchestra" filed on board past the Horseshoe Café and up the grand staircase with its wrought iron handrails to the Grand Ballroom. Grand Ballroom was a generous marketing description; in actuality the chairs were removed from the observation deck to create a dance floor and at 8:30 PM she would depart with revelers plying the waters of the Puget Sound until after midnight.

On the bridge, Captain Wallace Mangan was watching the weather carefully. It was just rain and wind now, not enough to scratch the sailing. At 276 feet long with a 22-foot draft and over fifteen hundred tons displacement, it would take more than a spring rainstorm to keep her tied up.

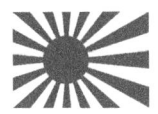

Commander Chosiro was navigating by charted waypoints now, using buoys and shore markers as they headed south. The American fleet they had been so concerned about had stopped dead in the water and seemed to mill about aimlessly for a while before getting under way again well behind them. The cold wind and steady rain had driven the small pleasure boats for shore, and he hoped, had obscured *Pufferfish* from the view of commercial vessels. He picked up the phone and called the bridge, "Captain, we will be in direct view of American military observation posts within ten minutes."

"Thank you, Commander. Clear the deck and prepare to dive," the voice of the Captain said from the other end of the line.

As the Captain gave the order to prepare to dive the Chief Engineer made his way to open the valve.

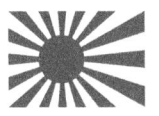

Rain does not deter Seattleites. If it did so nothing would ever get done, so it was no surprise that the party had started before *Kalakala* cleared the dock. It was Wednesday night so she wasn't as full as a weekend, but what they lacked in numbers they made up for in noise. The band was covering Glenn Miller at the moment, but before the night was over they would play every familiar big band song twice. In the engine room the three thousand horsepower Busch-Sulzer diesel engine was responding to the ministrations of the crew, who were in turn responding to instructions from the bridge. The direct drive engine began turning the shaft to which the single bronze propeller was attached and *Kalakala*, with her gangplanks lifted away and her lines cast off, eased away from the dock on another routine excursion around the Sound.

I-28 (Experimental) had been underwater for nearly five hours periodically sending out a tentative low-power sonar ping to look for rocks to avoid and occasionally coming up a few feet to allow Katsu to peer through the periscope. As darkness had descended, lights from houses on nearby islands had winked on and smoke from alder fires streamed out of chimneys to be whisked away by the wind. The Chief Engineer was keeping his crew busy with routine maintenance. He had given up looking for the problem wiring; they would find it when they got home.

In the battery room, which really supplies the heartbeat of the sub when she is underwater, engineering seaman Haruko Ryobi was removing the caps from all the batteries to maintain the level of electrolytes. He had noticed in the wiring blueprints that the port side ballast valve actuator wire traveled through here also. Since everything in the compartment was explosion proof—a precaution against a build-up of dangerously flammable hydrogen gas from the battery charging process—it seemed logical to him it must be enclosed by the conduit. Working carefully, he took a screwdriver from his back pocket and reached over his head to loosen the inspection ell. As the second screw was loosened, he tapped the cover lightly with the handle of the tool to loosen the paint. In a moment it swung away to reveal the interior. Haruko, standing on tiptoes couldn't quite see into the ell and realized he was going to need a flashlight. He left the battery room closing the bulkhead behind him.

Captain Mangan was pacing the bridge alternately peering out of the darkened windows into the gloom and restlessly glancing at his watch. Tonight he was keeping the *Kalakala* and her compliment of carousers in the main shipping channel of the Admiralty Inlet. It was deep water, well-marked with little chance of encountering small vessels. *Hell,* he thought, *I could have stayed tied up to the dock for all these people care.* His floating dance hall was going to take it easy. Nice and slow up to Admiralty Head, then turn around and come back.

"Jim, you have the bridge," the Captain said, "I'll be in the Horseshoe getting a sandwich."

"Okay Wally, take your time, this one will be a snoozer," Jim replied. Their familiarity came from years of working as Master and First Mate together. Jim would probably be getting his Master's rating this year and have a ferry of his own by Christmas.

Captain Katsu ordered the sub to put the sail above the surface. A fierce debate had broken out among the senior officers with regard to the wisdom of this action, but in the end there was simply no other way to determine when to launch the plane. It certainly couldn't be done in daylight and only the pilot could decide if the weather would permit flying. They might have to lay underwater for days for the right conditions, but each night they would have to come up to survey their situation and recharge the batteries. On the surface, the sail was crowded with the Captain, the first officer hoping to take some readings, Lieutenant Akagi and a seaman to stand watch.

"The weather is much better," Chosiro observed. "I'm going to try to get our exact location plotted." Without a useful horizon star charting wouldn't work, but a range finder to known chart locations would get them pretty close. After a few notations he disappeared down the hatch.

"Well, Lieutenant, what do you think? Can you fly?" the Captain asked.

"I think so. The wind is dying out and the clouds are breaking up to the south," he replied. "I would like to get the plane unloaded then I can go ashore after a few hours sleep and wait until first light."

All three men scrutinized the waters surrounding them. When it was assured no other vessels were within range, the Captain ordered the sub to fully surface. The launch crew worked rapidly. They opened the watertight deck hangar and rolled the plane into place. They extended the wings and sponsons, bolting them securely. Tonight's deployment was different. The catapult would be ignored; the plane would take off under her own power from the waters of Useless Bay. The men gently lowered the plane on a makeshift skid down to the waterline where lines were attached to rings in the forward part of the floats. The pilot, in one rubber boat, placed a watertight package inside the plane then attached a line to one of the rings and played it out to the other end, which he attached to a similar ring on his raft. Another sailor was duplicating the process on the other float, and on a signal from Akagi, each revved up their outboard motors and began towing the plane away from the submarine. As soon as they rounded the point and could see the shore, Akagi waved to the other boat. The second boatman waved back then cast off his towline and sped away, returning to *I-28* (Experimental).

The moment the sub had deployed the air snorkel, the engineer fired up the engines to begin recharging the batteries. Issuing new orders to his crew, he left the engine room and made his way toward the head. From there he intended to go to the Officer's Mess and have a sake, maybe a few. He had been involved in the officer's debate and knew staying submerged for a long time might be necessary. He wanted the batteries at full capacity even if he intended not to be.

The trumpet player aboard the party craft was making a hash of some sublime notes originally blown by Louis Armstrong but John and Louise didn't mind. They had gone to the aft observation deck to take a breather, look at the Sound and be alone together. Between rain squalls they made their way along the starboard promenade companionway, John pointing out landmarks, Louise noting how different they looked at night. It was a new moon, and the waning storm had left the night sky scrubbed to a crystalline transparency so that the stars shone brightly, winking on and off as clouds drifted by, hanging motionless in the black, bottomless inkwell of the sky.

In the sail, the seaman standing watch on *Pufferfish* sneezed so hard his glasses came off. *Damn this cold. I've been cooped up in this tin can for a month and now I'm stuck with the night watch in the conn.* He sneezed again, this one harder than the first, then spent some time blowing his nose and rubbing his watery eyes. *I'm a farmer.* He thought. *I grow rice and raise pigs.* He would get around to finding his glasses in a minute; right now he was busy being miserable.

Below decks Ryobi was off duty now but it had been hours since he had checked the batteries and he didn't want to leave it till he came back. The Chief had the next watch busy so they wouldn't get to it either. Armed with a flashlight and a short ladder, he entered the battery compartment. Securing the bulkhead behind him he put the ladder in position to take a look at the wiring in the ell.

During a respite in a sneezing episode, the man standing watch in the conn thought he heard music. It sounded strange to his ears and it played tricks on him, seeming to come from shore, then the water. *No, it couldn't be the water.* He stared out at the fuzzy points of light that surrounded him...confusing him...befuddling his bearings. He rubbed his eyes again; *there it is again, coming from the water. Where are my glasses?* He reached down and began feeling around the deck of the sail, finding them and raising them to his eyes.

With no moon, the waters surrounding the *Kalakala* were pitch black, only occasionally reflecting a stray light from onshore. On the bridge, Jim and Wally were discussing the relative physical merits of the ladies on board tonight. Both officers would make a show of parading around the Ballroom periodically. It was supposed to give the patrons a feeling of security. It really just gave the two of them a topic of conversation.

John and Louise were locked in a romantic embrace on the starboard promenade talking quietly, kissing; ignoring the world.

Now with his glasses in place the seaman in the sub conn finally focused on the source of the music. He was instantly rooted in horror as the *Kalakala* loomed ahead. Yellow light streamed from each of the over sized portholes ringing her upper deck and the din of the orchestra drowned out the noise of the motor. It looked like a silver-scaled dragon about to pounce on a hapless knight. The sailor grabbed the phone and shouted into the ear piece, "DIVE! DIVE! Emergency!" He dropped the instrument and jumped down the hatch pulling it shut after him.

"Huge boat forward seven hundred meters, closing fast!" he yelled in a panic. "On a collision course!" he finished.

Excited, confused, and not quite sure what to do, Chosiro, who was the duty officer, shouted into the ships comm., "Engine room, all astern emergency power. Officer of the deck blow all tanks, emergency dive!"

In the Officer's Mess, the Chief Engineer felt the sudden surge and struggled to his feet trying to clear his head on the way back to the engine room.

Haruko Ryobi didn't notice the tremor in the battery compartment. He was dead. Overcome by an atmosphere saturated with odorless hydrogen gas accumulated while charging the batteries. The gas, of course, was not dispersed by the failed blower fan.

It was at this particular moment; the moment when the dive officer pushed the button, that the molecules of the copper wire designated to operate the port side ballast valve finally failed. In a spectacular shower of sparks—which no one saw—the wire melted, shorting to the conduit. The volatile hydrogen of the battery compartment, finding a source of ignition, exploded with a sickening *thwump*, plunging everything into darkness.

Submarines are designed to keep from crushing from the outside. The massive overpressure caused by the explosion on the inside caused the hull to crack and splay out along three seams of the hull. With no power, no lights and no controls, the ship filled rapidly as water coursed through the stricken vessel. Most of the pressure tight hatches were still open as dazed, disoriented sailors trying to feel about for them. The water rushing in from the sea ran forward weighing the bow down and hastened the fifty fathom plunge to the bottom.

After securing his plane hidden in a tiny cove, Arimoto had just rounded the point when he spotted the ferry heading away up the sound. The submarine was nowhere in sight then a deeply muffled sound arose from below him and a huge expulsion of explosive gases set the sea under him churning. The wake of the *Kalakala* finished the task, overturning the rubber boat, casting him into the frigid waters.

Aboard the *Kalakala* the rail side couple broke their embrace. "Did you hear something, Fred?" Louise murmured, pausing their osculation for a moment.

"Only the beating of our hearts, *mi amour*" he replied.

"You are *terrible,"* she cooed, "but I like it."

"Me too, don't talk." They recommenced osculation.

On the bridge of the ferry Jim stopped for a moment in his conversation. "Did you feel that?" he asked the Captain.

"Feel what?"

Jim turned to the helmsman, "You feel anything, Peter?"

The man shrugged, "Just felt like a current eddy, that's all."

"Hmmph must be my imagination." He and Wally rejoined their conversation.

271

Akagi was still not completely certain what had happened. Clearly the submarine was sunk or badly damaged and unable to render any assistance. He himself had nearly drowned when the wake of the ferry dumped him unceremoniously into Puget Sound. Only a stroke of luck had saved him.

A wake wave tossed him into a mostly submerged rock slamming his shoulder heavily as he was swimming for shore. Clinging to the rock, he had squinted into the night to get his bearing and in the darkness saw he was only a few dozen meters from shore. Akagi then gathered his strength and flung himself into the water and flailed furiously with his right arm, eventually reaching land. Twice while crawling onto a small sand spit, wave action had crashed him against the rocks. He rested a few minutes then struggled first to his knees, both banged up and bleeding, then to his feet. He began to work his way along the deserted shoreline in the dark. The frigid waters of the Sound had set his teeth to chattering, but even in his weakened condition he knew it was imperative to get back to the plane.

With agonizing slowness he worked his way around to a point where he could make out the aircraft's hazy outline bobbing on its mooring in the dark. Wading out to where he had anchored it only two hours before, he opened the door and crawled inside. Again he rested for a while and then retrieved the small waterproof package he had placed aboard and searched for the life raft stowed behind the pilot's seat. Next he started the engine, deeming the risk of discovery to be minimal at this early hour, and slowly pushed the throttle forward for maneuvering speed. Arimoto took the plane out into the shipping lane positioning it so the tide would help push his life raft back toward shore.

Akagi clambered painfully out of the cockpit dragging the dinghy onto the float with him. When it was inflated he threw his package inside and fell in. He worked his way under the plane and opened the drain petcocks on both spare tanks, draining aviation fuel onto the sea. As he painfully paddled and drifted away from the plane, he took the flare gun from the raft, loaded the chamber and fired. Instantly the orange airplane became a huge fireball, moments later exploding with a resounding boom as the main fuel tanks ruptured. Within minutes the remnants of the little plane were spiraling down into the depths of the Sound joining the submarine in eternal rest beneath the waves. By daybreak, he hoped, not a trace would remain.

Kalaka'la made the turn at Admiralty Head and was five miles south of the point where the submarine had met her anonymous doom when an explosion and fire erupted in nearly the same spot. Captain Mangan, alerted by a crewman, made a notation in the ship's log, assuming erroneously that a pleasure vessel had failed to vent its engine compartment of fumes and blown herself up. It was a distressingly common occurrence and he radioed his observations along to the Coast Guard. An hour later he tied up uneventfully at Coleman dock and disgorged the night's happy but spent cargo of revelers.

When he got back to shore Akagi pondered what to do with the life raft, concluding he should just sink it where it was. Perhaps it would be found, perhaps not, but it couldn't really be associated with any of the people or events of the last hour. Exhausted and aching, he finally worked his way along the shoreline and hid himself in a tiny yellow sailboat.

Whidbey Island
Washington
March 27, 1941

It was a glorious day to be alive. Best of all for Ritchey Pearson there was no school today. Ritchey had catapulted out of bed at daylight and scurried about the small acreage doing his chores; feeding irascible hens then collecting their eggs, mucking out the stall where the cow and her calf stayed at night, then tossing hay from the rick to the manger. From there he raced into the kitchen to wolf down the bacon, eggs and toast laid out by his father. He guzzled down a glass of milk then fairly flew out the kitchen door heading down to his beloved little sailboat. He was reassuring to his father as the screen door slammed behind him, "Don't worry Father, I'll be careful and I'll be back later for lunch."

Arimoto groaned imperceptibly with every motion of the sailboat in which he was hiding. His body was stiff with cold and exertion, his head was throbbing and his left shoulder rankled painfully as he probed it gingerly with his right hand. Surreptitiously he lifted the canvas to survey the surrounding area and peered out into the shipping lane. Coast Guard vessels could be seen combing the area, but appeared disinclined to venture inside the bay. He checked his pistol once more and pulled the cover back into place. So far, considering the circumstances, he was doing okay. The sun had begun to warm the boat. The heat felt good and Arimoto drifted off to sleep.

Before he was halfway down the path to the little dock, Ritchey had already assessed what his sailing conditions for the morning would be. Wind; not much. Seas; pretty smooth, but the boat traffic seemed unusually high. In fact he couldn't recall a time when so many small boats were milling around out by the shipping lane. It was none of his business though; yesterday's storm had blown through and it was a beautiful day for sailing—even slowly—in his beloved little boat.

He bounded onto the dock and in three steps was beside the boat.

Hmmm, wind must have loosened the cover, he thought as he noted the untied canvas flap. *I'll have to tie it down tighter next time.* He moved quickly around untying the cover then flung the canvas back. Inside, a desperate Akagi pointed the Baby Nambu pistol at the boy from his position concealed in the boat.

"Don't shoot me mister, I didn't do nothin," a startled Ritchey blurted out.

As he lowered the gun, Arimoto's mind was racing. He needed a plausible cover story and a place to hide while he recovered.

"Relax, kid," he said, "I'm not gonna shoot you."

"Are you some outlaw on the run from the cops?"

"No, I fell off a boat last night, nearly drowned, too. I needed a place out of the storm until I could figure out where I was."

"You fell off a boat carrying a gun?" Ritchey was young, but he wasn't stupid.

"This?" Akagi waved the pistol carelessly. It's a souvenir. My brother sent it to me from Japan. I don't think it even works. *That part is probably true,* he thought, *these damn things jam up all the time.* With an aluminum magazine which was unsuited for a saltwater environment, the gun, when contaminated with briny water rarely worked properly. He had found it ludicrous that they were issued to naval officers.

"I have lots of Japanese friends," Ritchey said perfectly in Akagi's native tongue.

Now it was Arimoto's turn to be startled. He stared at the young man before him then addressed him in Japanese.

"You speak Japanese?"

"Yes, I do. You speak English, so what?"

"So it's a little unusual, that's all. Where did you learn it?"

"My father and my grandfather," Ritchey was getting a little impatient. If he wasn't going to be shot he wanted to go. "Listen, mister, I want to go sailing so could you get out of my boat?"

Still crouched in the bottom, the grounded flier peeped over the edge surveying the surrounding terrain. Satisfied that there was no imminent threat of discovery by a greater authority than a young boy he dragged himself into a sitting position.

"Hey, are you in the navy or something?" Ritchey had switched back to English, and had noted the uniform Akagi was wearing.

"What's your name, son?" Arimoto asked.

"Ritchey Pearson," he replied.

"Glad to meet you. I'm Paul. Paul Akagi. Reserves actually," he said referring to his uniform. "Listen, can you keep a secret?" He looked around conspiratorially.

"Sure I can, but why should I?" Ritchey responded.

"Because I'm on a secret government mission." *The truth so far as it goes*, Akagi thought. "And it's important nobody finds out how I got here. It could really mess things up in the War Department." *Also true, probably in both war departments.* So it's really up to you to keep this secret. What do you say?"

Wow, a real spy, and I could be one too! This appealed greatly to Ritchey. "So what do I have to do?"

"Well, right now I could use some food and water. Then you better go sailing because that's what people are expecting you to do."

"Okay, you wait here, I'll be right back!" Ritchey had already bounded off the pier and was racing up the pathway before Akagi could even stop him.

Arimoto, no, Paul, he corrected himself mentally, *what in the world are you going to do now?* He began undoing the buttons of his uniform but when he tried to remove the waterlogged woolen coat he was initially defeated by wracking pain in his shoulder. Slowly he shrugged the coat off his undamaged side then managed by degrees to remove the other side. He made a cursory examination of the injured area. Probing gingerly again with his fingers he discovered serious swelling and an ugly bruise, deep red in the center surrounded by dark purple. He had probably broken a collarbone and his adrenaline spiked activities of the previous night had driven the bone near the surface of the skin.

The clomping of running feet could be heard coming down the path. Paul turned in the direction of the sound and saw Ritchey roaring toward the dock with a canteen and a flour sack in tow. As he ran onto the dock he tossed the items in the boat and began to energetically fold the canvas cover to stow away: that done, he jumped aboard and untied the lines from the cleats, and pushed the little vessel away from the dock with an oar. Expertly he hoisted the sail and gathered what little wind there was and sailed out into the bay.

With every sudden jerk and rock of the boat, Paul groaned and tried to protect his damaged shoulder. His knees were pretty painful too and his head had a persistent ache he couldn't seem to shake. At least the knees didn't seem to have any serious damage. When they were finally adrift, he gathered in the canteen and the small sack. Paul took a deep draught of water then rummaged around in the sack withdrawing a thick irregular slice of bread with butter smeared on it. There were also a couple of strips of bacon and cans of salmon and applesauce.

"You don't look so good, Mister," Ritchey observed as he steered his craft to maximize the winds. "Maybe you oughta see a doctor."

"Mmmph," Akagi nearly choked on a piece of bread he was chewing. "Maybe later," he croaked, "after I rest up a bit." The last thing he wanted was to have to explain himself to some meddling doctor.

"Up to you I guess. But you don't look so good, anyhow."

"Sail out toward the sunny spots. That'll make me feel better for now."

"Aye-aye, Captain, prepare to come about," the young sailor shouted.

Akagi ducked his head in anticipation of the maneuver.

"Come about," Ritchey yelled and swung the boom from starboard to port. The patchwork sail fluttered momentarily then filled with wind. Pearson steered the tiller toward the sunniest point in the bay and the vessel and its odd crew compliment slowly plowed through the waters of Useless Bay.

U. S. Coast Guard Cutter *Tacoma*
500 Yards West of Double Bluff Point
Whidbey Island
09:15 hours, March 27, 1941

"How long are we gonna keep lookin', Skip? We been out here for two ana half hours already."

"Keep your shirt on, sailor. We're here until the Navy says we aren't. Just keep looking." Truth was the Lieutenant in command of the cutter didn't see much point in circling endlessly either. And why the Navy was suddenly in charge of a routine incident called in by a ferry captain was beyond his comprehension.

An excited call from his C.O. had suddenly put a charge in his crew and they had torn away from the dock at flank speed. They headed out to join a flotilla of assorted small vessels off Whidbey Island, where Captain Mangan had reported hearing an explosion and seeing the subsequent fire.

No big whoop dee-doo, he thought. *Some drunken idiot in an expensive Chris Craft had blown himself up with an unvented engine compartment. It happens all the time.*

Still, it was unusual he had to admit, that there seemed to be no evidence of any such disaster. No flotsam of varnished mahogany chairs or teak decking. No big sheen of petroleum on the water or the nearby rocks. Nothing. Definitely unusual.

"Skipper, bring 'er about and take a look at this."

"Helmsman, come about," the Captain of the boat said.

"Come about. Aye, Sir."

As the vessel made a one hundred eighty degree circle in the water, the bosun handed his commander some binoculars and pointed to a rock about 300 yards away.

"What do you make of that, Sir?" He asked.

The skipper peered intently through the binoculars at a small orange dot stuck on a rock near the island.

"Hell, Jack. It could be anything. But is sure doesn't look like part of any pleasure boat I've ever seen." Lowering the binoculars he studied the water between his boat and the object. "Let's get in a little closer for a look-see. George, you see that orange dot on the rock over there?" He was pointing for the benefit of his helmsman.

"Sure do Skipper."

"You think we can sneak a closer peek at it?"

"Sir, I can dock this boat next to a six foot two by four if you like. I can put you there, no prob."

"I'd just as soon not have to repaint the bottom of the boat when we get back, but let's move in slowly."

"Aye, aye, Sir."

Expertly the sailor at the wheel guided the boat through the jutting rocks getting to within about fifty feet of the object. The Lieutenant ordered two sailors to a dinghy to row over and retrieve the item.

Back aboard, the item was handed over and the examination began. The irregular piece was clearly a thin piece of sheet aluminum. Along one straight edge there was a series of holes where rivets had obviously fastened this piece to a larger construction of some sort. One side was poorly swabbed with a coat of orange paint, stopping at the overlap where two pieces would have joined. The other side had a flat sort of greenish gray paint.

"What do you make of it, Chief?" The Lieutenant asked his boson.

"Boeing, Sir."

"Boeing?"

"Yes, sir, they've been building all sorts of airplanes recently. This is probably part of a wing or fuselage assembly on some experimental job."

"You think we're out here looking for an experimental airplane?"

"Doubt it, Sir. If we were looking for a plane they would have told us don't you think?" The bosun opined, "Seems like that would be an important piece of information."

"Hmmm, I suppose you're right, Chief." While he pondered his next move he called out to his helmsman, "George, back us off these rocks, will you?"

"Aye, aye, Skip, Where to?

Before he could answer the radio squawked noisily.

"Attention all search vessels in vicinity of Whidbey Island attached to Navy Group Two; the search is suspended effective immediately. You are released to return to regular duties. That is all."

"Back to the dock to refuel, then we'll head out for a regular patrol." As the boat surged forward at his command, he returned his attention to the item in his hand.

"Well, Jack, what now?"

"Seems to me they don't much think there is anything to find. I think this is another snafu where the brass hats have us chasing our tails for their own amusement. But that's just me, Sir."

"Probably right, Chief, but what about this?" He held up the small sheet of metal. "You think Boeing oughta get this back?"

"Naw," the Chief replied. "By now they know it's gone when the plane got back. It's your call, but it just looks like more paperwork to me."

The Lieutenant mulled this over. None of the other search vessels he knew of had found anything. The Navy had called off the search and no one had said anything to him about any aircraft—orange or otherwise—that he should be looking for.

More paperwork, he mused, *just what I didn't sign on for, filling out more reports.* Stepping off the bridge he casually made his way to the stern of the boat and dropped the aluminum in the wake. For a second or two it could be seen churning in the foam then disappeared into the cold, deep waters of the Puget Sound.

In the ship's log he recorded his activities of the morning:

"Assisted U.S.N. from 06:45 to 10:15 hours in search for unspecified vessel possibly lost off Double Bluff Point. Small metal debris likely aluminum from aircraft seen but not recovered. Released to return to normal duties 10:15 hours."

Useless Bay

Whidbey Island
10:30 a.m., March 27, 1941

Ritchey had helped 'Paul' change from his uniform into the clothes from the bag he had rescued from his plane. Carefully he hung the uniform from the boom to allow it to dry and when it had, he folded it and stuffed it into the old flour sack.

By now, in clean dry clothes and some food and water in his stomach, Akagi had begun to feel a little better. He had watched as the search vessels outside the bay had broken up and headed off in different directions. Inwardly he sighed in relief. By now he could be relatively certain nothing important had been found.

The boy had been peppering him with questions nonstop since departing from the dock and he had mostly deflected them by asking questions in return. Now he was getting a little tired and the sun was getting a bit too warm. He felt hot and dry and he was having trouble focusing. Ritchey's voice was sounding distant and hollow.

"Hey Mister," Ritchey called, "you look really bad. I'm gonna head back in. My father is expecting me for lunch anyway."

Akagi barely heard what was said. His head was pounding, his shoulder was aching and his knees had stiffened up badly. By the time the sail had been reset and the sailboat was headed back to shore 'Paul' Akagi had drifted into unconsciousness.

"Hey Mister, wake up, wake up!" Ritchey was shaking his passenger trying to get a response. When he touched the stranger's face it was hot to the touch and he looked flushed. *Fever! I've got to get him back home. What am I gonna tell Father?* While Akagi was unconscious Ritchey gingerly removed the pistol from his side and put it with the uniform in the flour sack. He would worry about that later.

The wind was quartering his starboard so he had to return to the little dock by tacking and running, so it took almost an hour to sail the mile he needed to get home. When he finally furled the sail and leapt onto the dock it was nearly noon. Ritchey expertly whipped a few turns on the dock cleats both fore and aft and raced up the pathway to the house, bursting through the back door into the kitchen. His father was spreading butter on slices of bread to go with the soup already on the table.

"Father, come quickly!" He cried. "I found a guy over by Indian Point and he's real sick. He needs some help, hurry, run!"

The elder Pearson followed the younger as he ran down the hill toward the boat. Seeing the urgency in his son's demeanor he began running as well.

Ritchey reached the boat ahead of his father and noticed the flour sack in the bilge of the boat. He quickly grabbed it and stowed it under the seat just as Joshua Pearson arrived.

Pearson could see immediately the young Japanese was flushed with fever but he placed his hand on his forehead to confirm his initial impression. *Burning up!* He continued his brief examination discovering the damaged shoulder and knees.

"Son, run over to Mrs. Entwhistle's and call Doc Reid. Then ask Mrs. Entwhistle if she can send Amos down here quickly with the pickup. Go now, run!"

Ritchey dashed off to his assignment and Joshua returned his attention to his patient. That shoulder looked particularly bad and was probably the source of the fever, but oddly his clothes were clean and in good repair offering no hint of how these injuries had occurred. *Maybe he fell into the rocks at Indian Point. Still, you'd think the shirt would be torn or dirty.* Joshua rolled his patient on his side enough to access his wallet.

Inside was a driving license issued in California to Paul Akagi, a couple of photos, a Social Security card and six hundred forty dollars in cash. *Whew, this is a lot of money but it's not very informative,* he thought.

He could hear Amos backing the old flatbed Ford truck down the pathway and sliding it to a stop in the sand inches short of the dock. Amos, a huge black man with skin darker than coal and a smile as broad as the bay, stepped out.

"What's up, Mr. P?" He asked.

"Gotta sick man here, Amos. I sure could use a hand getting him out of the boat."

"Shouldn't be no kinda problem 'tal, Mr. P."

"We have to be careful of his left shoulder; it looks like a broken collarbone."

Amos lumbered down the dock and looked at the man in the bottom of the boat. Then he just stepped off into the water which was about waist deep on him and reached in and plucked Akagi out like a salmon. He slogged out of the water and gently laid his burden onto the flatbed.

"Iffen you get my jacket outta da cab, Mr. P. I'll make a little pillow for his head. This old flatbed be a pretty rough ride on the noggin I 'spect."

"Surely, Amos, and Amos, thank you very much."

"Ain't nothin' to it. You'd do the same for me, an' that's a damn sight more than most folks would do for me or this here Jap, either. You a good man Mr. P."

Working together slowly the two men managed to get the truck and passenger back up the hill and around to the front of the house. The handyman from next door once again gathered the unconscious man and carried him into the house, placing him gently in Ritchey's bed. Ritchey had returned and volunteered to sleep in the tiny loft of the house until the man was better.

Not knowing what else to do, Joshua had Ritchey putting cold damp compresses on Akagi's forehead.

Soon after, Doc Reid's '36 Dodge Coupe rattled into view. After it wheezed to a stop, wisps of steam escaping from beneath the leaping ram radiator cap, he stepped out with his black leather bag.

"Hello Amos, nice afternoon."

"Shore is Doc, nice to be greetin' you too."

"Joshua," Doc called, "Ritchey said you've got a pretty sick man here. Is that right?"

"Very much so, Doc; he's just this way, burning up with fever and a broken collarbone I think. Ritchey says he found him out by Indian Point. Maybe he fell onto the rocks."

"Well, let's take a look." The doctor's auburn hair was faded and brushed with silver at the temples. He sported a magnificent handlebar mustache twisted to fine points on either side of a long aquiline nose, and his green eyes were alert and clear with deep laugh lines creasing his congenial face.

He extracted a stethoscope from his bag along with a flashlight and a thermometer. First he listened to the heartbeat and respiration then peered into the eyes and ears. He took a small rubber block and placed it between Akagi's teeth then carefully placed the thermometer under his tongue.

"Keeps him from biting it in half in case he wakes up," the Doctor explained. "His breathing is shallow but clear and his heartbeat is a little irregular but that is probably the fever. Let's see just how high." Looking at the thermometer he whistled low. "One oh four and a half, we've got to get this down! Help me get him out of these clothes."

The two men wrestled the clothes off the man, discovering Akagi's battered knees, still oozing blood from the abrasions. Arising, the doctor went out to his car and brought back a bottle of rubbing alcohol.

"Ritchey, this is a job for you. Put some of this on a cloth and rub his arms, legs, chest and stomach. Be careful to avoid his shoulder and his knees. When you finish, start over again. Better open all the windows first. Josh, may I have a word with you for a moment?"

Joshua trailed the doctor as he headed back out to his car. Once outside Doc turned to Pearson with a worried look on his face.

"Josh that man in there is gravely injured. Infection likely is spreading from his knee injuries into his shoulder. He might very well have internal injuries as well. He should be in a hospital but I'm afraid the trip might kill him. He needs surgery on his shoulder right away."

"Yeah, I thought he looked pretty bad when I first looked at him," Joshua agreed. "What do you propose to do, Doc?"

"Get help, first. I'll call Sally and have her close the office and bring some extra supplies. Do you suppose Amos would be willing to go get her?"

"I'm sure he would, but so would I," Pearson responded.

"No, you need to be here in case I need your help. I'll go talk to Amos and call Sally. In the meantime run some cold water in the bathtub, we've got to get that fever down." The Doctor strode off toward Mrs. Entwhistle's house and Joshua turned on his heels and returned to the house.

Japanese Imperial Navy Submarine *I-28* (Experimental)
Fifty two fathoms below sea level
Two hundred yards west of Double Bluff Point
Whidbey Island
March 29, 1941

It took two days for the final submariner to succumb to the cold and the carbon dioxide poisoning in the only remaining intact, pressure tight compartment. Diesel fuel globules, leaking slowly, would occasionally drift out of the confines of the doomed vessel and float slowly upward. When they broke the surface they created tiny rainbow plumes on the water. Those would join the thousands of similar plumes created by the busy ship traffic in Puget Sound.

Dog sharks, sculpin and rockfish swam into, then out of the open wounds of the submarine among the broken teapots and tangled plumbing, endlessly searching for food or a place to hide. Sea stars were already dotting the hull and anemone eggs had begun to accumulate in every crack and crevice. An octopus was slinking behind a crab, as it scuttled along one of the broken seams of the death ship. In-rushing seawater had scrubbed away the last of the chalk markings that had christened her *Pufferfish*.

Battleship *Yamato*—C in C Flagship
Fleet Admiral Yamamoto's Cabin
Yokohama Harbor
14:25 hours, April 28, 1941

*N*ine *days overdue,* Yamamoto thought as he reviewed the report in front of him, *and only one submarine returns.* The Commander of the Imperial Japanese Navy read the brief communique for the fourth time:

Dear Nephew Eddie

No contact from three cousins. Cousin Judy reports unseasonably warm in the south. Good time for a vacation there. Should I extend my vacation to take in other sites of interest?

Regards, Uncle John.

The communication was stamped less than half an hour ago by the radioman on watch. The code wasn't particularly complicated, he was Nephew Eddie, the *Kobiashi Maru* was Uncle John and the cousins were the submarines. Sent in ordinary English rather than Japanese it was so vague that no intelligence agency would lend any credence or waste any time with it.

So one submarine reports good photos and thinks Long Beach would be a good target. Three other submarines have failed to return!

Yamamoto reached for a piece of paper and scrawled a reply:

Uncle John,

Looks like our cousins missed the train. Head back now, Aunt Mae needs your help on the farm. The cousins will have to find their own way home.

Regards, Nephew Eddie

With a sigh the Admiral rose to his feet, stretching his left side to loosen the stiffness, then walked to the cabin door and opened it.

"Deliver this to communications immediately. Tell them to send it with ordinary uncoded messages in English on the civilian frequency."

"Right away Admiral," said an Ensign waiting outside, and hurried down the companionway toward the radio shack.

Isoruku followed slowly, hands clasped behind his back. He made his way down the superstructure onto the teak deck. Ordinary seamen, unaccustomed to the Commander in Chief of the Imperial Navy wandering the decks, were startled into sudden salutes at attention. The Admiral ignored them all, deep in thought, as he headed for the bow of the gargantuan ship.

He gazed at the huge fleet assembled before him. The Shinano Bridge where he had chosen a life at sea flitted past his memory. He thought about sailors he would soon send to be with their ancestors when the dogs of war were finally unleashed.

After a long period of introspection he returned to his cabin and summoned his carrier strategist and planner Onishi Takijira, Chief of Staff of the Eleventh Air Wing.

"You called for me, Admiral?" Takijira asked when he arrived hours later.

"Yes, Onishi, find Kuroshima. Tell him it will be Pearl Harbor."

Whidbey Island
Washington
June 26, 1941

A spectacular spring day graced the Puget Sound, the morning sun suspended gloriously in the shimmering azure sky. White fluffy clouds scudded across the horizon and infinite shades of green cascaded down the hillsides to invade the valleys and meadows. Bright red and pink rhododendrons punctuated the landscape randomly as did volunteer roses and daisies that had migrated from nearby homes and fields in Mount Vernon.

Paul Akagi was sitting on a stump, shirtless and glistening with sweat as he looked over the waters of Useless Bay.

"Pretty big pile of wood you chopped there."

Akagi turned to see Joshua coming from the house with a glass of lemonade.

"Trying to get back in shape," he replied. "Chopping wood seems to be pretty good for my shoulder."

"Still hurt?"

"Not really." He unconsciously ran his right forefinger along the bright pink scar on his shoulder where the surgical incision had been made. "Sometimes if it gets cold it'll stiffen up some, but otherwise no. Doc did a real fine job."

Pearson handed Paul the lemonade, then squinted out at the bay.

"Is that Ritchey out by Indian Point?" He asked.

"Yes, it is," Paul replied. "I swear that boy will win the America's Cup someday. I've never seen a person so at home in a sailboat."

"He's certainly a better sailor then I am anymore." Joshua hesitated; then continued, "Paul, do you mind if I ask you a few questions?"

This was a moment Akagi had been dreading. Up till now no one had much asked about who he was or where he came from. Partly because he had been sick and partly, he supposed, because of the natural reticence of Americans to meddle in other people's business. But now, here it came.

"Sure, ask away."

"When you were sick you kept mumbling about an airplane," Joshua began. "What was that all about?"

"Airplane? What did I say about a plane?"

"Nothing specific, really, it just seemed…unusual, that's all."

"Well, I was probably dreaming about my uncle's old crop duster down in Salinas. He taught me to fly it when I was a kid."

"Where is Salinas?" Joshua asked.

"About a hundred miles south of San Francisco, maybe twenty miles inland from Monterey. I was born in Salinas."

"Hmmm" Pearson shifted his weight. "How did you end up in the rocks over there?" Joshua indicated Indian Point.

"Beats me, one minute I'm walking along the bluff, next I know it's a week later. I'm in a stranger's bed, weak as a kitten, with a four inch incision in my shoulder, and bandages on both knees."

Pearson mulled this over. It had been storming the night before and the ground along the bluff could be treacherous in the winter. Maybe he got too close and the wind blew him off, or the ground broke away under his feet and he doesn't remember. Maybe he never knew. "Why out there in a storm?"

"I like weather. It seems like I'm closer to Creation when I'm in it."

"That was a pretty thick wad of cash you were carrying," the inquisitor continued.

Paul laughed, "My dowry."

"Your dowry?"

"Money my father gave me before he and mom headed back to Japan. 'Son,' he said, "I wish you would reconsider and return with us," he mocked. "Consider the needs of the homeland just now."

"Why didn't you go back?"

"Couldn't; I don't speak Japanese well enough and can't write it at all. Ironic isn't it? I get saved by a ten year old white kid that speaks better Japanese than I do." Akagi hoped this particular red herring would be especially useful.

"Just a coincidence, Paul. Ritchey didn't set out to find a Japanese tourist piled up in the rocks. That was just your good luck."

"I suppose," he replied. "Still, that leaves me without a family, really. I can't write to Dad, he can't write to me. That was why I came up here. News on the grapevine said there was a nice community of Issei farmers on this island. I was hoping to catch on with one of them. I have a background in agriculture."

Following his father through all those fields, listening to all those farmers for all those years had given Paul a pretty good bluff if he had to talk shop with a field hand. It looked like now was about the best time to put this particular hand in play.

"Wrong island, Paul, this is Whidbey Island; mostly shellfish and timber over here. You were looking for Bainbridge Island. That's just across Elliott Bay from Seattle," Joshua explained. "Richey's middle name, Franklin, is after a good friend of mine, Frank Sakai. His family and several others live there."

"Does close count?" Paul smiled.

"In horseshoes it does," Joshua returned the smile, "which reminds me, I've invited Frank and his family to join us for the Fourth of July this year. You'll get a chance to meet him. Maybe he can find something for you."

"Maybe so," Paul looked across the water at the sailboat with the patchwork sail skimming back toward the dock. "Must be getting on toward lunch, here comes the Admiral now."

"In addition to being a great sailor," Joshua laughed, "he's a champion eater. Come on Paul; let's pick some vegetables from that garden you have growing over there."

Paul stood, placed the lemonade on the stump and pulled his shirt on. He fastened a couple of buttons then slugged back the remainder of the drink and fell into step behind Pearson. *I hope that's the end of all the questions,* he thought. *And I hope that kid can keep a secret!* He said a silent but fervent prayer to his ancestors, for he knew that his future currently resided in the hands of a sixteen year old boy.

Dick's Grocery and General Dry Goods
Oak Harbor, Whidbey Island
10:45 a.m. July 1, 1941

Dick Frost and his wife Abigail were both behind the counter near their vintage NCR cash register listening to the radio when Joshua and his temporary boarder came into the store.

"Hi, Dick, mornin' Abigail," he greeted.

"Joshua," the shopkeeper acknowledged. "What can I get for you this morning?" Dick was giving Paul careful scrutiny.

"Oh, just the Fourth of July groceries; probably need about twice as much as usual though." Pearson reached into his shirt pocket and withdrew a list which he handed to Abigail.

"Zat right? Why so much this time?" Dick was the island gossip, which rather annoyed Joshua so he was usually dismissive or evasive when questioned.

"Ritchey has turned into an eating machine," he laughed.

"Oh, I see. I thought maybe some a them friends of yours from Bainbridge was coming over." From his station behind the counter Dick was keeping his eyes fixed firmly on the Japanese stranger standing quietly nearby, his hands clasped behind his back.

"Now Dick," his wife scolded, "that's none of your business. You just hush and mind your manners!"

Joshua had seen this little melodrama played out many times before. Dick begins the interrogation; Abigail chides and then assumes the role of inquisitor. It was clever really: Who could resist the innocent questions of such a charming little woman?

"How is your grandfather doing these days?" Abigail continued seamlessly.

"He's fine, Abigail; coming for the Fourth as usual. Is it too early yet for Yakima peaches?"

"By a couple of weeks but we have some just come in from California. On a refrigerated train if you can believe it. We have four lugs. Should be perfect by the Fourth," she replied, "and how about his friend Thomas?"

"I imagine he's doing fine. I'll take half a lug. Corn any good so far?"

"Earliest we've seen just coming in from Tri-Cities," Dick answered. "It's a little puny and pretty expensive; two ears for a nickel but it tastes just fine."

"I'll get those," Paul said. "About twenty ears, please."

"I don't believe I got your name, son," Dick said.

"I'm sorry," Joshua interjected, "where are my manners. Mr. and Mrs. Frost, this is Paul Akagi, a guest visiting from California. Paul, this is Dick and Abigail Frost, proprietors of this fine establishment."

"Pleased to meet you," Paul said, extending his hand.

Dick hesitated slightly then extended his hand. "Likewise, I'm sure," he said noncommittally.

"What's on the news," Joshua asked, referring to the broadcast from Seattle radio station KOMO.

"Nothing much new, lots of talk about the war in Europe and the negotiations with the Japanese," Dick replied. "Call me crazy if you like," he said now staring openly at Paul, "but I think we'll be at war with the Japs before this is all over."

"Well, I certainly hope not," Paul responded smoothly, maintaining eye contact. "It seems like we Americans have enough to worry about in Hitler and Mussolini without adding the Pacific to the list. I hope they can talk things through."

"Yeah, maybe so, but by God we'll be ready for 'em if they do decide to make a war of it."

"Now Dick," his wife said, "all this talk of war will make our friends lose their appetite. You hush now and help me with this list!"

The two shop owners collected items from their shelves including two newspapers and a magazine Paul had requested. Dick tallied up the total of nine dollar and forty three cents. Akagi insisted on paying and the goods were carried out to the pickup and placed in the bed.

Dick and Abigail stood just outside the shop door watching the pickup retreat.

"You mark my words, Abby, we'll be shootin' at them sons a bitches pretty soon, and that whole damn Jap loving family can go straight to hell."

"Oh Dick, if you keep talking like that people will start going somewhere else for their goods. People don't like war talk, it upsets their digestion."

He stared as the dot disappeared around a bend and said no more.

Joshua Pearson Residence
Whidbey Island
10:00 a. m. July 4, 1941

"Pulleeezz, Father," Ritchey was pleading. "Let me take the sailboat. I'll be okay!"

"Son, there isn't a breath of wind outside. It would take six days to get to Mutiny Bay in a sailboat."

"But Father, you know the wind picks up out by the point. It would be fine once I got out there. Pulleeezz let me go."

"Well," Joshua hesitated, "let's go take a look." He grabbed his binoculars from the shelf and the two headed out the back door and down the path toward the dock.

Paul heard the door slam and looked up from his garden. He had been hoping he might find a ripe tomato or two to take along but it was just too soon for them, though there were plenty of green beans and spring onions. The lettuce was pretty good too. *Well, I guess we'll eat lots of salad,* he thought. Ritchey dashed past down the trail with his father following along behind taking his field glasses out of the worn leather case.

"Hey, Paul," Pearson called, "want to come along and see if we can convince the boy there isn't enough wind to sail today?'

"Sure, why not?" Akagi stood and dusted off the knees of his Levis and fell into step behind Joshua. "But what if I told you I was looking forward to sailing over with him?"

"I'd say it sounds like a conspiracy to gang up on old dad," he replied with a smile. "Then I'd say I feel a lot better about it if you go with him. He's a terrific sailor, but he's still just a child; hasn't developed adult judgment yet."

"I'm sure grateful for that," Paul replied.

"How's that?"

"Most adults would have left me out on the rocks and I would most likely be dead now."

"I'd like to think most adults would have done just what Ritchey did."

"Not now, not a Japanese. You've been reading the paper just like I have. You've heard the radio reports. You saw how that shopkeeper stared at me." Paul paused for effect. "I'd be dead."

Joshua had stopped on a little knob of land that gave a commanding view of the bay and Puget Sound beyond. He put the glasses to his eyes and swept them over the waterline. Sure enough, just past the mouth of the bay the wind was creating little waves. Not enough for whitecaps, but plenty for sailing.

"I think you're wrong, Paul. There are always guys like Dick around spouting off about something. Don't take it too seriously." Joshua replied, handing Paul the glasses; "looks like there's enough wind for the sail, if you don't mind rowing about halfway out."

"Good for my shoulder," Akagi said. "I hope you're right," he said, returning to the subject. "But I think he's probably right about one thing. Do you take anything in the boat for the party?"

"Not anymore. We just pick up the crab pots and shrimp traps and bring whatever might be in them. Ritchey can show you where we have them buoyed. Right about what?"

"About war," Akagi replied. "I think there will be war." *In fact, I'm certain of it,* he thought.

"See, I told you there was enough wind!" Ritchey was running back up the path skidding to a stop in the sand. "Pulleeezz, Father."

"Alright," Joshua relented, but only if you take Paul. "He can help with the pots and row you ashore when you get becalmed."

"Thanks, Dad!" Ritchey raced back down to the boat for preparations.

Joshua looked after his son as he ran down the path. He was silent and still as a tear slid down his cheek. Paul put the glasses back in their case after having surveyed the area for himself and noticed the sudden change of mood.

"What's up? He asked gently.

"First time he's ever called me Dad," Joshua said as he wiped away the tear. "until now I've always been father."

"Come on, Josh," Akagi said quietly. "I'll help you finish loading the truck."

What had once been a simple family picnic had turned into quite a production for this year. Sheets of plywood and a few sawhorses to create makeshift tables were loaded on the truck along with quarter cord of split alder and maple for firewood, food, plates, utensils and old newspapers to use as tablecloths. Paul stacked a couple of chairs on top and began tying things down. Joshua brought out some blankets and towels and put them in the passenger seat of the old pickup.

"Paul," Joshua called, "there is a big canvas tarp in the barn in the tack room, and some poles about eight feet long we need to take. Can I get your help?"

Akagi looked at the crystal clear blue sky. "Are you sure we're going to need a tent?"

"Not at all sure," he replied. "But if I don't take it I can guarantee I'll have needed it. You California boys just don't understand the weather up here. Too much sunshine addles the brain."

"Hmmph," Akagi grunted. "It was only two weeks ago that I had moss growing on my north side."

Pearson laughed. "Better than the black and green slime everybody else is covered with nine months of the year."

The two men were carrying the last of the tent poles trying to fit them into the puzzle they had created on the back of the truck. Ritchey arrived breathless, as usual.

"C'mon Paul," he said. "We need to get going so we can pick up the traps!"

"Okay, Ritchey, I'll be along in minute."

"Go ahead, Paul," Josh said, "I can finish the rest. I'd rather have you at the other end to help unload all this stuff."

"Sayonara, then until this afternoon," Akagi said.

"C'mon, Paul," Ritchey was tugging at his shirt, "let's go. See you later Dad." They headed down the path toward the little boat as Joshua watched. By the time they reached the dock, Joshua was headed back into the house to see if there was anything else he could find to cram onto the already overloaded truck.

Somehow Ritchey had miraculously managed to turn the few whispers of air circulating in the bay into a full sail and the sailboat with its two-man crew aboard was slowly heading for the first buoy, marking a crab pot. On the deck between the seats was a wooden box with a little seaweed in it and as Paul snared the first pot and hauled it aboard, the junior sailor shifted the tiller and headed for the second mark. Paul opened the trap and removed five crabs, tossing them into the box.

"Throw the little one back," Ritchey said. "It's a female. We let 'em get big enough to lay eggs."

Dutifully the small crab was returned to the waters of the bay and the process was repeated five more times, ending with a total of thirty two crabs. Paul had to put a rope around the lid of the box to keep them from crawling all over the boat.

"Okay, now we check the shrimp traps." Ritchey set the sail and turned the tiller heading for the narrow area between Double Bluff Point and the shipping canal.

How should I start this conversation? Akagi wondered. *Or should I bring it up at all?* Akagi hadn't really had a chance to be alone with the boy long enough to talk about the secret they shared. He wasn't even sure how much he might have told his father though he suspected he wouldn't be here alone if it had been much.

"I've been wondering," he started tentatively.

"About how much I told my father," Ritchey finished. "Don't look so surprised, Paul. I told you I could keep a secret."

"Where did you hide my uniform?"

"Someplace no one will ever find it, the gun too. But you aren't in the reserves. A friend of mine's father is in the reserves and his uniform is completely different. You're a spy from Japan, aren't you?"

Oh great! Now what? Akagi's mind raced searching for alternatives. *Do I kill him and claim he fell overboard? Perfect, Paul. He's a great sailor, its glassy smooth on the water and the only witness is a Japanese guy who washed ashore a few months ago.*

"Doesn't matter," Ritchey continued, "there's nothing much you could do now anyway. We don't have a phone and there isn't anything to see around here. Is being a spy exciting?"

I forget this is a kid. Paul breathed a sigh of relief inwardly. *He doesn't have any real notion of what being a spy is. I can handle this.*

"Well, even if I was a spy three months ago, I'm sure not one now, am I?"

"I don't know," the junior Pearson said simply. "You could just be hiding out at my house till you get better."

"I've been well enough to leave for more than month," Akagi countered.

"You could be spying on my father."

"Your dad is a custodian. How many government secrets do you think they have at Briarwood School?"

"Well," Ritchey hesitated, "probably none. I guess you're right. If you are a spy, you're not a very good one."

That much is true enough! Akagi pondered pursuing this line or letting it die.

"Our secret dies here?" Paul asked with all solemnity, hand on his heart.

"To the grave and beyond," the young voice returned. Ritchey was almost as good as his word for the next fifty years.

North Shore of Mutiny Bay
Whidbey Island
Early afternoon, July 4, 1941

It was shaping up to be a raucous gathering of three generations of dear old friends along the beach. It was part living history, part family reunion and part anyone else who wandered by.

Ritchey and Paul had put ashore with crab and shrimp a couple of hours earlier, and then helped Joshua unload the truck and begin setting up. Paul dug a fire pit and stacked firewood. Joshua tied a big driftwood log to the bumper of the truck and managed to drag it a few feet as a makeshift bench while Ritchey began spreading part of the tarpaulin on the ground to make a place for the chairs for the elders to use.

More people began filtering in about two o'clock. Frank and Eleanor Sakai arrived in a brand new Ford pickup truck. It was modern and sleek sporting a two-toned emerald green hood cab and bed over black fenders and running boards completed with varnished wooden side racks. Painted on the doors in an arc over artistic renderings of fruits and vegetables were the words "Island Farms". Below was "Bainbridge Is., Wash." Their three children piled out of the back, dusting themselves off.

"Uncle Frank!" Ritchey called, dashing off to meet the new arrivals. He ran straight into outstretched arms and was rewarded with a hug. In turn he took a hug from his Aunt Eleanor; shook hands with Steven and Mary then grabbed Benjamin and raced off down the beach.

"We won't see them again until dinner time, Frank." Joshua had made his way over to the group. "Gosh, it's good to see you. It's been too long." The two men shook hands warmly. "Eleanor, I swear you get prettier every time I see you!"

"Thank you, Josh," she replied with a smile. "But I think that just shows you live among too many men too much of the time."

"Alas, too true. Steven, you're looking fit these days."

"Thanks Uncle Josh. I think I lift too many cases of cabbages. Anything I can help with?"

"For starters," his father interjected, "you can unload the truck."

"Blindfold me first!" Steven said.

"Why?" Josh asked.

"Because I've done this so often I can do it with my eyes shut."

Joshua laughed easily. "Before you get started on that, I would like you all to meet a friend of mine. He's up from California looking for a fresh start. This is Paul Akagi. Paul, this is Frank, Eleanor, Steven and Mary. I didn't forget you Mary; I've missed seeing you too." He paused pointing in the distance, "that little dot down the beach with the red shirt on is Benjamin. You may see him later for ten or twelve seconds."

Paul shook hands with each new person making a careful mental note of each name. When he got to Mary he looked deeply into her eyes for a moment. It was very forward for a young Japanese man, and she shyly demurred. Mary was the reincarnation of her Grandmother Moriko at the same age. She was pretty now and would be a radiant beauty soon.

"I'm very pleased to make your acquaintance," he said as he bowed from the waist.

"Likewise I'm sure, Mr. Akagi," Mary replied returning the bow and blushing slightly at the attention.

"Please, call me Paul. Everyone please call me Paul."

Steven broke up the logjam by handing a lug of tomatoes to Paul and grabbing a couple of sacks of other vegetables and heading toward the fire pit.

"Well, come on Paul, these vegetables won't walk to the pot by themselves, let's get going."

"Tomatoes!" Akagi exclaimed. "How did you get tomatoes so early in the season? Mine are all still hard green baseballs."

The two young men wandered down the beach with Steven explaining the virtues of hothouses on getting early season produce.

"Come along, Mary," Eleanor said, "we have work to do as well."

The ladies reached into the back of the truck and retrieved their packages and headed down the beach as Josh and Frank circled the truck admiring the sleek new vehicle.

"She's a beauty, Frank. Vegetables must be pretty good money these days."

"Strawberries, Josh. We make more selling strawberries in two months than we make on vegetables the rest of the year. The co-op devised a way to freeze what we can't sell fresh. People are buying our berries all year long now."

"That's great! I'm so pleased for you and your family. Speaking of which, where are your Mom and Dad and what about Stan and Sarah?"

"Stan borrowed a boat from a friend of his and has been cruising around the Sound picking everybody up. Said he didn't want to spend three hours driving and two ferry rides to do this. So instead he's spending five hours cruising around picking up Mom and Pop and little Ambrose and Maryanne. Your Dad came over last night so he could ride along and save a side trip to Seattle."

No sooner had he said the words then a long whistle sounded and a small fishing boat hove into view, well around the point and headed for the beach. The distinctive sound of the diesel engine could be heard in the distance. Chuff, pause, chuff, pause, chuff...

"One lunger," Josh said referring to its single cylinder. "Probably wouldn't make ten knots with a thirty knot following wind."

"Just as well," Frank observed. "I doubt if my father, or yours, would appreciate those kidney pounders the rich kids are racing around Lake Union these days."

"No, probably not. Well, let's finish setting things up. Looks like they'll be about twenty minutes getting ashore." The two old friends loaded themselves with more gear and headed down the beach, passing Steven and Paul making another trip.

"Steven," Frank called, "I think the rice pot and the baseball gear is all that's left. We can leave the rest there and get it later if we need it."

"Okay, Pop, will do."

Stan beached the fishing vessel gently on the sand. The two patriarchs took off their shoes and rolled up their pants and with some assistance got off the boat and marched through the shallow water to dry ground. Steven easily carried his grandmother Moriko to shore while the children swarmed over the sides and charged up the beach. Sarah Davis *nee'* Sakai waded in with their contribution to the food table, two flats of raspberries. Stan was the last off trailing a long bow line behind him which he tied off on a huge drift log deeply embedded in the sand.

"It would be real depressing to see our ride float away with the tide," he said by way of explanation to Joshua.

"Especially when it isn't your boat," Josh laughed.

"Yes, there is that minor detail. Hey, when is it time to eat?"

"Stan thinks more about his stomach than any three men I know," Joshua said to Paul. "After the ball game, you know that."

When the trio got back to the main picnic area, now fully assembled on the beach, the women were doing a credible job of turning a mountain of jumbled stuff into an organized outdoor kitchen. Sarah was laying in the fire, Eleanor and Grandmother Moriko were peeling carrots and potatoes and Leta was sorting utensils; the perfect job for a thirteen year old. All were jabbering away in the pleasant gossip and conversation of familiar company enjoying a social occasion.

Frank and Mary were returning from the pickup with odd shovels and rakes over their shoulders.

"Hey, you guys," he called. "Let's go dig some clams!"

With the tide retreating, the men took up implements and headed for the beach. Mary came along too since there was little left to do at the campsite and she was interested in the newcomer.

The harvesters spread out along the beach at the retreating tide line some of them digging furiously when small bubbles appeared in the sand while others raked likely areas. Thomas and the Reverend

Pearson carried canvas buckets to and fro collecting the bounty of each successful effort.

As with the women, conversations ranged widely from the ongoing economic depression to Frank's new pickup to the harvest this year and inevitably to the war in Europe and politics in the Pacific.

"I fear the country of my ancestors and the country of my heart are coming to blows soon," Thomas said as he snatched up some butter clams raked from the muck.

"I'm not so sure, Thoma-san," Josh replied. "There is certainly tension, but there are negotiations and the radio says that both sides are hopeful."

"You speak the language of my homeland, Joshua," Thomas observed, "but you do not understand the customs very well."

"I'm afraid Thomas is right, son," Ambrose cut it. "America negotiates from misunderstanding. Rarely is anything in Japanese business or politics what it seems."

Frank brought a shovel full of Littlenecks and tossed them in a bucket.

"I sure hope there isn't a war," he said. "It's bad for business. People get jittery, do odd things. Act funny. What do you think, Paul?"

"Me?" Paul was caught off guard, not expecting or wanting to contribute to this particular aspect of the conversation given his current clandestine situation. "Well, to tell the truth, I'm not very political. I don't think about it very much. Especially recently, I've just been trying to get well enough to look for some work."

"Lucky man," Frank replied.

"Lucky?"

"Sure, war and money are just about anything anyone can talk about these days. It's a lucky man that can go through life without a worry."

"I didn't say I don't have any worries, I just said I don't think about it much."

Joshua looked at Paul curiously. Only a few hours ago he had spoken of how certain he was that there would be war, and how concerned he was that Japanese would be objects of fear and prejudice. He devours magazines and newspapers. *Now he doesn't think about it much? What gives?*

Steven came back from the tide line with more clams tossing them in with the rest. Both buckets were overflowing with a bounty of bivalves.

"Let's play some baseball! I'll carry the buckets back to the fire and get the equipment." Steven was directing traffic now, "Pop, see if you can get the teams figured out and a diamond laid out."

"Yessir," Frank saluted dutifully. "Mary, try to round up the younger children. We'll be on the flat part of the beach on the other side of the log Stan tied up to."

"I'll help her," Paul suggested.

"No, she won't need any help," Frank replied. "You come with me and help me measure out a diamond."

"Whatever you say, Frank." Paul had hoped to be alone for a few minutes with Mary. She was so pretty and he hadn't spoken to a girl anywhere near his age in many months.

Assignments given, the group split up and headed for their appointed tasks. After about twenty minutes, most of the families had been gathered, along with another family enjoying the beach. Teams were chosen and bases designated. The purple dead sea star was first base. A lid from a small barrel was second, the driftwood stick was third (runners must go around the outside of the stick but don't have to touch it) and home plate was an empty berry container buried in the sand. A home run was anything past the tide flow creek about one hundred fifty feet away from home.

Thomas and the older women served as the cheering fans. Ambrose assumed his customary position as umpire. Mary, in addition to her duties as a child wrangler, served as permanent catcher for both sides. She couldn't hit but she had a great arm and could catch pretty well too.

The game was hilarious. Tiny children swinging wildly as the ball sailed softly in their direction. Occasionally accidental contact would be made and the ball would plop a foot in front of the plate. People screamed in two or three languages and pointed toward first, encouraging the tyke to race toward the bag. Mary would pick up the ball and chase after them, always failing to catch up, eliciting the wild cheers of everyone watching.

Steven, a heavy hitter, would hammer the ball deep past the creek and scoop up slower children as he rounded the bases carrying them along as he headed for home.

Paul hadn't played baseball since he was seven, but he managed to make contact a couple of times and being fleet of foot he beat the throw to the sea star. By the time the old black pot was steaming and ready to be uncovered, almost everyone was covered with sand and grinning ear to ear. The scorekeeper had lost track somewhere past twenty runs and no one cared, except Steven.

"What's the point in playing if we don't know who won?" He groused.

"What's the matter son," Frank laughed. "Mad you didn't make the Courier League?"

"I could've played for the Western Giants, Pop. You know that."

"Unfortunately we don't have our own private ferry to get you back and forth to practice all summer," his father replied.

"Who, or what, are the Western Giants?" Paul asked.

"They are the elite Japanese-American team in the Courier Baseball League," Joshua answered. "They play mostly in the northwest. Some of those boys could probably play pro ball."

"They're playing today, probably right now," Steven said. "Tsuji probably hung another curve ball over the plate."

"I'm sorry you didn't get to go, son," Frank said.

"Oh it's okay, Pop, you can't play baseball for a living anyway. There isn't any money in it. Still, there should have been a winner."

"There is Steven," the Reverend Pearson responded. "Everyone who played, everyone who watched and everyone who laughed was a winner."

"My grandson is impatient to make his mark in the world," Thomas observed. "Everything must happen so fast. It makes me dizzy."

"It's a big world, Grandpa. I want to see it all and do big things!"

"What would you like to do?" Paul asked.

"Be an architect. Build tall buildings, bridges maybe, that sort of thing. It's my major at U-Dub."

"Very ambitious, Steven, I wish you luck." Paul said.

"America is a place where big dreams happen if you work hard," Steven said simply.

The cover was removed from the old iron pot with the breeze carrying away the steam. Gingerly the seaweed was removed and the crab, shrimp, clams, potatoes, carrots, green beans and corn were piled high on the newspaper covered plywood tables. The bounty of salads and fruit had already been prepared and after the blessing, the gregarious group fell to devouring the feast. Sake and beer appeared, liberally consumed by the adults, while lemonade, Coca Cola and iced tea were available for anyone not inclined to imbibe.

Afternoon drifted into evening. The sounds of snoring could be heard as elders took naps. Children playing in the distance lent a charming shrillness to the ambient sounds of the breeze in the trees, birds chirping and waves lapping the sandy beach. Quiet conversations murmured around the fire with occasional laughter punctuating the moment.

As the tide began returning, Stan roused and began to gather his passengers for the return voyage in the twilight. Ambrose chose to remain behind. He would spend the night with Joshua. Eleanor and the Sakai children would go home on the boat.

Steven carried Grandmother Moriko, Stan carried his wife and Paul carried Mary out to the boat and helped them onboard. After the children were placed aboard, Steven carried his mother out and got aboard. Frank had offered to take Ambrose home and Steven had no desire to repeat six hours in the bed of the pickup. There would be less to load since most of the food was consumed and the firewood burned. Ritchey and Joshua promised to help.

All the goodbyes and best wishes were exchanged and by the time the tide had lifted the vessel free of the sand, Stan had the engine running. Chuff, pause, chuff, pause; he backed off, executed a turn and charted a course for the setting sun.

The men loaded the trucks, secured the sailboat and headed back to Joshua's home to spend the night. They talked awhile and then fell into a deep and satisfying sleep.

At the twilight edge of sleep Paul marveled at the glorious day just passed. *This is an amazing group of friends, and an amazing country too. Freedom is an intoxicating thing in a country like America.* Akagi fell asleep and dreamed of Mary.

Special Code Room
Room 407, Unspecified Building
San Francisco
July 29, 1941

Months of diligent work by obscure but brilliant State Department mathematicians and puzzle solvers had yielded impressive results. The code used by the Japanese for encrypted communications between Tokyo and its embassies had been thoroughly unraveled by the Americans and so far as anyone could tell, the compromise was undetected. Much of the work now done in the office was routine decoding and translation, probably the same work repeated in the Japanese embassies. It amused some to imagine that the U.S. decoding effort was probably faster than the foreign counterpart.

Cable traffic had increased dramatically in June after Hitler had launched Operation Barbarossa breaking the non-agression pact with Russia. Japan, no longer fearing intervention by the Russian Bear, moved to consolidate and expand holdings in French Indochina forcing a 'mutual defense' agreement on a puppet government in Vichy.

The U.S responded swiftly with an embargo of munitions, oil, and raw materials. Events were beginning to take on an air of inevitability and Japan was feeling the pinch. U.S. contributions of men and war materiel to neighboring countries hostile to the Tokyo war machine further inflamed the army. All this put Imperial Navy Admiral Nomura (Ret.) in an impossible position. He had only been in Washington as the new ambassador for a few months and reports from his office were pessimistic. And now, only four days ago, Roosevelt had frozen all Japanese national assets in the United States, effectively severing all commercial contact and causing a run on Japanese-owned banks. Panic was beginning to set in and it showed in the cable traffic.

Faced with four negotiating conditions from the White House that the Imperial Palace would never accept, Nomura nonetheless kept trying to find a peaceful way to break the impasse. He never said so, but he believed his effort was futile.

Today's consular traffic was more of the same. Discouraging reports flowing to Tokyo from Nomura; return instructions from the Palace demanded he keep trying. Messages from the home islands were increasingly strident and belligerent and more than a few of the code breakers believed something big was in the wind, but they couldn't quite put their finger on it yet.

Island Farms

Bainbridge Island
July 29, 1941

Strawberry season was waning and raspberries were nearing an end as well so most of the field workers, including Paul and Mary, were harvesting second planting lettuce now for the weekend at the Pike Place Market. Moving rhythmically down the rows, workers would slice the head at ground level and toss it into a hopper towed behind a tractor, or pack it in a box strategically placed along the way.

Stripped to the waist, glistening with sweat, Paul stood, pulling a blue kerchief from his hip pocket and wiped his brow. He walked over to the tractor and took a dipper full of water from the small barrel attached to the side. He poured some over his head then drank down the rest.

"Lunch break, everybody!" Frank called out. As the word worked down the rows, labor stopped and the field hands walked to the row ends headed for the lunch table. Eleanor had set up the table with thick slabs of ham and homemade bread, mayonnaise and mustard for condiments, potato salad and pickles, and even some carrots from the next field over. Fresh lemonade would wash it down. She was rinsing a couple of heads of just-picked lettuce as the troops arrived.

Some washed their hands vigorously in the tub of water on the back of the pickup; others didn't bother so they could be early in line. In turn each worker would pick up a tin pie plate and make their way through the bounty, grateful for the food and the work, both of which were still in short supply throughout much of the country.

Paul had pulled on his shirt and was rinsing his hands when Mary approached and began washing her hands. They had talked briefly on several occasions since Paul had come back to the farm from the July Fourth picnic. Each was aware of an attraction between them but neither had spoken of it yet.

"Beautiful day, isn't it?" Paul thought it best to keep things light for now. He had been careful to make eye contact regularly, but not to stare openly at this beauty.

"Yes, it is lovely," she agreed. Mary looked up the fluffy clouds drifting silently through cerulean skies, "must be about seventy."

"Yeah, that's probably pretty close. Much warmer and this might be considered real work."

Mary laughed. "Some think this is real work anyway, don't you?"

"How could I? I've got a warm place to sleep, enough to eat and a pretty girl to talk to. How can that be work?"

Mary blushed deeply as she picked up her tin plate and moved down the line. *Too soon! Idiot, you'll scare her away!* Paul chided himself. "See what I mean," he said indicating Eleanor, "pretty girls everywhere, and bearing food too!" Eleanor looked over on hearing the comment and smiled.

"That won't get you any more food, but thank you anyway," she said.

He's a little flustered, Mary thought. She gave him her most innocent look and said with a bare hint of sarcasm, "I see, I am so flattered."

Maybe this is the moment, he thought. He screwed up his courage as he piled potato salad on his plate, then he caught Mary's eye and held it for some moments.

"You should be," he said earnestly. "You're the prettiest girl I've ever met and the smartest too."

Mary dropped a carrot as a diversion to hide another blush. *Now I'm a little flustered! What do I do next?* She stood and walked over to the lemonade pitcher to buy a little time. Paul followed, after building a mountainous sandwich.

"Thank you for what you said," she finally replied.

"Every word of it was true, Mary. You *are* the prettiest and smartest girl I've ever met."

"You're very nice too, Paul." Mary was very unnerved now and afraid to look at his face.

"I should eat lunch now." She moved away from him and sat in the truck. Paul hesitated for a moment, debating mentally if he should follow her. After a moment he slowly made his way down the crop row, sat down leaning against the wheel of the tractor and began eating his lunch.

Mary watched him in the side mirror as he walked away. Her heart was pounding and her breath was short. She only picked at her lunch.

Special Code Room
Unspecified Building
San Francisco
August 13, 1941

By now Oscar had decoded so many Japanese diplomatic cables that he almost didn't need the source code. He, like most of his clandestine companions, had noticed the increasingly rigid hubris coming from Tokyo and the almost desperate exasperation returning from the embassy in Washington.

Dutifully he worked the cipher and sent the translation forward in the system to destinations unknown. Initially he believed his work must have an ear somewhere higher up, but he had been unable to detect any sense of urgency in the public rhetoric or any movement of personnel that suggested a response. *Well, maybe the plans upstairs are as secret as we are,* he thought. *I hope to God somebody is paying attention.*

After work he walked down the stairs and out the front door of the building. He turned and walked three blocks, opposite the direction from which he had arrived that morning, and hopped on the northbound Powell-Mason cable car. He stepped off as it rounded a corner on Mason Street, just before heading up the steepest part of Nob Hill and waited a moment to see if anyone else stepped off this cable car or the next. When he was satisfied, he zigzagged a few blocks down to Grant Street, the central street of the largest Chinatown anywhere in the world not actually in China. He went in the front door of Wing Lee's Chinese Café. *Gawd, I feel like I'm in a*

Charlie Chan movie, he thought. Without consulting the menu he ordered a platter of Peking duck and a whole fish Szechuan style. The waiter was surprised when Oscar spoke in fluent Cantonese without even a glance up. By the time his supper arrived he had worked last week's *New York Times* crossword and started on math brain teasers he found mildly amusing. Occasionally as he ate he would survey his surroundings, making a mental note of the other patrons.

When he finished, he left through the kitchen out the back door, down the alley past the garbage pails and rickety stairs leading to warrens of opium dens and brothels. He emerged one street over and hailed a taxi which took him to the Sunset District beyond the Western Addition. Leaving the cab he walked four more blocks to a stairwell leading to a nondescript apartment above a Greek market and let himself in. In six months of code work he had never followed the same path to and from the office and had never kept the same hours.

Having paid for his small purchase, an olive-skinned young Italian man stepped from the market out onto the sidewalk stopping to light a cigarette. He casually tilted his head back to blow out the first deep puff of smoke and glanced at the window in the apartment above. He noted the lights were on and the shades were being drawn. He pulled his fedora down low on his forehead and walked around the corner to a waiting sedan.

"He's in for the night," he said to the driver.

"Okay, Tony, you stay for a while longer until Vito gets here. I'll send the message along."

"Hey, you tell Vito to bring along some pasta if you gonna leave me here all night."

"Always thinking about your stomach," the driver groused. "Get something from the store."

"Waddya think, I'm made of money? Besides, I hang around the store too much, mebbe they get suspicious. They wonder what this wop is doin' out in the avenues."

"Bambinos, they send me babies!" the wheel-man huffed. "Okay, pasta it is." He mashed the starter switch on the floorboard with his left foot. After the engine caught he depressed the clutch then engaged the gears and drove off, turning away from the apartment windows.

Watching from the back stairwell Oscar smiled as he saw a black Chevrolet fall in behind the Packard disappearing into the mist that rolled in from the Pacific Ocean. *These guys are too easy. How hard is it to follow a six foot Anglo through Chinatown? Well, I suppose I made it look hard enough to do for our purposes.* At least half the fun of this job was leading enemy agents around by their noses so the field operatives could pick them out and start following them. *Spy versus spy,* he thought. *If it weren't so scary it would be downright comical.* He went back into the apartment, read the paper and went to bed. He figured the poor Italian kid would be eating a cannoli and standing in the fog all night long. He was right.

Island Farms

Bainbridge Island
August 17, 1941

The single bulb hanging from the ceiling cast a harsh yellow light in the tack room of the barn. The only other source of light was from the window in the barn; an encrusted old sash window with a cracked pane, recycled from an old timber line shack abandoned on the island. Since the mules had been retired in favor of a tractor, the old barn had fallen into limited use. Now it was used mainly for storage of seed stock and equipment not likely to ever again be used. A layer of dust had accumulated on the worn leather riggings dry and cracked with age. Paul hauled things out, the air becoming thick with fine talc-like particles. Still, this would be better than the bunkhouse. There is no smell quite like that of a bunkhouse; redolent with stale sweat, weeks old unwashed socks and feet, cigarettes, kerosene lamps, beer and flatulent bunkmates. It made him almost long for the air of a submarine.

In just over a month Paul had diligently applied his accumulated early life experience to creating confidence within the Sakai family. Hard work, intelligence and natural leadership ability had paid off. Frank, with the approval of his father, had promoted him to labor foreman and that rated him a private space and a little more money. It was a good backwater cover until he could figure out what do with himself.

When the last of the equipment had been moved out, he surveyed the room. At about fifteen feet square it was plenty large enough, but come winter it would be hard to heat. He pulled his kerchief over his nose and began sweeping, first the ceiling, then the walls and finally the floor. Then he filled a bucket with water and came back with a scrub brush to repeat the process. Finally he came in with a fresh bucket of water and rinsed all the surfaces. Finished, he stood admiring his work in the center of the room. He heard a giggle and turned to see Mary standing in the doorway with a big grin on her face.

"There's a bank robber that needs a bath," she laughed.

Paul pulled down the kerchief revealing a two tone head. Dust brown and spattered in mud above the nose, Asian ochre below. He had to smile at himself.

"Don't you worry, Miss," he mimicked from western movies he had seen, "I'm not the varmint I seem to be."

"I came to see how the job was coming along, looks pretty sad to me."

"Not at all," Paul replied. "With a bunk, a box and a chair it'll be home."

"Needs a women's touch," Mary insisted. "And it wouldn't hurt to patch the holes in the walls either."

"No, I suppose not, but not too sissified. I wouldn't want to lose face with the other members of the gang."

"Still, you need a clean spot for a lady caller to sit."

"Am I likely to have a lady caller anytime soon?" He inquired staring at Mary.

"I'm sure I don't know Mr. Akagi," she said coquettishly, "I don't manage your social calendar."

"Mary," Paul asked impulsively, "would you like to go to a movie with me?" He waited in stillness. It was the first time he had asked for anything like a real date with her and he wasn't sure how she would react.

"I think I would like that very much," she answered softly. "I'm going to U-Dub tomorrow to pick up my schedule for classes for the fall. If you came along maybe we could go to a matinee."

"Congratulations, I hadn't heard; a college girl, and the University of Washington no less."

"Steven just finished his junior year this spring. He says it's a great school. He wants…"

"To be an architect," Paul finished. "He mentioned that at the picnic last month." They stood in an awkward silence for a moment. "So I suppose I can find a need to go to Seattle tomorrow that your father will approve."

"I suppose so." Her voice trailed off as she paused. "Anyway, I came out to tell you supper is ready, but you better wash up and put on some clean clothes first."

Frank Sakai was leaning against the door frame with his arms crossed next to his father who was sitting in his favorite chair on the porch. When Mary came out of the old barn headed for the house, Paul was right behind her covered in dirt and heading for the bunkhouse.

"I think my granddaughter has stars in her eyes," Thomas said to his son.

"We know nothing about this man's family, father."

"I knew your mother only from one photograph and some letters. At least we can take the measure of this person for ourselves. It is a different place and time."

"Maybe you're right. Mary is almost a woman now but it seems like she was a child only yesterday," Frank sighed.

"I trusted you, as you must trust her. If it is right she will know."

Mary reached the steps and bounded up to the porch headed for the door.

"Mary," Frank said, looking at his father, "something has come up. I'm not going to be able to take you in to Seattle tomorrow. I was thinking I would have Paul drive you instead. I have a few things he can pick up before you head back, sorry."

"Gee, Dad, I was looking forward to spending some time with you." Mary was trying very hard to sound disappointed but her insides were somersaulting with joy.

"We'll have another time. But keep track of Paul. I don't think he knows Seattle very well yet. I wouldn't want you two to get lost."

"Okay, Dad. I might give him a little tour. You know, so he can get his bearings; couple of hours maybe."

"Just don't miss the last ferry," he cautioned.

"Daddy, the last ferry is ten o'clock! We'll be home in time for supper." She kissed her father and bounced into the house.

The old man smiled and grasped his son's hand.

"Help me up, I hear it's time for supper," he said. "Tonight's menu is grilled boyfriend. One of your favorites I think." He winked and headed into the house.

"Thank you, father," Frank said. Paul was coming up the path. Another promotion perk was dinner with the family and tonight would be a meal he would remember a long time.

Port of Seattle
August 18, 1941

The *Kobiashi Maru* swung lazily at anchor in Elliott Bay waiting for her turn to load barley and Cascade hops bound for a brewery in Tokyo. Also on the manifest were a few machine tools, several crates with Philco radios, and seventy tons of brass and aluminum ingots supposedly destined for a forge that cast artwork. Since receiving instructions from Yamamoto to abandon the rendezvous with the overdue submarines, she had simply returned to her regular maritime shipping routine. This was the last cargo being allowed out of this port bound for Japan.

Paul and Mary stood near the railing of the ferry watching the water slide under the flat bottomed bow and occasionally looking at the ship traffic. Paul noticed one ship in particular that seemed familiar and was suddenly electrified to read *Kobiashi Maru* on the stern. *That's my ticket back to Japan!* He thought.

"I wonder where they all go?" Mary said.

Startled by her voice he said, "I'm sorry, Mary, what did you say?"

"Hmmph! Not even officially on our first date yet and already you're not paying attention. Not a good sign."

"Really, I'm sorry," he regrouped and focused on her. At least she was smiling. "I guess I was just daydreaming. What was it you said?"

"I said, I wonder where they all go."

"Wherever there is a port, I suppose. Should we guess?"

"Whatever for?"

"Just a game to waste some time. For example, that black cargo ship over there," he pointed at the *Maru*, "where do you suppose she's going."

Mary squinted a little to make out the name. "Well, Japan, obviously."

"Not every ship goes where her name might suggest," Paul observed. "She could just as easily be headed to San Francisco to pick up shovels."

"I think she's on a spy mission," Mary whispered conspiratorially. This caught Paul off guard but he recovered well. "She's stealing aircraft plans from Boeing and heading for Germany," she concluded.

"Very clandestine of you," Paul said. "I think she is carrying Ford pickups to Hawaii."

The ferry's horn sounded, warning drivers to return to their vehicles. Paul and Mary walked the thirty or so feet to the pickup and climbed in.

"Let's find out what she's really doing after we get off the ferry," Paul suggested, "just for fun. The Harbormaster's office could probably tell us."

"Sure, if it doesn't take too long."

Vehicles streamed off the ferry with the Island Farms truck ducking out as it drew near the Harbormaster's office. Paul found a place to park and jumped out of the truck, hoping Mary wouldn't follow.

"I'll just be a minute," he said as he dashed up the stairs to the office.

This is a very strange date so far, Mary thought.

Seated behind an oak desk near the counter separating the work space from the tiny lobby area, a reed thin man with sharp features and hazel eyes was just unwrapping the wax paper from a sandwich when Paul burst into the room.

"Can you tell me when the *Kobiashi Maru* is scheduled to sail?" He asked without preamble.

The thin man took a deliberate swallow from a Pepsi Cola sitting on his desk and carefully surveyed Paul.

"Ah, yep," he said in precisely clipped tones and then took a bite of his sandwich.

"Will, you tell me?" Paul was a little annoyed. "Please."

The man chewed carefully and swallowed. "Ah, yep." He looked at a chalkboard on the wall. "Scheduled to leave on the twentieth, but might leave early if she loads out sooner." He took another swig of his soft drink and then had another bite of sandwich.

"Has she made a mail drop yet?"

Another swallow then, "Ah, nope, but her skipper checks in before she sails. He drops mail then."

"May I leave a note for you to give to the skipper?"

"Ah, yep."

Paul searched his pockets. He had keys, a pocketknife some cash and a shopping list. No pencil, no paper.

"Would you have a pencil and paper I could use?"

"Cost you a nickel," the thin man said after swallowing.

"Fine, fine, a nickel it is." Paul reached into his pocket for some change.

"Each, a nickel each for paper and an envelope, I'll let you use the pencil for free." The thin man finished his drink and deliberately withdrew one sheet of paper and an envelope from a drawer in the desk. Standing, he brushed crumbs from his sandwich and made his way over to the counter, "ten cents please."

"Here's a quarter—keep the change," Paul said. He glanced out the window at the pickup hoping Mary wasn't getting too restless.

"Ah, nope, can't do that, throws off the books."

Paul took the pencil and the paper and started to write a note as the clerk stood watching. He stopped and thought for a moment then continued writing in kanji. Quickly he folded up the paper and stuffed it in the envelope. On the outside he wrote in English, 'Captain only, Kobiashi Maru.'

"Please make sure the Captain gets this." Paul sealed the envelope and thrust it into the hands of the clerk. The thin man handed him a dime and nickel from a small cash box in a drawer under the worn cedar counter.

"Got to keep the books straight."

"Right, thanks buddy." Paul threw the door open and raced down the stairs and back to the truck.

"Sorry it took so long, they were busy," Paul apologized.

"Not a single person came or went while you were in there," Mary said.

"On the phone; with his boss he said," Paul lied.

"Well, what is it?" Mary asked.

"What is what?"

"What is the cargo and where is it going?"

"Oh, that. You were right. Stolen aircraft plans headed for Germany." He started the engine and drove into traffic. "Kidding; its food headed for Hawaii."

"Speaking of food, let's get a bite of lunch before we head over to the U District," Mary said.

Paul's mind was racing trying to calculate the best way to get off the island and onto the *Kobiashi* before she sailed. It was probably the only hope he had in getting back to the Japanese homeland before the war began. He would need to take the ferry back to Seattle, grab a cab or even walk to the ship. Then he would have to hope the Captain had gotten and understood his message and was willing to take him aboard without putting him on the passenger manifest. Finally he needed the vessel to be going straight back to Japan, not to any other U. S. ports. It was a lot of coincidence to hang his fate on. *And what do I tell the Sakais? I can't just disappear. If I do, they may report me missing. If Mary tells the cops about my jaunt to the Harbormaster then the whole damn Pacific Fleet is looking for the Maru. And how do I feel about Mary? Damn!*

"What did you have in mind for lunch?" Paul asked.

"Meat loaf and mashed potatoes, a cold glass of milk and apple pie a'la mode: There's a diner three blocks away. The owner is Japanese, but it's strictly American food. It's pretty good and cheap too!"

"Oh great, now you think I'm a cheapskate!" Paul mocked.

"Tsk, tsk, now. These are thrifty times," she responded cheerily. "My grandfather says so, and he should know."

"And why is that?" Paul queried.

"My grandfather left Japan with the clothes on his back and what he could carry in the space of about half a lettuce box. He said he spoke not one word of English and was the first poor farmer from his village to learn to read and write."

"Really? That's fascinating!" Paul had heard stories of the first waves of emigres leaving Japan, but he had never known one. It was a story he genuinely wanted to hear. "Has he told you about his early life?"

"Grandfather and Grandmother have both told me stories of the old days. Grandfather went to Hawaii to work in the sugar cane fields. Grandmother came as a picture bride a few years later and two or three years after that they came to the United States. Apparently there was some trouble on the island, but they won't talk about it." Mary lapsed into silence for a moment. "There's the diner, ahead on the left."

Paul eased the pickup into a parking spot in front of a gleaming example of an Art Deco diner. It was resplendent, with flowing streamlined chrome, and glistened in the sunlight like a newly plated Packard bumper. He raced around to the passenger side and opened the door offering his hand to Mary. A bell mounted on the door tinkled loudly as they stepped inside, bouncing sound off all the hard reflective interior surfaces. The proprietor turned from the grill at the sound and spotted Mary. His face broke into a wide grin.

"Meatloaf and mashed potatoes, glass of milk, apple pie a'la mode!" He yelled with a thick accent.

Mary could feel the hot blush coming to her face.

"Don't get down this way much, do you Mary?" Paul jibed.

"No, he just has a good memory," she countered. The blush subsided as quickly as it had appeared.

"Make that two!" Paul called back to the blue collar chef.

"Honorable Harry Hoshimoto-san, let me introduce Paul Akagi," Mary said. "He works for my father. We are running a few errands today."

"*Hai*, very pleased to meet you." He wiped his hands on a towel folded into the waistband of his apron and thrust the right one toward Paul. He winked at Mary and said, "and very handsome too!"

The two men shook hands. Paul was surprised by the strength of the older man's grip.

Since it was after the lunch rush, and Mary and Paul were the only diners at the moment, they chatted amiably with Mr. Hoshimoto as he fixed their plates and placed the steaming food in front of them. When he had washed down the remaining crumbs of the apple pie with the last sip of milk, Paul put two silver dollars on the counter.

"It was a real pleasure to meet you Mr. Hoshimoto. I hope I get a chance to visit with you again," Paul said.

"You stick with Mary, I see you plenty!" He replied. "And call me Hank, easy to say for me."

"Okay, Hank-san, *arigato* and *sayonara*."

Back in the pickup Mary began giving directions. She had Paul driving all over Seattle, periodically stopping along the route to allow Paul to run in to buy something on the list he had from Frank. She explained as they drove what each of the neighborhoods was like, which ones were okay for Japanese and which ones they shouldn't linger in too long. Capitol Hill, then back downtown, over Queen Anne Hill and then west to the Magnolia District. Over the Ship Canal Bridge into Ballard, wander around through Green Lake then finally into the University District.

When Mary had concluded her tasks at the University of Washington, she and Paul headed for the Neptune Theater. A director named Hitchcock had a new spy thriller out called *Suspicious* starring Cary Grant and Joan Fontaine. Paul found the topic ironic given his situation. Finally the weary young couple climbed into the cab of the pickup and headed back for the ferry. They got back before the last ferry left for Bainbridge Island, but by the time they arrived home at the farm, dinner was long since put away and almost everyone was fast asleep.

"I had a wonderful day, Paul. Thank you for inviting me." Mary was standing next to the truck. She looked up into his deep brown almond eyes and he into hers. In the evening stillness they could hear a night bird making an occasional mournful cry and the odd *tink-tink-tink* sound of the cooling exhaust manifold on the pickup engine. In the distance, the ever present background sounds of ships and ferries criss-crossing the Sound, added a counterpoint.

"I had a great day too, really great." The words hung in the air for an eternity. Finally Paul gently cupped her cheek with the palm of his hand. Mary tilted her head into his hand and closed her eyes. For now they just stood together in the moment then he leaned down and caressed her lips with his.

She could feel the warm breath from his nostrils on her other cheek and it seemed to her that her heart stopped beating and time stood still. Finally he kissed her again gently and eased his hand slowly away from her cheek. Her face burned from the imprint.

"We should get some rest," he said quietly as he squeezed her hands.

"Yes," she agreed dreamily. "We should get some rest."

Paul gathered her into his arms in a tender embrace, holding her for a long time then kissing her on the forehead.

"See you in the morning," he said.

"Yeah, in the morning," she replied.

Paul disengaged himself reluctantly from their embrace and slowly started down the path to the barn. Mary floated toward the front steps of the house.

Grandfather Sakai had been watching from his favorite rocker near the window. He smiled as his granddaughter glided weightlessly up the stairs and across the porch. Toshio feigned the sleep of an old man when she came in, and he allowed himself to be helped to bed by the dutiful girl when she 'discovered' him in his chair. In the bed he had shared with Moriko for so many years, he stared at the ceiling as memories of the passion of his youth flooded back and the love he had shared for so long. He fell asleep with a sentimental smile of joy for Mary. She had found love.

Harbormaster's Office
Port of Seattle
August 19, 1941

The Master of the *Kobiashi Maru* was enjoying a leisurely stroll along the waterfront. It was a breathtaking day to be alive, blue sky reaching in every direction, a gentle breeze and mild temperature. He could see why Seattle was called the Emerald City. A profusion of greens of every imaginable hue set like an enormous jewel in a setting of sapphire waters. To his right, as he walked, he could see the jagged peaks of the Olympic Mountains still capped with snow at the highest elevations. In many ways the natural beauty reminded him of his home islands of Japan. He was thoughtful about going back again soon.

Reaching the stairs to the Harbormaster's office he climbed to the top and opened the door. The Harbormaster sat in an office enclosed with glass, speaking with someone on the telephone. The clerk sat at his desk making entries into a logbook occasionally taking a precise bite from a carrot stick. When the door opened, the clerk looked up and nodded in a businesslike way.

"Planning to hoist anchor soon?" He asked.

"Yes, today at five this afternoon." The Captain replied. "I have our mail drop here. Do we have any mail?" With only himself, three officers and twelve crewmen he didn't expect much.

"Ah, yep, young fella came in yesterday and wrote you a note. Nothing else for you, though. Here you go. Sign here for receipt of mail. Got to keep things shipshape you know." The two men exchanged the incoming and outgoing envelopes and the skipper signed the receipt.

"Thank you," said the clerk, "see you next trip."

"Okay, you bet. Bye, Bye."

The steamer Captain tore open the envelope as he was leaving and by the time he reached the bottom of the stairs his eyes were wide as saucers at what he read. He stepped onto the dock and headed for the road. Trying to look nonchalant, he was looking for a taxi or trolley. Finally he flagged down a taxi and jumped into the back seat.

"Where to?" The cabby asked.

"Japanese Embassy, and quickly please."

Special Code Room
Unspecified Building
San Francisco
August 19, 1941

"Dear nephew Eddie, Cousin Billy says Dad and the family have gone to the lake to live and won't be back." The Liaison Officer looked up from the paper in his hand.

"What in the hell is this, Oscar?" He demanded.

"Beats me Ed, but I know they interrupted other important traffic to send it," the Senior Analyst responded.

"What's the point of origin?"

"Seattle Embassy, less than an hour ago."

"Hasn't heard from Aunt Mae recently but he's homesick and wants to help with the harvest." Ed took his glasses off and tossed them carelessly onto his desk. Massaging the bridge of his nose with his right thumb and forefinger he looked back at his best code breaker. "This job is gonna make me crazy, and we don't even have a war yet. How long did it take you to decode this?"

"No time at all, it was sent in English."

"Now *that* is interesting!" He said emphatically.

"That's what I thought, Ed. They interrupt important coded traffic to send this in plain English. I did a little checking with the guys in signals. They vaguely remember a radio intercept that sounded something like this; again in plain English. Here's where it gets really interesting. That call was picked up by a cruiser patrolling near Hawaii…last April. No related intercepts we're aware of since."

"What's your gut telling you, Oscar?"

"Well, pretty clearly it's somebody reporting back to Tokyo. If you take it at face value it's probably reporting a failure of some sort and a need to get back to Japan. Problem is it's so vague it doesn't really tell us much. We need to know who all the players are. I've already asked signals to see if they can find the first transmission, but it may have been destroyed by now."

"I'll see if I can kick some brass and speed things up for you," Ed replied.

"You know, Ed," Oscar said, "there isn't anything going on in crypto they need me for. It's just routine traffic and decoding."

"You've got an itch, don't you?" Ed had learned very early after meeting the big man opposite him that if Oscar had a hunch about something it was good to let him run it to ground.

"Well, just a small one right now. But I'd like to spend a little time on it."

"What do you need?"

Oscar plopped down in the chair beside the desk putting his elbows on the arms and steepling his fingers. He slouched down and closed his intense blue eyes. In his mind he tried to imagine what little slivers and shreds of information might have importance. After a couple of minutes he sat upright and opened his eyes.

"All the west coast Navy, Coast Guard, Army and civilian law enforcement reports from the last six months that somebody smart in the office thought was unusual."

"Christ, Oscar, that's a damn tall order! It could take months just to assemble all that stuff."

"Probably not, remember, I only want what someone thought was very unusual. You know; a mystery."

"You and your mysteries, I suppose you want all this stuff to come by courier."

"Not really, that much courier activity across the board would raise eyebrows everywhere, even in Washington, and I don't think they've had an open eye in months.

Ed sighed heavily and leaned back in his oak office rocking chair clasping his hands behind his head. "Okay, I'll do the best I can, but this is going to take a while."

Oscar picked up the cryptic communication that was setting things in motion, turned to leave the office, then stopped and looked back at his boss. "You know, it might not be a bad thing if Seattle Customs decided to check manifests and ships for contraband. You know, check 'em all, but paying particular attention not to miss any that might be Japanese, German or Italian flagged. French too, maybe."

"Yeah," Ed agreed, "just routine, nothing special, I gotcha. I'll call it in right now. Good idea Oscar, thanks."

"Just another day in the pay of the U.S.A.," he responded as he shut the office door behind him.

Island Farms

Bainbridge Island
August 19, 1941
4:35 a.m.

The young man in the old barn had spent a short night of fitful sleep. His mind was in turmoil. His heart was telling him one thing and his conscience was confused. In the twilight of not-quite-asleep but not really awake, dreamlike visions and memories flitted to and fro like ghostly apparitions unable to rest.

His dreams, like his life, were in constant motion. Never reconciled to a particular path, his torture now was in deciding what to believe. As he lay in his bunk his life played like scenes from a surrealist movie: a childhood spent wandering the farm fields of the western United States. He struggled to remember his paternal grandparents but failed. He hadn't seen his grandfather since he was a small child. He had never met his grandmother: didn't even know her name. His maternal grandparents were a complete blank in his mind. Over two years had passed since he had seen or spoken to his father or mother and he didn't even know where they might be. His Japanese family was distant: a remote past without warmth or connection. How could duty and service to a passionless, mythical Emperor from a distant shore hold him?

His great-grandfather, grandfather and father had worked for the Emperors; he himself was recently trained as a naval aviator and spy for the Japanese Imperial Navy. He had taken orders directly from Yamamoto, yet to avoid embarrassment to the family, he'd had to take lessons in Japanese because English was his true first language. Arimoto was accustomed to the harsh discipline of service and the unquestioned fealty demanded by the Emperor, but Arimoto was his past.

It was his new life as Paul that was the future and embraced the ideas and freedoms of the United States. He liked jazz but was bored with Kabuki. He preferred American food and was not all that fond of rice, raw fish or seaweed. Paul was in love with a girl; an American girl. She loved meatloaf and apple pie. She swooned for Cary Grant, got angry about injustice and put her hand over her heart when the American flag went by in a parade. In his dream state he realized he was so much like her.

Fate has an odd sense of humor. Paul roused himself, had a sip from a glass of water on his lettuce box nightstand and padded barefoot and semiconscious up the path to the outhouse. It was while relieving himself, as the first hints of daylight appeared; he concluded what he must do. He walked back to his little room, got back into bed and fell fast and peacefully asleep in moments.

When he missed breakfast one of the farm laborers was sent to rouse him from his bed. He arose sleepily, splashed water on his face and dressed in his work clothes. With his own path ahead clear he wore a big smile and whistled a cheerful Count Basie tune as he reported to the field.

Late in the afternoon that day the *Kobiashi Maru* sailed without him, two hours before Customs had scheduled an inspection. The Japanese would fight the war without Arimoto Akagi. Paul Akagi had decided he was staying home; in America.

Home of Ambrose Pearson
West Seattle
Washington
September 3, 1941

It was a little early in the season yet but Ambrose could wait no longer. For two weeks he had delayed but now he was plucking the last of his late planting beet crop from his small garden in the back yard. He still went each Saturday to market to buy from his friend Thomas, but kept a small garden of his own as well.

Although stooped a bit now, he was still a tall man with a great shock of white hair. He carried his prized collection into the large kitchen that had been the sight of so many squealing children and grandchildren and so many meals shared with his beloved Marie. He placed the vegetables on the drain board of the sink and carefully took a paring knife from the drawer testing the edge with his thumb. The keenness of the edge satisfied him, something of a point of pride in his household. Edges should be kept sharp and tools well oiled, he had lectured often.

The old man bent to the task of rinsing the vegetables of the soil clinging from the garden, then carefully cut the tops off and set them aside. Since the beets were small he simply rubbed them hard with his fingers and trimmed the occasional errant root, placing them in a small saucepan with water. From time to time he looked out the kitchen window at the verdant trees and azure skies of the season and mentally gave thanks to God for living to see another such glorious day then the old minister sat down to rest some. The years had taken a toll on his joints and a little rest was a good thing. Presently the pain subsided and he returned to his supper. On the stove he set a small pot of rice to cook, then his beets. He would put the tops in when the beets were almost done. Finally he removed a small portion of beef steak from the ice box and began to fry it in a little cast iron skillet. His wife had carried that little fry pan all the way from Hawaii nearly fifty years ago. It was comforting to find little things they still shared, even in the separation of death.

Ambrose placed all the items of his supper on a cracked dinner plate and carried it into the dining room. He still took his solitary meals in the dining room. Marie had always insisted that dinner should be at the dining table and he had respected the habit all these years. He had a little trouble focusing but he could see the butter melting on the beet greens as he salted them.

The old preacher returned thanks to the Lord and quietly ate his dinner, savoring each bite, remembering times when food had been scarce and such a platter as was now before him would have been welcome indeed. After he finished, he took his utensils and plate back to the kitchen sink and washed them, along with the rest of the items he had used; carefully dried each in its turn and returned them to their appropriate places.

As the evening waned into twilight, Pearson listened to the radio for a while, enjoying some music while he slowly read the newspaper from yesterday. Each afternoon the neighbor would bring the Seattle Times from the previous day. This allowed him to stay current without the expense of purchasing a paper, an expense he could not spare from his meager pension.

Finally around nine o'clock he arose from his armchair and retired to the bedroom. Carefully he folded and hung each article of clothing as he removed it, and put on his pajamas.

The last thing he did each night was to read from the Bible. He had done so for over seventy years. Tonight he was in Psalms, specifically Psalm number eight:

Oh Lord our Lord, how excellent

is thy name in all the earth,

Who has set thy glory above the heavens.

Out of the mouths of babes and sucklings thou has ordained

Strength because of thine enemies,
That thou might vanquish the enemy and the avenger.
When I consider thy heavens, the work of thy fingers,
The moon and the stars, which thou has ordained;
What is man, that thou art mindful of him?
And the son of man, that thou visits him?
For thou has made him a little lower than the angels,
And has crowned him with the glory and the honor.
Thou made him to have dominion over the works of thy hands;
Thou has put all things under his feet.
All sheep and oxen, and the beasts of the field,
the fowl of the air, And the fish of sea and whatsoever passes through the paths of the seas.
Oh Lord, our Lord, how excellent is thy name in all the earth!

**Whoso hearkeneth unto me shall dwell safely,
And shall be quiet from fear of evil**
Proverbs Chapter 1 Verse 33
Holy Bible

It was a fine late summer day, sunny and mild with a southerly breeze. The only hint of impending autumn with its chill winds and rains, were the flaming red leaves of the vine maples and golden turn beginning to grip the birch trees. By this time of year the sun was arcing toward the southern sky and casting sharp shadows by mid-afternoon.

A small group of mourners were gathered around a grave site in the Forest Lawn Cemetery in West Seattle as a minister conducted the ceremony.

Thomas Sakai sat staring absently at the polished toes of his best black oxfords. He noticed a yellow birch leaf stuck in the shoelaces of his left foot and recalled the cherry blossoms on his feet over fifty years ago on a humble dock in Shimado. Thomas stared at the young preacher, aware he was speaking, but distantly unable to devote his attention.

The young preacher was going through the motions of the assignment given to him by the Presbytery, but he had only slightly known the old Reverend and knew virtually none of the mourners. Still, all the correct scriptures were read, the correct condolences conveyed. Reassurances of the redemption of the Resurrection were given with a final prayer spoken. His duty complete, the young man turned and walked away from the group, this mission fulfilled.

Most of the attendees began drifting away, planning to gather for a small reception in the home that Reverend Pearson and his beloved Marie had shared for so many years. Even now church Deacons were there, brewing coffee and arranging cookies and finger sandwiches on platters. Joshua did not plan to stay in the house, so he and Ritchey had mercifully been spared from an onslaught of well-intentioned covered dishes and casseroles.

"It seemed like a small group," Joshua observed.

"Well, I imagine your dad outlived a lot of his friends and parishioners," Frank replied. "And some probably can't get out anymore."

"No, I suppose not." Joshua stood silently beside the coffin for a minute longer. "He was a good man, you know."

"He was a great man," Thomas interjected firmly, "a great man with a great gift."

"Thank you Mr. Sakai," Pearson said. "I especially appreciate that coming from you." Everyone remained silent for another moment then finally the eldest Pearson said, "Come on Ritchey, people will be waiting for us." Stoic son and respectful grandson turned and made their way back to the old pickup parked nearby.

"Come on Dad, it's time to go," Frank said quietly. He placed his hands gently on his father's shoulders.

"You go ahead, help your mother to the car. I'll be along soon. I want to say goodbye to my friend."

"Okay, Dad. Take your time." Frank and Eleanor helped their grandmother to her feet and along with Paul at Mary's arm headed back toward the road.

Thomas pulled his chair close and sat next to the coffin for some time without moving. "Well, old friend, your journey is complete. Back with your Marie and in His glorious presence. I'm a little envious."

He unwrapped a small paper package and took out a bright red flower; an anthurium, for which Paul had spent an entire day searching area florist shops. He placed the Hawaiian flower on top of the simple polished wood coffin.

"A remembrance of where we began, old friend."

Thomas leaned, placing his right hand on his heart and his left on the coffin as tears slid down his cheeks and fell silently into the grass below. Finally he straightened and wiped away the moisture with the sleeve of his jacket.

"Goodbye Ambrose. Well done, good and faithful servant."

The old man turned and walked stiffly towards the car as the tears flowed freely again. He made no effort to conceal them.

Special Code Room
Unspecified Building
San Francisco
September 8, 1941

Oscar could barely see over the top of the mountain of file folders, letters, transcriptions and envelopes threatening to slide in hopeless disarray to the floor at the slightest provocation. Leaning back in his government-issue office armchair with his feet up on his government-issue gray metal desk with the linoleum top, he patiently opened the top file from a stack on his lap. Scanning quickly he would direct the contents to one of three piles: Yes; No; Maybe.

Ed stuck his head in the office door. The breeze from the open door set a pile tottering so dangerously he stepped inside quickly to catch it before it could collapse.

"How's it coming?" He asked.

"If you mean, 'How's it coming, have you figured it out yet,' the answer is no. If you mean 'How's it coming, did you know how many useless reports our government produces, and were you aware that virtually everyone who writes said reports believes them to be highly unusual and important,' the answer is yes. Resoundingly, unequivocally, irrevocably, irresistibly yes, yes, yes!"

"What is it you say?" Ed grinned, "Just another day in the pay of the U.S.A."

"Don't be a smart ass, Ed," Oscar groused amiably. "What can I do for you?"

"Well, it's really more along the lines of what I can do for you." He replied. "I have a first rate girl available—with all the clearances —to help if you need it. Whaddya think?"

"I'll take her. I don't even care if she looks like Sophie Tucker. If she can read, she can help."

"Great!" Ed stepped back to the door and stuck his head out into the hallway. "Come on in, Betty. I've got a new assignment for you."

Oscar struggled to get to his feet. "You son of a bitch, you could've told me she was waiting in the hall."

Betty Anderson stepped into the office just in time to see Oscar sprawling in a vain effort to prevent a huge stack from collapsing off the desk. She stood a generous five feet ten inches tall with flaxen hair, green eyes, and an eye-popping hourglass figure. She looked like she had just stepped out of the studio from a photo shoot for some glamour magazine.

"Sophie wasn't available," she said. "You'll have to settle for me."

Scrambling to his feet, Oscar tried with only marginal success to present a businesslike appearance. Extending his right hand he said, "Please don't mind me. I spend too much time in small rooms thinking dark thoughts. All for the government, mind you. I'm Oscar Lefwich, pleased to meet you."

"Betty Anderson." She grasped his hand with a firm handshake. "Ed says you could use a little help."

"Yeah, that's not all Ed says." He looked over with indignation.

"Yes, well I can see I'm not needed here any longer," Ed said backing out the open door, "so I'll be on my way. Betty, Oscar, you two play nice now and if you need anything be sure to let Uncle Ed know." He scurried out the door just avoiding a basketball hurled in his direction.

"So, now that the formalities have been dispensed with, where should I begin?" Betty asked.

"I don't know," Oscar said.

"I see. Well, what are we looking for?"

"I'm not sure," he admitted.

"This is going to be a more interesting job than I had imagined." Betty said.

"That's what I thought," he enthused. "That's why I love this job."

"Let's start at the beginning," Betty said. "Is there another chair?"

"Oh yes, it's right under here." He pointed to a three foot stack of unopened shipping envelopes.

"Why did you order all this stuff?"

"Oh that's easy," he said. While she picked up paperwork off the floor and began creating some sensible order he told her what he suspected.

"Whew!" she whistled. "That's some tall order. We better get to work."

"Great! But first I'm going to make Ed buy us lunch. How do you feel about ham and Swiss on rye?"

"With kraut, a cola and a Hershey bar." She said. "And a six foot conference table as a chaser. In fact, come to think of it, the table better be an appetizer."

"My kind of girl, er lady; There is a phone on this desk. I saw it last month."

"Follow the cord to the phone, Oscar. We'll have to see about the other. We'll just have to see." She flashed a gleaming smile and piled more folders on his desk. From the look in his eyes she knew she was already in his head.

Old Commons
University of Washington
Seattle
September 11, 1941

"I am telling you here and now: There will be war with Japan within a year and most of us will have trouble from it." Harry Matsomota had a habit of pontificating to his fellow students whether or not an opportunity presented itself. He was in rare form today but his friends usually indulged his idiosyncratic behavior because he was first rate at helping with homework.

"God save us from poli-sci majors," Mary said *sotto voce* to a school chum seated next to her. That earned a giggle from her classmate.

"I heard that!" Harry whirled around and gave Mary the evil eye. "You're *Sansei*; your family owns the land it farms. Others are not so lucky. Half the milk and three fourths of the vegetables eaten in Seattle come from Issei and Nisei farms, most of which are only leased. White farmers would love to have an excuse to break those leases. If there is war, there will be trouble for us all." He looked sternly around him. His round glasses reflected the sunlight adding a Little Orphan Annie quality to his countenance, despite his close cropped black hair. It made it difficult to take him seriously when he spoke. "Since Roosevelt froze Japanese assets, most of the banks our parents use have closed because of runs that drained them. What about you, Mary, where does your family bank?"

"Harry, where do you get such notions? My money is still good—isn't yours?" Another student in the circle spoke up. "What professor is teaching you this stuff?"

"Professor?" Harry harrumphed. "My professor is the newspaper, and the Congressional Record."

"My gosh, Harry, you make it sound like the cops are gonna send us all to jail." Mary replied, "Heck, we're Americans too, you know. They can't do that without any reason."

"You just don't get it," he lectured. "We may *be* Americans, but we don't *look* like Americans. You don't think it's a little odd that the Alien Exclusion Act excludes only Asians from emigrating here?" Matsomota extracted a newspaper from the inner pocket of his suit coat.

"How about this?" he began, clearing his throat. "This is from the *Nisei News & Record*. Dateline: Washington, D.C. August 20 1941." He paused for dramatic effect then continued to read. "The *Nisei News* has learned that Representative John Dingell of Michigan has recommended in a letter to President Roosevelt, made public today, that up to ten thousand Hawaiian Japanese be incarcerated to ensure 'good behavior' on the part of Japan.

This reporter pointed out to Dingell's office that such a measure would be unconstitutional. The response was that the Congressman was studying the issue further but was confident that should such a need arise in a time of crisis or national peril, the legal justification could be established.

Asked for a response, the White House said the President was 'studying the Congressman's recommendation and would have no further comment at this time.'" Harry slapped the newspaper triumphantly as if further doubt was inconceivable.

"You see, a white farmer from the middle of the country wants to round up citizens like criminals and throw them in jail just because they look like the enemy. If your grandfather hadn't moved away from Hawaii, this could mean you, Mary; locked up so that *real* citizens wouldn't have to worry!"

"My God, Harry, what are you spouting now?" It was Steven walking down the sidewalk toward the group, "Civil insurrection no doubt. Nobody here actually listens to him, do you?" Most of the group shook their heads and looked away sheepishly, feeling a little foolish. Steven was a senior now and knew Harry. If he didn't think much of what he had to say, why should they?

"Why Steven, how kind of you to stop by," Harry mocked. "I was just sharing ideas with the group about what was going on in the world of politics. From someone who is majoring in such things. With your vast political experience as a student of what? Bridges? How do you see the landscape?"

"Needs a little structural underpinning from where I sit," he refused to be needled, "Particularly in the undergrad liberal arts pontification department: Hey sis, about ready to hit the road?"

"Yeah, the mood is depressing around this guy!" She responded.

"Go then amid the unwashed and uninformed," Harry intoned melodramatically. "Someday the words of Harry Matsomota will ring truth in your ears."

"Maybe so," Steven said, "but right now the only ringing I hear is the class bell, which I believe makes you late for your last class, Harry."

"Damn!" Harry said. He grabbed his books and dashed off toward his hall. The group broke up and began to wander off to their separate pursuits.

"C'mon little sister, let's get you back to Paul."

"Oh stop it!" She protested. "He's just a good friend."

"Mighty good from where I sit," Steven changed the subject. "What was Harry screeching about this time? Land reform? Congressional accountability? Access to electricity from Bonneville Power when Grand Coulee comes on line?"

"Nope, Alien Exclusion Act and locking up all the Japanese in Hawaii to keep Hirohito in line."

`"You don't say?" Steven chortled. "How does he sleep at night with all those weighty worries? He sure is hot as a cheap pistol!" He laughed again. "Besides, where in the hell would you put tens of thousands of prisoners? How would you even feed them? Man, he is a hoot!" Steven continued chuckling as they made their way to the parking lot and climbed into the car for the ride home.

Puget Sound

Washington State
Mid-October 1941

The turn away from summer was evident everywhere. Leaves were falling in earnest now and the skies were filled with shrill honks as Canada geese and Tundra swans by the thousands arrived from their northern habitats to glean the remains from harvested farm fields throughout the area. Sudden cold downpours accompanied by swift winds could appear with little warning. Students had been recalled to school for over a month.

Joshua had returned to Briarwood for another year as the custodian. It was simple work, not intellectually stimulating, but steady and predictable, a bonus in lean and uncertain times. Occasionally he was calling on a pretty young teacher in the school, so he fussed more over the way he and Ritchey looked. He kept the little house they shared tidier too. He had put away all the photos of his dearly departed wife except one in his son's room.

Richard Franklin Pearson was starting his sophomore year. Precocious, genial and seldom challenged by studies, he would while away the school time with surprising patience. During recess he would often look out over Useless Bay making a survey of the winds while simultaneously doing mental calculations regarding how many knots he thought his little sailboat could carry. He did his homework while his father cleaned the school, then they would both head home in the battered old pickup for dinner.

Steven Sakai was now in his senior year at the University of Washington. True to his calling, he was already studying for an advanced degree in architecture. Although only a little less than two years younger, Mary was enrolled in freshman classes with no real focus of study except liberal arts; English maybe, or perhaps Drama.

Frank had given an old '34 Dodge Coupe to Steven and each school day he and his sister would leave the farmstead at six in the morning to catch the ferry to Coleman Dock. By five that evening they would be back on the island, prepared to recite a synopsis of what they had learned for their grandfather. Thomas took a keen interest in the education of his grandchildren and most nights managed not to doze off during their recitations.

Eleanor and Moriko patiently trimmed, washed, peeled, pitted or cored fruit and vegetables, cleaned salmon and sterilized Mason canning jars. For most of a month they would put up hundreds of quarts of food to store with the glassed summer eggs already in the pantry. Back in August they had made preserves from the wild blackberries that sprang up almost everywhere. Originally brought in by Russian emigrants in the nineteenth century; the berry—their seeds distributed widely by birds, raccoons, coyotes and bears—had become a pest, covering thousands of acres of the Pacific Northwest. But they did make good jam.

Paul was working the farm alongside Frank. Most of the seasonal workers had headed back south before the worst of the weather set in. It was a long trip on lousy roads and mud would not be a welcome travel companion.

The last of the late harvest was in—apples and potatoes—and the fields were being plowed or left dormant as suited the planting rotation for the next season. On days when wind or rain made field work impractical, Paul bent to the task of stripping machinery and implements apart for cleaning, painting and repair. There is never really a time on a farm when there isn't something to do and he was actually enjoying the rhythm of the seasons of work. Sometimes he even imagined himself as a farmer for the rest of his life.

It was honest work, fairly profitable if crops and expenses were carefully managed and offered great visceral satisfaction when those first green shoots appeared from the earth each spring. Mostly now, his previous life was a receding memory. He and Mary were becoming quite attached. Times seemed good and getting better. The rumbling drums of war seemed a solar system away.

Around the Puget Sound recreational boaters were making their last sailing or motorboat trips before docking safely in a slip and winterizing for the season. Coal trucks delivered basements full of the Newhalem fuel coming from Bellingham by train, and those using wood for fuel could be seen chopping and stacking cords of alder, maple, chestnut and birch. Housewives and hobbyists spread straw over planting beds; lawns were mowed for what many hoped was the last time before spring. People all around were settling in, hunkering down and preparing for the short days and the long cold nights just around the corner. It would be another winter to get through, not much different than most of the others which had preceded.

Battleship *Mutsu*

Admiral's Deck

October 1941

"Attacking Pearl Harbor as the opening strategy is a dangerous gamble!" Onishi Takijiro was Chief of Staff of the Eleventh Air Fleet of the Imperial Japanese Navy and had been making this argument for weeks now, apparently to no avail.

"Under other circumstances, I would agree with you." Yamamoto, in his capacity as Combined Fleet Commander was obstinate. "But we lost the initiative when we allowed America's Pacific Fleet to relocate to Pearl Harbor. Clearly if they can threaten the home islands, then we can threaten them." The C. in C. and Takijiro kept their own council regarding the failure of the submarines and the collapse of his even more audacious idea. There was nothing to be done about that now anyway. Kusaka, as with virtually everyone else, knew nothing of the aborted plan.

"I fail to see how we could have prevented the Americans from relocating their fleet without a premature declaration of war. Iso-san, I need hardly remind you that Onishi is not the only officer with this viewpoint."

"No, it is the dominant idea, but that does not make it the correct one." Yamamoto turned in his chair to get a better view of Kusaka Ryunosuke, Onishi's counterpart with the First Air Fleet. "If I were to do as so many suggest; to swing down into the South Pacific and conduct operations there, our flank would be wide open. Americans could attack from the east with little opposition. That's not all, you haven't been told yet but the army is planning to land a brigade on Malaya and drive the British out of Singapore from the land. Their operation is scheduled to coincide with our attack on Pearl Harbor. Now *that* is a risky plan."

"But Iso," Kusaka began.

"But Iso," the Admiral mocked. "Are you suggesting that having Tokyo and Osaka burning to the ground, so long as we secure oil, is an acceptable option?"

Onishi and Kusaka glanced at each other sharing a look of exasperation.

"You have a letter here signed by my friend Nagumo who opposes me in this, but so long as I am Commander in Chief we shall go ahead with the Hawaiian operation." Yamamoto sank back in his chair; his left leg was aching fiercely.

"Listen, my friends," the Admiral said, softening his tone, "I know you have difficulties with this...that it rubs the fur the wrong way. I'm asking that you go ahead with preparations on the positive assumption that the raid is on."

Reluctantly the two visiting admirals arose to leave having dashed the fury of their storm of protest against the unyielding rocky shore of the C. in C.

"Very well, Iso-san. We shall prepare for your mad gamble," Kusaka said.

"My reputation for enjoying poker and bridge is well known," Yamamoto said with a grin, "but I wish to hell you'd stop calling it a gamble."

The two flag officers left Yamamoto sitting in his leather chair, alone on the deck. *We haven't fired a single shot at the Americans and already this war is going badly.*

Special Code Room

Unspecified Building

San Francisco

October 11, 1941

It had been over a month and an impressive job of organization had been accomplished. Oscar and Betty had separated documents by a complex matrix that included geographical point of origin, type of report, date sequences, reliability of source and even the time of day. Even as they weeded through the reports in hand a month ago, more had flowed in until finally Oscar called a halt mostly in self defense.

"Damn it! It's so close my palms are itchy, but I just can't put a finger on it." He stared at the portable chalkboard where they had made notes of what they thought was salient. Mostly the scribbles referred to other documents in a sort of on-the-fly shorthand that only the two of them could really interpret.

"Well, I'm famished," Betty declared. She took off her glasses and stretched her long, shapely figure as she sat at the conference table. Glancing at the wall clock she exclaimed, "Gosh, no wonder. It's two-thirty. We've worked through lunch by a long shot."

Oscar fixed a vacant stare on her, then abruptly arose and walked to the coat tree in the corner of the office. He jammed his fedora on his head and began pulling his raincoat on.

"Come on," he demanded. "Let's get Chinese."

"You don't have to ask this girl more than once." She stood, stretched again then reached for her jacket and umbrella. She had long since given up trying to use feminine wiles on Oscar. To her utter amazement he had proven impervious to her subtle advances and even not so subtle ones. It wasn't that he didn't notice, for precious little escaped him, or even that he wasn't flattered by the attention. Oscar just happened to have the singularly most disciplined mind she had ever encountered. He had won her respect for that, and she was even getting used to his disheveled appearance. He had the unkempt look of having dressed using whatever he could find on the floor at the moment of need.

In other circumstances she would have liked to marry this guy. He wasn't Tyrone Power, but looks fade while a first-rate intellect would long be a source of pleasure and challenge.

"You first, I'll be six minutes behind," Oscar said.

"No way, buddy. You go first so you can order. Nothing weird either. I no speekee the language, yes?"

"Okay, I'll go left, you go right, Chen's Palace." He strode down the hall toward the elevator and disappeared behind its sliding doors.

Betty stepped into the ladies room to refresh herself. She hadn't been a minute when pounding suddenly thundered on the door from the outside.

""Betty! Are you in there?" It was Oscar startling all occupants. "Betty! I've got it, I've got it! For crying out loud get out here!"

"Good Lord, Oscar you scared everyone nearly half to death," she said coming out of the lounge to stand in the hallway. "You've got what? Chinese food I hope, I'm starving."

"No, no, no," he said. "It's that damn orange airplane. It's the key to the whole thing. Come on, let's get back to work."

Oscar's eyes were glowing now; he could sense victory and was moving in for the kill. Betty's eyes were red and tired.

"Okay Mister Lefwich, after I pee." She hoped the little vulgarity would send the message she wanted, mainly that she needed a break.

"Fine, fine, fine; soon as you can." He yanked the hat off his head and was tugging at the sleeves of his overcoat as he disappeared back into the office.

355

After a few minutes, a splash of water on her face and a little rouge and fresh lipstick Betty returned to the office. Going directly to Oscar she reached over his desk placing her breasts square in his face. She picked up the phone and waited.

"Ed, its Betty, call Chen's and get us some lunch. Oscar's onto something."

"You know, you are really a very attractive woman, Betty," Oscar remarked.

"Why thank you, Oscar." Betty was caught a little off guard. She thought for a moment then realized, *of course! Puzzle solved. Everything is just leg work now. He has enough space in his brain for thinking about other things. I'll let him think about this puzzle for a while.* She leaned over just a bit further and kissed him. She kissed him seriously and he kissed back.

Bainbridge Island
October 14, 1941
Late afternoon

"I love coming here," Mary said. "It's so peaceful and pretty." Paul looked out to the southwest gazing at the last rays of autumn sun. Sunset came early this time of year in the Pacific Northwest and the last beams glistened off the raindrops of a recent shower which had coated the trees and ferns. They looked like tiny gemstones scattered about in the fantastical fractal garden of a fairy tale. The overall effect was truly magical.

"Me too." He held Mary tightly in his arms as they leaned against the fender of the old Dodge. "How did you ever find this place?"

"Grandpa used to take us here when I was a kid. He said he found it wandering around the old logging roads on the island and that it reminded him of Japan a little."

"Yes, I can see how he would imagine that." Paul searched across the small passage that separated the island from the Kitsap Peninsula as the last of the sun slipped below the horizon, the soaring cedars and distant Olympic Mountains casting long, dark shadows.

"How would you know what Japan looks like?" Mary asked, looking up at him. "You said you were born in California."

"I was, in Salinas. But Pop took Mom and me back to Japan a couple of times. He worked for the government as an agricultural attaché." Paul was not being fully accurate, he knew, but it was true as far as it went and Paul wanted as few secrets between he and Mary as was possible.

"You don't talk much about your folks."

"No; well we don't really speak the same language, literally. He's old school Japanese, Mom wouldn't dare to contradict him openly, and I grew up in the U.S. I'm not even sure if I'm a Japanese citizen." The last was an open lie—he knew full well what his real citizenship status was—but if ever there was a doubt he wanted everyone he knew to believe what he told them. "I don't want to talk about the past anyway; I want to talk about the future."

"Oh really," Mary smiled. "And which future would that be?"

"Our future, yours and mine," Paul said softly.

Mary turned to face Paul and gazed into his eyes; "Our future? You want a future with me?"

"With all my heart, Mary," he leaned down to kiss her, "If you want one with me."

She kissed him. Tenderly at first, then with increasing ardor. They held each other so tightly that it was hard to breathe—or maybe it was just hard to breathe anyway. In the gloaming of the evening and the verdant greens of the forest their passion arose. Paul gently caressed Mary's breasts at her encouragement; she pressed earnestly against his rising manhood. Just as the moment was about to overwhelm them both Paul broke off their embrace.

"Mary, I love you so much—let's not begin this way." His breath came in short gasps; his voice was husky with lust. "Let's begin when we can be open and honest about how we feel and declare ourselves to the family. I owe your father that much respect and you too."

The young beauty regarded him with admiration. Her moment of passion was replaced with a great respect as her breathing returned to normal and the flush of her face, invisible in the darkness, subsided. She tugged at the blouse she was wearing, rearranging herself into a semblance of restored dignity.

"Paul, you're a good man and I appreciate your strength. You're right, of course. Thank you." She reached up and took his face in her hands and kissed him one more time, with passion tempered with affection. "God, I do love you."

"Let's go home," the young lover said. "It's dark and I hear there are bears in these woods."

"Yeah, I hear that too. Big Japanese bears named Paul. Yes, let's go home." Mary couldn't wait to tell her mother about tonight. Actually, it might be better to tell her grandmother first. Moriko had a way of making these things easier. Paul fired up the car, Mary slid in next to him on the seat, and the two of them traced the dim yellow headlights out of the bush and back toward the house.

King Street Railroad Station

Seattle

October 19, 1941

Oscar and Betty stepped off the *Cascade Flyer* onto the train station platform. They were traveling as husband and wife—George and Maggie French—while on this assignment. They had shared a Pullman sleeper compartment from San Francisco, very cozily it turned out, and now here they were, hot on the trailh. By now they had a better idea of the quarry, but even with weeks of sorting and speculating it was still possible they were chasing the proverbial wild goose.

"Well, let's head to the hotel." Oscar pulled his fedora low over his forehead and fastened the top two buttons of his raincoat before picking up the bags and heading into the station. Three cars down, a lone man stepped off the train and lit a cigarette, blowing the smoke skyward as he looked up.

"Okay by me, honey." She picked up her hat box and fell in step with her partner. "When do we get to work?"

"First thing in the morning, love, I need my beauty sleep."

"You men, obsessed with your looks!"

Oscar laughed. "Yeah, that's me alright, a regular dandy." He tapped on the window of a cab occupied by a dozing driver. "Hey, Bud, you open for business?" The cabby awoke with a start looking around in bewilderment for a moment.

"Yeah, sure," he said scrambling out of the car; "Where to, Mister?"

Oscar handed the bags to the man as he opened the trunk; "Pacific Hotel, downtown."

"Right, that's only about ten blocks from here, Shouldn't take five minutes." His passengers clambered into the back seat and he hopped into the driver's seat, started the engine and pulled away from the station.

Emerging from the shadows, the man with the cigarette waved for the next cab in line, opened the door and sat in the front seat with the driver.

"Hello, Tony, how's things in the City these days?"

"Bellissimo, Angelo, how's about here?"

"Couldn't be bettah, couldn't be bettah." Angelo pulled into the street and fell in—at a reasonable distance—behind the other cab.

Island Farms

Bainbridge Island
8:30 a.m.
October 20, 1941

Wearing brand new Levi's pants and a jacket, coupled with a new plaid flannel shirt, Paul moved around the barn stiffly like the Tin Man from *The Wizard of Oz*. Breakfasts came a bit later and life on the farm was beginning to settle into a relaxed rhythm as dormancy fell across the region. Salmon fishers, he had heard, were following the harvest of Kings up the coast and crabbers were gearing up for another dangerous season in the deadly waters off Alaska.

Today was building day for him. Frank had decided living in the barn wasn't suitable for the Foreman so last week a small slab foundation of concrete had been poured next to the barn, complete with stubs for running water and a toilet which would connect to the septic tank. Three rooms, about six hundred square feet, consisting of a bathroom with a shower, a living/sleeping area with a small cooking stove—useful for heat as well—and a tiny office where he could conduct business with the laborers and buyers he would manage.

Paul pulled on his worn leather gloves and peeled the tarp back from lumber he had purchased a couple of days ago. Everything was covered with moisture. The fog that blanketed the area looked as if it wouldn't likely burn off before afternoon, if at all. He built a fire from scraps to have a place the take the chill off while working and took four likely pieces for a mud sill. He mixed a batch of one-third kerosene and two-thirds creosote in an old Folgers coffee can. The creosote was stiff in the chilly morning and it took a while for the ingredients to soften near the fire and fully blend. He was about half done applying the concoction when Frank came down the path from the house, his breath creating little clouds of personal fog which swirled behind him.

"You think we need to let that set up before we start?" Frank asked.

"Only if you want to wait till next June to build."

"Yeah, it's pretty wet now; if we wait it would be next summer. Oh well, it's just the Foreman's house."

"Ouch," Paul rejoined. "That cuts me like a knife."

"Speaking of cutting, why don't I get started on the studs. You figure out how many we need yet?"

"About fifty to frame the outer wall, another twenty-five for inner rooms; we'll cut stringers and headers as we need them."

"Man, my arms are tired already." Frank picked up the Disston crosscut saw and tested the sharpness with his thumb then looked down the blade to check the kerf angle. Satisfied, he measured a piece of timber, placed it in the cutting cradle and sawed it off. When he had finished he used the cut piece to set up a stop. That completed he could now saw multiple studs without measuring each one.

For a couple of hours the two men went about their labors. When Paul had finished applying the treatment, he consulted his crude drawings then measured each sill piece to the appropriate length and sawed them off. As the wood was cut Paul would move it into position then cut a few cripples. Finally actual construction was ready to begin.

"Frank, let's take a break, okay?"

"Sounds good to me, I'll go get us some tea." Frank said.

"Hold on a minute before you go." Paul took a deep breath. "I'd like to talk to you…about something…important."

Frank paused, waiting for more. Then finally he said slowly, "Okay, go ahead."

"Well, I'm not sure where to begin," Paul felt awkward and it showed. "Listen Frank, you've only known me now for what, three months?"

"A little more than that."

"But my point is, not very long, and already you're building a space for me as your foreman. And I'm appreciative, really I am."

"But..." Frank had a sinking feeling that Paul was about to announce his departure. That would break Mary's heart, but if it were going to happen, better now than later.

"But I think you ought to know that I love your daughter," Paul blurted.

Frank worked very hard not to smile. "I see," he said, struggling to maintain a serious demeanor. "And what are your intentions?"

"I would like your blessing to marry her." Paul hurried on, "I was thinking that perhaps I could stay on as Foreman. I like farming. Steven doesn't really want to work on the farm after he graduates and I could look after things until Benjamin is older. You know, manage things; give you a little more time off."

"Good morning." Thomas Sakai broke in as he approached the two men carrying a tray with a teapot and cups. "I saw that you had stopped for a break. I thought you might like some tea."

"You honor me, Thomas-san. I should be bringing you tea." Paul said bowing.

"Very polite, isn't he?" Thomas said to Frank.

"Indeed! He has just asked for Mary's hand. What do you think I should do, Father?"

"Give him a raise. He doesn't earn enough to support my granddaughter on what he makes now. Maybe make the foreman's house a bit bigger too."

A broad grin broke across Frank's face as he looked at a bewildered Paul.

"Just a warning to my future son-in-law, Mary is the worst secret-keeper on the planet. Oh, and by the way, this has been a foregone conclusion among the rest of the family for more than a month."

"But you hardly know me," Paul protested.

"A man reveals himself not just in words, but in deeds," Thomas said. "Your feelings have been apparent for some time and your actions remained honorable. You cannot hide so big a secret from those who have grown to love you."

Oh brother! If he only knew how wrong he could be! Paul thought.

"So it's settled: a raise, a marriage, and a new family partner." Frank extended his hand. Paul, smiling broadly grabbed it with both of his, pumping vigorously, then grabbed Thomas' hand and repeated the exercise more gently.

Frank turned to the house with his thumbs up. Mary was the first down the stairs onto the path flying toward Paul. Eleanor helped Moriko along and soon everything was a confusion of hugging, laughing, crying, bowing and shaking hands. Smiling, Thomas sipped his tepid green tea and nibbled on a ginger snap.

Port of Seattle

Harbormaster's Office

October 20, 1941

Midmorning

An interrogation is a touchy thing. Particularly if the inquisitor does not wish for the subject to realize it is happening: A ticklish feeling out of the personality. Are we voluble or reticent today? Would a couple of drinks loosen the inhibitions, so to speak? Should the interrogator be a friend or an authority figure? Perhaps just being perceived as nosy will suffice. Oscar didn't get much time in the field and he liked this puzzle. Sometimes Betty presented as his wife, beautiful but demure. Sometimes she played her sultry siren while he blended in the background. So far not much had turned up and he was beginning to think he was on the wrong track.

"Well, Doll. Let's try the Harbormaster's office before we break for lunch."

"What's the story?" Betty asked.

"Not much, just Federal Agents asking a few routine questions." He thumbed through his cards finding one that identified him as a Special Agent of the FBI. *J. Edgar would shit a brick if he saw these*, he thought.

"Pretty flimsy cover story, Bub."

"I don't expect to find much, but you never know."

The twosome trudged up the stairs and stepped into the small foyer of the office. The man sitting behind the desk looked up from behind his glasses.

"May I help you?" he said.

"George French, Special Agent with the FBI. This is Maggie, my assistant. I have a few routine questions if you have a minute."

"Ah yep, just a moment," The man finished the last bite of an oatmeal raisin cookie and washed it down with a gulp of milk. He carefully brushed the crumbs from his desk then crossed to a small sink where he rinsed the bottle and placed it in his lunch box which he then placed in a drawer of his desk.

"Got to be tidy, you know, more efficient. Now what can I answer for you."

"As you know, the President has imposed an embargo on all cargoes bound for Japan. We're checking to see if you have had any activity with a Japanese flagged vessel recently."

"Hmmm, seems that ought to be a Customs question," the man countered.

"Yes; well, Customs is concerned about cargoes, we're concerned about persons looking to enter or leave the country illegally."

"Ah yep, isn't that usually the Immigration Department?"

This guy is getting on my nerves! Oscar thought.

"Actually," Betty leaned over displaying some cleavage with just the barest hint of lacy bra, "we think this person may be a spy." She checked around conspiratorially giving the clerk a good long look.

"Well, ah yep." He put a nervous finger to his collar. "I see; serious business is it?"

"Very serious," Oscar cut in, "Also very secret. You must not speak of this conversation with anyone, even your wife."

"No, no, of course not."

"Now, do you remember my question?"

"Yes, yes I do." The clerk said. "Not much activity on that regard that I would be aware of up here, you understand. Last Japanese flagged vessel to leave here was the *Kobiashi Maru*." He withdrew a ledger from beneath the counter and opened it, flipping through the pages. Pointing to an entry he said, "Here it is. August 19. Hoisted anchor about five in the afternoon. Sailed with the tide. Not many worry about that anymore."

"Is there anything about her that stands out in your mind, anything unusual?"

"Ah, nope, sorry. It was a completely ordinary sailing. Routine cargo, here's the manifest."

Oscar and Betty looked at the manifest and the crew report: Nothing in the least out of place, another dead end.

"Well, we appreciate your time, anyway. Thanks." The couple turned and walked out the door headed down the stairs.

"Damn! I thought August nineteenth would be something here." Oscar said.

"Me too, isn't that when the 'Cousin Billy' intercept came in?"

"Ah, yep," Oscar mimicked.

"Ah, wait just a minute!" A voice called down the stairs to them. They turned to see the clerk standing with the door open. "I don't know if it means anything but I just remembered something a little unusual."

Oscar bounded back up the stairs leaving Betty to manage in her heels.

"There was something unusual with the mail," the clerk said when the couple had regained the foyer.

"Unusual how?" Oscar asked.

"Day before she sailed a young Japanese fella came in asking if he could leave mail for the Captain."

"Is that common?" Betty asked.

"Well, it's not common, but it's not rare either. Folks leave mail for ships pretty regular."

"What made this stick in your memory?" The pseudo-Fed asked.

"He didn't bring a letter to mail. He wrote it here, on the counter. Bought a piece of paper and an envelope. Five cents each. Paid with a quarter. I have that in the petty cash ledger if you would care to see it."

"Does it have his signature on it?" Oscar asked.

"Ah, nope, just my entry."

'Never mind then. Did you get a look at what he wrote?"

"Ah, yep, couldn't make it out though. Written in all them squiggly lines they use in China. He sealed it in the envelope and I put it in the mailbag for the Captain."

"When did the Captain pick up the mail?"

"About this time the next day."

"Did he open it in front of you?"

"Ah, nope, he just took it and left."

"Could you give my secretary a description of the man that wrote the letter?"

"Ah, yep, be pleased to." Betty took out a notepad and began writing down what details the man remembered. Oscar ambled over to the window and peered out at the traffic both on and off the water. *Watch your back, Billy. I'm getting close.*

Joshua Pearson Residence

Whidbey Island

October 20, 1941

Late afternoon

Mrs. Entwhistle was positively beside herself with anticipation by the time Joshua and Ritchey got home from school. As soon as the old truck rumbled into view she was out in the driveway waving a frilly hankie.

"Looks like Emma is trying to surrender." Joshua laughed.

"Missus Whistle sure looks excited," Ritchey said.

"Guess we better stop and find out what's going on." Joshua pulled up beside the plump widow and slid down the window. "Howdy Emma, what's all the fuss and feathers?"

"Oh Joshua, just the dearest news," she gushed. "You remember that nice young man you found injured last spring?"

"Well, actually, Ritchey found him. You're talking about Paul? What about him?"

"He and Mary Sakai are going to get married! Isn't that just darling?"

"Married! He certainly works fast. She's only known him for three months."

"Oh it's so romantic." Mrs. Entwhistle continued, ignoring him. "Eleanor called to invite us to the wedding. Well, to invite you and Ritchey anyway." She looked over the top of her reading glasses.

"She says they will mail invitations but that the wedding is soon so they wanted people to save the day."

"And when is that day?" Joshua asked.

"December sixth. It's a Saturday at their house on Bainbridge. One o'clock."

"Well, thank you. That is interesting news. I'll write that down when I get to the house." He looked wistfully in the direction of his own driveway.

"Oh, no need Joshua. I have it all written down on this piece of paper for you." She handed a slip of paper to him through the window. He plucked it from her sausage-like fingers.

"Well, thanks again, Emma." She waved her hankie at him as he drove away.

"Shall we go to a wedding, son?"

"Paul is going to marry Mary?"

"It seems like that's the case. We'll need a wedding gift. Maybe Louise can help us with that."

"Will Louise be going with us?"

"It would be customary. She is my steady lady friend now."

"I miss Mom," Ritchey said quietly.

"I do too, son. But Mom is gone and we both have to get on with our lives." He paused and then continued, "Just like Paul is getting along with his."

Ritchey thought about the gun and uniform he had hidden away.

"Dad?"

"Yes, son?"

He remembered his secret pledge. "Nothing, Paul seems like a nice guy."

Coast Guard Station

Seattle

October 20, 1941

Early afternoon

"The report said a small piece of aluminum debris was spotted but not recovered. If it wasn't recovered how could you describe it as aircraft aluminum?"

The Coastie looked down at his fingernails for a moment. "If I say anything it'll go hard on the Skip'."

"Who needs to know? It's just you and me and Maggie here; goes no further. What's the scoop?"

"Ah, jeez, I knew this was a bad idea. You swear this goes no further?"

"Absolutely," Oscar pledged, "on my grandmother's grave."

"We brought the boat alongside a small piece of aluminum stuck on a rock. It didn't match anything we were told to be looking for so we threw it back. The Navy called off the search and we went back on routine patrol. Honest to God, we thought it was another one of their damn exercises. Excuse me Ma'am."

"Don't worry about it, sailor." Betty remarked.

"What did the piece look like?" Oscar asked.

"Well, it was about twelve inches by about eighteen inches, shaped kinda like a rectangle with the corners sanded off; about a sixteenth of an inch thick."

"Any marking or writing?"

"No. A few rivet holes along one edge, green primer on one side, shiny orange on the other. Funny thing about that orange paint though."

"Yes," Betty prompted.

"Well it looked fresh," he said looking at her. "You know, new like. Around the edges there was kinda greenish brown underneath."

"Anything else?" Oscar was wildly excited but was keeping his outward demeanor as controlled as he could.

"One other thing, it didn't look like crash debris usually looks. It looked more like explosion debris. It was bowed out in the center and the rivet holes were ovaled out like they'd been pulled apart. I didn't get a very long look at it but that was my first thought when saw I it."

"Can you show us where you found it?" Betty was indicating a navigation chart on the table.

"Yes, Ma'am; right here," he said, pointing with a pencil, "off Double Bluff Point on Whidbey Island."

"Could you take us there?" Oscar asked.

"Not without getting the Skip' in hot water, you promised."

"Let me worry about that. Nobody will get poached, really."

"Sure then, it's about an hour to get there. All we need is an okay from the Duty Officer to reassign a boat."

"I'll take care of that," Betty said. She walked out of the little conference room and crossed to the nearest officer she saw. "Who do I talk to about getting a boat?"

The Lieutenant looked her over then said, "Business...or pleasure?"

"Business, Mister, strictly business."

"Too bad, the pleasure would be all yours."

"Are all officers this ill-mannered, or are you a special case?" She handed him a card which identified her as a Special Assistant to the President. His eyes widened then he handed her back the card and saluted smartly.

"My apologies, Ma'am; I was out of line. How may I be of service?"

"We need a boat to go to, uh, Double Bluff Point."

"Whidbey Island, yes Ma'am. I'll have one alongside the pier in ten minutes, anything else?"

"Absolutely, this is a routine—I repeat—routine patrol. Do you understand clearly?"

"Routine patrol, yes Ma'am. I understand completely."

"This conversation never took place, dismissed."

The sailor saluted again, turned on his heels and began to set the wheels in motion to fulfill her request. *Damn, I hated to bust his chops like that! The pleasure would have been all mine!*

An hour later the boat slowed to a crawl maintaining only enough speed to maneuver and began circling the area. "What can you tell me about this area, son?" Oscar asked his reluctant informant.

"Not much. Very little pleasure craft activity. Big ships come real close to the land here. The shipping channel is fifty fathoms or so deep but it shallows out very fast and wake action can swamp small boats easily."

Oscar scratched his head and looked at the island. He looked at Betty and she shrugged. "Can you take us into any of these bays?"

"Partway into Mutiny Bay, it's low tide and there are mud flats; most of the way into Useless Bay."

"Let's go in there first." He pointed to the nearest one.

"Useless Bay, Skipper."

"Helm, come about to zero-eight-five," the Captain said. "Hug the inlet dead slow."

"Zero-eight-five, dead slow, aye Sir."

Betty walked back from the bow where she had been getting the freshest air possible. "What are you thinking?" she asked.

"Trying to imagine what all the pieces mean. Messages in the Pacific, messages from Seattle. By whom? To whom?"

"Let's examine the premise," she said. "A clandestine mission: Who are the suspects? Germany, Italy, Japan most likely. Who do we eliminate? The Germans are probably preoccupied with the Atlantic. The Italians? Please, they can't even get out of the Mediterranean. What's left, the Japanese? How? Submarine no doubt.

Three hundred feet of water would leave plenty of room to sneak in."

"I still can't figure the plane." Oscar was warming to the task. What are the possibilities? Aboard ship? Hardly likely. Stolen? Too obvious. Left for a pilot by an internal sympathizer? Too complicated. Why not just assign the task to whoever was delivering the plane in the first place?"

"It doesn't matter," she said.

He looked at her quizzically. "Why doesn't it matter?"

"You're too focused on solving the entire puzzle when you only need to solve part of it. Take a few things for granted. Imagine it was submarine carrying a plane. Where was the orange plane first sighted?"

"Astoria, Oregon."

"Flying east from over the open ocean. Next seen where?"

"Portland, then Yakima, then it disappeared."

"Did it? Orange aircraft aluminum debris found right here. Explosion reported the night before, nothing of interest discovered. It seems to me the most pertinent question is whether or not the pilot survived. Either way, the sub would likely be back in international waters by now."

"By God, Maggie, you're a genius! Now we just need to see if our mystery man made it out alive." Oscar kissed her on the lips. "Skipper, get us back to the dock, pronto if you please."

"Aye, Sir. Helm, head for home best speed, set an appropriate heading."

"Aye, Sir. Home it is." He gunned the engines and headed back to the Coast Guard dock at full speed.

Island Farms

Bainbridge Island
October 21, 1941

Life was suddenly in high gear on Island Farms. A dazed Paul and a radiant Mary were the center of an intense maelstrom of wedding planning. Paul had expected a quiet civil ceremony with close family. Mary, aided and abetted by Eleanor and Moriko, had other plans. By lunchtime yesterday the date had been set, and telephone lines were melting with the volume of calls.

Early December had been chosen because it had the least impact on the farm schedule, was far enough away from Christmas festivities, and there was at least an outside chance the weather might be fair, if cold. Little matter though; the barn would be the place in just under seven weeks.

Paul and Frank were working on the little Foreman's quarters, framing the walls and setting rafters. A hasty reworking of the floor plan had eliminated the tiny office, enlarging it slightly to become a bedroom instead. The office would occupy the room in the barn that Paul currently called home. Meals would still be in the main house for the most part so no provision beyond the small heating stove was made for a real kitchen. The tarpaper vapor barrier and sheathing along with three sash windows, vermiculite for insulation and a solid fir door sat in the barn, waiting their turn at installation.

Before that though, plumbing would have to be installed and wiring as well. Neighbors had promised to help with the lath and plaster and it was expected that if the weather held, the little love nest would be completed within a week.

Paul had other things on his mind as well. He needed to send to Salinas to request a certified copy of his birth certificate. He had never seen it and hoped desperately that it bore no information regarding his status as the son of a member of the Japanese Embassy delegation in San Francisco. That would cloud any citizenship claim he might make but nothing could be done about it. If it was bad news he might just ignore it. He might be able to get by with his newly minted Washington State Driver Certificate.

There seemed to be an endless stream of women coming to the homestead today. Every time he looked up another car would disgorge one, two or three women who would disappear into the house. Paul was sure the house would burst any second, yet it held firm.

Inside the women formed a beehive of activity around Mary, Moriko brought out her wedding kimono, which she had kept for so many years. Mary was enchanted at the sight.

"Oh Nana, it's beautiful!" She exclaimed.

"Do you like it?" Moriko asked.

"I love it!"

"Here is picture taken on my wedding day." Moriko held out a faded, sepia toned print. From the center of the picture Moriko looked like a priceless porcelain doll of exquisite beauty staring out at the ladies assembled.

"Where is Grandfather?" Mary asked.

"Silly girl, you know I was picture bride. Honorable Toshio-san was working in Hawaii on our wedding day."

Mary had a sudden insight into what it had really meant to be a 'picture bride' and had new warmth for the strength of her grandmother.

"Mary," Moriko continued, "if you like kimono you may wear for your wedding. It is old fashion now so you may not want."

"Nana, I would be honored to wear your dress. But I've never worn a real kimono. I have no idea how to put one on."

Several of the older women laughed at this. "Don't worry honey; there will be twenty women to help you dress, all of whom know exactly what to do." Eleanor said.

"Oh Mom, I'm the happiest girl in the world right now!"

"And I'm happy for you, my darling. Now let's concentrate on invitations."

Pacific Hotel

Seattle
October 21, 1941
9:15 a.m.

"How in the hell does anyone get anywhere up here?" Oscar asked in a clearly rhetorical flourish. He pushed aside the room service dishes with their breakfast remainders and turned the page of the *Seattle Post-Intelligencer*.

"Snorkel, sweetie," Betty called out from the bathroom.

Oscar snorted a laugh. "And rowboats. You ever see so damn many boats in your life?"

"Well, I did notice one or two in San Francisco. You have any luck yet?"

"I'm not sure, Miss Smarty Pants. It looks like there are a couple of ferries that run to the south end of the island but it's probably at least an hour drive just to get to the terminal. Some place called Mukilteo, probably Indian for 'twenty miles past the end of the line.'"

"We mustn't keep the government waiting, let's get going." Betty stepped from the pages of a magazine once again and earned a whistle.

"I can't believe my luck," Oscar said, "What a beautiful woman you are, and bright too, a real bonus."

"A bonus babe; great, just great!"

"No offense intended I assure you."

"None taken, you big lug; let's go."

Oscar picked up the phone by the bedside and gave instructions to the operator, then picked up his hat and headed out the door behind Betty.

It took nearly four hours to get to Whidbey Island. Allow time to get lost once or twice. Ooh and ah at the scenery. Wait at the terminal for the next ferry and then cross. They drove around the island speaking to just about everyone they met, casually inquiring about any newcomers. They had been at it for several hours and needed to head back to the terminal to await the last ferry back to civilization, which Oscar defined as any place with a hotel that had room service. Whidbey Island did not qualify.

"Oscar, let's stop here. I need to freshen up. Be a sweetie and buy me a Coke and a bag of peanuts, will you?"

He pulled in and parked the car. The sign read *Dick's Grocery and Dry Goods.*

When Betty returned to the car he handed her the soft drink.

"Let's make a beeline for the ferry. I got an earful from good ol' Dick there. He doesn't seem to care much for Japanese. Thinks there's going to be a war. I agree with him there, I just don't know when."

"That's great information if you've been living in a cave for two years," Betty replied. "Did he tell you anything actually useful?"

"I have a name; couple of names, actually. Our Cousin Billy is probably Paul Akagi and he moved to Bainbridge Island to work for a farmer named Sakai at some place called Island Farms. It's the family business."

"My, my, we have been busy, haven't we?"

"Just another day in the pay of the U.S.A," he retorted.

"They are definitely going to have to give you a raise."

The ride back to the dock and thence to the hotel took half the time as the morning since they had the lay of the land. Oscar's mood was jovial. Another puzzle solved. All that was left now was to turn over the information to the real FBI and let them round up the suspect.

In the hotel they dined on the best steaks and toasted with almost the best Champagne and danced for an hour before retiring to their room.

"What a fabulous day!" Oscar exulted. He tossed his hat and coat on the bed and flipped on the lights as Betty closed the door behind them. He embraced her, kissed her passionately and died, shot in the back twice.

Betty screamed as the lifeless body slid from her grasp onto the floor. She looked at the assailant in astonishment.

"Vinnie, what are you doing here?"

"Following orders, Betty, just like you."

"Well, Jesus, we better get out of here before the house dick shows up with the cops." She started to gather her purse.

"Sorry Betty, they punched your ticket too."

"Why, Vinnie?" she said desperately. "I'm doing good, I'm all the way inside with the code people. Why?"

"I don't know, honey. I really don't."

Betty didn't hear the gunshot that killed her. Vinnie methodically searched through both victims' pockets, leaving only that which identified them as George and Maggie French; on vacation and doing a little business buying fish. He took their money and scattered a few pieces of costume jewelry around, pulled out a couple of dresser drawers. Custom made to look like a senseless double murder after they caught a burglar in the act.

The killer checked the hallway then strolled casually to the elevator. "Lobby, please," he told the operator. Vinnie walked through the lobby, stopping outside to light a cigarette, drawing the puff deeply then tilting his head back to exhale. He got into the waiting cab and Angelo pulled away from the curb. He saw the police cars beginning to converge on the building.

Too bad about Betty, he thought. *I bet she was a great piece of tail.*

Special Code Room

Unspecified Building

San Francisco

November 17, 1941

"**Y**our best code man and his top assistant have been missing for a month?" The teeth-clenching tension in the disembodied voice on the phone made Ed wince inwardly.

"Well, no, not exactly. They were on assignment. I didn't really think much about it until I hadn't heard from them for a couple of weeks."

'Wild' Bill Donovan had been the Coordinator of Information for FDR exactly four months and six days and already had a comprehensive grasp of just how disjointed the intelligence community was and why the President was so frustrated.

"Okay," Donovan said tightly, "Your best agent and his top assistant have been missing for two weeks. Can you elucidate any further? I'll presume you've started a discreet inquiry so let's just skip ahead to the good parts, shall we? Do you have any idea what happened to your best field agent?"

"Actually," Ed groaned inwardly, "Oscar wasn't a trained field agent. Neither was Betty." He waited for the explosion.

"I see." Donovan said with preternatural calm. "You sent an untrained but brilliant code breaker and his secretary into the field on a wild goose chase to Seattle, haven't heard from either of them for a month, and only just now decided to inform your boss."

"No Sir, I called the Undersecretary two weeks ago and followed that with a memo. Your call is the first response I've gotten."

"I see. Stand by for a moment." Ed could hear something cover the mouthpiece and then an animated but muffled conversation began at the other end of the line.

Ed hadn't met Bill Donovan. In fact, he had only gotten a coded message from his boss, the Deputy Secretary of State, yesterday with a heads up about who this guy was and what his charter encompassed. 'Wild' Bill's bio had been an eye popper. Business bigwig, Medal of Honor recipient, candidate for Governor of New York and recommended to FDR by his close personal friend the Secretary of State.

According to the secret poop sheet Ed had, he had already brought the Office of Naval Intelligence and the War Department's G-2 operation into his portfolio. Now, obviously with the blessing of the Sec State, Ed was working for him too.

Scuttlebutt was that Congress had approved—at Roosevelt's insistence—a massive budget for the new department that required only Donovan's signature and created no audit trail. If this guy decided he needed a ski lodge in the Colorado Rockies to fight the war, all he need do was sign for it and building would start the same day. In other words, this guy had some serious horsepower.

Ed had been at State for twenty three years. He had worked his way into senior intelligence management from junior clerk mostly by learning how to sense which way the tide was flowing and always keeping his career pointed toward the flood tide.

"Okay," Donovan said, "I got it." That steely calm voice was unnerving as it snapped Ed's attention back to the moment. "Let's not quibble, tell me exactly what you know."

"Well, we run a pretty compartmentalized ship here. Agents are allowed to run their operations pretty independently, so all I can give you is general information. He didn't share specifics on this covert story." Ed was equivocating, but it couldn't be helped.

"We know the two of them took the train to Seattle. We know he was trying to pin down some leads regarding unusual communications from Japanese sources and possible reports of espionage. We have all the files he was looking at, and we have his notes, but so far we haven't broken them."

"You haven't broken his notes?" Donovan sounded incredulous.

"No, Sir, he was our most gifted code man and it was a private joke of his to keep his notes in his own personal code. It's infuriating, but it keeps everyone on their toes."

Donovan allowed a touch of exasperation to creep into his voice.

"Call in all the help you need from anywhere you need it. Break that code—soon."

Or it's my ass, Ed mentally filled in the unvoiced implication.

"Yes Sir, I'll get Krause from Princeton and Jacobs from MIT. They worked with Oscar, they might have some insight."

"I'll have the President call 'em; they'll be there in two days. Don't waste them," Wild Bill said evenly.

"No Sir, thank you sir."

The line went dead. Ed leaned back and realized he was shaking with tension. He took a deep breath and exhaled unevenly. *Sweet Mother of God* was all he could manage to mutter to himself.

Across the continent Bill Donovan placed the handset back in the cradle. What he hadn't—couldn't—tell Ed was that of the three obvious possibilities: One, that Oscar had been turned by the enemy; two, he'd been kidnapped; or three, he'd been killed. Information the freshly minted COI had seen suggested that the most likely scenario was the last one.

Island Farms

Bainbridge Island
December 6, 1941

Broken clouds and gentle breezes from the south greeted Mary as she looked out her bedroom window. Much better than yesterday's rain and last week's windstorms. She stretched and scratched her head trying to shake off the cobwebs. At first she didn't think she would ever get to sleep last night. Her excitement level was on overload. But finally weariness had overtaken her and she fell into a deep slumber.

This morning she could see Grandfather outside pointing here and there, Frank and Steven were finishing the last details in the barn where the reception would take place, and her betrothed was putting up some stakes and ropes to direct traffic and guests upon their arrival.

From downstairs she could smell the aroma of family dishes that would be served, along with the foods many friends and guests would bring. It would be a time of great feasting. Mary looked at the Big Ben alarm clock on her bedside table; nine-twenty-five.

Nine-twenty-five! Oh my gosh, I'm getting married in five hours! "Mom!" she yelled down the stairs, "I'm getting married in five hours!"

"Yes dear, I know." Eleanor smiled at Moriko. "You should probably take a bath now."

"Bath...yes, I'll be right down." She grabbed some clothes and raced down the stairs past her mother, grandmother and three other women already there to help, and into the bathroom, slamming the door behind her.

"She's an eager one," cackled one of the women in Japanese. She had lived here and been a friend to Moriko for more than twenty years but still spoke almost no English at all.

"You would be eager for one such as Paul too if you weren't such a wrinkled old prune like me!" Moriko retorted.

"Even a wrinkled old prune like me would like a ripe plum now and then." The woman made a vulgar gesture which collapsed all present into paroxysms of laughter.

In the yard the old Ford carrying Joshua and Ritchey wheezed to a stop and disgorged its riders. Joshua was wearing the only suit he owned. It was the suit he had worn to his own wedding. Ritchey had new dungarees, a long sleeved white shirt, and an uncomfortable looking necktie. His hair was slicked down with lanolin pomade. It was the first time he had ever been to a wedding and he had no idea what a groomsman was, or why he had been asked to be one.

"Hi Josh, Ritchey, it's great to see you again." Paul said. "Where's Louise?"

"Wouldn't miss it," Josh said. "She was previously committed, sorry."

"Me too, I was looking forward to meeting her. And look at Ritchey! I'll bet he even washed behind his ears." Paul folded back an ear for a cursory inspection.

"Aw Paul, don't do that," Ritchey grumbled pulling his head back.

"Sorry you couldn't sail over for this."

"Couldn't anyway," Ritchey said. "The boat got messed up in the last storm. It'll take a while to fix it."

"That's too bad; it was a good little boat."

"It still is a good boat," Ritchey said defensively. "It just needs some fixin'."

At that moment Benjamin emerged from the barn and spied his friend. Making a beeline for the little group he yelled, "Ritchey! Ritchey, over here! C'mon!" Ritchey dashed down the path to meet him.

"Don't you get dirty now!" His father called after him. "I mean it."

"Okay, Dad. I promise." He hollered back.

"Come and take a look at the barn. You won't believe it. I watched it, and I hardly believe it myself."

The two friends strolled down the pathway on the ten inches of sawdust hauled in to forestall a muddy quagmire from developing. Opening the small door they stepped into the old barn and were greeted with a blast-furnace-like wave of heated air. Two huge cast iron Franklin stoves were ominously glowing deep carmine from fires raging within.

"I guess Benjamin was a little over enthusiastic. His job was to stoke the stoves and keep it warm in here."

"Well he surely succeeded!"

"Toshio-san! Frank! Steve! Look who's here."

Three generations of Sakais came to greet the visitor.

"What do you think?" Frank asked.

"It's amazing! I mean really amazing." Joshua looked around in awe. Gone were the tools and implements of farming and in their place was a rustic Japanese courtyard. Colorful paper lanterns of all sizes and shapes hung at different heights from the ceiling. Chairs borrowed from probably every neighbor in a one mile radius were strategically place around the expanse. Paper scrolls wishing the newlyweds good luck in both Kanji and English festooned the walls. Toward the back, tables covered with freshly pressed cloths were lined up awaiting the bounty of food soon to come, and a mule stall had been converted into a beverage serving area. Toward the farthest reaches of the barn a small dance floor and bandstand had been hastily built.

Most amazing of all, however, was the central theme. Constructed in the middle of the outsized building was a miniature Japanese garden. At the core was a koi pond fashioned from an old oval galvanized watering trough. With floating plants and brightly colored fish it was completely disguised. Arching over the top was a miniature Japanese style footbridge, painted in the bright red lacquer so often favored for such things. Surrounding, and on differing levels and platforms, were dozens of bonsai. The tiny trees had been arranged to depict nature beautifully, and even dormant varieties like maples—sans leaves—were represented.

"Absolutely stunning, I'm speechless." Joshua said.

"Yeah, me too, Mary hasn't seen it yet. I hope she likes it."

"Paul there is no chance she won't like it. None."

"My friend from 'Mountain in the Clouds' Nursery brought almost every bonsai he owns." Toshio said with satisfaction. "Nobody will forget my granddaughter's wedding."

"Gonna have live music." Steven said. "I promised some friends of mine free food and ferry rides if they would play. They mostly play big band and jazz: 'The biggest sound from the smallest band in town'. That's how they bill themselves."

"Is there anything at all I can do to help?" Joshua asked.

"Absolutely," Frank said. "You're the best man. Get this guy out of here and make sure he gets to the church on time. Don't forget the ring. I have the paperwork for the minister."

"Can do, Frank. Okay Paul, time to say farewell for now."

They stepped from the barn into the chilled December air and headed for the new foreman's quarters Paul now occupied.

At the church, Mary had spent nearly two hours getting dressed in Moriko's kimono with the aid of several older ladies and the distraction of several friends who shared her ignorance of the sophisticated garb and traditions. Finally all the guests had been seated; the parents and grandparents of the bride were in place as were the groom, best man, groomsman and minister.

The minister nodded to the organist who began the treadle. The bellows-powered reed organ whispered to life and she began playing the processional march. As the bride came into view all that could arose as she made her way down the aisle.

Her radiance and beauty poured forth like incandescence from the golden sun. Upon seeing his granddaughter, Toshio's eyes welled with moisture threatening to cascade down his face. He clutched his beloved Moriko and whispered in her ear, "She is you!"

Paul had an audible intake of breath when he saw her. His knees weakened and sweat formed on his upper lip. *My gorgeous bride, how I love you.*

The ceremony went off without a hitch. The wedding party and invited guests streamed from the church and headed for the reception. Tables groaned with a multitude of dishes: Japanese, American, and of course, Hawaiian. The couple was feted, toasted, kissed, hugged, danced, greeted and congratulated to exhilarating exhaustion, and at eight o'clock retired to the Foreman's quarters for their first night as husband and wife.

Lying together on the bed, still in their wedding clothes, they held each other saying nothing, listening to the sounds of guests as they made their farewells to the Sakai family. A starter motor would grind, an engine would spring to life and depending on the skills of the driver, a transmission would be engaged smoothly or with a fearsome gnashing of gears. Finally the sounds of the last departure faded in the distance.

"I'm glad we waited." Mary whispered.

"So am I." Paul replied. Slowly, tenderly, the lovers undressed each other, taking time to savor each nuance of the other and finally consummating their love with unabashed ardor into the wee small hours.

The sound of rain on the roof and wind whistling through the barren trees outside awakened Paul. He looked lovingly at his new bride sleeping soundly, wrapped up tightly in a wad of blankets and sheets. He slipped out of bed and stuffed a few sticks of firewood in the stove, hoping they would catch from the banked coals of the previous evening. Paul padded across the bare floor into the bathroom where he relieved himself. *Indoor plumbing!* He thought. *What a luxury!* He slipped on shorts and Levi's and looked for his shoes and socks.

Looking at his clock he couldn't believe his eyes. *Eleven o'clock! Have we really slept that long?* He filled a teapot with water and placed it on the now blazing stove. He warmed his hands for a moment, then retrieved a shirt and put it on.

"Hey, sleepyhead, time to get up." Paul gently shook his bride.

"What time is it?" She looked up groggily.

"Eleven o'clock."

"Middle of the night, let's get some more sleep."

"Eleven o'clock; in the morning, it's the next day. We're married. You do remember who I am, don't you?

She propped herself up on one elbow surveying the scene.

"Sure I do. You're the guy that delivers the milk."

Paul laughed. "Tea is on in five minutes."

After sipping a little tea and consuming some of the food Joshua had insisted on stashing, the couple chatted for a while, made the bed, and thought about repeating last night's performance. Cooler heads prevailed, and about two p.m. they finally emerged from their cocoon and headed up the sawdust walk to the main house.

Mary climbed the stairs to the porch, holding Paul's hand as he fell in behind. She opened the door and they stepped inside. Immediately they sensed something was different: Bad, somehow.

Frank looked up from the table where everyone was seated his faced etched in anxiety and fear. "Come in, close the door behind you." He said.

"What's wrong?" Paul asked.

"The Japanese have bombed Pearl Harbor," Frank responded gravely. "It's war."

Part Three

"Silent enim leges inter arma"
Law stands mute in the midst of arms
Marcus Tullius Cicero

Fear isn't something measured or quantified. It creeps eerily up your spine making your hair stand on end for no apparent reason. Sometimes it constructs itself from accumulated misfortunes, unintended slights and misunderstandings. Small doubts arise and niggling fears fill the void. Little fears gnaw and burn and irritate and explode into wracking panic. Often it comes when an unexpected incident challenges the assumptions upon which single lives or entire societies are built. It may come in a blinding, disorienting, disruptive moment touching primal chords of basic instinct. The simple truth is when it comes it erupts from within the deepest, oldest, most primitive part of the human experience. Fear. Fear of loss of home and hearth and wealth and life and culture—visceral fear was what gripped the United States at this moment.

From grandest mansions to humblest ramshackle cabins an icy iron fist gripped the heart of the nation like it never had before. Even as the first wire reports of the sudden massive attack on the Pacific Fleet at Pearl Harbor were being relayed by radio announcers struggling to sound dispassionate and molten zinc coursed through Linotype machines to form up the newspaper flash editions, citizens reacted in whatever way their fear led them.

Along the West Coast resolute WWI veterans dusted off old Springfield rifles and Doughboy helmets to make their way out to the coastlines with binoculars. Impromptu committees formed to search for incoming enemy aircraft, ships and submarines. Citizens made runs on grocery and hardware stores buying both guns and butter and all the ammunition they could carry. Military leaders were besieged with requests for instructions on what to do and police and Coast Guard officials were swamped with hundreds of reports—all false—of enemy planes, ships and troops.

By the time the initial shock had worn off and the President had called for and received a war declaration from Congress, fear was being supplanted by a sense of determined outrage. Tens of thousands and more men began flooding military recruiting offices to sign up for service against this implacable and perfidious enemy. They sought to redeem the lives lost in Hawaii in a great effort to repel the repulsive. The ponderous machinery of government suddenly lurched out of lethargy and into motion as a provoked leviathan inexorably began to set a new course toward crushing the Yellow Menace. Here was an enemy it could see both across the Pacific and here at home; an enemy easy to recognize. The enemy at home and beyond the blue waters was Japanese.

Island Farms

Bainbridge Island, Washington
December 10, 1941

The days since the attack had been nerve-wracking for the Sakai family and the Japanese American community at large on their island and all along the West Coast of the United States. Like most Americans, they were incensed by the attacks. Steven wanted to charge down to the Navy recruiting office and sign up and Mary was discussing what she might do for the Red Cross. Paul, acutely aware of how precarious his position was as a spy without a country, kept his own council, carefully avoiding any but the most superficial discussion. Thomas and Frank had greater worries beyond the new war in the Pacific. Thomas had decided it was time to try to make some plans and had called his family together around the kitchen table.

"It is very worrisome," the old man began without preamble, "this new war with the homeland of our ancestors."

"It's not my homeland!" Steven blurted. "I was born right here in the good ol' U. S. of A! Right here on this farm, in fact."

"I was born in the U.S. too, son." Frank pointed out. "That's not the problem here."

"What is the problem, Dad?" Mary looked at her father then to Paul. Paul in turn detected significant glances between Moriko and Thomas. Concern was deeply etched in the weathered old faces.

"The question isn't whether or not we are American." Frank responded. "The question is do we look American?"

"What does that mean for crying out loud? We're all Americans! Gosh, I can barely speak Japanese." Mary said.

"White," Paul said.

"What do you mean, white?" Mary insisted.

"Right now in the U.S., an American is someone that doesn't look like you or me." Paul said softly. "That's what I mean."

Mary looked startled. She looked around the table at her family: Her grandparents holding one another's hands; her father standing behind her mother his hands on her shoulders. Steven was pacing like a caged lion, running his right hand through his hair in frustration. Paul sat next to her quietly.

"This is ridiculous." Steven declared. "I say to hell with the Emperor. Let's go kick Tojo's butt all the way back to Tokyo."

"That will undoubtedly happen," Thomas interjected. "But you will not be among those that do the kicking. I have lived among these Americans for fifty years. Many are kind folks and faithful friends like Joshua Pearson and his father and mother. But many tolerate us only so long as we keep to our place. We can harvest their food, clean their houses and mow their lawns if we keep to ourselves otherwise."

"My husband is right." Moriko spoke rarely about politics and racism. "I remember how bad it was in Hawaii and California, and here too when we first came."

"But why Grandmother? What could anyone possibly want to do against us? We just grow vegetables." Mary looked from one family member to another for an answer.

"Mary," her father said, "I'm already hearing about vandalism against Japanese businesses and threats against families. The FBI has arrested four fishermen right here on this island. Men I have known for years and who have no interest in anything but providing for their families. If this becomes a long war people might get hurt or even killed here at home just for looking Japanese."

"So what are we supposed to do?" Steven asked. "We can't go into hiding, Mary and I have midterms next week at U-Dub."

Eleanor concluded the conversation by saying, "We go about our business. Quietly without any fuss or calling attention to ourselves. We'll go to school, go to church, go to the store and the marketplace. We listen to the radio and read the newspapers and try to be invisible for now. Time will tell us what we must do." Paul and Mary left the main house and walked back toward their little home by the barn.

"What do you think will happen, Paul?" Mary asked.

"I expect there will be a lot more Japanese arrested. Questioned probably, maybe get cameras, guns and binoculars confiscated."

"Who would do that?"

"The government, FBI probably; maybe the Army or local cops."

"Whatever for?"

"Prevent espionage." Paul could well imagine how that would be a concern in high government circles right now.

"Well, I think everybody is worried about nothing; it's five thousand miles to Japan. I think the war will be over before it even gets started. We'll be fine."

"I hope you're right, honey." Paul replied, and he did hope so, but he also remembered the vast fleets of the Japanese Imperial Navy and the steady flow of military equipment streaming out of the homeland factories and knew in his guts that the sentiment was the triumph of hope over experience.

Western Defense Command U.S. Fourth Army
General John L. DeWitt, Commanding
Headquarters Company Command Office
Presidio of San Francisco, California
December 19, 1941

Like the placid eye of a hurricane John DeWitt sat daydreaming behind the desk in his office. Lying amid a clutter of papers covering its top were his wireframe glasses. Like his spectacles the General himself was wiry. His thin lips neither smiled nor frowned but simply cut a straight line across his ascetic face. Having begun his service in the U.S. Army as a fresh-faced eighteen year old Lieutenant in the Spanish-American War he had steadily risen in the ranks winning the French Legion of Honor for his service as a quartermaster during the Great War. He had been promoted to Quartermaster General of the Army then served another stint in the Philippines finally coming home to command the Army War College. His posting to the Presidio had come about three years ago and until December 7th he had been looking forward to retiring.

He had traveled the world with the army for more than forty years and seen many beautiful places but he especially liked San Francisco. Like a faceted jewel glittering atop the hills, the city was picturesque. In fact, but for the fog shrouding the Presidio, he could see Angel Island and Alcatraz through the office window from his desk. If he walked over to the window and looked a little more to the northwest he could see the recently opened Golden Gate Bridge. The General imagined he might be able to see the south tower today but probably not beyond. The veteran was shaken from his reverie by a crisp rap on the door. Wearily he rubbed the bridge of his nose then replaced his glasses on his face.

"Enter," he said.

"Excuse me, General," his Aide-de-camp said, "Washington on the line for you, Sir."

"Swell, thank you Major." DeWitt picked up the phone as his aide quietly closed the door behind him. "General DeWitt." he said into the receiver.

"John, George here. How are things out there?" George C. Marshall was the U.S. Army Chief of Staff, and DeWitt's commanding officer.

"They'd be a damn sight better if the Japs hadn't bombed Pearl," DeWitt retorted, then retreated. "Sorry, George, I'm a little cranky these days."

"Yeah, just about everybody's shorts are in a knot right now. Listen, I'm three thousand miles away from your situation but I can tell you the political heat coming in about the Japs out there is becoming intense. Frank Biddle at Justice is giving me nothing but grief about what I'm going to do about the them."

"I thought that was a Justice thing all the way." DeWitt felt a little defensive. "Hell what ever happened to Roosevelt giving alien investigation to the FBI?"

"Well," Marshall replied, "as you noticed things are a damn sight different than they were two weeks ago."

"True enough."

"Anyway, we're gonna need some recommendations about what to do out there and I'm counting on you to give us some clear ideas."

General DeWitt thought how instantaneous had been the collapse of the two distinguished careers of Kimmel and Stark in the wake of the disaster in the Pacific and absolutely did not want his career to end as ignominiously.

"I've been giving it a lot of thought lately, George. I have some ideas that I'll get out to you today. I can tell you this though; there is a lot of hubris floating around out here in the civilian population about the Japanese. It bears watching closely."

"Well, I'll look for your report. You're a good man, John. I've got confidence in you."

"Thanks, George." DeWitt hung up the phone then depressed a button on his intercom. "Major, can you come in here please." The officer entered the office. "I need you to take a letter. Secret or I'd have one of the sergeants handle it."

"Yes sir, go right ahead."

The old man began dictating, his aide struggling to keep up. The General waited patiently on a couple of occasions for him to catch up then concluded, "... that action be initiated at the earliest practicable date to collect all alien subjects fourteen years of age and over, of enemy nations and remove them to the Zone of the interior. You get all that?"

"Yes, Sir, I believe so," the officer replied.

"Fine, type that up—one carbon only—and bring it in for my signature. Top priority. And I don't need to remind you I don't want anyone reading over your shoulder do I?

"No, Sir, I understand completely."

"Fine then, dismissed. Oh and Ed," the General said less formally, "this is going to the Chief of Staff; try to keep the typos to a minimum for my sake." The aide cracked a wry smile, "I'll do my best, Sir."

"That's what I'm afraid of," DeWitt shot back with a smile of his own. When the officer had retreated to the outer office the General once again took off his glasses and rubbed the bridge of his nose. How in the hell am I going to defend the entire West Coast, he wondered.

Joshua Pearson Residence
Useless Bay, Whidbey Island, Washington
6:00p.m. December 19, 1941

"Ritchie! Get washed up for supper now.'

"Okay Miss Watson," Ritchie called back from outside. "I just have one more thing to do; it'll just take a minute."

"Well, the table is set and we're ready to say grace."

"Okay, I'm coming."

"I got a call from Frank Sakai today." Joshua said while they waited for Ritchie to join them. "He's worried about how all this is going to affect them."

"Well I shouldn't wonder," Louise replied. "I certainly hope you won't get involved."

"How do you mean?" Joshua asked.

"For heaven sake, Josh," she looked around as if someone might hear then half whispered, "They're Japanese! We just can't be involved with anyone like that now." Ritchie dashed in from washing his hands and sat in his customary place.

"Frank is my best friend in the world. We grew up playing together as kids." Joshua's voice was quiet but strained. "My son is named for him, his middle name anyway," he said indicating the new arrival. "Exactly what do you expect me to do, pretend he doesn't exist?"

"They are Japanese," Louise insisted firmly. "They are the enemy and we are at war. We can't be involved with them at all. What would people say?"

"Louise, I speak Japanese better than Frank. Ritchie speaks it better than Steven or Mary." Joshua deliberately poured a glass of milk from a tall pitcher giving him a moment to think before continuing. "The Sakais are my friends. What's more, except for Thomas and Moriko, they are all U.S. citizens and entitled to the rights of a citizen. Besides, I don't really care what people say."

"Well, you certainly can't expect me to embrace them with open arms," Louise said with finality.

"No," Joshua said with a weary sigh. "I suppose not. Let's have grace, Ritchie, it's your turn."

"Father, thank you for this food, thank you for our friends, and please watch over the soldiers. Amen."

"Thank you Ritchie." Joshua carved a chicken drumstick and placed it on his son's plate as Louise piled mashed potatoes and carrots on the other plates.

"I mean, good grief Joshua, I have a reputation to uphold. I'm a single woman in a small community. I work with people's children almost every day." She stuffed a bite of chicken in her mouth.

"Yes...a reputation..." Josh twirled his potatoes around with his fork.

She swallowed and continued, "We've got to do the right thing here." She concluded with implacable finality, "I'm glad we've settled that." Louise wiped daintily at the corner of her mouth then spread her napkin in her lap.

Thereafter supper was eaten in unusual silence. Dirty dishes were collected, washed, dried and placed in the cupboards. Louise retrieved her purse and wrap and Joshua fished around in his jeans for the key to the old truck.

"Say goodbye to Louise, Ritchie. She won't be coming back."

A look of astonishment fixed itself upon her face at hearing the words. Ritchie looked surprised as well.

"What do you mean by that?" She asked, clearly at a loss.

"Ritchie and I are a package deal Louise, and that includes our friends; all of our friends. I'm afraid there isn't going to be any we as long as you feel the way you do about the Sakai family. They're our friends and we're going to stick by them now more than ever. We are going to do the right thing"

"I see," she said as a single hot tear rolled down her flushed cheek. She refused to wipe it away. "Then I suppose you should take me home."

When they drove away in the darkness Ritchie stood on the porch for a moment watching the taillights recede. Absently he thought, *Darn, I kind of liked her. Oh well.* He turned and went back to work on his homework.

The ride back to Louise's rented cottage was made in stony silence. When Joshua pulled up outside she got out of the truck and strode to her door and walked inside without even looking back. Inside she collapsed into a tearful heap, one of the first and surely most unexpected victims of the stateside war of ideas that had just begun.

On the return ride the old Ford bounced along, its feeble headlights dimly illuminating a few feet of the road ahead. Joshua spent most of his time second-guessing and trying to imagine other ways to have gone about it, but by the time he rolled into the driveway of his little house he was sure his father would have approved.

Western Defense Command U.S. Fourth Army
General John L. DeWitt, Commanding

Headquarters Company Conference Room
Presidio of San Francisco, California
January 5, 1942

"Gentlemen, I thank you all for your contributions to this conference. It is most helpful that we are getting the cooperation and coordination required to address this problem." This problem, General DeWitt thought, is on the brink of spiraling out of control. "Please convey my appreciation to your colleagues at Justice and the Provost Marshal's Office. I'm particularly pleased that the Attorney General will entertain the Army's input on specific alien strategic military exclusion zones in this theatre of operations." *My ass! We should have had exclusive control without having to come hat-in-hand to Biddle for permission.* "In any event the Attorney General and the Provost Marshal's Office should have those recommendations within the week."

The conference broke up with attendees and functionaries gathering papers, congratulating one another in little cliques and the General striding back to his office trailing junior officers like litter whirling behind a speeding staff car.

Standing in his office he began issuing orders and majors and chicken Colonels began assigning the work to their lessers. "I want to make sure Biddle understands that we want all enemy aliens excluded from these zones. I don't think this system of passes is very practical but if we have to live with it for a while, so be it."

"General, there are going to be thousands of people who will be considered enemy aliens," his Chief of Staff observed. "Are you going to propose that they all be sent to holding facilities in the interior?"

"Damn right I am!" DeWitt retorted.

"What exactly is an enemy alien going to be?"

"Well, Justice will probably have to define that, but right now I imagine it will be any German, Italian or Japanese alien living in this theatre. It's not just them I worry about though. How in the hell can you tell which one is a loyal citizen and which is sending signals back to the homeland?"

It would turn out to be more than a rhetorical question.

"It is at night that faith in light is admirable"
Edmond Rostand

The darkness falling over the landscape wasn't a lack of light but an absence of vision. The cascade effects of the events of December 7th were beginning to careen out of control. Business relationships of years standing were broken. Friends and neighbors suddenly viewed each other with suspicion. Rumors flew, loyalties were questioned and worse. The innocent habits of decades, like writing home to friends and family took on a sinister sheen. Print media regurgitated untrue speculations and whipped up a frenzy of fear among the readers, egged on by every group that thought they had a score to settle. White supremacists, farm cooperatives—particularly in California—and fishermen, which felt threatened by the industrious Japanese before the war, took the opportunity delivered by Yamamoto to agitate and race bait against their competitors.

Some important newspapers were particularly incendiary, publishing jingoistic columns and calling on legislators and military leaders to imprison any and all persons of Japanese descent regardless of citizenship, age, gender or religion. Washington DC found itself in an impossible position; intensely pressured to 'do something serious about the Yellow Menace and fifth columns at home'. General DeWitt was against the notion of even attempting to incarcerate 120,000 people. Having spent most of his career as a quartermaster he had particular insight into the massive logistics involved in managing and supplying such a program in a time of war. He thought it was a better idea to leave ethnic Japanese in place, except in the immediate areas of military sensitivity, and let neighbors and local police keep a watchful eye. He certainly was no friend to the Japs and harbored his share of paternalistic racism, but he believed it illegal to so treat citizens—even Japanese ones. Enemy aliens were another matter. Enemy aliens, including German and Italian nationals should be sequestered for the duration and he said so in communications with superiors.

In the nation's capital the sweeping authority exercised by the Executive Branch was applauded on most fronts and new Administrations of This or That Wartime Military or Civilian Necessity began sprouting like mushrooms, nurtured in the dark humus of distant cannons.

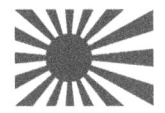

One evening Joshua heard a knock at the door of his little home while he and Ritchie were eating their supper. Two men in gray pinstriped suits introduced themselves and flashed badges: FBI men—asking lots of questions. They had information that Joshua and his son were known to speak Japanese, even had Japanese friends they had known for years. The local store owner reported a new Jap had been around for a few months then mysteriously disappeared. Did he know anything about that? A local schoolteacher had reportedly identified you as saying your best friend was a Jap: Any truth to that? Do you own any binoculars? We notice you can get a pretty clear view of the shipping lanes from nearby. Do you own a radio transmitter? How about a camera? You don't mind if we take a look around, do you? Weren't you born in Hawaii? Where did your father and mother spend most of their time as Church missionaries? Japan, wasn't it? Who owns that sailboat by that little dock down there?

Joshua finally had had enough when they started to question Ritchie and pulled the plug on any further interrogation when he resolutely insisted that without specific charges he was done answering questions and the G-men were politely—but firmly—sent packing. They promised to return with warrants but they never did.

Steven was running a few minutes behind when he got to U Dub, the ferry had a problem getting docked in choppy waters. When Steven walked into the classroom he expected everyone to be hard at work on the exams scheduled for the day but instead they all looked up nervously at him as he entered. No papers, not a single pencil in sight. Two men in suits were standing next to the Professor. One fidgeted with a broad brimmed black fedora he held in his hand, the other was studying a well-worn notebook he was carrying and looked up when Steven came in. Mr. Sakai, he presumed and Steven confirmed. Steven looked around, and noting the looks on his classmate's faces and the serious demeanor of his Prof wondered aloud what was going on. The two men flashed badges and identified themselves as FBI men. They had some questions to ask him, quite a few, in fact.

A navy staff car followed by a black Ford coupe *skuddered* to a stop just at the gate of the farm. The vehicles disgorged a Lieutenant in khakis under a raincoat, a seaman second class in a pea coat as his driver and two men in suits, wearing overcoats and fedoras. The navy man headed for the front door of the house. Two of the men headed for the barn and the staff driver waited by the car trying to keep warm as he smoked a cigarette.

In the house the officer had more than a few questions. In the barn the two men identified themselves and flashed badges. FBI men and they had a few questions for Frank and Paul, substantially more for Paul.

After half an hour or so the Lieutenant stuck his head out the door and called for the Seaman to come up. He had ransacked the house in a haphazard search and had some 'contraband' he was collecting. Thomas Sakai signed the receipt for his old box Brownie camera, two pair of binoculars, a radio transmitter that hadn't worked in several years, and two boxes of correspondence between him and his sister in Japan dating back nearly half a century. The naval men, leaving the dishevelment of the search for the family to clean up, retreated from the house back toward the car as Eleanor held Moriko in her arms and Thomas held Mary's hand watching them go. About the same time the two FBI men emerged from the barn flanking Paul and headed for the cars that had brought them. Frank followed closely behind and dashed up the stairs to his family. They were taking Paul in for closer interrogation. There seemed to be some questions about his citizenship that needed to be cleared up. Mary broke away from her grandfather's restraint and ran toward the cars, but it was too late. All she could see were retreating tail lights disappearing in the distance taking her new husband to places unknown.

FBI Field Office
Seattle, Washington
February 7, 1942

"So explain to me again how you ended up on Whidbey Island." Special Agent Sam Klein looked at his interrogation subject with infinite patience. His training with the FBI had taught him many techniques for questioning suspects, including some that weren't very polite, but it had been his experience that patient repetition was most effective. It was an extraordinary mind that could repeat the same lie time after time with just enough variation but without mistakes and discrepancies creeping into the recitations. With patience a good questioner would find cracks and drive a wedge of confrontation into them with vigor. Eventually even the most skillful liar tripped himself up; which is why he was inclined to believe what this man had to say.

Paul looked up, past the bright light in his eyes, trying to make out his accuser in the dim recesses of the claustrophobic, overly warm, windowless square room. Two oak chairs without arms, a small table upon which sat a bright lamp, a stenographer sequestered in a gloomy corner and his inquisitor were all the room offered in the way of clues.

"Is there even the remotest chance I will get back home before Valentine's? Has anyone told my wife where I am?" Paul was tired of playing this chess match.

"Maybe, and no," Klein replied. "Now tell me again how you ended up on Whidbey Island." Sam took off his jacket and neatly folded it over the back of the vacant chair revealing a muscular build on his five and a half foot frame. He loosened his necktie and ran his hand through his closely cropped blonde hair. Reaching into his shirt pocket he took out a pack of Chesterfields, pulling one out for himself, then offering one to Paul. Paul declined. Sam snapped open a Zippo lighter and struck the thumb wheel sparking a flame to life. He took a deep drag, held it in his lungs for a moment then exhaled. He leaned over the table into the light, placing his face within inches of Paul. His calm demeanor was showing just a hint of frustration and Paul looked right into his blue eyes and repeated his story one more time.

Special Agent Klein allowed himself a little sigh and straightened up. This Jap was either the best trained liar in all recorded history or he was telling the truth, but in either event nothing had turned up in his background check so far that would allow the FBI to continue to hold him, wartime rules or not. He was going to have to cut him loose.

Klein left the room and Paul relaxed in his chair then took the opportunity to stand and stretch for a moment. His technique, of course, besides maintaining the discipline to keep his mouth shut when he had made his statement, was not so much remembering the lies correctly—he had been telling them so long now they seemed more real than the truth anyway—it was never volunteering anything but the shortest answer, without elaboration. On that basis most of what he had told them was true in the strictest sense and therefore easy to remember. So far his most important ally had been the questions they were asking. The agent was asking the wrong questions, which revealed to Paul what they didn't know or even suspect at this time.

Sam Klein returned to the room after a few minutes and Paul prepared to take his seat once more.

"You're free to go home," the Fed said. "One of the agents will drive you back to the ferry dock. You'll be home in plenty of time for fish and rice."

"Rib steak and mashed spuds; that's Valentine's dinner at our house; maybe a Hershey's bar or two. I'm not much for raw fish and rice, personally," Paul replied.

"That's all for now Edith, thanks," the agent said to the shadowy figure in the corner. They waited as she gathered her pad and pencil and excused herself from the room. The agent turned the switch for the overhead light and switched off the lamp.

"Look," he said half apologetically, "this is nothing personal. I'm just doing my job. Everybody's scared as hell right now about your people."

"My people," Paul mused. "Klein, that's a German name isn't it?"

"Yeah, my grandfather came over to work in a brewery in Milwaukee around eighteen eighty," he replied.

"Well, it seems to me," Paul said, "that everybody's scared as hell right now about your people too." Paul grabbed his coat and brushed by the agent and out the door. The FBI man stood staring at the door for a moment then picked up the case file and headed back to his desk to trade it for another.

Western Defense Command U.S. Fourth Army
General John L. DeWitt, Commanding
Headquarters Company Command Office
Presidio of San Francisco, California
February, 1942

This was definitely not going the way the General had envisioned it. It had taken weeks, not days, to define the military exclusion zones. The Provost Marshal and Justice wanted one set of boundaries; the Navy wanted different parameters extending essentially everywhere within a hundred miles of any navigable West Coast waters, fresh or salt. Worse than that was the intense pressure being applied by politicians for a wholesale evacuation of anyone with a Japanese surname or even physical appearance.

Racial hysteria had run high since Pearl but now it was dangerously close to collapsing into vigilante mob violence. Incidents and threats increased daily. Banners and signs hung from business of Korean and Chinese ownership declaring 'We Are Not Japanese'. Senators, Congressmen, Governors and Mayors, each with increasingly shrill constituents filling their ears and offices and flooding their mailrooms with voiced denunciations and barely veiled threats of violence toward any Japanese, were clamoring for action.

The Governor of Idaho, for example, made a special point of declaring he would fight any effort to voluntarily relocate any Japs in his state. If they came, he insisted, they would come as 'detainees' confined to a reservation of some sort, under military guard. Idaho would do its part in the war effort if necessary but by

God the damn yellow menace would have to go elsewhere after the war.

General DeWitt sat behind his desk staring at the information in front of him. They included reports from the coordinated task forces that had been conducting raids and interrogations of alien citizens of belligerent nations, memoranda reporting ship-to-shore radio communications thought to be directed to enemy submarines lurking in the coastal waters of the North American Pacific. Not to mention transcripts of phone conversations with dozens of military, elected, and industrialist types. These and more littered his desk as did coded cables from General Headquarters in Washington.

Even police reports from cities up and down the coast were represented. Everything he looked at pointed in a single direction he did not wish to go. In his mind he rationalized it was for their own protection. Without some way to remove them to safe locations even local agencies with unclouded judgement and pure motives—a rarity to be sure—could not guarantee their safety.

He reviewed the agreed upon exclusion zones and the registration reports. Too many people to be left in place: Too many people to be moved away. The logistics facing this problem were a nightmare, not the least of which was the breakneck timetable for implementation.

The General took his glasses off and tossed them on the desk, closed his eyes and rubbing the bridge of his nose leaned back in his chair. For a long while he stared aimlessly at the ceiling fan taking notice of dusty spider webs collecting on the motionless blades. Finally he sat upright and picked up his glasses once again. He removed a white cotton handkerchief from his hip pocket, misted the lenses with his breath and carefully cleaned them before putting them back on his face.

He shuffled the papers on his desk looking for one in particular, Executive Order 9066. He read it again and noted Roosevelt's signature on his copy. Opening his desk drawer he removed a file folder and took out its contents. He read this document over as well, very carefully. The old soldier was cornered. The worst possible solution to this problem was the only one left to him. He took a fountain pen from the pencil drawer of his desk and dipped it in the inkwell sitting to the right of his telephone. With the stroke of that pen he signed the enabling orders which would set in motion the forced evacuation and internment of 120,000 Americans of Japanese ancestry. Two-thirds were U.S. citizens.

Bainbridge Bellwether
Editorial Office
Bainbridge Island, Washington
March 19, 1942

"Captain, tell me this is some kind of mistake or sick joke." Harold Painter was the publisher, editor, reporter, typesetter, salesman, printer, delivery boy and janitor of the only reliably published newspaper on the island. He printed on Friday and then spent Saturday with his wife distributing copies to subscribers: All four hundred twenty one of them. He sent a few to the school and had a few more for sale in the grocery near the old Anderson Dock store building. By virtue of the nature of his enterprise, his gregarious good humor and door-to-door delivery he knew virtually everyone living on the island and counted most as friends and neighbors. If his hair hadn't already been snowy white what he was currently reading would certainly have turned it so.

"No sir, it isn't. It comes straight from General DeWitt." The officer thought it best to keep his own counsel regarding the chaos that was surrounding this dress rehearsal and the internal turf wars being waged between new and old agencies. The principal upshot of those battles seemed, to him at least, more about passing the buck than solving the problem. But he was only a Captain and those problems were well above his pay grade.

"My God, most of the people affected by this are just farmers and fishermen! They aren't any more of a threat than my dog Sally." Hearing her name the dog opened one eye to look at her master and tentatively thumped the floor with her tail a couple of times. Seeing nothing of interest she closed her eye and went back to sleep on her blanket in the corner under the type drawer.

"That, Sir, is not my problem. I'm just here to ask you to run this on the front page of your next edition. I'm just following orders."

"Hmmph! Following orders has been used to cover a multitude of sins, son and I think this is one of them." The old editor finished reading the document. "I suppose that if I refuse, the War Department will probably wallpaper the whole damn island with posters, won't they?

"I imagine they will do that in any event, sir," the Captain said.

"Yes, that would be the Army way. Well, alright then, I'll publish it. On the front page right beside my editorial excoriating those who created it and reminding every single reader that these are all people we have known and trusted for years. I may print the Constitution on the front page as well."

"Thank you sir, print whatever you like next to it," the Captain added. "It's a free country."

"Not today it isn't," the newspaperman retorted angrily to the back of the retreating khaki uniform. "No sir, not today it isn't!"

Island Farms
Bainbridge Island, Washington
March 24, 1942

Frank was reading the notice for the third time trying to comprehend the meaning. It wasn't that the words were unusually difficult, it was just that they were so unbelievable.

"What does this mean for the farm?" Eleanor asked her husband.

"I guess it means we have six days to arrange our affairs and leave voluntarily to some 'approved' location before we involuntarily get shipped out to...well, somewhere else."

"Where are they sending us?"

"According to this we are going to..." Frank scanned the document in his hands, "...here it is. Quote; on March 30, 1942, all such persons—that's us—who have not removed themselves from Bainbridge Island in accordance with Paragraph 1 hereof shall, in accordance with instructions of the Commanding General, Northwest Sector, report to the Civil Control Office referred to above on Bainbridge Island for evacuation in such manner and to such place or places as shall then be prescribed. End quote."

"But that doesn't tell us anything at all," his wife protested.

"No it doesn't. Not where, not what we can take, not what the weather might be, not anything useful at all. Just show up at the dock to be shipped out to oblivion. It also doesn't explain how we are supposed to be able to relocate voluntarily when the government has frozen all our bank accounts." His voice strained with bitterness. "I was ten years old when I came here with my mother and father. My whole life we have worked this farm to make a living for the family and now the government is just going to yank us right off our property and send us away. It just isn't right to treat citizens this way."

Outside the house they heard the sound of the truck rolling down the driveway and skidding to a stop. The door of the truck slammed and almost immediately the front door of the house flew open and Steven stormed inside wild with frustration and anger.

"There are armed military guards at Eagle Dock! Nobody Japanese can leave the island without a permit," Steven raged. "A *responsible* member of the family has to go down and register at Anderson's and fill out a bunch of paperwork about where you're going, why you're going there and when you're coming back." The young man paced the floor like a caged animal seeking some civilized manner in which to vent his pent-up emotions. "Armed guards! Like I was gonna try to sink a damn battleship by ramming it with the pickup!"

"That's not the worst of it," his father said, "read this." Frank handed his son the copy of the exclusion order. "I guess it's a good thing Dad doesn't trust banks all that much," he concluded.

As Steven was reading the document Thomas came into the house.

"I've been talking to Bill Tanaka and Fred Yamura," he began without preamble. "They don't think it's legal if you're a U.S. citizen."

"Hmmph!" Steven grumped. He looked up from the pages in his hand, "they oughta try to get on or off this island right now."

"What do you mean?" Thomas asked his grandson.

"The army has posted guards at the ferry. No Japanese comes or goes without a permit." Steven raged.

"Hmmmm, this is very bad business. How can we get planting seeds if we can't get off the island?"

"Dad," Frank said, "I don't think you understand. We can't get to any money we have in the bank and in six days we have to be gone somewhere or they are going to remove us by force."

"Yes, my son. I know that. But we will need seed for the planting season."

"Dad..."

"Frank, listen to me. I have arranged to lease the land to Warren Farms. We have enough cash to provide the seed. They plant, harvest and sell the crop and we split the proceeds."

"Warren Farms? Jim can barely keep his own ground planted, how is he going to take care of ours too?" Frank was mystified.

"He says he will hire Filipinos. We probably know most of them anyway from working for us. He thinks there will be lots of government contracts for food and that lots of people will want to work to win the war. He seems pretty sure he can do this. Besides, what choice do we have in only six days?" Frank opened his mouth to reply when the telephone rang. Eleanor got up and answered it then held it out gesturing to her husband. He got up and took the phone.

"Hello. Oh, hi. Uh-huh...Uh-huh...Okay, well that's mighty generous of you. You're sure it won't be an inconvenience...okay then. Well, I guess I'll see you day after tomorrow then. Okay, bye." He hung up the phone carefully in the ebony Bakelite cradle, walked back to his seat and sat down. "That was Josh Pearson. He's coming over in a couple of days to learn how to watch after the farm and the buildings. He's insisting that he be the caretaker while we're gone."

Steven looked up from his reading, anger etched on his face. Frank sat with Eleanor in a sort of stunned torpor and Thomas stood looking out his favorite window at the fields arrayed before him, unable to cry, unwilling to give up.

Bainbridge Island

Puget Sound, Washington State

March 26, 1942

The old black Ford pickup trundled off the ferry at Eagle dock and pulled into a parking spot next to Anderson's. Joshua got out and looked around. Military guards lounged nearby, carbines slung casually over their shoulders. A couple of trucks and a staff car were parked nearby. Japanese men formed a line disappearing into a building. Joshua recognized some of them as friends and neighbors of the Sakais and nodded an acknowledgement when a couple of them made eye contact.

Making his way into the little store Josh politely shouldered aside a gaggle of men in animated discussion in the doorway. He made his way to the counter and handed his list to the clerk.

"What's with the hen session?" He inquired in an offhand manner, indicating the ongoing discussion group.

"Don't know, don't care; 'taint none a my business." The clerk began collecting the items on Josh's list.

"I don't recognize anybody in that bunch," Josh mused.

"I don't reckon I recognize you so much either," the clerk countered in a clearly irritated voice.

"I'm sorry, where are my manners? Joshua...Joshua Pearson. I'm a friend of the Sakai family." Josh thought he detected a flash of warmth from the clerk but it faded quickly. The man behind the counter stacked Josh's small order in front of him.

"That'll be one dollar and nineteen cents," he said rather loudly, then sotto voce he said, "I you're a real friend of Frank's you'll hotfoot it out to his place and help beat back this new breed of vultures nesting on the island." He nodded slightly toward the group near the door. Josh looked at him quizzically. "You'll catch on quick enough, now git." The counterman handed him his change and box of groceries and turned back to survey the remaining inventory till the next customer came forward.

Back in the truck Joshua and Ritchie sat for a few minutes watching the line of Japanese creep forward. The men entering the building looked worried and animated. The men leaving looked stunned with resignation.

"C'mon, Dad, let's go, I'm hungry," Ritchie complained.

Joshua shook off his morbid fascination with the unfolding spectacle, started the truck and headed off in the direction of Island Farms. Even Ritchie had noticed an unusual number of incoming passengers on the ferry and as Pearson drove the short distance towards the farm it began to become clear what the clerk had meant by his comment. Pickups and flatbeds seemed to be everywhere piled high with household furnishings, appliances, beds, radios and clothing. One old vehicle even had a few ornamental plants obviously just dug from the wet spring soil and crammed in amongst the other items. As he turned into the driveway at Island Farms he could see an animated discussion ongoing between Frank and someone he didn't recognize. He braked the truck to a halt and as he and Ritchie got out he gave the groceries to his son with instructions to take them to the house. He would be along soon. As he walked toward his friend he could hear the conversation.

"That is not the arrangement you made with my father, Jim," Frank said. "I expect you to honor your word."

"Well, it seems to me you're not in much of a position to be driving any hard bargains right now," the man retorted.

"We've lived here for over thirty years, Jim. I'm not just going to hand you the keys to the tractor without a fight."

"I shouldn't think so," Joshua said, interjecting himself into the conversation.

"Who are you?" Jim asked, annoyed at the interruption.

"Jim Warren, this is my best friend Joshua Pearson," Frank said. "Josh, Jim Warren, Warren Farms. He wants to change the agreement he made with dad."

"Now Frank, you know nothing was in writing about this. Your dad just misunderstood what I was offering, that's all."

"Thomas Sakai agreed to allow you to work the farms, sell the crops and split the profits after expenses. He shook your hand, Jim." Frank said firmly.

"Thomas agreed to allow us to work the farm," Jim countered emphatically, "do the maintenance and sell the crops. If there was any money left over I would send enough to cover the property taxes to wherever you want. That's what we shook on. The rest of this mess is just your bad luck. I'm sorry for it, but that's the way it is."

"Seems to me," Josh pointed out, "that there is a difference of opinion with regard to the terms and you're just being an opportunist..."

"Now see here..." Warren began sputtering in protest.

"...and as you noted, Jim," Josh continued, "there is no paperwork to document the agreement so therefore no obligation exists on either side. I suggest you pack up and go back home. I'm offering a better deal."

Jim looked at the resolute face of Frank and the congenial expression but steely eyes of Josh and shrugged his shoulders.

"Suit yourself, Sakai. It won't matter in a year or two. I'll buy it at tax auction for a song anyway." Perfunctory goodbyes were grunted and the old farmer stomped his way back to his truck and roared off down the road.

"What was that all about?" Joshua asked.

"That was all about panic. Come on down to the house for lunch and I'll let you know what's going on. I could use a bite to eat anyway." The two old friends headed down the path toward the house comfortable in the silence of the walk.

"Ritchie and Benjamin, you wash your hands before you come to the table. Wouldn't hurt you to wash your faces either," Eleanor said.

Frank kissed his wife on the cheek she presented and Joshua did likewise.

"Are you wearing a new perfume?" Josh asked.

"Stop teasing me, you know perfectly well that it's eau de mustard from making sandwiches!" Eleanor smiled.

"Positively bewitching," Josh took his seat at the table and looked around at the faces of his friends. Frank sat next to Eleanor on his left, Thomas at the head of the table. Moriko, Steven and Mary sat opposite, with Paul at the other end to his right. Benjamin and Ritchie had gathered up plates ready to sit on the front porch with their lunches when grace was finished.

"Let us return thanks," Thomas said. All present bowed their heads and the old man continued, "Bless the Lord, oh my soul and forget not all his benefits; having food and raiment let us therewith be content." Amens were murmured and the boys headed for the porch, glasses of milk sloshing precariously on plates as they opened the door.

"I haven't heard that prayer since Dad passed," Josh said pensively.

"I have recently been thinking about your father," Thomas said. "It was a favorite of his. I think I first heard him use it in Hawaii. It seems so long ago."

"It was a long time ago you sentimental old fool." Everyone saw the smile on Moriko's face and the twinkle in her eyes. "You were such an earnest young man, how could I help loving you?"

Thomas reached over and patted his wife's hand, his eyes clouding up with tears. "And you are still so beautiful." His voice trailed off.

"Well," Frank finally said breaking up the intimate moment, "What do you hear from the outside world, Josh?"

"Most of the discussion about this problem seems to revolve around Roosevelt's constitutional authority under the war powers as the Commander-In-Chief. There is a fierce debate about whether or not this 'relocation' order is legal but no debate about whether or not it will actually happen." Josh paused to take a bite out the huge sandwich on his plate.

"You think they're actually going to move all of us to some secret location?" Steven asked.

"Mmmmph huh," Josh swallowed, "no doubt at all. Someone will surely mount a legal challenge, but they'll have to do it from wherever they end up."

"What about our things? What about our farm?" Mary asked. "Are they keeping families together?"

"I talked to the military commander yesterday," Frank interrupted. "He said families would be kept together as much as possible but they might separate men and women for a little while till they sort things out. They gave me list of what to pack, and an even longer list of what they considered contraband that we couldn't take."

"Like what?" Steven wanted to know.

"Weapons, radios, cameras, binoculars; mostly what they've confiscated from everybody already, even flashlights." Frank replied to his son.

"There are people coming over on the ferries, I saw them at Anderson's. They're hitting every Japanese family on the island according to the clerk." Josh said. "Is it all stuff like that Warren guy?" He directed his question toward his best friend.

"Yeah, that and worse, pretty much. Most of our neighbors have been great but the others are all over, offering pennies on the dollar for cars and appliances. A lot of Japanese here don't speak much English and are getting fleeced but good. Most of our friends can't get their money out of the banks so they're selling out, taking almost anything so long as they get paid in cash," Frank sighed. "What I don't understand is how the government expects us to close up all our business affairs—without any money—get packed, say goodbye and tend to all the last minute chores with only six days' notice. I'll tell you Josh, if you weren't here Jim Warren would be right. I would have had to take his offer, however bad."

"You might still have to," Josh reminded him. "Remember, I've never run a farm before. I have no idea where to start or what to do."

"That's where I come in." Everyone turned at the sound of Paul's voice. "The last couple of days I've been writing down a list of what needs to be done. It's sort of a schoolbook. It's got schedules and suppliers, buyers and a list of what assets the farm has and where they are."

Mary looked at her husband in surprise. She had seen him working on equipment and repairs every day and had no idea where he found the time for such a project.

"I couldn't sleep," he said sheepishly, acknowledging her questioning look. He reached back to the sideboard behind him and picked up the college theme book he had used for his project. It was left over, unused from Mary's college classes. He handed it to Frank.

"You might want to check this over and make sure I haven't forgotten anything," he said.

Lunch continued as Frank thumbed through the impromptu discourse on his family farm. When he finished he closed the notebook and handed it to Josh.

"With this book you could run the farm if you didn't know the difference between a radish and a rutabaga." He looked at Paul with genuine admiration; "better than I could have done, without a doubt."

Once again Paul's childhood experience of being dragged up and down the farm fields of the West Coast was unexpectedly paying dividends. He could scarcely believe that less than a year before he had been a badly injured, highly trained pilot and spy for the Imperial Japanese Navy who had narrowly missed death when his submarine sank. For a brief moment he thought of his shipmates lost in fifty fathoms of water not twenty miles from where he sat eating his sandwich. It's a rich irony, he thought, not a solitary soul knows what I was or what I was doing, but I'm going to end up in a concentration camp anyway. What a strange world this is.

The ladies began clearing away the dishes. Mary went out to the porch and retrieved the abandoned dishes left behind by the boys.

"You better go find out what kind of mischief those kids are getting into," she said to Paul. "I'd hate to see them get hurt."

"Come on, Josh," Frank said. "We have a lot to teach you and not much time to do it. We still have to get you a power of attorney too. There is supposed to be a liaison from some government department to help us with this stuff."

"Well, if the line at the dock is any indication we better plan on two or three hours in line before they tell us we we're in the wrong line. Ladies, Thomas-san, if you will excuse me I have to learn how to run a farm. Don't wait up, this might take a while." Joshua and the other two men headed out the door and towards the barn, presumably to find the boys and thence to the temporary government offices to get whatever bureaucratic paperwork was required in the works.

"I got a call from Stan yesterday," Eleanor said to Moriko and Mary. "He said the Army is going to send Leta and the baby along with us. He was heartbroken. I could hear it in his voice. He said that living in Bremerton was 'not an option for Japs, even if they are married to a white'."

"What do they expect him to do, just abandon his family?" Mary asked.

"You know how it's been for them. This is just more of the same, only with the approval of Uncle Sam," Eleanor replied.

"To endure the unendurable is real endurance," Moriko said repeating an ancient proverb she had known since childhood.

"Endurance yes," Mary replied, "enjoyment no."

"These are difficult times my family," Thomas said. "We will all bear hardships but let us be thankful for friends. My old friend Ambrose," Thomas mumbled, looking heavenward, "you have a son to be proud of." The women nodded respectfully as the old man got to his feet and shuffled over to his favorite rocker by the window. He stared out at the steel-gray sky for a few minutes then fell fast asleep for his afternoon nap.

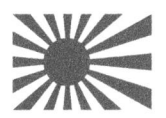

"Can you keep a secret?" Ritchie asked his friend. Benjamin nodded solemnly while crossing his heart with his right forefinger.

"Paul is a spy for the Japs, a real live spy, with a gun and a uniform and everything!" Ritchie poured out the whole story as viewed from his now sixteen year old perspective while his wide-eyed friend listened with rapt attention, occasionally glancing around conspiratorially.

"You're foolin' me," Ben finally concluded. "My sister didn't marry a spy. Besides what is there to spy on here? This is just an old farm."

"He's not a spy right now, of course. But he was, I mean before he married Mary. But now everybody is talking about the war and how bad the Japs and the Krauts and the Wops are and now I don't know what to do," Ritchie said.

"It's confusing, isn't it?"

Startled by the voice the two boys turned to find Paul leaning in the doorway of the old shed where they had sequestered themselves.

"I thought you said you could keep a secret." Paul looked at Ritchie sternly and he hoped just a little menacingly as well. "Who else knows our little secret?"

"Nobody Paul, honest, just me and Benjamin."

"Benjamin and me," Paul corrected. "It seems hard to know who to trust, doesn't it?"

"It sure does," Ritchie affirmed. "Dad quit goin' out with Miss Watson cuz he's friends with Benjamin's dad and old man Frost won't hardly speak to us down at the store anymore. He looks mad all the time."

"Are you a real spy, Paul?" Benjamin blurted, "With a uniform and a gun?"

This is a damn ticklish situation here Paul old buddy, he thought. *I can't screw this one up or the whole ball of yarn will come unraveled.* He took a deep breath, stepped into the room and sat on a bale of straw.

"I was," he confessed, "until Ritchie here found me in his boat. But I'm not anymore. My mission was a failure so I quit."

"But didn't you want to go home?" Benjamin asked.

"I am home, Ben," Paul answered honestly. "I was born in California. I've only been to Japan twice. I had to take lessons to learn better Japanese. That was an embarrassment to my father and grandfather."

"My teacher says Japs are the enemy now and it's our patriotic duty to hate them," the youngest Pearson recited.

"Do you hate Benjamin, or Mary, or me?" Paul asked.

"No, of course not."

"Why not? We're all Japanese."

"Naw, you aren't Japanese. You just look like them."

If only the world could see with the eyes of a child, Paul thought.

"Well, in a few days everyone on this island that looks like Benjamin or me or Mary is being sent..." he paused as he realized he didn't actually know where they were all going, "...somewhere else. Away from our homes and our land and our other friends, like you and your father. It will probably be very different from here and we won't be able to leave when we want, or have visitors."

"Like going to jail?" Benjamin asked.

"Probably very much like that," Paul said.

Ben's eyes got wide and welled with tears as an expression of fear came over his face. He looked at his friend and blinked then looked back at Paul.

"I don't wanna to go to jail, I didn't do nothin'! Can't we just tell them we didn't do nothin'? Dad doesn't even know where Pearl Harbor is. He said so." His distress was palpable. "I can't see Ritchie again? Or you or dad or mom?"

"You won't see Ritchie again for a long time, Ben. But you'll be with your family. This is why it is so important to keep this little secret between just the three of us. Other people might not understand that I quit and they would take me somewhere else. I wouldn't be around to help your sister or watch over you when your dad or mom has to go to a meeting or something."

"You would be in bad trouble, huh Paul." Ritchie said.

"The worst," Paul replied. He thought this might be the decisive moment so he continued: "I could get shot if you told anyone. If you told your dads..." he looked both boys in the eyes in turn, "...and anyone found out they knew and didn't say anything they could get shot too, by a firing squad."

"But won't they shoot us if they find out?" Benjamin quaked.

"They can't, you're too young. They couldn't even put you in jail."

"I'm already going to jail, you just said so!" Ben retorted.

"We're going to a different kind of jail, I think." Paul eyed his young conspirators once again. "Well, what do you say? Is this our secret?"

Ritchie looked at Benjamin who returned the stare.

"I don't hate you, Ben, our secret."

"I don't hate you either, Ritchie, our secret."

"Okay then," Paul said. He fished around his pockets and found a safety pin. *This is perfect. I want it to hurt just enough to be remembered.* "Hold out your hands." The boys each held out a hand. Paul grabbed Ritchie's and jabbed the point into his index finger, then did the same with Benjamin and himself before they could protest further.

"Now each of us puts our fingers together," he said, "and swears to be blood brothers in all things forever, especially secrets."

The three fingers came together and the blood flowed across racial and generational lines as each solemnly promised to be true to the other no matter the consequences. The ceremony completed, Paul stood up and dusted off his trousers and put the pin back in his pocket.

"Okay then, there is lots to do around here in the next couple of days so let's get going and look like we're getting some chores done before your dads get back."

The boys looked chastened and serious as they left. He knew that wouldn't last very long. He desperately hoped his secret would.

Bainbridge Island
Puget Sound, Washington State
March 30, 1942

Buck sergeant Jimmy Joe Jackson had joined the army six years ago mostly to escape the Great Depression. He stood six foot five inches tall and the raw-boned Texan had a drawl deeper than the cleft in his chin. His wide shoulders contrasted with a narrow face and a shock of short red hair was visible under his uniform cap. Surprisingly his fellow NCOs called him 'Triple Jay' rather than the obvious 'Tex' or 'Red', and that had naturally evolved to TJ over time.

Standing at the entrance to the ferry traffic lanes TJ wondered at the spectacle unfolding before him. A line of deuce-and-a-half trucks led a forlorn parade of private vehicles and Japanese pedestrians headed toward the *Kehelokan* ferry. Their path was flanked on both sides by white folks. Many seemed to be there to wish friends goodbye, some were crying, some seemed angry at no one in particular and a very few showed smug satisfaction as their countenance.

As a young man in Texas, TJ had seen a few niggers lynched. A dozen or so whites wearing sheets would shove some darky up on the back of a mule, throw a rope over a tree limb and tie it off, then loop a coil or two 'round his neck. He'd be screamin' real scared like, that he hadn't done nothin', hadn't hurt nobody when some guy, sometimes TJ's own daddy, would yell back at the hapless prisoner 'It don't matter none, boy, you'z black as blazes and that's good enough reason.' The owner would whack the beast out from under him and victim would swing back and forth and jerk with little strangling sounds comin' out his mouth. Eventually he'd be dead and most everybody would wander away just leavin' the poor bastard there to hang. It made TJ a little uncomfortable, just leavin' him there like that. Didn't seem proper but it was just the way things was. His daddy had always said that you couldn't let them niggers get uppity; had to keep 'em in their place. TJ understood, of course. Niggers and Spics was inferior to whites; not suited to much else 'cept farm labor or maybe domestics. He hadn't ever seen a Jap in the flesh until a week ago but it seemed like as not they was like the rest. No moral character either, sneakin' in on Pearl Harbor like they had. All the same his momma had always told him to be kindly to the lesser races as they couldn't help bein' what they was.

Like so many things in the Army his principal occupation this morning seemed to be to stand around. His .30 caliber carbine complete with bayonet was slung over his shoulder and he stood or rather shuffled from foot to foot surveying the scene. Some General in San Francisco had decided all the Japs had to be rounded up, so a flurry of activity had been ongoing for a week. Which is how he; a Texas country boy through and through, had ended up here in a company comprised almost entirely of city swells from New Jersey, more or less in the relatively calm eye of a cyclone of politics and paranoia.

The column slowly ground to a halt on the landing and Japanese clambered off the trucks. The younger more nimble aided the elderly and the children and the private vehicles disgorged their passengers and began unloading baggage.

It kinda reminded TJ of the Okies that had flooded into his home town while he was just a kid in the Dust Bowl days. Old vehicles piled high with boxes, children perched precariously on top. Some folks dressed in their Sunday go to meetin' clothes, others in dungarees and plaid shirts. Women here and there wearing fur trimmed coats and once fashionable hats with long plumes that looked like pheasant tail feathers.

Jimmy Joe had seen this sort of thing before: Folks milling about aimlessly waiting for someone to be in charge. Finally a Major started spouting off, as officers were wont to do and a line began to form beside the jumble of disparate drayage.

The brass leaf droned on to the assembled group about making sure everyone was wearing their family number and had written same on each article of baggage making the trip. For TJ the trick with officers was to look like you were paying attention as they flapped their jaws while picking out what really meant something. This was mostly just jaw-flapping so he ignored most of the speech.

With his military eye he surveyed the crowd gathered on either side of the approach. Now that the lines had begun to form, the white folks had started to separate themselves from the passengers leaving them to form a desultory parade of sorts leading to the water's edge. His Captain's instructions had been to the point this morning. He and his fellow soldiers were here to make sure things went smoothly. Everybody gets aboard the ferry safely, the whites don't create any disturbances and for God's sake, don't shoot anybody.

As the line moved forward onto the ferry TJ and the other soldiers began collapsing along the rear and flanks creating an orderly retreat. It was oddly quiet, a man struggling with baggage finally got help from a tight-jawed soldier instructed to keep the line moving. A dog held by a young white boy strained at his leash and barked at one of the retreating families, a small Japanese boy waved goodbye wistfully and shouted back a farewell to the boy and the animal.

Finally it was done. All the baggage and bodies were on the ferry. TJ stationed himself near the railing in the stern as the ferry crew buttoned up the boat and the Master eased the vessel away from the dock for the short ride across Puget Sound to Seattle. Here and there a few people still waved to friends left behind on shore but he could see that most everyone was headed back to wherever they had come from and within minutes it was impossible to see any people. He was amazed though at how many of the Japanese continued to stare at the island as it receded into a green blur of trees and rocks.

Less than an hour later the ferry eased up to Coleman dock and the shore crew secured lines and opened the gates. No vehicles were coming off so the Japanese families began streaming off dragging what they could carry. The scene was surreal. A special train, guarded by more stern armed soldiers, was sitting on a siding, the tired old engine hissing steam periodically and all the windows on the Pullman cars covered or painted over. Overhead, on an elevated walkway, idle spectators had gathered to watch. Some were mostly silent, others jeered and heckled shouting out racial slurs as the modest group worked its way toward the train. Military men checked family numbers against seat assignments and pointed either forward or backward to indicate which car a particular group was to occupy. A reporter or two; a photographer or two and some government functionaries, looking desperately for some function to perform, milled about. An old Japanese man in traditional clothing sat erect but disconsolate on a large wooden crate marked "Family 49".

When it became clear that the families would not be able to load all the materiel themselves some of the soldiers leaned their weapons against the train and helped heave things into the freight cars then they would retrieve their guns and go back to their posts.

For Thomas, the patriarch of the Sakai family it was a bitter moment. Here he was, along with all his family, being loaded onto a train in the shadow of the market where his family had sold vegetables and fruit for three generations. Soon it would carry them to an unknown place for an unspecified time. So very long he had worked for the little piece of land he and Moriko called home; so swiftly it had all seemed to disappear.

For Frank, Paul and Steven the moment was no less bitter, but for different reasons and because there was so much to do in these last frantic minutes they wouldn't begin to reflect on their situation till after the train got underway.

Moriko, Eleanor and Mary were moving up and down the train looking up old friends, not really sure if they would see them again but constantly interrupted by soldiers trying to herd them onto their cars so the train could leave. The ladies finally gave up in frustration, found Leta and the baby, corralled Benjamin and got on the train.

Ambrose Sakai and his wife Maryanne had boarded several cars ahead. Ambrose had chosen not to work in the family farming business and had become a radio repairman. His was the only repair shop on Bainbridge so when all his equipment had been confiscated by the FBI it became a hardship not just for his family but for everyone on the island, Japanese and white alike.

Most heart-wrenching of all had been the goodbyes between Stan and his family; Thomas' youngest daughter Leta and their three children. Here was a hulk of a man, accustomed to long hours of hard work in poor circumstances—hardened in so many ways by life—inconsolable as his wife and kids were literally torn from his arms and marched aboard the ferry at Eagle Dock. It had been bad enough since Pearl putting up with the innuendos and downright scorn directed toward them but this was unbearably worse.

Inside the train chaos reigned. Soldiers with clipboards speaking no Japanese desperately trying to communicate with the elderly who spoke no English found that children were suddenly in great demand as interpreters.

"Little girl," one Corporal asked. "Can you tell these folks they are in the wrong car?"

"My name is April," the child announced. "April Sakamoto."

"Well now, April is a pretty name; pretty month too. My name is Corporal Vincenti, can you help me out here?" He tucked the clipboard under his left arm and extended his right hand into which Miss Sakamoto's tiny hand disappeared as they shook.

"Where should they be?" April asked.

"Three cars forward, that way." The army man pointed toward the front of the train.

Miss Sakamoto turned to the elderly couple and spoke with great deference to the smiling gentleman. She listened to his response politely, bowing when he was finished then turned back to the soldier.

"Mr. Mutsui says he and his wife were given the paper by the man with the golden leaves on his uniform that showed which car to board and this is it."

"Does he still have the paper with him?" April turned to ask the question while the Corporal thought *just great, now the Major is giving out seat assignments.*

The old man, after rummaging around in a raincoat with too many pockets, finally produced a three by five file card which had typed in the upper right hand corner of the horizontal aspect 'Mitsui car 6'. Scrawled in vertical aspect was a big grease pencil 6. It seemed plain enough to Vincenti until April looked at the card.

435

"May I show you?" She asked. The army man handed the little girl the card and she turned it in her hand. "The older folks who don't read English read Japanese this way. She indicated top to bottom and when held in that manner the card clearly indicated a nine. "And this is Mr. Mutsui who lives over the barber shop, Mr. Mitsui lives by the old sawmill."

Just then the steam whistle sounded twice and car doors closed with soldiers stationed at each one. *Just another Army fubar,* the Corporal thought.

"Miss Sakamoto you've been very helpful." The soldier handed the card back to the man. "If you could do me one more favor and ask them to please take a seat, the train will be leaving soon."

Once again the girl turned to the old gentlemen and conveyed the message. The couple smiled broadly, bowing to the soldier then the little girl. Then the old man spoke to April before sitting.

"Corporal Vincenti," April said without any hint of an accent, "Mr. Mutsui and his wife were wondering when lunch was going to be served."

Vincenti stood there for a moment at a total loss for words until the little girl stepped in between the soldier and the old man.

"They are very old people, sir. It has been a very long time since they had their breakfast and they don't understand this. They don't know we are going to jail."

This stood Vincenti straight up as the simple honesty of this child, enemy or not, touched something deep within him. "Thank you again, April," he said quietly. "You can tell them I will personally see to it that they get their supper right away."

The noise of the steam pistons of the engine filled the air and the clank of the cars ahead being pulled taut shuddered down the train and slowly this Special, the first of hundreds to follow, began chuffing on its somber journey. Fifteen minutes later Corporal Lorenz Vincenti presented Mr. Mutsui and his wife with the promised lunch...swiped from the Major's mess.

"What's with the windows?" Steven was leaning against a seat as he stood in the aisle. The train was lurching forward and the tempo of the rhythmic click-clack of steel wheels rolling over section joints was steadily increasing. "We can't see a damn thing."

"Steven, you mind your mouth," his mother warned.

"One of the guards said it was to keep us from seeing where we're going," Frank replied.

"That's stupid, Dad. We're on the train, it's moving at a relatively high rate of speed and there are soldiers with guns to keep us on board." Steven's frustration level had been very high the last few days and it was getting harder for him to maintain his civility. "What can they possibly expect; that children and old women will overwhelm them and force the train to head for Japan? This is just ridiculous."

"I don't think that's the real reason Frank," Paul said to his friend. "I think they don't want anyone outside to see inside the train. Wherever we're going we're probably considered dangerous cargo to the government."

"I'm scared." Mary had finally given voice to what everyone was thinking.

"So am I," Paul admitted. "Everyone is scared."

"I am not scared," Moriko declared flatly. "I spent years living in a shack next to a railroad track in the sugar fields. Wherever they are taking us, it can't be any worse than that." She patted Thomas' hand and he smiled at her distantly.

"Grandmama, tell us the story of how you and Grandfather met." Mary had heard the story a dozen times a dozen but it still gave her a sense of warmth to hear the old voice tell it, and a reassurance that everything would be alright.

"Well now, that is a very long story," Moriko began.

"Looks like we'll have plenty of time for it," Steven said with more than a little sarcasm. His father and Paul both shot him a 'that will be enough of that tone' look and Steve understood immediately. He calmed down and said softly, "Go ahead Gram, I like that story."

As she spoke, before the train had even cleared the Seattle city limits, little penknives, secreted in ladies hats and men's pant cuffs had been retrieved and tiny holes began to appear in the paint on the windows. Most of the windows had been painted on the inside due to a ladder shortage so even fingernails would do to scrape off a little paint. Black eyes peered out at the landscape as it slipped by. By nightfall all the familiar landmarks had been left far behind and ahead lay only undiscovered country.

Seattle Police Department
Pioneer Square Precinct
Seattle, Washington
March 30, 1942

Something just didn't add up. Two victims—white male shot twice in the back—the other a white female and a real looker, shot once in the heart. No powder marks on either decedent so probably shot from six feet away or more; no evidence of a struggle; no apparent motive other than a rifled room, wallet and purse: Looked at first blush like an interrupted burglary but things just weren't lining up that way. No matter how long he looked at the photos and read the reports it just didn't make sense.

"Lieutenant, Cap'n wants to see you."

"Thanks Sarge, tell 'em I'll be right there." He looked up briefly with a disarming smile on this face at the uniformed cop in his office doorway.

"He said now, Howie, I think he means it and he's got company."

"Company?"

"Yeah, some college type in pinstripes. Diapered ass lawyer maybe."

Howard sighed inwardly as he rose from his chair. If there was a picture somewhere of the quintessential pencil pusher, his Captains mug would be at the center. He followed the Sergeant out through the bullpen winding through the maze of desks and file drawers.

The Sergeant stopped to answer one of the phones ringing incessantly as the detective continued toward the office of his boss through a thick haze of yellow-grey cigarette smoke hanging at about eye level. Here and there suspects sat in hardwood chairs their heads hung down. Next to each occupied chair there was a desk, at which a cop sat typing a report, usually one finger at a time. The dregs: Rapists, killers, thieves, hookers, drunks; life's losers, this was where they all eventually landed. *This is a miserable stinkin' job,* Howard thought.

"What's cookin' Boss?"

"Hey, Howie, come on in, close the door behind you."

The Lieutenant looked around the familiar office. The requisite number of citations was displayed on the wall, a calendar, files, books and a few personal photos on the desk and wall. A flag hung limply in the corner of the room. It, like everything else, was covered with a yellow veneer of nicotine. There was also a young man in a black suit with a thin grey pinstripe standing quietly in another corner.

"Sit down, Howie." The Captain indicated a chair. The detective sat wondering what the hell was going on.

"Should we close the blinds, Agent?" The Captain asked the young man.

"Can anyone hear us?" The young man asked.

"Probably not," Howard offered. "It's noisy in the bullpen and half the time you can't hear the guy sitting right next to you." The Boss nodded his agreement.

"Then let's not, that might just draw extra attention."

"Listen Cap, what's all the dark shadows stuff here?"

"Are you still working that double murder at the hotel? Late October I think," the Captain asked, deflecting the question.

"Yeah, but I'm not very hopeful."

"May I ask why not?" It was the agent.

Howie made a quick survey. The guy was maybe five-ten, about a hundred sixty-five pounds, sandy hair, blue eyes. Well dressed, well groomed, inquisitive and running the show in his Captain's office. Not a lawyer. An agent the Captain had called him, probably

Bureau; a G-man. Howie glanced at his superior and got a nod of approval.

"Well, I learned a long time ago that when the facts don't seem to fit the crime you either need a new crime or different set of facts. So far the facts don't fit the crime. By the way, who exactly are you?"

"I'm sorry, Eldon; Harvard Eldon. I'm with the Bureau."

"Howard Seabourne," Howie extended his right hand. "I guessed you were a Fed." Howard couldn't resist, "Harvard?"

"My Dad's alma mater, friends call me El. You were saying," he prompted.

"Yeah, well things don't add up. It looks like double homicide during an interrupted burglary but the facts don't fit. First, we haven't been able to I.D. the bodies yet."

"No I.D. after five months?" The Special Agent sounded incredulous.

"Not one that I believe. The information at the crime scene identified them as husband and wife. Papers they were carrying indicated they owned a small fish company and were here on a buying trip."

"What's unusual about that?" The Captain asked.

"Nothing if the fish company existed and anyone had ever heard of it, or them."

"Where was this fish company supposed to be located?" The Fed asked.

"San Francisco. I called the Frisco P.D. for leads," Howie noted with a little satisfaction the wince from Harvard after the word Frisco. *They don't like that down there*, he thought, *they're all hoity-toity and want it called the 'City'*. "When they called me back they said they couldn't find anything on the people or the business."

"I remember that now," the Captain said. "Didn't we send you down there on the case to look around for yourself?"

"Yep; turned up nothing; well, almost nothing. One Chinese guy recognized a picture of the guy but didn't know his name and didn't know the girl."

"Was this Chinese working at a restaurant in Chinatown?" El asked.

"Yes as a matter of fact. Hey, you got something that'll help me?" Howie was beginning to smell a rat, or maybe a bad beat coming that he couldn't do anything about.

"Not sure yet, what else do you have?"

"I figured maybe it was an affair. You know, checked in under a false name for a few days of whoopee then off on their separate ways; seemed plausible."

"Didn't pan out?" The Fed wondered aloud.

"Nobody was reported missing. I checked with almost every department on the Coast but no hit on either victim. It's like they didn't exist. And the fish story stinks too. Who goes from one major west coast seaport to another to buy fish? Seattle doesn't have fish that San Francisco doesn't catch too. One other thing; the clothes on the guy were expensive, from a big San Francisco men's store...Ross Brothers I think."

"Roos Brothers," El corrected.

"Yeah, that's it. Well I figured with the positive hit on the photo and the clothes he had to be from somewhere in the Bay Area, but I'm damned if I could ever make a connection. The dame was wearing clothes from Paris. I couldn't make anything on that angle."

"City of Paris, Detective?" Howie nodded. "It's a department store—an expensive department store—in the City. You got anything else stuck in your craw?" Eldon was apparently on a fishing expedition of his own.

"A couple of things bothered me," Howie confessed. "First no sign of any forced entry or a struggle. I mean, it figures to me that if the guy and the dame come back from a night on the town—lots of witnesses to that—and walk in on a burglar, they would both get it from the front and the bodies would be near one another. Not so. Second, nobody sees anybody in a hurry to go anywhere. Elevator man takes one well-dressed guy down to the lobby between the time of the shooting and the time people in the next room call the front desk."

"What happened to him?" The Captain asked.

"After he got off the elevator nobody knows. He just disappears."

"Did the elevator man give a description?" Harvard again.

"Yeah; big tipper, medium height, medium build, medium complexion, brown suit, brown Fedora, brown shoes, Italian accent he thought; Mr. Almost Everybody."

"What about registration?" the G-man asked. "Was the elevator guy registered at the hotel?"

"Nope, everybody registered was accounted for and none were identified by the elevator operator as the man he had taken down from the 6th floor. And before you ask, everyone with reservations for the previous night, that night and the next, showed up. None met the description of the Elevator Man."

"Italian accent, hmmm." He mused a moment then Harvard turned to the Boss, "I've heard enough, Captain. Howard, I'm going to need all of your files on this case. Photos, autopsy reports, ballistics, field notes, physical evidence, basically everything written down, collected or photographed since you started the investigation."

"Hey, wait a minute. This is my case, if you've got something you give it to me—not the other way around."

"Not this time, Howard. This is a national security matter now. I need those files so I can get going."

"Captain?" Howard looked helplessly at the pencil pusher who was his boss.

"Out of my hands Howie, orders from topside."

"Anybody ever call you 'El Federale´?" Howard asked as he arose.

"No, not really," Harvard replied.

Island Farms

Bainbridge Island, Washington
March 30, 1942

Josh and Ritchie had watched the ferry carrying their friends away until it was just a dot lost in the clutter of the Seattle waterfront then walked slowly back to the Island Farms pickup.

"How long are they going to be gone, Dad?" Ritchie asked on the short ride back.

"I don't know, son, but probably until the war is over. That may be several years." The two lapsed into silence and remained that way until the truck had been parked and they had gone into the house to try to imagine settling in for a long haul.

Joshua wandered around the house trying to come to grips with what was happening. Every room was slightly disarranged; clothes left in a heap on a bed—considered then rejected—utensils sitting out that couldn't go because it put them over the weight limit or was on the excluded list. The breakfast dishes were dry in the rack next to the sink waiting to be put up. It had the eerie quality of a house expecting its occupants to return and resume their lives at any moment; it gave him the heebie-jeebies.

He shook off the feeling then began to tidy up. It was uncomfortably personal handling intimate apparel and putting away makeup. It reminded him of his wife. Unexpectedly all the pain of her loss suddenly crashed against him like waves driven by a Pacific storm. It was overwhelming and for several minutes he just stood there captured in the past, haunted by the present.

Finally Joshua choked back his feelings, putting them in the dark place in his soul he rarely visited and went back to the business at hand. He made the beds with clean linens and set out the laundry to be washed later. He imagined that everything would need washing at least every couple of months so he started making a mental checklist of how he and his son would see to that chore. It helped him impersonalize the process if he could reduce it to just another chore.

As he went about that business in Frank and Eleanor's room he pulled a dresser drawer out too far and it crashed to the floor. Upside down in a heap he could see a large envelope taped to the bottom, something clearly intended to be hidden. Joshua peeled the envelope from its hiding place and removed the contents. It was a photo, taken less than two years ago at the beach. Pictured were Joshua's father, son and himself along with the entire Sakai clan. Paul had taken the picture of all these smiling and happy Americans celebrating the Fourth of July.

Clearly, Frank had hidden this photo to protect Joshua but hadn't the heart to simply destroy it. Joshua stared at the smiling faces until they were blurred by his emotions.

Stan and Leta's Residence
Bremerton, Washington
March 30, 1942

Glass shards crunched under his shoes as Stan walked through his little home. Every window in every room; every mirror; every plate, cup, saucer and dish were smashed to the floor. All the clothing was cut or rendered useless; every piece of furniture broken; every photo destroyed. Splashed crudely on most walls in red paint were the words 'Jap lover'. The giant of a man bent over retrieving a few pieces of photos he thought he could maybe patch together. He found an earring his wife favored and—incongruously spared from destruction—a teddy bear baby Sarah loved. Each of these items he placed in a box retrieved from his car. When he had carefully gathered what he felt was most important from the wreckage he took the box back to his trunk.

In the small building that ostensibly served as a garage, he nearly vomited when he went inside. Hanging from a thin twine was the family cat; strangled, with its viscera trailing ghoulishly from the abdomen. A piece of paper with the sentiment 'this is what happens to Jap lovers' was attached.

Stan stared at the devastation then took a can of coal oil and methodically poured it, first in the garage, then throughout the house starting at the back door and working forward making sure every room had a good dousing. At the front door he deliberately wiped his hands on a rag which he then set alight and tossed into the house. At a distance he watched, detached from any emotion, as flames consumed the little home. Thick black smoke and little bits of flying embers carried away the love and joy that had been his life here and replaced it with emptiness. He watched as the flames grew high knowing that on this evening, in this place, the fire department would not arrive to save the house.

When the home was reduced to smoldering ruins and the darkness and cold damp air began to set a chill, he got in his car and drove toward the only place he could think to go. It was time to go home to the farm.

My God, my God, why hast thou forsaken me? Why art thou so far from helping me, and from the words of my roaring?
Psalm 22, Ch. 1
Holy Bible

The initial shock had worn off, the ignorant excitement of the children had abated and the butt numbing ride clacking across switch points and rail section joints overwhelmed even the bad food and inadequate facilities. The passengers were prohibited from changing cars for the trip and the windows couldn't be opened. Over the course of two days without showers and plenty of wiped baby bottoms mixed with the motion sickness of the first day the cumulative stench was pretty bad without quite bringing tears to one's eyes.

Thomas Sakai had been in almost a dreamlike state for most of the trip. Although no one could tell from looking at him, he was reliving life in the hold of an old whaler he shipped aboard over half a century ago.

Frank had tended to his family to the point of distraction, Steven had spent most of the time peering through a small peephole at the countryside rolling by, periodically reporting what he saw to no one in particular. Paul tried to ignore the malodorous similarities to a cramped submarine and find a comfortable spot but randomly jumped to his feet and paced the length of the Pullman; his frustration and anxiety palpable to any who bothered to observe. Thus most of the men did what men do best; they chafed, kept mostly to themselves and when they did talk they spoke of superficial things. Would the Giants beat dem bums da Dodgers and would anyone ever beat the Yankees again? A few, deeply enmeshed in the politics of the day, passed the time in earnest debate about the legality of it all and the differences between the demands of the Constitution and the realities of a shooting war. Heated rhetoric would rise to the level of red faces and shouting, then it would subside to sullen silence when a guard took special note.

The women had done what women often do in situations like this. They talked about their feelings among themselves and the other ladies in the car. They talked about what the weather had been like in Seattle; they wondered where they were going and what the weather would be like wherever there turned out to be. They talked about how bad the food was and how cute the guards were and how much they all wanted a bath and a clean towel. And a place to lie down and stretch out; a real bed and real privacy once again. They talked about anything that wasn't connected to the new circumstances.

What almost everyone did was talk about how long they might be held in this camp so far away from their homes and what would happen to all the belongings left behind. With the windows mostly blacked out it became slightly disorienting to many, losing track of day and night a little; old habits disrupted and the occasional glare of sunlight when a guard opened & closed a door. Periodically the old train would pull sluggishly onto a siding to let another train pass and occasionally it stopped for a few minutes to take on water and coal or an hour for passengers to debark for a hastily cobbled together soup line on a siding but mostly it just rolled slowly on.

The guards had been instructed not to fraternize with the passengers, but as the second day dawned on the rails some of that formality was gone. A small piece of chocolate appeared for a favored child; a friendly conversation transpired between a soldier and a pretty young high school girl and even the Major relaxed some allowing a couple of windows in each car to be opened—from the top—while the train was traversing countryside away from the prying eyes of the public. By now the eternal constant of the clacking rails seemed to be the only past anyone could remember and the only future anyone could imagine. Then it stopped.

Lone Pine station consisted of a hastily constructed wooden platform, a small depot building and an assembly area of sorts—an unpaved parking lot really—with buses and trucks standing by. The passengers began coming off the train, squinting out at the bright sunshine that filled the cloudless sky and stretching out muscles aching from three days aboard a cramped train. Children scampered about relishing this sudden freedom chased by mothers and older girls. The doors of the freight cars slid open and local guards herded the men coming off the train right back to the open baggage cars. Cargo began pouring out as the passengers and a few Japanese men who had volunteered to come to the site early and help build facilities swarmed over the drayage.

Almost instantaneously a huge pile of personal paraphernalia comprised of hastily packed suitcases, wooden boxes with names stenciled on the sides, duffel bags and even a few pillow cases tied with twine and trailing labels jumbled itself onto the platform. Guards then directed passengers fresh from the train to climb aboard and cram the waiting buses. Not to worry, they reassured; all the baggage will come along in the trucks in a few minutes. Just move forward onto the buses. Now aboard the even more confining buses and still with no real idea of the destination or how long this leg of the journey might be, the dispirited group commiserated collectively as their misery quotient rose another notch.

Finally the pastiche caravan of heavily laden vehicles hastily pressed into service by the Western Defense Command began rolling out of the station. To the weary passengers it seemed as if the drivers of the straight-axle buses made a special effort to find every bone-jarring rut and pothole in the road. Those riders in the lead vehicle could see a little of the barren countryside as they rolled out toward US Highway 395; to those following behind, the countryside remained shrouded in mystery as they were engulfed by great clouds of dust billowing from the vehicle ahead. Presently the road surface changed and there was a merciful relief from train sections clacking and potholes as a ribbon of asphalt stretched into the distance. Barely ten minutes later the passengers were disgorged from their conveyances and stood milling about, unsmiling guards carrying carbines with bayonets at the ready, stationed around them.

"Welcome to the Owens Valley Reception Center." A man standing on a makeshift little platform said loudly. Everyone turned toward the sound of the voice. "This is the intake area. All of you will register here and receive your apartment assignments. I recognize this is not an ideal situation but we will try to process everyone as quickly as possible. Please gather your family groups together and line up at the tables here behind me so we can get going."

A familiarity with the process led to lines forming quickly and families gathered themselves together searching for the shortest line. As things inched forward Frank Sakai and Paul Akagi assumed the role of family leaders. Moriko clung to Thomas who had affixed his stare to the right sleeve of one of the clerks as it dragged across the forms scratching out names and information. *Sakai Toshio is my name* he thought as he moved as an automaton with his children and grandchildren.

Steven surveyed the area. To his left stood a new building shaped in an ell, just now getting a coat of white paint with a small makeshift sign attached describing it as the administration building. There were fences beyond with barbed wire enclosing a large area in which construction workers sawed and hammered away, building what could only be described as tarpaper shacks in the size and shape of barracks. At each corner of the enclosure stood a sixty foot tower; Searchlights on the topmost platform were manned with more serious-looking guards. Each was armed with carbines, and patrolled a narrow walkway surrounding a guard shack just below.

To the west loomed the knife-edged granite mountains he would later learn was the Sierra Nevada range soaring rapidly upward from the valley floor. Clearly these were young mountains in geologic terms while to the east the older, lower, rounded mountains rose less impressively to form the White-Inyo range. He guessed the floor of the valley was maybe ten or twelve miles wide and ran roughly north-south as far as he could see. Like many weary travelers before him, Steven was a poor judge of distance in the desert; the distance between the ranges being more on the order of forty miles.

As families were being processed and given quarters assignments the trucks with the baggage rolled in through the open gates stopping just inside. Unceremoniously the suitcases and parcels were dumped in a jumbled heap on the ground and the trucks rumbled away.

"Okay everybody, we're in Block 5, Barracks 4, apartments one and three," Frank announced. "Let's try to find our stuff and get going. One of the guards said it's straight up this street toward the mountains."

Paul and Mary began searching through the belongings strewn about by families ahead of them, Steven and his mother searched also. Benjamin stayed with his grandparents helping Leta with the children as she struggled to manage the three.

"Hey," Steven called out, "here's Grams suitcase, and Mary's too!"

"I've got a couple here," Paul said.

Eventually all they were looking for was found and divided up among the able bodied and the march began toward their new home. Block 5 turned out to be two thirds of a mile straight as an arrow up a road that had only been graded a week before. It had been, and still was, highly traveled by supply trucks carrying building materials. More than once they were startled off the road by one of those trucks, its horn blaring at them. All around were the sounds of hammering and sawing. By the time they reached their assigned quarters everyone was thoroughly exhausted, covered in a gritty dust, and ravenous.

"Oh my God, there must be some mistake. They can't possibly mean this place," Eleanor groaned in incredulity.

Frank checked the form in his hand against the chalk marking scrawled on the building. Block 5, Building 4. "No mistake, this is it."

They stared at the building. It had walls covered with tar paper secured every couple of feet with a strip of lath. Where there should be windows there were just framed openings and the roof joists were in place but no roof actually covered it. There were, however, short sets of three step stairs and doors about twenty feet apart. Thomas broke away and went over to the building. To everyone's amazement he struggled down to his hands and knees and disappeared underneath, emerging a few moments later. He climbed the stairs of the first door and went inside, testing the floor gingerly. *Good, Sammy-san, we won't need to fix the floor in this one.* He peered around seeing four steel spring beds. *We will need copra to fill the sacks for mattresses. Where is the copra?*

"Dad, are you okay?" Frank asked.

"Ayee, Sammy-san. Watanabe won't have much to do here," the old man said in way of reply.

"Sammy? Who is Sammy?"

The old man stared at him intently for a long moment, not noticing the other members of the family making their way into the apartment. "I am Sichou Thomas Sakai, who are you?"

Moriko let out a little hiss and hurried to her husband's side. "He was called the Sichou in the little camp he worked in, in Hawaii. I haven't heard him say that in almost forty years." Everyone heard the fear creeping into her voice and it was infectious. "Come my husband, you must rest." She led him back outside and sat him down on a box then sat with him, holding his hands in hers.

"What was that all about, Pop?" Steven asked.

"He's, er...a little disoriented from the long trip. He'll be okay when he gets some food and a decent night's sleep." Frank was trying to sound upbeat but his stomach was tied in knots of worry.

"Well, it won't be much of a sleep tonight. Where are the mattresses?" Mary wondered.

"There aren't any. I checked all the apartments, four sets of springs and nothing else. Two apartments, eight beds, twelve of us," Paul reported. "Math doesn't work very well."

"The three babies can sleep on one bed frame for now," Leta replied. "If we put Benjamin on the floor tonight everyone else gets a set of springs. No wait; that still leaves us one bunk short."

"Nobody home in any of the other apartments yet, I say we scavenge one before anybody notices."

"Great idea, Steve, let's do that right now." Paul headed for the door, Steven right behind him.

"Steven! I'm ashamed of you! Other people are going to need a place to sleep too." Eleanor had a look of shocked consternation on her face. "It's not the right thing to do."

"Maybe not, my dear," Frank spoke up. "But under the circumstances it maybe the only thing to do. Paul, did I hear you say each unit had the same number of bed frames?"

"Yes, four sets each."

"They just crammed the same amount in each room. I don't think they gave any thought to how the numbers would work out. Anyway for tonight at least let's grab one from each of the next two rooms. We can sort this out better in the morning. Maybe by then our benefactors will have conjured up some mattresses to go with these springs. Go ahead Steven." Frank saw the disapproval remaining in his wife's face. "Just for tonight, love; tomorrow we can fix it. I promise."

"Go see to your parents," the weariness in her voice palpable, "we will try to make something out of this for the night. You might see if you can find some food and water." Frank headed for the door, "and try to find a bathroom too. We're all gonna need that for sure."

Now the women had a chance to survey the situation. Each space was twenty by twenty feet. Assuming they would eventually have a roof and windows it was about the same size and not any better built than one of their garden sheds back home, framed with two by fours two feet apart with one by eights hastily nailed up at a forty five degree angle from the studs as sheathing. Here and there nails which had missed the stud poked ominously into the little room. Beyond the bed frames there was no furniture of any description. The floor looked to be ship lap two by six. Already the green wood was shrinking, desiccated by the low humidity of the desert.

For a long moment they all looked around hopelessly in stunned silence; overwhelmed by the circumstances and situation they found themselves in.

"I sure hope it doesn't rain tonight!" Mary said staring through the roof joists to the blue sky beyond. Then she began to laugh; a nervous giggle at first then soon all the women were laughing heartily, struck by the absurdity of the moment.

Island Farms

Bainbridge Island, Washington
April 2, 1942

Joshua and Stan were studying the primer Paul had written on farm operations and had been for a least an hour. Finally Stan ran his hand through his hair and let out a sigh of frustration.

"I was almost always shipped out somewhere when this was going on. Leta never told me it was this complicated to farm."

"It's not all that complicated, Stan. It just needs perseverance and some decent weather. We'll get the hang of it." Joshua was trying to sound more upbeat that he felt. Truth be told, he was a little daunted by all that had to happen so quickly in the spring. According to the charts they were already behind nearly two weeks. In the last few days before the Sakai family—along with every other Japanese farmer on the island—had been marched off to parts still unknown, nearly nothing had been done in anticipation of planting.

The war had changed everything. Supply sources Paul had cited were suddenly being diverted to production of war materiel, tens of thousands of laborers and skilled equipment operators were enlisting. Gasoline and diesel fuel were becoming expensive—when it was available at all—and it seemed likely that their lack of experience in the fields would soon put them hopelessly behind for at least this season.

"Well, I can certainly learn to run a tractor," Stan began, "but I doubt if strawberries make much sense as a crop. Besides, even with Ritchie helping, the three of us can't plant a hundred acres by ourselves before Christmas."

"No, not strawberries, that's true. But we might be able to get two crops of lettuce in one season; or maybe plant carrots and potatoes." Joshua contemplated the situation. "Carrots are pretty easy, potatoes are too."

"Not much money in those crops. California grows lettuce and carrots by the trainload and Idaho, Oregon and the East Side here in Washington do the same with potatoes."

"True enough," Josh admitted, "but if fuel keeps getting harder to come by our produce may be competitive locally. And if we can plant something that takes less labor to handle, we don't need to make as much money."

"Frank has grown carrots here before and they did okay. I don't know anything about potatoes." Stan stared out the window that Thomas had favored so long then finally turned to Joshua. "Well, Hell; we can't just sit around forever hoping it will do it by itself. Let's choose something and get started."

"According to this inventory list we have a seed drill and we even have twenty pounds of seeds left over from last year. Let's try carrots."

"Frank should be here to do this; the whole family should be here. Grandfather should be in this chair taking his nap." He fell silent. Joshua let the moment linger, sharing the same thoughts. Stan sat in the old chair touching the worn cloth on the arms staring out the window again. "I miss my family," he whispered.

Owens Valley Reception Area
Inyo County, California
April 3, 1942

The substantial heat that accumulated during the daytime fled with the sun each night escaping to the stars. Huddled into two tiny apartments, crowded on springs with no mattresses, covered with towels and the few sheets they had brought, and each wearing all the clothes they could get on, the Sakai family shivered under the thin wool blankets issued by the Army as they checked in.

Paul spent the night staring into the black skies seeing stars more brilliantly than ever; marveling at the clarity and taking notice that here in the desert the stars hardly ever seemed to twinkle. Mary had burrowed into his side for warmth, cramped together on the same single bed frame listening to the green lumber crackle as it shrunk. Frank and Eleanor tried to sleep but found only short naps possible, waking up continuously to check on the rest of the family, adjusting blankets here and there as the temperature plunged to the freezing level.

Moriko suffered the most on this first night, desperately needing a bathroom but horrified beyond words that a ditch with an outhouse on a sled was the only 'facility' available. Finally her needs overwhelmed her shame and in the dead of night she carefully made her way to seek her relief. The dim illumination of a single light bulb on a pole near building four and the starlight were her only help and twice she stumbled, once her knees on the decomposed granite and k. Had it not been for the extra clothes urely would have skinned her knees badly. As it was, Moriko painfully managed to become upright again and return to her husband. She was worried and fretful over Toshio. He had reverted to speaking Hawaiian pidgin learned in the cane fields and seemed to be lost in the past. Moriko feared he was becoming unreachable but didn't know what she might do for it.

In the middle of the night, while most of the family slept fitfully, Paul thought he heard sobbing. Carefully he disentangled himself from his bride and listened intently. Muffled by layers of clothes, Benjamin was crying softly. Paul gently shook him by the shoulders and whispered "Come with me." Benjamin followed Paul outside, down the steps and stood in the cold air, his breath coming in gasps.

"You're scared, aren't you?"

Benjamin nodded, wiping the tears from his eyes.

"Look up. What do you see?" Paul asked.

"Stars is all." Benjamin said plaintively.

"That's right, stars. Do you see the Big Dipper? Where is Ursa Major? Where is the North Star?"

Benjamin peered more intently, scanning the sky then pointing. "There's the North Star, and the Big Dipper. I could never find Ursa Major at home."

"You saw those stars at home, you see them here. As long as you can see the stars you can always be home in your heart." Benjamin and Paul stood looking at the stars for a long while. Finally Paul pointed to the stairs, indicating it was time to go back to try to get a little more sleep.

"Thanks, Paul," Benjamin said simply, "you're a great blood brother." Paul watched the boy head into the unfinished room then glanced at the gemstones scattered in the sky and wondered absently if his father ever looked up in the night in wonderment.

As the sky brightened and the sun began to pour in through the window framing and open ceiling joists, the adults began to stir, trying to bring life back to frigid extremities and loosen painful cramps and rusted joints. Within minutes the sounds of saws and hammers began filling the air as construction workers got back to the business of building more warehousing for people. Trucks began rumbling by sending clouds of dust into the air which began settling inside the unfinished space. The children; being among the most adaptable creatures on the planet, slept on: oblivious to the world reawakening around them.

It had been four days now since anyone of the group had had anything near a decent night's sleep and the deep fatigue was beginning to take a serious toll.

"I've got to do something about this." Paul said. "This is just intolerable."

"What do you have in mind?" Frank asked as he tried to stretch out a particularly stubborn cramp in his left calf.

"I don't know," Paul admitted. "But at this point I'm beginning to think getting shot is better than another night like last night."

Frank took the time to survey what could be seen from the front of their building. Toward the main gate a fence topped with barbed wire had been erected along what he supposed was the front perimeter. It made a corner near the southeast guard tower and headed west for about a hundred yards then just stopped. A few stakes marked where the fence would be continued he supposed but there was nothing really between the camp and freedom on three sides; nothing except the desert.

"Well, before we do anything rash, let's count noses and see if the crowd over there knows something about breakfast we don't," Frank said.

"Yeah, I wouldn't want to get shot on an empty stomach."

"Who's going to get shot?" Mary had joined the two men, and the rest of the family began to stir and head toward the advance clique already formed.

"I'm considering volunteering," Paul smiled. "It seems like light duty compared to last night."

"I think I'm offended," Mary replied, feigning high dudgeon.

"No, no, Princess, no reflection on you only the accommodations."

"Very well then, vassal, I suppose you are forgiven."

"Will the King and Queen of the Desert care to accompany the rest of the family to breakfast?" Frank noted the arrival of the family, Leta carrying the baby; the children wiping sleep from their eyes while yawning widely.

"Lead on fair knight," Mary replied with a giggle. As Frank and Paul led the way toward what they assumed was the mess hall Eleanor leaned over to Mary and asked, "What was that all about?"

"Giddy with fatigue, Mom."

"I can believe that well enough."

If the previous night's supper had been a study in mish-mash cobbled together tinned fruit, meat and vegetables it at least had the virtue of being served a few meals at a time as internees were processed and made their way to their new homes. This morning however was best characterized as a riot being managed by a rabble. People who had never prepared anything more complex than their own ham sandwiches were overwhelmed trying to manage a crew feeding three hundred people what was essentially an encore of the previous night's supper.

In a shocking display of disrespect, young toughs from the Terminal Island region of Los Angeles pushed aside elders and children, forcing themselves to the head of the line, then commandeering utensils from hapless servers and heaping their plates full without regard to others. Steven and Paul had to be restrained by Frank or a real riot might have ensued.

"It's the first day, and we don't know the lay of the land," Frank cautioned. "Too soon to start something we may not be able to finish."

"Damn it, Dad, those bums shouldn't get away with that." Steven's fair play threshold had always been high, but this time Paul was nodding vigorously in agreement.

"No they shouldn't," Frank agreed. "But now is not the time. First we have to look out for the family before we can go crashing headlong into managing the entire camp. Let's do that first and then start thinking about forming some alliances among other folks."

It was evident at the outset that no real order was in place so chaos reigned as the clustered little family wormed its way to and fro through the throngs, always polite but always moving forward. In the hour it took to get to where food was being served all the women and children had taken turns finding and using the outhouse and on one of the return trips Leta informed the group that there were workers swarming over their apartments adding a roof and putting in windows.

Finally they began passing through the service line where they were served lukewarm corned beef hash, canned pears and tomatoes and a sort of watery coleslaw. There was reconstituted evaporated milk, but only the mothers of young children seemed to be taking any, and then only reluctantly. It was certainly not the kind of breakfast that farmers were accustomed to, but it was sustenance after a fashion so everyone ate it, if not with gusto at least with determined resignation.

It was the walk back to the barracks that congealed their situation for them. There was nothing for them to do and nowhere for them to go. No planting, no school, no shopping, nothing; nothing but being livestock in a yard awaiting their fate.

The sun was warm, much warmer than the Puget Sound and the sky a shocking bright blue from horizon to horizon. The short walk back to the assigned apartments was the first really leisurely moment for the family in two weeks. By the time they got back, the construction crew had moved on, having slapped on a rudimentary roof and filled the cut outs in the walls with sash windows. It certainly wasn't inviting, but at least it was enclosed. Four bales of straw and two dozen gunny sacks had appeared, evidently thrown off a passing truck.

Inside everything was covered with sawdust, bits of tarpaper and grit and in complete disarray. Bed frames shoved around, possessions rifled and anything that looked useful or the slightest bit valuable was gone. Like most of the others arriving now, that really didn't amount to much, but with so little available the loss seemed to sting all out of proportion. Predictably Steven flew into a rage. That seemed to be happening a lot lately. Frank reasoned with his son that since the perpetrators were unknown, his ire—however justified—was nonetheless impotent.

"Unknown! I know damn well who did this, and so do you, Dad. It's the stinking United States Government. If anyone in Washington had bothered to read the Constitution none of us would be here!"

"It's war, Steven. Things are different in wartime. Rules are different; they have to be. You've read the stories in the paper, heard about the violence against Japanese Americans on the radio. The government says this is as much for our own protection as anything else," Frank concluded.

"Yeah? Our protection?" Steven grabbed his father and pulled him outside then pointed to one of the guard towers in the distance, "If they're so damned anxious about our protection why are the guns pointed at us?"

"It's a fair point, Frank." Paul said, having followed them outside.

"Don't you think I know that?" Frank exploded. "Don't you think I know this stinks? Don't you think I see the damn guns too? What do you want from me, Steven? Should I march down there and get my brains blown out raging about how unfair it all is, how I'm no threat and neither is anybody else here? Whaddya think, Paul? Maybe I should just pack everybody up, go the main gate and say 'Excuse me, my family doesn't like it here, we'd like to go home now." His steam vented he concluded, "These are the cards we play, son. I have my family and Stan's family to look after and shaking my fist at the heavens won't help them or me. What do you want from me?"

Steven searched his father's eyes then looked around at the grim faces of his family who had gathered when the shouting had begun. He toed the desiccated gritty soil and surveyed the barren landscape and drew in a big breath.

"I don't know, Pop. I guess I just wanted someone else to be mad too."

"Son, everyone in this place now, and everyone that comes here is mad; angry and worried and frightened. Everyone wonders what will happen next. Everyone wonders what to do to protect themselves from all these strangers."

"Take the straw and fill the mattresses."

The words and their source were so totally unexpected and seemed so irrelevant to the conversation that everyone turned to stare at the speaker.

"What do you mean, Thomas-san?" Paul asked.

"I mean make the beds. That's why it's there." The elder Sakai was renewed with energy now that he was in what seemed to be familiar surroundings.

"Gather nails and wood. Try to find a hammer and a saw. We are going to need shelves and chairs and quarreling about the guards won't help."

It was a mixture of relief and amusement felt by Moriko. She had been so frightened that her husband might be irredeemably addled that her joy was palpable.

"You heard your Shichou," she said cheerfully. "Let's get busy."

Costello Estate

Somewhere in the Catskills
New York State
April 6, 1942

Wild Bill Donovan needed answers and he wasn't going to be too particular about where he got them—or what he had to promise—to get them: Just this minute he unambiguously had to know if U.S. code breaking had been compromised. He was playing a long shot.

"Mr. Luciano, as you know, is serving a prison sentence right now. I can assure you, he is highly unlikely to know anything about the unfortunate demise of this couple in Seattle." Consigliore Frank Costello was certain he wanted nothing to do with any federal inquiries, particularly regarding espionage. "I'm sorry I can't be of any assistance." He handed the crime scene photos back to Donovan. "Genovese is back in Sicily, I can't help him."

Wild Bill was determined to elicit—or intimidate—some sort of response. "Well, I might be able to do something for him."

"Mr. Luciano is a loyal citizen and I am sure he would be willing to aid his government, but alas, his circumstances are limited by his incarceration." Costello began to rise, signaling that this meeting was over as far as he was concerned.

"I can get him out." Donovan said, making no effort to arise.

"I can as well, in thirty to fifty years, sir. How might you be able to improve on that period?" Costello settled back down on the divan.

"I can get him out of prison, but he would have to return to Sicily. Probably doesn't want to go there right now. Il Duce is not a friend to the families." The chief of intelligence for FDR and the manager of Lucky Luciano's enterprises beyond the prison walls regarded each other. The Capo clearly wanted more, Donovan wanted assurances. Costello spoke first.

"I suppose discreet inquiries could be made," he said.

"Perhaps Mr. Luciano could be granted greater access to the outside world," Wild Bill countered.

Costello picked up the photos and scrutinized them, then signaled someone from a nearby room. "You don't mind if I keep these, for the time being, of course."

"Not at all," but I ask for discretion. I'm sure I need not remind you these are perilous times and our national security is paramount."

"Of course," Frank Costello said. "I will confer with my associates in the business world. Perhaps they can shed some light on this troubling crime."

"I look forward to hearing from you. You know how to reach me." Donovan arose, shook the gangster's hand and was shown politely to the front door of the sprawling grounds.

A Letter

April 7, 1942
Inyo Valley Reception Center
Block 5, Barracks 4, Apartment 1
Lone Pine, Calif.

My Dearest Stan,

    Well, we've been here now for four days, it took nearly three days on the train to get here. You'll have to look on a map to find us. I still don't know for sure where we are. Everyone got here okay except we were all dog tired and worried about father for a while. He seemed lost in the head.

I put our address at the top of the letter so you can write. Joshua can send mail too. When we first arrived there wasn't even a roof on the building! We slept in all our clothes and blankets on springs with no mattresses and no water or toilets. It is freezing cold at night in the desert and much warmer than Seattle in the daytime. It was 85° yesterday! It is very dry, everyone's lips are cracking and our sinuses are dry and itchy too. I have a list of things we could use here if you could send them.

Each barracks has five apartments and the family has three in this building. We started with only two but Paul was able to talk the administration into another one claiming that there were really 3 families here and putting 12 people in 2 rooms was just too much. We were surprised when they said ok. Paul is pretty good at talking people into stuff. They are all 20' square with one light bulb hanging down from the center and one plug on the wall. Each has one door to the outside and two windows with no coverings. One is next to the door and the other is on the opposite wall. The inside walls only reach to 8'high between apartments so the space in the rafters is open. It's not very private. Some of the children climb over the walls instead of going outside through the doors. Sometimes we can hear Mr. Kasemata snoring at night clear from the other end of the barracks.

We decided that we would put all the children in one apartment. They are in apartment 2 and Steven usually sleeps with them, but sometimes it's me. The baby still sleeps with me for now, along with Mom, Eleanor and Mary in #1. Father, Frank and Paul sleep in #3. This is how things ended up because we couldn't figure out any other way for the men and women to have any privacy so it just ended up like a dormitory.

The food is horrible and the bathrooms are even worse. There is one latrine for the men and one for the women in each block but there are 15 barracks to each block. That's 75 apartments for each bath house, and half of them aren't even working yet so we still have to wander around looking for the outhouse on the sled. There are long lines, especially for the women and the smell is terrible.

I miss you very much my love and I wish this awful war had never happened. I can't wait to get home to our little house in Bremerton. We will pretend none of this was ever real. Everyone says hello and says how much they miss you and love you, but me most of all. Everyone says hello to Joshua and Ritchie too. Frank and Paul want to know how the planting is going so if you see Josh or talk to him let him know so he can write.

Don't forget to try to send the stuff on the list on the next page, especially the Vaseline for our lips.

Your loving sweetheart, Leta

"She doesn't know about the house?" Joshua looked up after he had finished reading the forwarded letter Stan had offered.

"No, not yet; we didn't know where to send mail so there was no way to let anyone know much of anything."

"What are you going to tell her?"

"Just that there was a fire and I'm living here now, helping you and Ritchie. I'll tell her the cat ran away scared off by the fire.

Maybe he's living with a neighbor. I don't know; something like that."

"Lone Pine, I wonder where that is?" Josh wondered aloud.

Stan took out a U.S. map and carefully unfolded it on the kitchen table. He pointed to a tiny black dot in the middle of a long thin black line snaking up the eastern part of southern California. "Right here," he said, pointing.

Joshua studied the map for a little while. "Good grief," he exclaimed looking up at Stan, "that's only about eighty miles from the Mojave Desert. If it's already eighty five degrees in April what's it gonna be like in August?"

"Warmer," Stan said simply.

Federal Bureau of Investigation
Seattle Field Office
April 8, 1942

Harvard Eldon had taken the station he preferred in situations like this; he was standing quietly in a corner of the room. He watched carefully while Special Agents pored over the files and photos he had collected from the Seattle P.D. last week. Eldon had told the police he was 'Bureau', but he had neglected to specify exactly which bureau he may have meant. He had done the same here, suggesting, but not really saying, he was with the San Francisco field office. He looked the part, spoke the lingo and knew all the drills. Nobody had actually asked for his bona fides and he hoped maintaining a low profile would keep it that way. A turf war was not something he relished.

"So what are we looking for, here?" Sam Klein's eyes searched around the room until he picked out Eldon in the corner. "It's a local double homicide. Tragic, but why are we looking at it?" A couple of other agents looked up and Harvard could see the similar questions flashing through their minds.

"Well," El spoke slowly, buying a little time to organize in his mind exactly what he could and couldn't say. "We lost touch with a couple of agents working an undercover assignment. Their work is related to the Pacific War theatre. We were hoping they may have checked in with you." He knew that last part was an outright lie, but it would seem reasonable enough to the other agents. "And we were hoping that perhaps someone had interviewed a Japanese that stuck in their memory."

The room erupted in raucous laughter. It was so hearty that a couple of men were actually gasping for breath before it died down.

"Agent Eldon," Sam said, trying unsuccessfully to wipe the smirk off his face, "In the last three months I have personally interviewed about a hundred and fifty Japs. The six of us here, maybe nine hundred or a thousand; about half of them spoke enough English to get through a rudimentary interview. The other half either didn't speak it, or didn't let on if they did, so yeah, about five hundred or so stuck out."

It was clear to Eldon he was going to have to leak a little more information out: Which was good, he supposed, since it was really all he had. Nobody back at the code room could figure out Oscar's shorthand. That idiot Oscar had done it in his own private code and it had cost him his life. Eldon sighed inwardly and moved to the table where the other agents sat. Quietly he revealed what he could and hoped for the best.

Admiral Yamamoto's Quarters
Battleship Yamato
Somewhere in the Pacific Ocean
April 17, 1942

"Isoroku-san, you are too much of a pessimist. The attack on Pearl Harbor was a great success. We are successful at every turn and two thirds of the Pacific is at the command of the Imperial Navy." Yamamoto's Chief of Staff was quite pleased with the way things were going and was dismayed by his boss's persistent gloom.

"Pearl Harbor will turn out to be the worst disaster to befall the fleet since the first keel was laid." Yamamoto was not sanguine about the future and was tired of the empty praise heaped upon him for what in truth had been his fallback plan. "We attacked before the notification was presented to Washington. That made the Americans righteously angry—and more indignantly dangerous—plus we didn't sink any of the carriers. Worst of all the second attack was canceled, so the fuel stores remain intact. I don't care what the rest of the Naval Staff thinks—and Tojo-san's plans are lunatic, battleships are the naval heroes of the past. This war will be won or lost with carriers, and we didn't even damage one. With the western ports of the United States intact, they will begin building ships at an unbelievable rate."

He paused for a moment, considering what he was about to say and wondering how long it would take for his words to reach the Emperor's ear. *Well, no matter, I've been telling everyone who would stand still the same thing for two years and still no one lis-*

tens. "I think at best our navy can hold off the Americans for maybe a year and a half. By then we will be overwhelmed by sheer force of numbers. Still, we will do the best we can."

"*Hai,* Admiral, for what else can we do?"

"We can pray to the gods, my friend. We can pray."

Admiral's Deck, *U.S.S. Enterprise*
650 Nautical Miles East of Tokyo
Pacific Ocean
April 18, 1942

"Are we calling it off, Sir, over?" The Colonel sounded disappointed and tinny in the earphone.

"The Captain thinks we should. We've been spotted and the enemy got a message off before they were sunk, over." the Admiral responded.

"I think we should launch now and fly through to the mainland. Ditch the planes if we have to. Chang's waiting for us in China and if some of us get lost his underground will help us get out, over."

"That's the conclusion I've reached too, Jimmy." He tried to sound upbeat and hoped it came through radio. "I can't stress how important this mission is." Bull Halsey pictured his flight commander's face. "You and your men have trained your asses off and some of you probably won't come back. But, hell, you know that, over."

"Yes Sir, I do." Static crackled on the ultra-low power ship-to-ship transmission as Colonel James Doolittle was silent for a moment. "Sir, If we can put even one plane load of bombs in Hirohito's back pocket it would mean a lot to the folks back home. And with any luck maybe scare the hell out of Yamamoto, over."

"It would mean a lot to the sailors out here too, Jimmy. We're badly outgunned right now and Chester is betting a lot on this little raid slowing Yamamoto down. Give him something in his backyard to think about, over."

"Doesn't it seem a little unusual, Sir. I mean Nimitz getting the fleet. I thought he was a submariner, over."

"No more unusual than an artillery guy getting an infantry command. You know how the military is—become an expert in one field and they're sure to put you in command of something entirely different—anyway Nimitz is the CINC-PAC now and better he than me, over."

"I suppose. Hell, I'm Army anyway what do I know about running a navy? Well, Sir, if you'll excuse me, I have a flight to make, over."

"Godspeed Jimmy, for all your men, over."

"Ten-four Sir and thank you, over and out," Doolittle turned to the Captain of the *Hornet*, "it's a go, Sir: With your permission?"

"By all means Jimmy, and good luck."

As the flight commander left to join his crew the Captain picked up the shipboard phone and called the bridge. "Get ready to turn her into the wind, lift off is in seventeen minutes."

Twenty minutes later sixteen United States Army Air Force B-25 bombers stripped of everything inessential except the black broomsticks where machine guns had once been, lumbered into the skies laden only with fuel, bombs and guts and headed for Tokyo.

Federal Bureau of Investigation
Seattle Field Office
April 12, 1942

Klein flipped open another file, read the notes then mentally tried to put a face on them. Occasionally he would recall something, but mostly they were just routine interviews. All the same questions, mostly similar answers; personally he didn't think there was much of a threat from the Japs living here, but he had avoided actually saying so. He imagined most of the other agents were experiencing much the same result.

Taking a pack of Chesterfields out of his shirt pocket, he leaned back in the office chair and lit up. After a couple of deep drags he tossed the current file on the already-looked-at pile and grabbed another from the he-hadn't-looked-at-since-the-interview pile. *Akagi, Paul-Bainbridge Island 02-14-42* was typed on the label glued to the tab. He opened it and began reading.

A Letter
April 18, 1942

Dear Frank,

Stan was sure happy to get that letter from Leta. He's writing back to her right now and we'll probably send these both out at the same time. Stan is living here now, you'll find out why when Leta reads his letter, but I'm glad to have him. I have been having a hard time getting much help. Since the war started it seems like everyone is enlisting. Everybody with a farm is having a hard time getting help.

We left the strawberries on the south side twenty three acres, but we decided we just didn't have enough know-how to try to plant any more. I'm not so sure there will be much demand for berries either. We are planting carrots using the seeds we found in the barn. If we can get some seed cuts we might plant a few potatoes. Some reds might sell here better than the russets from the east side of the hills. If we have trouble getting help during harvest I hope they will last in the ground a little longer. So long as we can beat the rains we should be okay.

Stan and I are sending a couple of boxes with the items on Leta's list along with a few things we think might be useful now that we know where you are. The Bainbridge Bell *has* one of the island internees working as a reporter so his first report in the paper lets us hear what's happening and what people might be needing. I rummaged around in a couple of boxes and found some cloth remnants that might make decent drapes and sent along some needles and thread. I hope that keeps the ladies happy for a little while.

I don't know if you hear any war news but XXXXXX XXXX XXXXX XXXXXX (censored) XXXXXXXXXXX XXXX XXXXXXXXXXXXXXXXX XXXX XXXXXX. Anyway that's how it seems to me.

I can't imagine the frustration and anger you must be feeling, but if it is anything like mineXXXXXXXXXXX XXXX XXXXXX XXXXXXXXXXX (censored) XXXXX XXX XXXX XXXXXX XXXXX.

We're doing our best here but it would be better if you were all here to look after things. Perhaps this will be a short war and everyone can get back to normal pretty soon.

Ritchie says hello to everyone and to tell you he is taking good care of the dog. He says he misses Benjamin and Paul and for them to never give up. I have no idea what he is talking about but I suppose it will mean something to them. I miss you and your family and send my best.

Your friend,

Joshua

Frank handed the letter to Eleanor who read it in silence then passed it to Steven. He harrumphed acidly when he got to the censored portions. "I guess we pose a threat too great to risk telling us how things are," he said.

"No need, really; we know how things are." His father replied.

"Bad enough to lock us up, not quite bad enough to shoot us yet," Steven replied.

"Don't get started with talk like that," his mother chided. "Things are hard enough without hearing that sort of thing." Secretly it was her greatest fear but she held it in abeyance for her family's sake and her own sanity as well.

"Hey everybody!" all sets of eyes turned to the doorway where Paul was standing laden with boxes. "It's an early Christmas!" He clambered in and put the two boxes on an unoccupied bed. The boxes had been opened and a paper label had been attached stating 'Inspected/Passed'. Eleanor began going through the contents, occasionally holding up a piece of cloth or an article of clothing that had been requested. She made little piles, based on for whom or for what the item was intended, and handed out the small stacks accordingly.

"Boy am I glad to get these," Frank laughed easily as he donned a pair of sunglasses. "The sun in this desert is sure bright."

Moriko and Mary each took their little prizes and even Steven was happy to have two more pair of socks. Eleanor handed a folded piece of floral print cloth to Leta and a jar of Vaseline. "I think this would make a pretty set of curtains for the girls dorm room. What do you think?"

"Isn't that the fabric you picked out to make a new dress?"

"Well, I think I would rather have curtains just now, wouldn't you?"

Leta thought about it for a minute then nodded. "Curtains would be nice," she conceded. With this the assembled group fell into gossipy talk, Benjamin snatched a treasured Tootsie Roll retrieved from the small part of the box with his name indicating it was a gift from Ritchie. Thomas was already chewing thoughtfully on some dried apples from Wenatchee; a treat he had enjoyed for years. Paul stood in the doorway reading Josh's letter then surveying the scene in the cramped room crowded with people. A smile crept over his face as he looked at Benjamin.

"What's funny?" Mary asked.

"We'll be okay," he responded.

"How so?" she looked at him quizzically.

"Think about it, three weeks ago we were all in a panic. Now we find pleasure in new socks and stale Tootsie Rolls. A scrap of fabric with flowers, a pair of sunglasses and Vaseline for our dry lips; my God we are durable and adaptable. Whenever this damn war is over and we get back home we will be fine."

"Amarimono ni wa fuku ga aru"

Fortunes exist among leftovers

Japanese Proverb

The trickle of evacuees had become a torrent with a thousand new inhabitants flooding in every week. Flimsy buildings to house all these people were flying up at an astonishing rate and infrastructure—roads, sewers, power lines, water mains, a hospital, washrooms, warehouses, theatres, mess halls and even a canteen—followed close on their heels. The new arrivals were now coming in from what the government was calling 'assembly centers'. Places with names like Tanforan and Puyallup; Horserace palaces hastily pressed into service to hold the thousands of prisoners—for they couldn't really be considered anything else—waiting for space in concentration camps.

In Puyallup in Washington State, spring rains had transformed the entire area into a smelly, slippery, slimy sinkhole of mud. Families found their 'assigned housing unit' was often a horse stall into which half a bale of straw had been thrown. In other locations, in hot climates, thousands of churning feet turned the ground into a talc-like dust which the slightest breeze churned into a choking, cloying, gritty aerosol which covered everything and everyone. The whole thing was almost an equation; misery times anxiety equals fear plus rage squared.

Paul stood near the front gate chatting with the camp administrator. Paul was a positive genius at getting concessions from him for his family group and had become an unofficial spokesman for most of the Bainbridge Island contingent.

"So what are we this week?" He asked.

"We are this week, and hopefully until we throw open the front gates and everyone goes home, the Manzanar War Relocation Center of the Owens Valley. I am now working for a civilian agency and the Army—thankfully—is in blessed retreat headed for where the real war is happening."

"Not a big fan of the Army I take it."

"Oh hell, Paul; it's not that really. They're damn good at the mechanics and logistics of this kind of operation but they somehow expect military order and discipline from mothers, babies in diapers and toothless elders with arthritis and gout." The camp administrator looked over the bustling acreage with what seemed like a sense of satisfaction, "You know, in different circumstances we could all be pretty damn proud of how quickly this has gotten done."

"Maybe so, Al," Paul said. Silence fell between the two men for quite a while then Paul spoke again. "But these aren't different circumstances, are they?"

"Nope, they sure as hell aren't," Al agreed. "But I suspect you aren't here to discuss war, politics and philosophy with me. What do you need?"

"We need to be somewhere else. There is a lot a friction right now and I'm worried it could escalate into violence."

"Your family," Al wondered?

"No, the entire group from Bainbridge Island; we've heard from friends back home that the rest of the evacuees from around Seattle are being shipped to somewhere in Idaho."

"Minidoka," Al confirmed nodding his head. "Near some tiny little town named Eden." He thought a moment about the irony in that name for the people being sent there.

"Well, the California Japanese are a rougher group. Their culture is different, even their dialect is aggressive. They have a few hoodlums that are making life difficult for us. We'd like a change."

"That's a pretty tall glass of lemonade you're asking for, Paul. We barely have you here and already you want to be shipped somewhere else sight unseen."

"I'm just trying to imagine how you would write the report," Paul replied. "After refusing a request for transfer, several elderly internees from Bainbridge Island, Washington were bludgeoned to death by assailants unknown but suspected to be from the Terminal Island region. In the ensuing riot several more casualties occurred, including at least one military guard. The investigation is ongoing."

"I'll give you one thing, Paul; you have an uncanny knack for reaching the deepest fears of a bureaucrat and turning them to your advantage."

"It's that inscrutable Oriental thing I have working," Paul replied with a grin.

"Yeah, from the deepest heart of enemy territory—Salinas, California, no promises, Paul, but I'll see what can be done about your request. Meantime, I'll have the camp police keep a special eye out for trouble in your area." Al stood erect and businesslike, a clear indication the session was ending.

"Thanks Al, that's really all I could hope for."

The two men wandered away from each other nonchalantly and in no particular hurry stopping here and there to chat inconsequentially with other people they encountered. It was how business was done and jealousies avoided by masters of the craft.

"You've been gone a long time," Mary noted as Paul walked into the little square room that now constituted home.

"Yeah, talking to Al about the Terminal Island group," he replied. "He's gonna see about getting us transferred to some place called 'Minidoka' in Idaho."

"That Los Angeles bunch scares me, but I don't want to be all alone in a new camp either."

"Nope, whole Bainbridge group goes or nobody goes."

"Well, that might not be so bad."

"Where is everyone?" Paul asked.

"Moriko and Eleanor took the girls and went to do the laundry. Frank went to some JACL committee meeting and Grampa and Steven took Benjamin scrounging," Mary said. "It was my turn to have some time alone with my husband, who was nowhere to be found!" she added petulantly.

"How much time do we have left?" Paul asked.

"Probably half an hour, forty five minutes tops."

"Plenty of time," Paul said stripping his shirt off, "anybody else home?"

"Only old Kasematsu, but he's so deaf he can't hear anything anyway," she giggled.

Paul turned his beautiful bride around to face him as he pulled the makeshift drapes closed and hung a towel on the doorknob outside as he latched it. "I remember the first evening we watched the sunset over the Olympics." He drew her closer into an intimate embrace. "My God how beautiful you were that night, and how beautiful you are now." He lifted her easily in passionate embrace and carried her to the bed. In a few minutes they were completely unaware that everyone within fifty yards could hear the loud, rhythmic squeaking of the springs of their narrow little cot.

When Thomas and Steven burst breathlessly into the little room it was stifling hot and smelled vaguely of musk. Paul and Mary turned to look. Paul, buttoning his shirt, was seated on the edge of a cot, Mary pulling back curtains preparing to open the window.

"Look at all the swell stuff we found," Steven exulted. The grandfather and his son, with Benjamin slowly bringing up the rear, dumped their pocketed collections on a nearby cot. Included in the inventory were miscellaneous tin can lids, nails of several sizes—both bent and straight—a few soft drink caps, a dozen or so boards of random length and width, pieces of wire and scraps of tarpaper. But there in the jumble was the real jewel—a broken saw blade.

"Where did you find all this stuff?" Paul wondered aloud.

"Shush," Thomas said nodding toward the open windows and doors. He whispered, "Over in Block 20, they're still building there and no residents yet."

Everyone knew that most of the stuff on display was officially considered 'contraband' and subject to seizure and discipline if discovered. But it was also widely ignored by the administration of the camp since most of the items of this nature were being used to cover knotholes and joints as the green construction material became desiccated in the arid desert conditions. By the time one of the completed barracks was a month old it was common for knotholes as big as a silver dollar to appear in the floors and walls. Floorboards developed gaps as much as half an inch and when the wind blew, an occupant could actually watch the sand form tiny dunes on the leeward side of the holes. In the winter of course it would be drifting snow.

And the wind did blow. It howled in one direction for half the day then reversed itself and blew the other way at night. It was almost like a tide, Paul thought. In, then out with a slack tide as it changed direction; perpetual motion. Mostly the internees just thought of it as 'that damned wind' and made the adjustments they needed. That was what the treasure hunt was about and everyone in camp was on the lookout.

"Let's put some of this stuff to use," Paul said. He lifted a loose board and withdrew a hammer head that had been discarded by a framer too busy to take the time to install a new handle. Thomas had found a piece of sturdy apple branch from the old orchard within the camp and with Steven's penknife had fashioned a new handle. Not pretty, but it worked well.

Steven picked out several lids and tentatively found holes that corresponded in size. Thomas had already begun measuring for chairs. That was the biggest need now, shelves and a table would have to come later. Paul had begun to straighten the bent nails as quietly as possible considering he was pounding away with a hammer. It was noisy in camp though and no one was likely to notice the noise of just another hammer. For half an hour everyone worked at making their little black boxes just a bit more like a home.

Steven heard it first; the sound of a car pulling to a stop alongside the barracks. "Shhh," he warned, "listen."

Everyone stopped and listened intently for something out of the ordinary but for a moment nothing seemed amiss. Suddenly a car door opened and slammed shut and barely seconds later a sharp rap was heard at the door.

Before anyone could even think what to do the rap sounded again accompanied by a voice: "Administration, I'm coming in." With that the door opened and there everyone stood contraband in hand.

"Al?" Paul was startled to see him standing in his barracks. Then he suddenly realized, rather sheepishly, that they had been caught redhanded so to speak in forbidden activity. "We were just, uh, plugging up a few holes." Then he regained his composure, "Al, I'd like you to meet Toshio-san and his wife Moriko. This is his son Frank and grandsons Steven and Benjamin and this is my wife Mary, Frank's daughter. Frank's wife Eleanor is with Leta and the other kids, doing the laundry." The administrator alternately bowed or shook hands as he deemed age appropriate. Paul casually laid down the hammer next to the saw blade Thomas had tossed on the furthest cot. "What can we do for you?" Paul asked.

Al pointedly ignored the infractions and came right to the point. "I think I can do something for you, actually," he said. "I've heard from Minidoka Relocation Center. They think they are going to have enough space for your group when all the other Washington evacuees have been settled. That's still at least a few months away—and unofficial—but I think there's a good chance."

"That's great news, Al, but you didn't drive down here to tell us that. You could have done that at the fence any day."

"That's true, Paul," he conceded, "but what I am about to say can't be risked being overheard or repeated." He stared purposefully around the tiny room.

Mary was first to get the hint. "Excuse me. Honey, I'm going to go help Eleanor and Leta with the laundry. Steven, I thought you and Grandfather were going to look at the apple orchards. Maybe you could take Benjamin."

Al moved out of the doorway as people began leaving to be out of the way. When he and Paul were alone he carefully closed the door and motioned for Paul to close the window.

"Have a seat, Al," Paul motioned to one of the cots. "What's up with the cloak and dagger?"

"Paul, have you ever heard of the *Kobiashi Maru*? It's a Japanese freighter that worked Hawaii and the west coast here before the war."

Paul hoped that the dagger of ice that cleaved his heart wasn't apparent in his face. His mind was racing now, but he answered as casually as he dared. "I think I may have seen it tied up once or twice somewhere; San Francisco maybe, or Seattle. I saw lots of ships as a kid. After a while they all start to look alike. Why do you ask?"

"I am not telling you what you are about to hear, and if anyone ever says I did I will deny it and denounce you as a traitor. Am I clear?"

"Crystal," Paul said somberly.

"The *Kobiashi Maru* was intercepted by a navy Destroyer Escort about three weeks ago. Among the documents that were seized was one on letterhead of the Japanese Imperial Navy. Your name—Arimoto—was on it. It is coded in a way likely not to be broken because it isn't a cipher it's just a substituted phrase code. Everyone who needs to know what it says has it memorized probably for a one time usage. Why would your name be on that paper?"

Paul was furious. No one in the submarine operations were supposed to use actual names, and certainly the Captain of the freighter should have known to destroy documents like that. Calm on the exterior Paul decided a limited truth was better than a wholesale lie.

"Gosh, nobody has used my given name in a long time," he tried to look thoughtful. "Probably my family," he said. "My grandfather in Japan is the head of the Imperial Household Staff. I met him once about six or seven years ago."

"Your grandfather works for the Emperor?" Al was incredulous and nonplussed.

"I don't know if he still does," Paul answered truthfully, "but he used to. My family goes back eight or nine generations in that job."

"How in God's name did you not end up at Heart Mountain or Tule Lake?" Al asked himself rhetorically.

"Heart Mountain?"

"Heart Mountain, an internment camp, well POW camp really, up in Wyoming. Tule Lake is in northern California. High security risks mostly get sent there," Al replied. "What about your father? What about you?"

"Dad was an agricultural attaché attached to the embassy in San Francisco. He dragged Mom and me up and down the west coast for years. I saw more fertilizer by the time I was ten then most farmers will see in a lifetime."

"Where are they now?"

"Dad got recalled before the war so we went back to Japan for a while. I was the proverbial fish out of water. The only thing I had in common with my 'people' was eye shape and skin tone. As far as they were concerned, I was an American. The more I thought about it the more I thought so too, so I came home. That's the whole story." Paul had neglected to report that his return had been aboard an Imperial Navy submarine as an officer and a spy. He hoped that tidbit of information was still eluding notice.

"I'll be damned," Al whistled softly. "How'd you get back in? You were a belligerent alien at the time on a Japanese passport."

"No, I was born in Salinas. I'm a citizen. I applied for a passport before I left and traveled on that."

"Children born of foreign nationals on diplomatic status in the U S are not automatically citizens." Al observed.

"Really? There isn't any notation like that on my birth certificate, I was just coming home."

"Maybe so, Paul, but someone out there has been sifting through a pretty big haystack looking for your needle. Geez Paul, what am I gonna tell these people?"

"That is a really butchered metaphor, Al. What people?" Paul asked.

"FBI people I think. Some agent called me about twenty minutes ago said he talked to you in Seattle on Valentine's Day; wants to talk to you again. He says there are some 'irregularities' he would like to discuss." Al shook his head as he stood up. "God Paul, why didn't you tell him this before?"

"He didn't ask," Paul said simply.

"I haven't decided what to do about this. I figure I have maybe three days before I have to respond. Meantime just keep your head down and don't make any waves." He nodded at the collection of contraband scattered around the room.

Paul nodded back and the administrator opened the door to step out then turned back inside. "I like you Paul, and what's more I'm inclined to believe you. But there won't be anything I can or would do to help if any of this is a lie."

"I know Al, and listen, thanks for the warning. Really, I appreciate it."

Al nodded and left Paul standing in the doorway as his car worked its way through the gears around the rest of the camp. Paul knew he would stop several more times for long heart to hearts with others so his visit here wouldn't seem so pointed. Paul appreciated a subtle man like Al.

Admiral's Quarters
Battleship Yamato
April 19, 1942

"It was just a few bombers, no real damage was done, Admiral." Instantly the Ensign snapped to attention with the realization that his comments were astonishingly inappropriate given his rank in relation to the man seated before him.

Yamamoto looked up blankly at the young officer that had delivered the dispatch and the optimistic outlook. *He can't even begin to comprehend what a catastrophe this is,* he thought. Blandly he responded, "I certainly hope the Emperor shares your viewpoint, Ensign, dismissed."

The dispatch revealed the short message sent from the Japanese surveillance picket before contact was lost: *Two enemy carriers with four cruiser escorts approx. 1300 kilometers off eastern coast of Kyushu. Heavy bombers visible on deck.*

Isoroku rubbed his knee, changes in barometric pressure often made it uncomfortable. Mentally he charted exactly where the latitude and longitude in the message would have put the bombers and tried to imagine how the U.S. Navy had gotten long range airplanes with full bomb racks off the short decks of the carriers. *Hornet* and *Enterprise* he imagined; Halsey's battle group. *The best U.S. commander in the Pacific Fleet and yet they put Nimitz in charge, a submariner! Amazing, perhaps I might yet win this war,* he thought; *perhaps not.*

His problems with submarines that didn't return had jaundiced his opinion of their potential and he had largely turned his sub fleet into covert troop and resupply ships. They still had torpedoes and certainly were to attack targets of opportunity but he couldn't imagine they could have any real impact on the outcome of the war. Airplanes were the key. He had grasped this instinctively even while watching flies at the naval academy, and truth be known it was why he never really let the *Yamato* wander too far from the home islands. The sailors could call it 'Yamamoto's Yacht' all they wanted, he was not about to send the largest battleship on the planet out to engage an enemy that had somehow managed to launch sixteen heavy bombers which delivered their loads from more than six hundred miles offshore. The Admiral knew that the battleship's days as masters of the seas were over. He himself had proved that. *Any sailor aboard the Arizona could have told him that,* he thought with a shiver.

"When you look for rocks, don't ignore the stones"
Old Saying

It had been a cold spring night and Lieutenant Colonel Jimmy Doolittle and the crew of his Tokyo raider had spent it hiding in the countryside of China after bailing out when their Mitchell bomber had run out of fuel. Shortly after ordering his crew to bail out he had seen his airship crash into the rugged terrain of the nearby mountains. Now it was morning and he and his crew had traversed the rock-strewn hillsides searching for his lost craft, finding it in a crumpled heap in the morning sunshine.

"The skipper looks like shit." Paul Leonard, Doolittle's gunner and engineer sat with his crewmates watching as the Colonel surveyed the wreckage forlornly. They grunted in what Leonard assumed was an affirmation. He stood up and walked nearer, then clicked a picture of the disheartened pilot.

"What do you think they'll do when you get home, Colonel?" The engineer was trying to cheer his commander up a bit, after all, they had put bombs on Tokyo and that wasn't nothin'.

"Well, I guess they'll court marshal me and send me to prison at Fort Leavenworth," Doolittle replied dispiritedly.

"No sir. I'll tell you what will happen," Leonard replied. "They're going to make you a General." Doolittle looked up with a wan smile on his face, "and they're going to give you the Congressional Medal of Honor."

"That's a nice sentiment, Paul. Thank you. But it's not the way to bet. C'mon fellas, there's a lot of hiking to do to get back home, we may as well get started."

With the help of Chinese sympathizers the Colonel was back in Washington in a month where he was promptly awarded a General's star, skipping full Colonel altogether and cited with the Congressional Medal of Honor for valor.

For their part, the Chinese of the district, which helped the raiders escape, endured retribution with the slaughter of a quarter of a million men, women and children at the hands of the enraged Japanese Imperial Army.

"Tsuki ni maragamo, hana ni arashi"

Clouds over the moon, a storm over the blossom

Japanese Proverb

It happened so fast that Paul barely had time to react. The camp administrator was set to send him off to Idaho, giving him a running start, so to speak, from the FBI. Now all five and a half feet of blonde-haired, blue-eyed Special Agent Sam Klein was waiting, smoking a cigarette as Paul was escorted under guard to the small conference room in the admin building.

"Nice to see you again, Mr. Akagi, have a seat." Klein indicated a grey steel chair sitting beside a small table.

"Wish I could say the same," Paul said.

"Well, I suppose I understand how you might feel. Let's pick up where we left off, shall we?" His piercing blue eyes were better informed now, Paul could tell. He wouldn't be casting blindly hoping to snag an inattentive fish; he would have a net stretched across the river. Paul tried to relax mentally to prepare for the ordeal. "You were telling me how you ended up on Whidbey Island."

"No steno this time?" Paul wondered aloud.

"Not this time, with the war on you won't be in court anytime soon; not as an enemy combatant. It'll be straight to a P.O.W. camp for you. You can appeal after the war is over." The hint of menace in Klein's voice caused Paul to shiver internally.

"Enemy combatant?" Paul tried to sound as incredulous as possible but now he was truly frightened. The only glimmer of hope he held out was that the G-man hadn't mentioned a firing squad. It wasn't much, but it was better than nothing. "I haven't done anything more aggressive than plant carrots and harvest strawberries in more than a year."

"Are you Arimoto Akagi?" Klein asked abruptly.

"That is my given name, yes."

"Have you ever been on a freighter called the *Kobiashi Maru?*"

"It's possible. My father sometimes took my mother and me back to Japan on freighters. One of them might have had that name, I don't remember."

"What did your father do?"

"Agent Klein," Paul sighed, "we've tilled this ground many times before. Let's not beat around the bush anymore. Ask me what you really want to know."

"Fair enough," Klein said, "do you work for the Emperor of Japan or the Japanese military in any capacity?"

"No." Paul again relied on the specifics of the question. Paul didn't currently work for anyone; he was incarcerated for the duration in a relocation center.

"Your father work for the Emperor or the military?"

"At this point I don't know. Before the war he was assigned to the Diplomatic Corps as an agricultural attaché so I suppose he worked for the Emperor in the same way that you work for the President."

"What about your grandfather?" Klein asked.

"He was a middle bureaucrat in a rural province. I never actually met him before he died. This is what my mother tells me." Paul was purposely referring to his maternal grandfather.

Klein opened a file and studied its pages for a few moments. A smile crept onto his face. He looked up to study his adversary more closely. "You're a clever one, Mr. Akagi. What about your *paternal* grandfather, your father's father?"

"Last I heard he was in charge of the Imperial Household. That was two years ago. I've only met him twice, actually."

"In charge of the Imperial Household? How is it you neglected to mention that before?" Agent Klein was closing the trap.

"You never asked," Paul replied blandly.

"No, I didn't," Klein acknowledged. "But now I know what questions to ask, don't I?"

Paul resisted the temptation to rise to the bait. He shrugged innocuously and looked at his inquisitor blankly.

"How do you explain this?" Sam lit another cigarette from the butt of the first while Paul looked over the document that had been handed to him.

"I can't, except to suggest there is likely more than one Arimoto Akagi in Japan. Neither name is particularly rare I'm told." Paul handed the document back. It was a bit of trivial bureaucratic housekeeping from naval headquarters. Not important in any way except to establish a link between the freighter and the military, and therefore by inference himself and the military.

"So now, let's go back and include the little trip to Japan you made several years ago. When did you go back?"

"We went to Hawaii first. I went to high school in Honolulu my senior year. Dad sent me to Tokyo after I graduated so I could 'learn proper Japanese'."

"You don't speak Japanese?" Klein was incredulous.

"I speak American Japanese. Do you speak German?"

"Enough to get by with the family," the agent responded.

"Same with me, I had conversational Japanese, I could read a little bit, but I had an accent. Not a good thing with the folks in the homeland."

"Why should that matter once you're back in Japan?"

"You don't know much about Japanese culture, do you?"

"Why don't you enlighten me," The G-man said.

"Japan is probably the most class-conscious nation on the planet. They have elaborate rituals to insure that no one loses face and centuries old traditions that keep everyone in their place. Having a foreign accent is like having the mark of Cain. You just aren't going to crack the barriers and no amount of money or connections will change that."

"So Daddy sent you back to the Motherland for lessons on how to be Japanese; that still doesn't explain how you ended up back on Whidbey Island."

"I hung on as best I could, mainly so my family wouldn't lose face in the eyes of the Imperial Court, but man when I 'graduated' I headed back home almost immediately."

"And the island was home?"

"No, no—United States. I was up and down the whole west coast as a kid. I liked the Puget Sound so it's where I came."

Klein scratched behind his left ear while he studied Paul. He opened his file once again and peered at it just long enough to create some nervous tension. He was hoping Akagi would get a case of verbal diarrhea; it happened more than most people would imagine. The pressure of silence would overcome a suspect and he would spill his guts just to fill the void. It wasn't working this time.

"How did you get back into the U.S.?" Sam finally asked.

"Well, it wasn't easy what with the embargo. I had to sail to Mexico then I caught a bus into California then took a train to Seattle a month later."

"Where's your passport? It would make it much simpler to see all the correct stamps corresponding with the correct dates, wouldn't it?"

"Sure would," Paul agreed. "But I must have lost it when I took the header down the bluff. There is a week or so in there I don't remember very well."

There was something missing and Special Agent Klein couldn't quite put his finger on it. He liked Akagi for the murders in the Seattle hotel of two intelligence operatives, but the descriptions of the only known suspect didn't match at all. He had only a vague notion of the significance of the mystery airplane, but he liked Akagi as the pilot. It was like putting together a jigsaw puzzle with no picture and most of the edge pieces missing.

"When did you start flying?"

"About three years ago..." Paul scrambled mentally to retrieve the mistake, "...I rode in a plane for the first time. I hated it, I was sick for hours after we landed. I make a lousy sailor for the same reason."

Gotcha! Klein moved in for the kill. "This is what I think happened a year ago. You re-entered the United States illegally, flew a clandestine reconnaissance mission in an orange airplane, crashed in the Sound & managed to drag yourself ashore where you were later rescued. How do you like it so far?"

"As a dime novel, not bad; as a description of what I did it's pure bull." Paul had stumbled badly and was shaken by the stunning accuracy of the FBI man. He hoped a little bravado might save his...life, really. Espionage was a capital offense and he wasn't looking forward to thirteen turns around a loop of prickly hemp rope or a volley of thirty caliber rifle rounds anytime soon.

"Oh, I think it's better than that. I'm recommending that you be transferred to Heart Mountain until the end of the war. Meanwhile, we'll be assuming custody for your transfer." Klein had noted the guilty stumble. It wasn't evidence, but it would be enough to move him.

"I can't go to another camp; I've got a family to look after." Paul let just a bit of resignation creep into his face and his shoulders slumped almost imperceptibly.

"You *can* go, and you will."

"How soon?" Paul asked.

"It'll take a couple of hours to get the paperwork finished and authorization on the phone, then we go." Klein looked the thorough professional but he was gleeful on the inside. *Gotcha you yellow bastard!*

"Two hours!" Paul was visibly distraught now, "Can I at least say goodbye. Will I have an address where family can write? Jesus, two hours is all I get?"

"Consider yourself lucky, Akagi. If I had a single eye witness we'd be telling your family when the hanging was going to take place. By the way, I'm still looking for that witness."

The men shuffled toward the conference room door, Sam turned Paul over to his partner with instructions then headed for Administration to get the ball rolling on the transfer.

"Okay Akagi, let's get going." The other agent gave him a push. Just as they were leaving the room Klein stopped him and looked into his eyes.

"Why did you kill those two people in the hotel in Seattle?"

Paul looked at the G-man, truly perplexed.

"You think I killed someone?" he asked incredulously.

"I'm tying up loose ends, Akagi, that's all."

"I have no idea what you're talking about. I won't bother to say you've got the wrong guy. Actually, on second thought I will say it, you've got the wrong guy; really."

The other agent pushed again and they walked back out toward the main gate. On the way the G-man stopped and talked with the guards. A truck with three armed guards was hastily fetched to carry the prisoner back to his blockhouse.

Sam picked up the files from the table thoughtfully. *He's the flyer for sure but not the shooter. He was genuinely surprised by that question.*

Thomas was napping in the sun, Moriko quietly sitting by his side mending trousers, when the flatbed truck ground to a halt in front of the pair, gray dust billowing behind it. Paul jumped down from the back, followed by two guards and walked to Moriko. Bending down he whispered in her ear. Her eyes widened in shock then fear and quickly she shook her husband awake.

"Toshio-san, wake up. Something terrible is happening," she said. "The soldiers are taking Paul away!"

Paul's whispers were recounted again and Thomas roused himself in indignation intending to protest.

"No time, Thomas-san," Paul said. "I need to gather the family so I can say goodbye." Moriko thought Eleanor and Leta were doing laundry. Frank had probably taken the boys to the orchards to work on the apple trees. No one was quite sure where Mary was. Moriko thought maybe taking a walk, Thomas remembered something about the infirmary but couldn't recall if that had been today. Ultimately they set off in different directions as fast as their aging legs could carry them searching for the rest of the clan.

When it is least desired, bureaucracies have an annoying habit of sudden efficiency. Barely forty five minutes had expired when

Agent Klein, papers in hand, rolled up next to the truck. By now Eleanor, Leta and the baby had been retrieved and Frank could be seen coming up the road with Steven and Benjamin. Mary still had not been found, though by now half the Bainbridge contingent was searching for her. Paul was sitting disconsolately on a battered brown leather suitcase which contained a few clothes and toiletries, a photo of the family and another of Mary.

Klein waited impatiently by his sedan, his partner still hovering around the outskirts of the little family gathering. The guards had taken up stations around the area halfheartedly trying to get the small crowd that had formed to move along. Finally Sam's patience was exhausted.

"Okay, Akagi, let's go."

"It hasn't been two hours yet, in fact it's barely more than an hour," Paul pleaded. "I haven't seen my wife yet."

"Sorry pal that was an estimate. Let's get going."

"Now see here," Frank protested in Paul's behalf, "this man may not see his family again for months, years even. You can damn well spare a few minutes more."

Klein stared hard at the man for a moment then sighed heavily and hung his head, shaking it briefly. He looked up, deliberately took out a cigarette slowly and lit it. Exhaling after a deep drag he said, "Okay, ten more minutes, that's it."

The time slid by, hugs were shared and tears were shed and still no sign of Mary. Benjamin had a wide eyed look of shock, so evident that Paul took him aside to reassure him he would be okay, and more importantly, that their blood bond of secrecy had to remain intact. Finally Paul reluctantly climbed into the sedan with the two agents, the truck re-embarked its guards and together they formed a slow, short caravan headed for the main gate. The gates swung open as they approached and in the dust Paul could see Mary running to catch up.

"Stop!" he yelled. Instinctively Klein slammed on the brakes. Paul jumped out of the car, the G-man leaped out drawing his gun. The truck following nearly slammed into the back of the car and sent its guards sprawling in the bed. Tower guards swung carbines around ominously and drew a bead on the young husband as Mary ran into his arms, her face streaked with tears.

Sam relaxed and put his revolver away signaling others that everything was okay and they returned to their respective routines. The truck backed up a little and the three guards tended to minor scrapes and bruises tossing dirty looks alternately between Paul and agent Klein.

Paul tried to wipe away her tears with his thumbs as he held her face gently but they continued to flow unabated. He kissed her tenderly, reassuring her that he would be all right and that he would write whenever he could. Mary was crying so hard she couldn't breathe normally or even speak she was so overcome.

The two Federal officers stood nearby uncomfortably, trying to ignore such a private moment all the while making sure no one was about to try anything stupid. Finally it was Paul who reluctantly disengaged himself. It was time to go.

"I've got to leave now, Mary. Take care of everyone till I get back, okay?" Mary nodded, involuntary spasms still racking her chest. Paul brushed her black hair back from her face and traced the trail of tears through the dust on her cheeks. He kissed her one last time then climbed back into the car.

"Okay Sam, let's go; and thank you," Paul said.

"My pleasure," he replied without a trace of irony in his voice. Paul rolled the window down and held her hand as the car started moving. She ran alongside and pounded on the roof.

"You can't go right now, you just can't!" She was crying hard all over again.

"I have to honey, they're going to take me and I can't stop them, neither can you."

A guard stepped between the lovers as the car moved forward past the gate. She yelled at Paul as he craned his neck for a last glimpse, "You can't go. I'm going to have a baby!"

"Asu no koto o ieba, tenjo de nezumi ga warau"

Talk about tomorrow and the mice

in the ceiling will laugh

Japanese Proverb

Vocation Siding seemed literally like the end of the world. It consisted of a typical small wooden station. A pit toilet inside an even smaller wooden enclosure was perhaps a hundred feet away. Like Lone Pine, it featured a one lane dust-choked dirt road. This one made a beeline up a low rise and disappeared onto a huge natural plateau just above a basin. Paul stepped down from the rail car along with a dozen or so other men and looked around.

Stretching for miles in every direction was a barren landscape of sage-dotted desert devoid of trees or even rocks much bigger than a fist. This seemed to Paul to be the ultimate in desolation. At the urging of the guards he and his fellow inmates; Paul was no longer simply an internee but a bonafide prisoner, shuffled toward the back of one of the ubiquitous flatbed trucks. There they were instructed to toss their bags on the back, and watched in disbelief as their luggage headed toward the administration building atop the knob of the plateau. At the urging of the guards they were left to trudge the mile up the hill afoot.

It was late June. The bleak Wyoming landscape was set off by a crystalline blue sky and the sun seemed closer and brighter than he had ever seen it. Paul spied the unusual geological formation that had given this new camp its name; Heart Mountain. Looming as the dominant—indeed the only—feature in what he judged to be the south it looked like a gigantic broken tooth anchored in an eroding fragment of jawbone jutting up from the floor of the Bighorn basin. In the distance to the west a string of inconsequential mountains were visible in a purple haze.

It was depressingly familiar. Tarpaper barracks being thrown together by work crews swarming like ants, guards with guns placed in strategic locations, admin buildings, latrines, mess halls. It struck him that this was the penultimate example of the banality of bureaucratic efficiency: Hastily cobbled together, inferior materials, poor workmanship with leadership by committee. It would no doubt still be standing a century from now, maintained to no purpose at taxpayer expense simply because it existed. He imagined it as a desultory monument to a long ago conflict; an icon to ignorance.

The process proceeded at its predictable pace, paperwork and people shuffled, until he found himself being escorted to his new assigned quarters. His new status as an enemy alien meant more than a change of address. Paul no longer had the run of the camp. He was restricted to his area. Across a barbed wire barrier he noted there were white prisoners. This puzzled him until he heard German being spoken, then later from another sequestered section, Italian.

As the days wore on other differences were discovered. The food was much better. He learned he was now subject to all the rights accorded him by the Geneva Convention. Visits and even packages from the International Red Cross became routine. Most peculiar of all to him was the fact that he now had a lawyer.

"So let me see if I understand this," Paul said. "When I was just an ordinary American citizen of Japanese ancestry the government could lock me and my family up just because the President said so. Now that I'm considered an enemy combatant I get a lawyer?"

"The paradox of this situation is not lost on me, Paul." John Hobart was jut-jawed, unusually tall, a tonsure-fringed bald head with an angry looking brown mustache sprouting beneath his aquiline nose. When he knitted his brow, as he often did, his umber eyes seemed capable of boring holes through solid steel. "Yours is an unusual case. Until the specifics of your citizenship are cleared up you are entitled to legal counsel. I think I can get you out of here. Well, reunited with your family anyway."

"Can I take the chow with me?"

John looked up blankly for a moment and then a broad smile broke across his face.

"I doubt it," he said through his grin. "Look, this is gonna be interesting from a legal point of view. Because of the war a lot of procedures are being sidestepped, but I think the first task, is to make the government prove you are not a citizen."

"Not a citizen? How does that help?" Paul asked.

"Well, if they can't prove you're an alien then ordinary Constitutional rights should be honored notwithstanding the outcome of *Hirabayashi* in the Supreme Court. They would be required to present the evidence against you in a court and I would have the chance to examine their witnesses. It's called habeas corpus; Article one, Section nine of the Constitution."

"Okay, say you succeed and I'm a regular guy again. Now who pays your bill?"

"Good question. I suppose, technically, if we win the first part then you cease to be an alien and therefore lose your status with the Convention. You're pro bono for me at this point."

"Hmmm...I don't want to be beholden to anyone." Paul wasn't sure what this guy's angle was but he wanted to draw him out some.

"Look Paul," John was very serious, "there are a lot of us out there that think your people are getting a raw deal; that think this entire internment is illegal. Some of us have joined a group to protect citizens from abuse by the government. It's called the American Civil Liberties Union. It's not about the money. It's about the principle of the thing. I'm doing okay financially, so let's get your situation squared away. Don't worry about me, or my fee."

Paul studied the man as he pondered his situation. It wasn't an easy decision. If he let sleeping dogs lie, eventually the war would be over and irrespective of which side prevailed he could hope he would just drift into the bureaucratic milieu of a post-war euphoria and go home. If he pursued this strategy and won he could be back with his family. If he lost he could face a firing squad the next day.

Paul took a deep breath and held it, then slowly exhaled. "Okay, John, let's go."

"I was hoping you would say that. We won't let you down. Oh, by the way, I have a letter for you from your wife. Sorry it's been so redacted."

"Redacted?"

"Sorry, legalese for censored. Here you are." Hobart handed the opened letter to Paul and gathered up his papers. "I'll be in touch as soon as I can, Paul."

"Thanks Mr. Hobart, give my best to your family." Paul clutched the letter close to his heart till he reached the privacy of his bunk. Thick black lines blotted out so much of what was written that it was useless to try to make sense of it. Only two lines were left intact and as he read them a lump formed in his throat. They said simply, *I miss you. I love you, Mary.*

Combat Bridge, Battleship *Yamato*
800 nautical miles Northwest of
Midway Island, Pacific Ocean
June 5, 1942 (Tokyo Time)

Yamamoto's stomach was churning and he was pale as he stood on the combat deck of his flagship. He had been stricken with some elusive intestinal bug for a couple of days and it was contributing to his general dyspepsia as his part of his fleet maintained way in support of Nagumo's attack carriers while a large contingent had been dispatched toward the Aleutians for the planned invasion there. By his calculation Nagumo should be preparing to launch bombers against Midway Island at this very moment.

As he quietly held onto a chart table his mind drifted back to the incident with the cook: As the planning for this operation was being concluded he had been served sea bream broiled with miso paste. The Admiral wasn't particularly superstitious, but the name for the dish was *miso o tsukeru* which in culinary terms simply meant "to serve with miso". It was the other meaning the phrase had that bothered him, especially in light of the illnesses among key personnel and when fifty-one sailors were killed during exercises by the explosion of a gun turret aboard the battleship *Hyuga*.

His left hand and leg had shuddered involuntarily when that news had reached him, recalling a similar incident that had maimed him so many years ago. The other meaning of the phrase was "to make a hash of something".

A report came in from the radio room indicating a scout plane had spotted an American carrier group under way two hundred forty miles away from Midway. This was totally unexpected and unplanned, but Yamamoto thought perhaps it was a singular opportunity to deal a harsh blow the U.S. Navy in the Pacific. Only a few minutes later the radio room reported traffic from the *Tone*: "Attacked by enemy land-based and carrier-based planes. *Kaga, Soryu* and *Akagi* ablaze".

The news was greeted on the bridge with stunned silence as the import of this information sank in. Coming from the *Tone*, the ship second in command of the fleet, it raised the specter that *Akagi* and Admiral Nagumo might be lost. Yamamoto only grunted through compressed lips and silently left the room to the appalled officers of the watch.

Letters

Dear Frank,

Well, according to Paul's instruction book, Stan and I plowed fields and planted carrots and potatoes a couple of months ago. Now I should be running down the rows to loosen soil and in a perfect world I would be doing that. But right now the tractor is just about axle deep in mud. Old man Sweeney is on his way with his tractor to haul us out, but obviously after this last rain the fields are still too wet to work. I guess we'll wait a week or so and hope they drain some.

It's getting harder to find extra workers. Just about every able bodied man in the area has joined up or is headed for a factory somewhere. There are rumors about rationing, but the only thing I really worry about is fuel. Can't farm these days without a lot of machinery and it all needs gas! It's really quiet on the island since everyone was shipped out. It's strange, I just expect you to walk in any moment and then I remember that won't be happening anytime soon.

Stan sometimes thinks he may be drafted into the Navy since he was a Merchant Marine, then other times figures that since his wife is Japanese, probably not. Anyway it would be almost impossible to run the farm without him so I hope he gets to stay here. Maybe we can get him a critical job deferment.

Ritchie can't wait for school to finish this year. He's been learning to drive the tractor and imagines himself quite the farmer.

Truth is he's been a real help. I suspect by harvest time he'll know as much about things as I do. Not that that will take all that much work!

Well, Sweeney is here so I better close and go help pull your tractor out of the mud.

Give our best to everyone and stay strong. This war can't last forever.

Sincerely,

Josh

PS, great news about Mary and the baby, sorry to hear about Paul's situation.

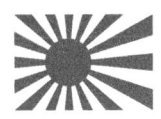

Dear Mommy,

You can't possibly imagine how much I miss you. In some ways this spot could be described as glorious isolation I suppose. There is almost nothing in any direction for miles except a few rocks and scrub. More barren even than Manzanar, still they've managed to find a decent water supply and some of the regulars have started to do some farming. I can't help because there is apparently some Geneva Convention rule that stops prisoners of war from being used for labor, even if I want to. So instead we mostly sit around being bored.

It was a weird day yesterday, though. The Japanese prisoners formed a baseball team and challenged the Germans to a game. The guards weren't quite sure what to do about that but finally decided it couldn't hurt so they let us play.

I'll say this (if it doesn't get cut by the censors) the krauts may build a mean tank but they're lousy at baseball. It was hilarious to watch, almost as funny as the 4th of July on Whidbey. God that seems so long ago.

I dreamed about our son the other night, at least that's what I'm imagining. It seems so unfair that he'll be born in a XXXXXXX

XXXXXXXXXX (censored) XXXXXXXXXXXXX XXXXXXX. But I know you and the rest of the family will take good care of him (or her!) and so I don't really worry about it.

I wish I could send you some of the chow we get here. Being a XXXXXXXXXXX XXXXXXXXXX (censored) XXXXXXXXXX XXXXXXXXXXX XXXXXXXXXX XXXXXXXXXXX XXXXXXXXXXXXXX XXXXX XXX XXXXXXXXX XXX XXXXXXXXXXX has its benefits.

My lawyer says he's hopeful but that these things tend to go slowly so not to expect anything real soon. It's too bad; I really wanted to be there with you when the baby was born.

Time to go, they're sounding the dinner bell and the guards get real testy when we're late.

I love you with all my heart my dearest,

Daddy

My Darling Stan,

It's only been a few months but I miss you so and want to come home. Sarah cut her first tooth yesterday on the bottom in the front. She's been fussy all week and now I know why! Mary is just starting to show. She hasn't been sick once since she started, what a lucky girl! Mom and Dad have been settling in. Dad is trying to bring some scraggly old apple trees back to life a few cell blocks over. He says they look like they were part of an old orchard that may have been on this property years ago.

Everybody is getting used to the lousy food, but it sure isn't what we like. Frank and Steve are working like fools along with some other farmers from the Imperial Valley to plant crops that will get us fresh vegetables soon. They have about five acres in spinach and lettuce. It's not much but it grows quick and at least it's fresh. They have big plans for lots of other crops but they probably won't be ready till Thanksgiving. One thing about farming in the desert, they get lots of sunshine!

I kind of hate to say it but everybody is sort of getting used to being here. The weather is always clear. We could all go for a dose of Seattle sunshine (you know, rain) about now, but it doesn't look like it rains here more than a few minutes a year.

Mary got a letter from Paul last week but he couldn't put much in it because of war restrictions. He did say he has some lawyer helping him now but I don't think that made her feel any better. She is so blue and lonely with him gone. We all try to cheer her up but the truth is we're pretty lonely and sad too.

Anyway I was sad to hear about our little house burning but I imagine Josh probably needs you more at the farm anyway.

Well, time to go do the laundry now so I will close. I miss you so much and can't wait for this damn war to be over so we can come home and be a family again.

All my love and kisses,
XOXOXOXOXO

Dear Daddy,

I gave mommy a great big kick this morning. She was eating oatmeal, and I don't think I like it very much! I think I like kicking her though, because I'm doing a lot of it now. It's warm and cozy in here, but it is starting to get a little cramped. I think I hear voices outside and sometimes I kick when I hear ones I like. I wish you could talk to me sometime. I have no idea what time it is but I think it may be time to come out and meet everybody around Halloween. I'm just going to grow in here for a while so bye bye.

Love, baby Paul(ette!)

Hi Honey,

We just found out from Al that everybody from Bainbridge is getting relocated (again!) to some place in Idaho called Minidoka.

It's just like the government isn't it! We just start to get settled into something like a regular life (well, as regular as it can get behind barbed wire) and now they are going to ship us off again.

Dad is a little irked I think. The farmers have almost 200 acres working now and somebody else will get to eat all the food. Oh well, isn't that what farmers do anyway? I think Grandfather will be the most disappointed though. He has made quite a few friends here and his old apple trees actually look pretty good and even have a small crop of fruit for the fall.

I'm not looking forward to two or three days on a train. I can't see my feet anymore and I'm starting to waddle around like a mallard hen. Maybe its best that you can't see me right now, I feel like a fat old cow. I'll send along the new address as soon as I have it.

I miss you my love,

Mary

"When you find yourself trapped in a hole the first course of action should be to stop digging"

Anonymous

"This is ridiculous!" Special Agent Klein studied the paper spread over the hood of the car in front of him. "We are both trained investigators with the FBI; we should be able to read a map!" His partner scrutinized the surroundings, focusing on a road sign marked *Black and Yellow Highway* pointing in one direction and *U S 116* pointing in another. Finally he looked at the Conoco Oil Co. road map Klein was leaning on.

"Black and Yellow isn't even on here," he pointed out unnecessarily. "But if this is 116," he gestured to the road snaking off into the distance, "then we must be on 16 now. If we follow the marker for 116 it should take us to Sheridan pretty soon." It was getting on toward late afternoon and he didn't relish traipsing around in this godforsaken wilderness after nightfall.

"Seems about right," Sam agreed. "I'm hungry." It just popped out like an afterthought, but now that they had chosen a course of action is seemed like a good time to eat one of the sandwiches the mess hall at Heart Mountain had packed for them. "Here you go," he said, handing one of the waxed paper wrapped morsels to the man across the hood. "You get a choice of baloney and cheese or cheese and baloney."

"Swell, my favorites," he retorted. Using the grill of the car for leverage he popped the top off of a couple of Cokes, spewing brown sticky foam on his pants. "Damn, I'll be stuck to everything till we get to Sheridan. Remind me again why we are in such a hurry to get this paperwork to Casper?"

"It's part of the litigation over the internment of the Japs. Some group of bleeding heart lawyers wants to use Sakai's case as a habeas corpus trial. I don't see it myself; he's straight up espionage in my book." He took a swig from the bottle to help slide the sandwich down. "But we're just couriers now, time to let the real legal eagles earn their dough."

By now the spilled soft drink had begun to attract unwanted attention from nearby yellow jackets so the two men piled back into the car and headed up the road marked as U S 116.

"Those damned hunters!" Joe exclaimed. He got out of the road maintenance truck he was driving and looked at the sign. "They must think it's funny as hell to change that sign. Well, I'll put a stop to this once and for all."

"What are you whining about now, Joe?"

"Look at this Mark, I'll bet it was Jeff again. He's doin' this kinda shit all the time. He's gonna get somebody good and lost someday."

His workmate looked at the sign and snorted. "Hell, Joe, everybody knows one-sixteen has been closed for five years and they haven't called this road the Black and Yellow for what, seven or eight years now?"

"Yeah, well, not everybody is from around here. Let's finish this stinkin' thing so we can get home."

The two men went about their business, Joe removing the bogus signage while Mark got started on a barrier across old 116, much sturdier than the previous ones that had been removed so many times by local hunters. When they left there was no signage at all since there was no intersection to mark and no way to access the old road without tearing down its substantial new impediment.

Old Apple Orchard
Manzanar War Relocation Center
Lone Pine, Calif
June 23, 1942

Thomas peered over the top of his glasses at the tortured trees he and a few other old men had nurtured back to some semblance of productivity. This was currently his favorite spot in the camp. A chair and small side table had been formed with a few old cantaloupe crates, and most days he would spend time just watching the trees and daydreaming of home. He had no idea what variety the apple trees might be and wouldn't even hazard a guess until the green nubbins got closer to maturity in size and color, but he knew the trees were old. Probably fifty years old if the ring count was right on one of the deadfalls.

He tried to imagine who would have planted and tended a fruit orchard in this heat blasted, windblown, barren desert. And from where the water could have come or how they had managed to survive untended all these years. But the unforgiving climate reclaims its harsh terrain quickly, leaving only the woody clues to ponder.

The fact that the Owens Valley had relatively recently been lush with crops was wholly unknown to him, as was the fact that most of the water rights had been bamboozled from local inhabitants by far away developers. As happens so often, politicians, lawyers and accountants with sharp pencils had snatched a precious resource. In this case, to feed a growing monster called the Los Angeles Basin.

The warm sun lulled Thomas into a sort of stupor and he drifted between the here and now, and the long ago past as his mind painted gossamer dreams in his semi-consciousness. Distantly a rhythmic tapping droned out a syncopated beat. In his mind he was back on Maui, the trade winds swaying the sugar cane stalks. It was the sound of the chopping as workers harvested the sweetgrass. *No, that's not it. The rhythm is wrong—the pitch is wrong.* He frowned, trying to place the sound. That he couldn't nagged at him until finally he realized it wasn't from long ago, it was from right now, here in Manzanar. What was so familiar about that sound? Now fully roused, he concentrated on trying to figure out from where it was emanating. Thomas labored out of his chair and followed the tap-tap-tap, pause, tap-tap-tap-tap out of the orchard, through a walkway between barracks and across the road into the firebreak clearing. The noise got louder as he approached a hunched figure from behind. Muscles flexed in time to the taps. What was evidently an old man stood for a moment, then hunched over and began tapping again.

Suddenly the image of a dragon winding around the mast pole between the decks of the *Hawaiian Sunrise* flooded Thomas' memory.

"Watanabe!" He exclaimed. "Watanabe, can it truly be you?"

Startled, the figure stood erect and spun around to inspect his accoster. He studied the old man as he approached and slowly a big grin broke across his face. He put his carving gouge and mallet aside and moved to greet his old friend.

"Sichou Thomas-san, what are you doing here?"

They looked at each other for a moment then collapsed into each other's arms in laughter as the silliness of the question sank in.

"I'm waiting to die or for the war to end, same as you," Thomas finally managed to say. "Where is Tatsuyo? Tell me about your family, what has happened to you all these years?"

"She is probably helping our daughter with laundry. Today is our barracks day at the washroom."

The two old workmates fell into a dialogue as Watanabe; a master carver, now of world renown, collected his tools. Then they began to walk back towards their barracks.

The reunion was joyous, Moriko and Tatsuyo relived their voyage from Japan and the two men spoke at length of their life in the cane fields. Time had granted them the blessing of nostalgia to blur the harsh conditions, long hours and brutal treatment. It gave the entire era a romantic patina.

Long after most members of the families were asleep and the camp had fallen into silence they talked, occasionally lapsing into the old patois of the island. Each wanted to know everything about the other, how the years had treated them, what they thought about the war and if they would return to their old lives after the camps.

Finally as the first fingers of light appeared behind the mountains to the east they reluctantly parted and retired to their respective beds. It was the first of many such evenings shared in an effort to ease the sting of their current circumstances.

> "The miserable have no other
> medicine, But only hope"
>
> *Wm. Shakespeare*

"This can't possibly be right," Klein announced abruptly. "Look at this road, nobody is using this regularly." His FBI partner, Hoody Marks, had been visually scanning the road for the last five miles and had reached the same conclusion, but since it had been he that had suggested this route, his stubborn side was reluctant to admit it.

"Yeah," he finally acknowledged, "I think you're right." Sam pulled the sedan over to side of the road, set the parking brake and switched the engine off.

"Let's look at that map again," Klein said. They unfolded the colorful paper carefully and peered at various lines winding across the area depicted.

"It's too dark in here to see anything," Marks said.

The two men got out of the car and spread the map across the hood. Sam searched the road behind them, then ahead to the bend in the road about three hundred yards forward. The roadway was peppered with leaf litter from the trees and weeds that had taken root and grown to maturity in the cracks of the pavement, apparently uninhibited by traffic. Through a clearing to the side of the road next to the car, was what appeared to be a foot path down to a stream perhaps hiding a fishing hole guarded by a few jagged boulders and scraggly willows. The stream was low, but running clear.

"Look at this, Hoody." Sam had his foot on the bumper and was leaning over the map trying to make out details in the waning light. "If this isn't the right way then the only thing to do is go back the where the road forks and go the other way. According to this map it's a longer route but still gets there."

Marks finished his survey of the terrain then leaned on the car to take a closer look.

"How old is this map?" He wondered aloud. He turned it over and checked the date. "Copyright nineteen thirty four. Well, hell, how many roads could they have built through here since thirty-four?"

Both men heard the sharp *thwang* and felt the car lurch backwards as they were tumbled to the pavement. The emergency brake cable had snapped, and to their horror, the car was rolling backward, quickly gaining momentum down the path heading for the creek bed. Sam was first to spring to his feet and give chase with Marks scrambling behind him. Klein was nearly there, when the car made a sickening screech over a jagged rock, creating a tiny spark that instantly ignited a fireball of volatile fuel vapors from the now ruptured gas tank. In a matter of seconds the entire vehicle, and the dry grass surrounding it, were engulfed in flames and the two men were forced to retreat.

They managed to beat back the flames in the grass to prevent a range fire from erupting, but when the inferno in the vehicle had subsided it was clear that everything was a total loss. Daylight was waning fast in the mountains, the two men were afoot in unfamiliar territory, and no one else knew they were there.

"Damn," Hoody said.

"What?" Klein demanded in exasperation.

"We lost the rest of our baloney sandwiches."

Island Farms

Bainbridge Island
July 4, 1942

"Well, this is certainly a better crop of strawberries than I expected to see!"

"Nature does have its ways, Josh." Stan surveyed the tidy rows of lush green leaves on the plants laden with crimson jewels with some satisfaction. "We even have decent weather on the Fourth. That in itself is darn near a miracle."

"They taste great, too, dad!" Ritchie, with red stains on his fingers and lips, carefully worked his way up a row trying to avoid crushing any of the fragile berries.

"All this is wonderful, except for one minor problem," Joshua paused for effect. "We have no one to pick them, and maybe no one to buy them. So I guess it's a lot of strawberry shortcake for a while."

"Maybe not, dad. Old man Sestus who took over the Mitsui place didn't plant any berries. Almost nobody did, so right now they're paying hands that don't have much to do. They might let us borrow some of them, especially if they don't have to pay them for a few days."

"We've become quite the little farmer here, haven't we?"

"Hey, Stan, I'm almost seventeen, I'm not a kid anymore. I pay attention."

"So you do, young man. Well, so do I. There might be a small demand for a few fresh strawberries at the Pike Place Market, but there is a rumor going around that frozen is the next big thing. I might look into that."

"Frozen! Who the hell would want frozen berries?" Stan scowled as he peered at the fields then at Joshua.

"The army, for one," Josh said. "Imagine getting a taste of home to the troops on the front lines. Ya can't can 'em. I suppose we could contract to make preserves out of them, but there's not much profit in that. Nope, I think we should take a chance on freezing. There's a new facility in Poulsbo that froze fish. They're looking for other things to process since most of the trawler crews are signed up for the war. Maybe they can do some berries. Frank mentioned they had done it before with some success."

"Too bad we can't run it by Frank or Paul. They'd know what to do." Joshua caught the lingering sadness in Stan's voice.

"Yes, I suppose they would. But by the time we got a letter back all the fruit would be rotted on vine. Either way it would be a shame not to try."

"Hmmph, well, it's Saturday, so I better see about rounding up some hands, before everyone is snagged by Boeing or the new shipyard in Bremerton. Won't get anyone till Monday and those berries need picking real soon. Maybe I'll start with Sestus. He might know who else has too big a payroll right now. See you later. You too, sprout." Stan turned and headed back to the main house.

"Who you callin' a sprout, you big moose?" Ritchie yelled at the back of the massive man as he retreated. Stan looked over his shoulder with a smile and continued without reply.

"Dad?'

"Yes, son?"

"Is it really just a year since we were all together on the beach in Mutiny Bay?" Instinctively Joshua's eyes looked to the northeast. He couldn't actually see the island beach, but the laughter was still ringing in his ears, and the fellowship of family and friends was sorely missed. The image of the photo carefully hidden by one of the Sakai family flashed through his mind

"Yep, just a year ago," he replied.

"Dad?"

"Yes?"

"It's a crummy war.

"It is that, son. It is that, indeed."

U.S. District Court for Wyoming

Casper, Wyoming

July 6, 1942

Riddled with mosquito bites, their feet blistered from hiking miles in street shoes, cold, bedraggled and ravenous the two G-men looked more like tramp rail riders than professional FBI officers when they finally flagged down a rancher and got a ride back toward civilization. After gulping down endless cups of coffee and devouring a couple of hamburgers each at Peggy's Café (and Post Office) Klein finally found a telephone and made the call he had to make to the home office.

By the next day, a federal prosecutor and an ACLU attorney representing Paul Akagi were standing before the district court judge in his courtroom.

"So, Counselor," Justice Thomas Blake Kennedy intoned, scowling down at the prosecutor, "the continuance I granted—reluctantly I might add—so the government could produce its evidence, is no longer needed?"

"Uh, no, your honor. The government will be prepared to begin at the court's convenience."

"Your honor, the prosecution has failed to produce the documents required by our discovery motion. The defense can hardly be expected to proceed blindly."

"Well, Mr. Prosecutor, what about that? Where are the discovery items and when do you expect to deliver them to the defense counsel?"

"We will be proceeding on direct testimony. There will be no documents presented. Our witness will be here tomorrow morning." The judge shuffled through some papers settling on a few pages which he studied closely, his scowl deepening as he read. The defense attorney was rummaging around in his briefcase, apparently looking for the same paperwork.

"According to the indictment, there are supposed to be interrogation notes, original documents to support the charges being laid, and witness statements. Where are these documents?"

"Well, uh, there seems to have been a problem during the transport of the documents. We will be proceeding without them."

"Your honor," the defense counselor broke in, "defense would like to know what, specifically, happened to these so-called documents."

"So would the court, counselor. Well?"

The prosecutor shifted uncomfortably under the gaze of the judge, fingering the file in his hand.

"There was a problem, an accident actually, while two FBI agents were bringing the files here. There was a fire."

"And..?"

"And all the documentary evidence was destroyed."

"So you propose to continue on the basis of the direct testimony of witnesses?"

"One witness, your honor, yes."

"Your Honor!" the defense counsel began to protest. Kennedy held up his hand.

"Who is this witness?" The judge asked.

"Joseph Klein, a special agent with the FBI."

"What do you anticipate his testimony will reveal?"

"He will testify to his interrogation of the defendant and on the contents of the evidence lost in the fire."

"Your Honor, I must protest. In fact, the defense moves for dismissal on the basis of habeas corpus. It is hearsay—at best—for an agent to testify about documents not in evidence."

"You propose to prosecute an American citizen for espionage solely on the basis of the memory of a single, overworked government investigator without any corroborating evidence?" The skepticism in the judge's voice was palpable.

"Yes, your honor. Well, not exactly, we believe Mr. Akagi is not actually a United States citizen."

"And your evidence for that?" the defense counsel asked.

"The direct testimony of our agent."

"Actually, counselor, I don't think you are." The judge tossed aside his glasses and pinched his nose before he continued. "I am inclined to grant the motion for dismissal. If you think the loss of your evidence is just a bothersome detail, you clearly haven't attended a trial in my district court. I expect both counsels to be ready to begin on time, and to move forward. Absent the evidence cited in the charging documents, the indictment is fatally flawed, and I doubt the government would have brought this case. This isn't a parking ticket in a municipal court; this is a capital espionage case in a federal court."

"Your honor, perhaps a continuance would be in order so the government can assemble more witnesses for this case." It was a hopeful suggestion from a clearly disappointed prosecutor.

"Mr. Prosecutor, the government may have as long as it likes to try to assemble a case, just not this case. The defense motion to dismiss is granted with prejudice. Start over if you like, but any evidence cited in the original indictment is excluded. You are free to pursue an appeal, but as far as this court is concerned this case is ended." He replaced his glasses on his nose then scribbled something on a paper and handed it to his clerk.

"Next case."

Admiral's Deck aboard the *Yamato*
August 10, 1942
Somewhere in the Pacific

Yamamoto studied the engagement report carefully. The war in the Pacific had been going badly for Japan despite the inflated boasting of General Tojo about successes by the army. In fact, Tojo's co-opting of the resources of the navy to transport troops left the door open to Allied vessels pouring in barely challenged to the western and southern Pacific. This decisive blow at Savo Island by Vice Admiral Mikawa, the sinking of several American warships and damaging others engaged in defending resupply efforts to U.S. Marines on Guadalcana,1 was a serious blow to enemy plans. It had crippled the marines stranded on the island and forced Admiral Turner to withdraw. Still, he knew it was a temporary reprieve at best. He was haunted by his own experience witnessing the unending supply of coal and iron ore feeding U.S. industries now turned into war machines. Worse still were the reports that shipyards were churning out transport ships at the unthinkable rate of nine ships per week. As he had warned Tokyo on many occasions it was now just a matter of time until the Japanese Imperial Navy was overwhelmed by the sheer numerical advantage the Americans could bring to bear.

The nagging feeling that Mikawa had retired from the engagement too early and should have pressed the attack lingered at the edge of his thoughts as he reflected on the Battle of Tsushima so many years ago. As an Ensign he had learned the lessons of pressing an attack when the enemy was in retreat, badly damaged and in disarray.

Yamamoto rubbed his aching knee with the mangled hand he sustained during that distant battle. *It won't matter in the end,* he thought, *we will lose this war. But I am a sailor for the Emperor, so I will plan for the war I am given and pray for the peace that I hope for.*

"Bushi desu honshitsu-teki koto no okodoeshita"
A Samurai is a man of action
Minidoka War Relocation Center
Hunt, Idaho
April 19, 1943

As the sun rose on the barren skyline of the basalt plateau of the Snake River Basin, a cold, dry wind whistled around and through the low tarpaper barracks and other assorted shops and buildings perched thereon. The icy dirt streets of the winter had thawed bringing plains of mud throughout the camp. Women had begun asking for *geta* clogs to be fashioned to keep their feet clean as they shuttled back and forth to the showers.

This was the Magic Valley, whose name Harry Hashimoto found particularly galling. He along with the rest of the Bainbridge group had been transferred to this garden spot of desolation from Manzanar last August. Harry was standing on the banks of the Northside canal near Swimming Hole #3 watching some old-timers fishing from the bank and silently seething about the state of things in the political world.

"Hey Harry, anybody catching anything?" Harry turned and was surprised to see Steven Sakai approaching.

"Haven't noticed, really. Not paying much attention."

"Yeah, I understand. Listen, I owe you an apology."

"For what?" He eyed Steven curiously.

"For busting your chops on the Quad that day. You were fulminating about how things would go south for us and I dusted you off. Clearly I was wrong. I just wanted to say I'm sorry."

"Thanks. It's water under the bridge. Or down the canal, I suppose. Just so you know, I had no inkling it would end up being this bad. But I think it may get worse."

"How so?"

"Nothing travels faster than a rumor and yesterday I overheard the guards talking about Topaz. It's the place in Utah."

"I think Paul is there. Or maybe Heart Mountain, I'm not certain. He got shipped there before we were transferred. Not likely he'll be here when Mary's baby arrives. Anyway what about Topaz?"

"A guard shot an old man. A cook, I hear. Killed him. Guard says he was trying to escape but even our keepers here don't believe that. Might be a show trial, but I would bet a year's pay he'll beat the rap."

"Jeez, I hope nobody here gets trigger happy. Technically we're out of bounds at the canal, the fence is on the other side of the levee road. This can't last forever and I, for one, would like to get out of this alive."

"How did you answer the loyalty questions?"

"Yes to both questions if you mean 27 and 28, but praying I don't get drafted."

"I still can't believe they gave us a loyalty test. It's insulting, infuriating and useless. What's the point?"

"Well, I guess they want to give out passes to leave camp. For jobs and farm work so they say. And of course, they're forming up a Japanese army unit. I don't imagine they'll be shipped out to the Pacific though. How did you answer the questions?"

"Left them blank. I'm a natural born citizen of the United States of America, and until they start asking everyone those questions they can damn well kiss my ass for an answer!"

Steven edged over to one of the fisherman and tapped him on the shoulder. "Come on Gramps, time to go. Breakfast is ready." He turned back to Hashimoto, "I thought about answering no. Dad and Paul talked me out of it. Said the nail sticking up is the one that gets hammered. So I work on finishing my degree by mail and dream of building skyscrapers taller than the Empire State. Even if I get drafted I'll probably end up in an engineering detail. Meanwhile I just swallow my pride and keep my head down. It burns like hell, though." He helped Thomas to his feet and took the tackle from him, offering his arm.

"Mark my words, Steven, a raging fire is gonna sweep through these camps before it's all over."

Steven nodded as he walked away. "That's what I'm afraid of, Harry."

Costello Estate

Somewhere in the Catskills
New York State
Mid April, 1943

As his car wound its way along a quiet country road OSS Director William Donovan scanned the letter which prompted the bucolic trek to the estate of mob boss Frank Costello. It was only a few lines suggesting that the 'research effort' initiated by Wild Bill had yielded results with an invitation extended to discuss the matter privately in person. That request had been over a year ago and Roosevelt's spy chief had been very, very busy since then. So busy, in fact, he had forgotten the initiative altogether until the letter arrived. Now, as his driver pulled up to a guarded gate and rolled down the window, his curiosity had been piqued and he was anxious to see what the acting head of the Luciano crime family had to offer.

"Mr. Donovan for Mr. Costello," the driver said. "He is expected."

"Of course. Good afternoon, sir. Please follow the drive to the main house. Mr. Costello is waiting for you Mr. Donovan." Redirecting his eyes to the driver the gatekeeper said, "And you will remain with your vehicle while on the grounds. I'm sure you understand. Mister Costello values his privacy." The chauffeur nodded and drove toward the house. The full glory of early springtime in the mountains was on display with carefully cultivated flowers in full bloom, lawns immaculately manicured and trees dressed with the bright green of a new season. Standing in the *porte cochere* was the Mafioso himself, no doubt alerted to the arrival by the gatehouse.

"Your grounds are lovely this spring, Mr. Costello." Donovan said, alighting from the car. He was no stranger to the forced formality and politeness these sort of meetings engendered. Nor would he be dissuaded by the likelihood that the conversation would be laced with vague allusions and overly broad language which nonetheless made the point.

"Thank you. Yes, the gardeners have excelled this year. Perhaps I should give them a raise." He smiled and continued, "and a beautiful day as well. Shall we step inside?" Donovan followed as Costello led him into the same room their last meeting had occurred. "May I offer you a beverage? Iced tea, perhaps?" He gestured to a man stationed nearby, "and some fruit would be nice." Bringing his focus back to Wild Bill, Costello said "perhaps we should dispense with the formalities and get to the reason for your visit. After your request we looked into the circumstances of the unfortunate murder of your colleagues in Seattle. A very unsavory affair to be sure."

Donovan doubted the mobster was much bothered by a killing. He shifted in his armchair, recalling the circumstances of the loss of the best code breaker west of the Mississippi and his assistant. Shot in their hotel room by an unknown assailant while pursuing a hot lead on a suspected spy. That trail had gone cold. The team assigned to deciphering the notes left by Oscar something, the name had vanished from his memory, had failed and more pressing events swept the effort away. Everything had dead-ended thereafter. Maybe the crumbs he got here would heat things up again.

"Our resources in the Pacific Northwest are meager but a cab driver recalled your couple and was persuaded to share his information with my associates." Left unsaid were the beatings and torture that had yielded the results, nor his killing thereafter. It turned out the frigid waters of the Puget Sound were a great place to dump a body.

"So you have news for me," Bill said.

"Indeed, I do." The goon had returned with a silver tray laden with items. "Thank you Michael. Your tea, Mr. Donovan. And please help yourself to some fresh fruit. Michael, see to it that his driver has some refreshment provided." Costello continued, "The cabbie directed our researchers to a small organization in the United States whose mission was espionage and mischief to disrupt your efforts at code breaking enemy communications. To our shame this effort was traced to the old country."

Donovan sipped his tea and popped a juicy strawberry in his mouth. It gave him a moment to consider his response. "Excellent. If you could provide me with the names, and addresses if you have them, of these operatives we'll take it from here."

"Alas, but that I could. A series of unfortunate revelations led us to believe that no time could be wasted in rooting out this group and their operatives. Naturally, they resisted and we insisted."

"Naturally."

"It seemed members of that organization had become entangled with our business activities and to protect our own assets we acted, as you would do, to protect our interests."

"I see. Yes, that is unfortunate. They could have provided some important information."

"To the extent we were able we did conduct interrogations on your behalf. You will find the relevant results in this report." He handed Donovan a file folder that had been lying on a nearby casual table. "You will, of course, appreciate unimportant names, dates and places have been omitted in the interest of clarity."

"Of course."

"We are loyal citizens, Mr. Donovan. It was painful for us to learn of this clandestine effort to undermine our country. You can rest assured that our measures have ruined their organization both here and in our homeland. Permanently."

Donovan arose and offered his hand, "On behalf of the President, thank you."

Costello took his hand firmly, "And the other item we discussed earlier?"

"I'll see to it. It might take some time, war and all that, but it will happen." On the drive back to D.C. the driver, who was also a trained agent, wondered aloud about what the result of the meeting had been.

"Luciano found a good excuse to strike a blow for democracy while ridding himself of some competition. He had them all killed. Not the way I would have done it, but hey, problem solved."

Operation Vengeance
Solomon Islands, South Pacific
April 14-18. 1943

It was a Wednesday and Fleet Radio Service could scarcely believe their luck. Three separate listening stations had intercepted a series of encrypted Japanese transmissions. As the code breaking team read the results of their collated efforts they realized it was the itinerary of Imperial Fleet Admiral Yamamoto as he planned visits to the Solomon Islands within the week. This news—held closely as top secret—was at the office of the President within hours. FDR wasn't there, and ever the politician, he demurred—at least officially —leaving the decision about a seek and destroy mission to an anxious Secretary of the Navy and his CINC-PAC Admiral Chester Nimitz.

Such a mission ran a significant risk of exposing the Allied code-breaking capabilities, which would be disastrous to the war effort not just in the Pacific theater, but throughout the war-torn world. After an excruciating examination of the chance of ruining cypher secrets versus the high value of the target, and with consultation with Bull Halsey, Nimitz issued the go ahead on Saturday.

The effort was daring, complex and long range. Almost anything could wreck the mission, and a lot had to go right for any chance of success. The flight team was assembled and planning began.

Yamamoto gazed at the first hint of light in the morning sky and sighed. The recent air efforts to retake Guadalcanal, or at least deny the use of its airfield to the Americans, were going badly. Almost certainly the casualty reports he was receiving were fantasies meant to save the face of field flight commanders. The enemy and its new twin boom configuration fighter plane was exacting a terrible toll on the Imperial Air Force and not suffering nearly as much. His judgment that Japan could not win this war, or at this point even plausibly sue for peace, was intact. But so was his *bushido* code determination to fight to the end for the homeland, however hopeless. So this farce of rallying the army and boosting morale by his presence must go on. The sun emerged to light a clear and fair day. He sighed once more, then returned to the airfield to board his plane for the flight from *Rabual* to *Ballale*. At precisely 6:10 a.m. the two Mitsubishi G4M Medium bombers and six Mitsubishi A6M Zeroes that comprised his staff and air cover group lifted off the runway for the three hundred mile jump to the next stop.

Intramural rivalries among the services threatened to derail the assignment before it could get off the ground. Neither the F4F Wildcats or the F4U Corsairs available to the Navy and Marines had the range for such a mission. The only fighter that was mission capable was the recently delivered P-38 Lightning assigned to the Army Air Force. Admiral Marc Mitscher, air operations commander for the entire region, had been part of the initial planning and with some reluctance called in the XIII Fighter Command leader. With a quick assessment and a few calls, another team was assembled and designated P-38 pilots of the Cactus Air Force were ordered to report. An emergency call for wing tanks to extend the range of the aircraft, its urgency boosted by Mitscher's signature on the requisition, went out and yielded the fuel cells.

Working through the night, maintenance crews scrambled to repair battle damage and affix the range-extending tanks. Meanwhile 339th Squadron Commander Major John Mitchell pored over maps and charts to calculate the navigation details, all of which were dependent on pinpoint speeds, timing and headings. Emerging from the planning tent before dawn, he got some chow and reported to the flight line. At precisely 5:10 a.m. eighteen P-38s lined up. One blew a tire on the runway and retired, another had fueling issues and returned. The sixteen remaining planes took flight and after forming up, the squadrons dropped to an altitude of fifty feet skimming the waves and enduring the intense concentration required so close to the water. The sauna-like heat the broiling tropical sun created in the cockpits made the task doubly difficult. Struggling to stay awake, Mitchell focused on the navy compass a Marine had supplied, his airspeed and his watch. The rest of the formation wiped sweat from their eyes and cursed the design that graced this normally high altitude fighter with a canopy that couldn't be opened in normal flight. Radios silenced, they flew in tight formation another two hours before they could begin ascending for the hunt for the target.

The P-38 squadron arrived just as the Japanese planes were lining up and in a gliding descent prior to landing. Two Zeroes spotted the planes and began an attack dive. Splitting up, the Allied planes engaged the fighters and targeted the two bombers preparing to land. The first bomber was struck and trailing black smoke went down in the water off the island. Unsure which plane carried Yamamoto, the battle was carried to the second bomber. Riddled with bullet holes and belching white smoke it crashed into the dense jungle of the island miles short of the runway. Flush with victory the American pilots broke off the engagement and returned to base having lost a single plane and pilot.

Yamamoto's bullet ridden body was discovered the next day by a Japanese search party. Having been thrown from the plane, still strapped to his seat in an upright position next to a tree, he was found clutching his *katana* in his hand, his head leaning forward as if contemplating his own death.

For the Admiral the war was over but his remains were still useful to the Imperial Armed Forces. Following an elaborate procession and ceremonial extravaganza worthy of an Emperor, half his ashes were interred at the Tama cemetery in Tokyo. Nearly beatified, the rest of the earthly remains of Isoroku Yamamoto were returned to his childhood home of Niigata and laid to rest. As the procession crossed the rebuilt Bandai bridge, red *tori* flitted among the cherry trees just as they had when he was a child.

Minidoka War Relocation Center
Hunt, Idaho
May 10-12, 1943

The ink on the form authorizing Paul's transfer back to his family had barely dried on Friday when he was given a pass and told to be on a Greyhound bus Saturday night to begin the journey to southern Idaho. The bus rumbled into Vocation Siding about eleven p.m. and the lone departing passenger, Paul, boarded an empty vehicle. The driver barely acknowledged him but gave a nod to the guard that had delivered him, pulled the door shut and drove out to Highway 14 for the long journey to Salt Lake City.

In Cody the driver turned east into the featureless plains until reaching Highway 20 when he headed south. Paul wondered aloud about the route and the driver said bus service was about the only way to get around with the gas rationing so they had a circuitous route to get anywhere. Every Podunk town they came through might have a passenger.

"Sit back and enjoy the ride, he said, "it's gonna be a long night."

"Thanks," Paul replied. "I hope you had a good nap today." The driver snorted and kept driving.

Mile after desolate mile crept by deep into the darkest hours of any day, uninformed by the feeble light of the waning gibbous moon. Periodically they would heave-to at some wide spot in the road for a solitary figure waving a lantern and embark another passenger. Each would settle into a seat and the bus would trek on once again. Across the flat land it passed tiny farm towns most notable for the presence of a U.S. Post Office in the back of a gas station or small mercantile, often with the living quarters in the same building. Village sign posts with names like Worland, Kirby and Thermopolis emerged from, then disappeared into the gloom. In Shoshone the driver pulled into a deserted city park where he announced a meal break and half hour rest stop. Paul noticed he bolted down a sandwich and stretched out on a park bench. He was sound asleep in a moment. Pulling out his own meal provided by the mess hall at Heart Mountain he surveyed the thick slabs of canned corned beef crammed between two generous slices of bread slathered with mustard. Along with the two sodas it was enough for a couple of meals so he carefully divided the sandwich and ate half. A few of the passengers had eyed him curiously but with Japanese internees helping with farming and harvesting now the novelty had worn off, but not the animus. Mostly people would throw a scowl his way or just ignore him.

With legs stretched, nature's call answered and a nap for the driver the 1936 GMC Model 719 hit the road again. Winding southwest it worked its way along extended stretches of gravel roads skirting the foothills until once again the countryside opened onto trackless savanna. When Paul was certain the sere landscape must change soon the road disappeared beyond the headlight beams into more of the same as far as the eye could see.

The sun had risen behind them a couple of hours earlier when Kemmerer was reached. A coal town and the seat of Lincoln County, it boasted a Union Pacific Railroad station, a J.C.Penney Co. department store and an authentic bus depot. Everyone piled out, some having reached their destination, others to transfer to other buses and the rest waiting for the refueling and driver change. It would be another hour until the tarmac began to unspool beneath them once more.

More hours scrabbling through the desert, winding through the foothills and snaking through the Wasatch Mountains at length delivered them to Salt Lake City. From there, though the roads were better, the bus would stop every few miles to embark or disembark passengers. The bus filled with people then disgorged some and trundled slowly north toward Idaho.

In Burley, Idaho, Paul switched buses. The one he had spent over fourteen hours on was headed on its great circle route through eastern Idaho, north into Montana and eventually southeast back into Wyoming. His new conveyance drove to Twin Falls then north over the Perrine Bridge spanning the Snake River Canyon four hundred eighty seven feet above the river and a few miles later into the Minidoka War Relocation Center. It was late afternoon but it would be several hours before the sun fell below the horizon. He was exhausted, covered in road grime and smelling like one of the road kills they had driven by, but soon he was surrounded by his family and friends, laughing, crying, holding his wife and child in his arms and, unbelievably, happy to be back in a prison with barbed wire fences and tarpaper shacks.

Minidoka War Relocation Center
Hunt, Idaho
May 23, 1943

The ecumenical Protestant church service had ended. The Sakai family with Paul and Mary Akagi were walking along the crushed red cinder road from the rec hall-cum-church to their barracks assignment for a change of clothes then lunch in the cafeteria. Thomas had slowed considerably over the last year and Moriko clung to his arm to support him as they made their way periodically stopping so he could rest.

It was a pleasant day. The blistering heat of summer was a month away, the overcast and mud of March and April a memory. Across the sage-dotted landscape beyond the barbed wire, desert wildflowers bloomed and the scent of sagebrush gathering energy to blossom later in the summer wafted through the air. Life within the camp had settled into a routine. Packages from friends and relatives helped prisoners spruce up their barren quarters. Mail-orders from Sears Roebuck and Montgomery Ward brought specialty items and the canteens and barber shops were busy each day. However normal it might have all seemed one only needed to look at the menacing jagged wire and basalt stone walls surrounding the grounds with eight guard towers looming thirty feet over the camp to know that circumstances were anything but normal.

Most of the family had made their way to the cafeteria by the time Thomas and Moriko returned to their room. Thomas sat outside on a chair built from scrap lumber and melon crates from Hagerman about fifty miles due west. When Moriko emerged from the room in fresh clothes she carefully stepped the three stairs to the ground and smoothed her dress.

"Come along Tosh, let's go for a meal."

"I think I'll stay here and rest for a while. You go ahead, bring me back a piece of bread with butter. And maybe some soup."

"I'll wait here with you then."

"No, no my love. Go be with the family. It's Sunday supper. I'll still be here when you come back."

Clearly reluctant to leave, Moriko kissed her husband of forty-five years on his bald head and squeezed his hand. "As you wish," she said and started down the path, glancing over her shoulder as she went.

Other internees making their way towards the dining hall would smile pleasantly or acknowledge Thomas with a nod or hello. Some who had come from Bainbridge Island or Seattle and knew him would pause briefly and exchange greetings with their friend of many years. Kiyoshi Abe had known Thomas since Hawaii and sat on the steps to chat for several minutes. Though he had trouble recalling who all these people were, Thomas was nonetheless polite and smiled at all who passed by.

Across the firebreak in a nearby barracks block someone had planted rose bushes, their blossoms bursting in blazes of red and yellow. Struggling to his feet Thomas set out to smell those roses and wonder at the vibrancy and hopefulness they represented in the drab sameness of the camp. He marveled at the beryl blue sky above as it contrasted with the soaring snow clad peaks of the Sawtooth mountains to the north. The sky swirled in circles, changing, sparkling like a kaleidoscope, making it impossible to grasp the motion of his dizziness amidst the featureless heavens above as he sank to the ground his eyes fluttering closed.

Eternity, yet no time at all, had passed when he again opened his eyes. Staring up into the harsh light of a hospital lamp he could see his family gathered around. They seemed to be speaking but he could not hear the words. They seemed to be touching him yet he could not feel their caress. He wanted to speak. To tell them he was fine, that everything would be okay and that life was an adventure to be lived, but he could not find his voice. The image of his modest home and farm on his faraway emerald island paradise, verdant with lush crops and ringing with the laughter of his grandchildren, floated tantalizingly just beyond his reach. He smiled serenely and his heart whispered "I'm coming home, I'm coming home" while the vision drifted away enveloped in comforting darkness.

The funeral service for Toshio Sakai was well attended despite warnings from the camp administrator that its size would constitute an unlawful assembly. He was an honored elder with many friends wishing to pay their respects to the family. Flowers grown in the camp were arranged and lay atop the casket and remembrance wreaths fashioned by students from crepe paper stood nearby as the homily was given and the prayers and blessings were anointed upon the faithful and all present. At the family's request the Sacrament of Christ was offered to believers and when the ceremony ended, the simple wooden coffin holding his earthly remains was placed in the hearse contracted by the camp and began the slow, dusty crawl to the cemetery.

A plot of land bulldozed from the sage-covered mesa past the west end of the camp boundary served the inmates with graves clawed through the hardscrabble earth with picks and shovels. With the recitation of ashes to ashes and dust to dust complete, the mourners filed away and the earth received its offering, a rudely chiseled monument of basalt to mark the spot. Of the Sakai family generation born into the bondage of social strictures, that fought their way across the Pacific Ocean through backbreaking toil, racism and intolerance to a new life in a promised land, only Moriko remained in her grief, once again a prisoner of circumstances beyond her control.

Minidoka War Relocation Center
Hunt, Idaho
June 13, 1943

"Are you out of your mind? You've only been here for a month and now you want to join the army? You're a father with a baby that's only eight months old, you don't have to do this! Good grief, three months ago they were trying to hang you and now this?" Mary was beside herself with a mix of anger and incredulity.

Paul was certainly conflicted about his decision. At one level he was trying to prove to himself his loyalty to his adopted country. He had, after all, been a spy for the Japanese Empire and while his efforts had yielded no results it was yet a stain on his conscience. At a practical level he had checked both boxes on the loyalty questionnaire which meant he was eligible, likely in fact, to be drafted. He hoped that volunteering would put him in something other than frontline infantry.

"I'm not crazy. I've explained this before. It's already done, I ship out Monday for basic training in Camp Shelby."

Tears, rage and fear spilled from Mary's eyes burning holes in Paul's heart as he held her close. The weekend flew by and on Monday he departed for the train that would carry him to Mississippi. All the family had gathered to say goodbye and Godspeed but Mary turned away. She couldn't bear to watch again as he disappeared as the bus drove out the gate.

Camp Shelby
Mississippi
June 16, 1943

It had been another butt-numbing ride for Paul. Stopping every hundred miles or so for coal and water the Baldwin 2-8-0 Army locomotive clambered along the landscape back down to Ogden, headed east to Omaha then on to Kansas City, St. Louis and Memphis before rolling into Camp Shelby about three in the afternoon. It was only mid-June but temperatures were already in the mid 80's and the humidity was oppressive. His travel mates were mostly Nisei, volunteering from western region internment camps and others not subject to confinement living outside the exclusion zone. As they disembarked into a ragged line a waiting drill sergeant barked out orders snapping everyone to a semblance of attention. The new recruits were then marched to the intake center where they were shaved, injected, inspected, deloused and issued uniforms. After that they were quick marched briefly to barracks to stow their gear and then to the commissary for their first Army meal which Paul found delicious. From there it was a march back to barracks, two hours to settle in, then lights out.

The time in basic passed quickly for Paul. Having been through the Japanese version of training he concluded it was much less harsh and while intensive, probably created better soldiers. The advanced training was next and that was when he would learn what his role in the US Army would be.

Island Farms
Bainbridge Island, Washington
September 18, 1943

The first season at the farm had been a tooth and nail struggle to get a crop. With no experience and most of the resources Paul had outlined either shut down or re-allocated for the war effort Joshua and Stan had scrounged every spare seed from every farmer on the island that was fully planted. They ended up with two acres of carrots, ten acres of potatoes and three acres of peas. Including the strawberry planting it left nearly forty acres fallow and after expenses had made barely enough money to pay the taxes and set aside cash for the next season's supplies. Ritchie, now a junior in high school, was a seasoned veteran on the tractor, Stan had become a skilled mechanic and Joshua—to his own amazement—was running the operation as well as could be expected. The second full growing season was drawing to a close at Island Farms and every acre planted was with crops in high demand. His harvesting crew, shared with other farmers on the island would be moving in soon to begin reaping the benefits of their collective efforts.

"It's pretty rewarding, really. I can understand why Thomas was so happy here," Joshua mused.

"Yeah," Stan replied, "it's a damn shame he didn't survive to see it again."

"Yes it is. I hope Moriko outlasts this damn war. She deserves to spend her remaining years here."

"My last letter from Leta said she was sad and lonely but still strong. The Allies have landed in Italy. The paper said the 100th Battalion was included. That's an all Nisei unit, so maybe the beginning of the end for Germany."

"I hope so for Mary's sake. Paul is still training in Mississippi. They don't expect to ship out till late spring next year. We'll probably just be done with the planting."

"Probably," Stan concluded. "Hey, I'm about to close up the goody box to ship to Frank. You got anything more you want to put in there?"

"No. But you should check with Ritchie, he might have something for Benjamin."

"Okay, can do." The box was shipped, the harvest was made and after the potatoes were harvested, men and boy alike settled in for a winter of rest and repairs in preparation for another cycle in the never ending story of growing food for humanity.

Letters

My Darling Mary,

I miss you my love. Training here in camp is pretty routine now. Most of the marching, running, crawling, shooting and camping in the woods is behind us. We are spending most of our time learning our specialties. I've been assigned to the 232nd Engineer Combat Company. We're learning how to blow up enemy bridges and build good guy bridges. I'm sure Steven will be thrilled to hear that. Some of us are trying to play catch up since the company formed back in February before I got here. Our unit is apparently the only one entirely commanded by Japanese officers. Our captain is named Pershing Nakada if you can believe that. Named after a WWI general.

I read in the Irrigator *that Minidoka looks half deserted because so many are out doing farm work. More than any other camp apparently. Because there are so many of us here from different spots I get a chance to look at most of the other camp newspapers. We see the* Manzanar Free Press, Topaz Times, Poston Chronicle *and the* Heart Mountain Sentinel. *It's pretty eye-opening how different the cultures are in each spot.*

I expect by now baby Tom is beginning to trundle through the camp on wobbly legs, eating dirt and throwing silverware. I wish I had been there for that first step. Maybe you were right. Maybe I should have stayed and taken my chances at getting drafted. But I guess I've blown that bridge up now, so perhaps I was foreshadowing my training here. Anyway Army chow is pretty good in the mess hall but the meals they give us in the field are nearly inedible. The army calls them K rations, we're all pretty sure it stands for krappy. It's been upper sixties in the day and not much cooler at night. Almost no breeze or rain, and, mercifully, a lot fewer mosquitoes.

It's almost time for lights out here in the barracks. Tomorrow is Sunday so we'll have a day off after church. Some of the guys get a pass to go into Hattiesburg but I just relax in the camp library and read. Working my way through Tolstoy right now—War and Peace. Napoleon tries to rule the world.

Anyway, give my love and affection to the family and know how much I hold you and the baby dear. Above all, keep a candle in the window for me. I promise I'll come back to you.

All my love,

Paul

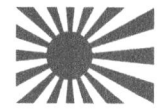

Sweetheart,

Luckily I'm not quite to the stage of chasing Tom yet but he scoots around on the crawl pretty fast now. He's pulling himself up to stand so it won't be long before he will be waddling around. Choosing Thomas to honor Grandfather was a sweet idea. Don't worry, we'll have a Paul Jr. too.

You're right, Dad and lots of other people are working in the local farms, some have even gone as far away as eastern Idaho and Montana to work. Getting passes to go in to Twin Falls to the movies or to go shopping has been getting easier and at least some of the folks that live there seem to be nice. We try to stick together when we go though. You never know what might happen.

Administration has been sending out messages trying to get people in the camp to consider moving out and to the east. Places like Michigan and Ohio even all the way to New York and New Jersey. Most are pretty resistant to the idea. The people I talk to just want to go back home. Maybe sending farmers to work in Blackfoot and Pocatello is a subtle way to make it easier to swallow the idea.

Subtle, now there's a word I never imagined I would use to describe the administration.

I'm glad you're not slogging through swamps anymore, that must be miserable, but come to think of it barracks life must look pretty easy. You've certainly had enough practice at it the last couple of years.

Grammy Moriko has been so blue since Grampa died. We all try to cheer her up but it's been hard for her. At least she's still eating. Rumors are swirling that turkeys will be shipped in for Thanksgiving but to tell you the truth I think we'd all be happy with some decent chicken and fresh veggies. Lots of the Issei really miss the old food like rice for mochi, tofu and Japanese vegetables. But this being Idaho, at least we have potatoes.

Today is our day for laundry and I've got diapers aplenty to do so it's off to the washeteria for me now. If I can just wrangle that child of yours! All my love and kisses, be safe.

Mary

PS The candle is in the window, come home to us soon.

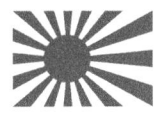

Dear Frank,

The first of the early storms blew through last night. Lots of leaves on the ground and a sea of mud in the fields. We're done out there this season anyway. Stan is tearing down the tractor to clean and grease all the bearings and weld up a few places where metal fatigue is showing. Needs paint too but with all the shortages who knows what color it will be by the time you get home. Did I tell you before that I bought a used welder? Turns out to be a handy thing to have. We've fixed the disc plow frame and built a seed rack with bits that we hoarded from the scrap metal drives. We have enough seed stock to plant everything next season, including probably two crops of peas on the one field. Peas are in demand since they can so well. I'm not going to plant carrots next season. It's a long growing season and a difficult harvest for the little money they bring in. I'm doing corn instead. We can sell the sweet corn at Pike Place Market and there is a small cattle operation here on the island that said they would be interested in the silage.

I imagine you get an overview of things on the island from the Bainbridge Bellwether *but from my vantage point it's gonna be a tough row to hoe for some of the people coming back. Since you left there has been an influx of new people with a chip on their shoulder about Japan and all things Japanese. Mostly we keep a low profile and they just assume we own the farm. When it's time to come home you may need to prepare the family for a difficult readjustment period. At least you have someplace to come back to. I'm afraid many won't have a home or a job.*

Sorry to end on a down note. Keep the faith, eventually this will all fade away.

Joshua

Aboard Liberty Ship *Thomas Cresap*
Somewhere in the Atlantic
May 17, 1944

The days leading up to the boarding had been frenetic for the 232nd Combat Engineers Company. It seemed like every sergeant in the Army had gathered to oversee the preparations for war zone assignments. Tons of equipment—bulldozers, deuce-and-a-halfs, trailers, a command car, bridge making materials, bridge destroying munitions, barbed wire and a thousand other things required to equip the group—had been assembled. Finally, after every soldier had been inspected and deemed fit, every duffel checked and all the personal equipage accounted for, the 232nd left for Newport News where they embarked and the ship slipped out to join the forming convoy at 02:00 hours.

The first few days consisted of landlubber seasickness, then fire, lifeboat evac drills and a rotation on KP. Tomorrow would mark two weeks at sea with no one in the battalion knowing where they were headed. Bets were being laid for England, Italy or a bivouac somewhere in Africa. If the officers knew, they weren't letting on. So the days were spent doing drills or security patrols, joining the ubiquitous floating crap games, playing checkers and chess for the more cerebral and a lot of exercise and manual reading. However else they felt, as a part of the 442nd Regimental Combat Team, they all wanted to embrace the motto, *'Go for Broke'.*

Paul had been circumspect in his letters to Mary. He omitted the grueling days spent in the field in the cold, wet miserable conditions of simulated combat. It had been a grind, even for the physically fit like himself. He hadn't had time, really, to ponder the irony of his situation until the unit had put out to sea. What a chain of events, born and raised in California yet trained by the Imperial Japanese Navy Air Service as a pilot and a spy. Inserted by a clandestine submarine mission to fly recon over the northwest U.S., his sub sunk almost beneath his feet, injured, saved, loved, married, incarcerated, tried as a spy and now—unbelievably—aboard a cargo ship as a soldier headed to combat for the Allies. *What a life!* He thought. *I'm not even sure I believe it myself and I'm living it!* Once the convoy had sailed past Gibraltar and tracked slightly to port it became clear what the destination was; the 'Go For Broke' boys were headed to Italy.

May 26, 1944

The *T. Cresap* moored to a makeshift pier fashioned from a half sunken passenger liner in Napoli Bay. Streaming off the ship directly into the destruction and carnage of the ancient city was sobering and a sudden gut check that this was no longer a drill. Naples had endured weeks of bombing by Allied forces, the civilian uprising against Nazi and fascist forces and the final push by the British Kings Dragoons and Royal Scots Greys supported by the All Americans of the 82nd Airborne. It had left much of the city in ruins. After gathering at a rally point, the 232nd of the 442nd marched to a train station where they were transported to the new bivouac area in Bagnoli.

Ten days later, fully equipped and trained up some more, the unit began the northward trek toward the front lines. First via an LST bound for shellshocked Anzio. Then the column found itself wandering aimlessly around Rome in search of Route One. Finally, by the middle of the night they were once again on the way to war.

Paul checked his watch; 1400 hours. His unit had been attached to the 109th engineers and had been receiving specific instructions on disarming or disabling German booby traps and land mines for several days, with the rear area moving forward every day or so to stay within reach of the infantry advance. Now it was time to head to the front lines and clear the way.

"You nervous?" It was his mother hen sergeant working his way through his chicks.

"No, not really. Well, maybe. Not sure really. I guess I don't want to screw up and get somebody hurt."

"Really?" Sarge laughed. "You do remember this is a war zone and the bad guys are shooting at us don't you?"

"You know what I mean, I don't want to be the guy who blows up half a platoon of dog faces because I was careless."

"Relax, Flyboy. You'll make more mistakes overthinking something. Sometimes doing is better—and safer—than thinking." Paul had acquired the nickname when he had been waxing poetic about how beautiful the Puget Sound was from the air. "We'll be moving out pretty soon, better button up for the ride."

"Thanks Sarge, will do."

"Let me leave you with this bit of wisdom; You'll never hear the bullet that kills you."

"How reassuring." Paul smiled. "I'll keep that in mind."

June 15, 1944

Two weeks of 24 hour a day efforts split into 12 hour shifts kept the engineers busy. The retreating Germans had laid mines and booby traps on every road and at any spot where they imagined any bypass lane might be carved. The 232nd had meticulously removed or disabled everything along the way up to and including being under enemy fire at the front lines. One squad found themselves in a fire fight and had to call the rest of the platoon to surround and destroy the resistance. The work was exhausting and dangerous with even the rear areas within reach of Nazi guns.

Atop a mostly enclosed heavily armored Caterpillar D7 bulldozer sweltering in the midday sun, Paul was grading a road bypass after he had pushed a disabled Mercedes staff car into a ravine. All the enemy ordinance had been cleared and now it was essential to open an artery for supply trucks to bring materiel to the point of conflict.

Shells had been sailing over his head toward rear areas for an hour and small arms fire had peppered the landscape. Now it seemed, there was a lull; *Maybe the Krauts are having bratwurst and beer.* He thought. *Probably not.* His dozer jolted to a sudden stop. Stepping out from behind his armored control seat he walked on the track so he could look over the blade. Lodged solidly against the blade he could see a substantial rock impeding the way. *Well, crap, this is just Jim Dandy.* Jumping off his machine he went forward to get a better look. Maybe he could dislodge it, if not he'd have to call up some dynamite. As he stood there he heard the mortar shells flying again so he scrambled up onto the track. As he neared the cab an artillery round screamed into the ground about thirty yards away. Paul felt a massive concussive blast with a searing hot stab of pain in his lower back. His last thought before he blacked out was *You lied to me, Sarge. I did hear it coming.*

Minidoka War Relocation Center
Hunt, Idaho
August 4, 1944

The heat was oppressive. Even in the shade Mary was sure it must be a hundred degrees. Baby Tom and Sarah's baby were dozing fitfully in a crib Joshua had sent from the Sears Catalog. She read the casualty list of the 442nd in the *Minidoka Irrigator*. Even the flies and grasshoppers were taking a break and the only winds stirring were the dust devils popping up across the shimmering atmosphere of the Snake River plateau.

The population of the camp was a third less than it had been a few months ago. Those men who hadn't joined the Army were farming as far away as Blackfoot and Pocatello in eastern Idaho. A couple dozen, including Steven, had volunteered to fight a sagebrush range fire in Shoshone about fifteen miles north. Others had been granted furloughs to relocate in the east. Some deemed dangerous or unpatriotic had been shipped off to Tule Lake in northern California. Among those was Harry Hashimoto, a classmate of Steven's at U Dub in Seattle. Mary knew him slightly and knew that he was a No-No boy, which is what had landed him a ticket out of the desert.

Her dad was part of the committee working with the JACL planning how the camp would eventually be vacated, although Mary had trouble understanding how the Japanese American Citizens League would find a role. Leta's other kids were in school and she and Moriko were at the arts and crafts building working on something Mary was pretty vague on. She couldn't imagine how oven-like is must be indoors right now. *God, I can't even read it's so hot. I wonder where Paul is right now?* She tossed aside the paper and glanced up to the window of their barracks where the Blue Star Family flag denoting a member in service hung limply. The last letter she had gotten from him had been sent two days before he was to ship out and that was more than a month ago. New correspondence would come as a V-mail. A photo of the letter printed stateside from film shipped back from Europe. It was apparently more efficient than sending the real thing. Anyway, she was hoping something would come her way soon.

"Hello Mary, I thought you might like a cold drink. I brought you a Coke from the canteen."

Mary jolted out of her daydream and blinked vacantly for a moment. "Thanks Sakura, I feel like a statue in an overheated wax museum." She took the proffered beverage and had a sip. "Hits the spot!"

"Have you heard from Paul? I still haven't heard from Haru and it's been two months."

"Nope, not a peep. But they say it takes six weeks to get mail to the processing center from the front lines, then another three or four to get it back stateside." She felt a little better knowing she wasn't the only one waiting for mail from a loved one.

"I saw another one of those dreadful Western Union Specials come in yesterday. They drove to one of the barracks towards the rear, spent five minutes and drove right back out again. Every time they drive in my heart skips a beat."

"Me too," Mary answered. "It feels like a vice squeezing my whole chest until it goes by."

The two friends chatted aimlessly for a few minutes then Sakura ambled away stirring tiny dust tornadoes with her feet that then hung motionless in the air.

Mary got up and checked the babies; Still sleeping, so she went inside to change her blouse which was damp with sweat. As she buttoned up she heard a car downshifting and slowing to a stop outside. Two doors opened, then closed and she heard a sharp rap on the door.

"Hello, is anyone home?" A soft male voice, clearly trying not to wake the children.

"Just a moment." She opened the door to step outside and there was the dreaded Western Union Special courier with an envelope in his hand.

"Mary Akagi?"

"Yes, that's me."

"I have a telegram for you." Mary felt her knees go weak and tears welled up in her eyes. Her breathing became ragged. She nearly fell as she stepped down to the ground and sat in the chair that her grandfather had used. Her hands were trembling as she took the yellow envelope. Mary grasped the notice and looked up at the messenger and his military escort. "Thank you," she managed to croak out past the thickening in her throat.

"Is there anything we can do for you, ma'am?"

"No. Thank you." Mary paused. "Maybe say a prayer for us on your way back. For all of us, here and there."

"Yes ma'am, we will surely do that." The two men reclaimed their car and slowly drove away headed for the front gate and the rest of their lives. Finally Mary took the slip of paper and opened it.

Regret to inform you your husband Paul Akagi was severely wounded in action in Italy 15 June 44. You will be advised as reports of condition are received. Per Adjutant General.

Mary stared at the telegram. Her breathing steadied and she wiped her eyes. She stared again at the Blue flag in the window. *At least we won't be swapping it for a Gold Star.*

8th Evacuation Hospital

Cecina, Italy

July 4, 1944

I am swimming toward the light. It seems so far away and I'm running out of breath. Please help me, I need to breathe. No, don't go away! I need to get to the light. It seems so far away.

"Come on, Corporal. Wake up now." The doctor switched off the flashlight he was using to check Paul's eye response. "I know you're down there, you just need to want it enough, son. Don't give up."

"I don't know, Doctor. He's been like this since he was wounded. Do you really think he'll wake up?"

Doctor Sam, as he liked to be called, surveyed his nurse. Like everyone else on this field hospital staff she was a battle casualty with no visible wounds. Functioning on adrenaline, too much coffee and not nearly enough sleep, she was competent, experienced and a reasonably attractive brunette in what he guessed was her late thirties. But the last three months could well have added years to her looks. "I don't know, Anne. His post-surgical wound is healing and there doesn't seem to be any secondary infection but with a lacerated kidney repair there is a lot of fragility. Even now there would be risk in moving him further back. Will he make it? I suppose it's in God's hands now. I just don't know."

"Well, leave it to us Sam, we will do our damnedest to get him safely back home to his family."

"I know you will. When you finish your shift find me in the mess tent. I'll buy you a bourbon."

"Make it a double and you've got a deal."

"Done and done." He replied. Anne went down the line of patients in one direction, Dr. Sam headed back to the operating room. He had heard the rumble of trucks rolling back from the front lines and they usually had casualties that needed care.

I hear voices far away. They seem to be speaking to me but I don't know what they are saying. Speak louder, come closer. I can't quite hear you.

Nurse Anne was sitting bedside reading Shakespeare's Sonnet number 116. It was something she did with all the comatose patients in her off hours. Somehow the notion of ideal, unchanging love appealed to her wish to give these soldiers a fighting chance to recover. "Let me not to the marriage of true minds admit impediments. Love is not love which alters when it alteration finds, or bends with the remover to remove."

She sighed and closed her slim volume of poems. Reaching over she took Paul's hand in hers and caressed it gently. "Sleep on good knight, tomorrow will bring a new sunrise." She started to rise when she felt a twitch, then a squeeze of her hand. "C'mon soldier!" she cried. "Come on, we're all waiting for you! Dottie, go find Dr. Sam, I think this guy is coming around." Nurse Dottie raced out of the ward and minutes later ran back in with the doctor in tow. He immediately pulled out his flashlight to check Paul's eyes.

I see the light! I see the light! It's closer now. I'm swimming up, please don't go. I'm coming to the light, I'm coming to the voices.

"Anne, tell me exactly what happened." Dr. Sam looked directly at her. "Every detail."

"I was reading, like I do and I was stopping for the evening. I patted his hand, as I also do and he squeezed me back. I'm certain of it. He squeezed my hand. That's when I sent Dottie running for you."

"Okay, keep reading, I'll check his eyes while you do it." Anne opened her book and took up where she had left off. "Oh no! It is an ever fixed mark that looks on tempests and is never shaken;

I'm closer, I can feel it. Swim toward the light, listen to the voices.

"It is the star to every wand'ring bark, whose worth's unknown, although his height be taken. Love's not Time's fool, though rosy lips and cheeks within his bending compass come, Love alters not with his brief hours and weeks, But bears it out even to the edge of doom."

"Snap to, soldier, you can do this!" Dr. Sam exhorted. "Dottie, rub his hand, let's get this G.I. back in the land of the living."

Paul's eyes fluttered open for a moment then closed. He clenched his hand around Dottie's then opened his eyes again.

"Welcome back, son. You've been gone for a while. Welcome back!" Dr. Sam checked his eyes one more time, listened with his stethoscope stood up, ran his right hand through his graying hair and let out a deep breath. It was always a great moment when one of these cases rallied because so many didn't. Dottie gave his hand a robust squeeze to which Paul responded with his own.

"I heard a voice," Paul croaked out. "I heard an angel calling me."

"You certainly did Corporal." Sam said, "Finish the poem, Anne."

"If this be error and upon me proved, I never writ, nor no man ever loved." She closed her little book with tears of triumph streaming down her face.

Hospital ship *Emily H. M. Weder*
Napoli Bay, Italy
July 13, 1944

Post-coma, Paul improved quickly. Within a couple of days of putting three squares in his belly he was up and moving around. Gingerly to be sure, but out of bed at any rate. A trip to the latrine was still an adventure in pain management. "Hey, Dr. Sam, when can I get outta here and get back to the front with my brothers?"

"No more war for you Corporal Akagi. As soon as we can get you aboard that hospital ship you'll be headed home." He pointed to the converted transport ship now wearing white livery with huge red crosses painted on the sides. "And you need to be damn careful, too. If you reopen the wound while you're in transit it could be your corpse coming back to your family." Dr. Sam had been rotated back to Third Army General Hospital the same day Paul had been transported by rail. The ship was anchored in Napoli Bay. A round trip for Paul, just another posting for the doctor who had started his tour in north Africa.

"Well that's a brilliant bedside manner, doc," Paul chuckled.

"Perhaps not, but it's good advice just the same."

"I wish I had gotten a chance to thank Anne. She really saved my life. I really wanted to thank her."

"Is it impertinent of me to suggest I may have helped save you too? Most soldiers with serious kidney wounds don't survive. As it was I was experimenting on you, hoping to find a better way for your type of injury so it's up to you not to keel over and make me look bad."

Paul laughed out loud then winced. "No, I guess you helped some."

"You don't worry about Nurse Anne. You should have seen how she beamed when they carried your litter onto the train. She knows you're grateful. And so do I. For what it's worth, I think the treatment your people have gotten since Pearl has been disgraceful. I'm proud to be a fellow soldier with you, even if I am behind the lines."

Paul nodded thoughtfully. *What a story I could tell you.* "Thanks. It means a lot."

Two orderlies in spotless whites were heading their way, one consulting a clipboard. "You Paul Akagi?"

"Yes that's me." Paul reached out and shook hands with Dr. Sam. "It's kinda corny to say but if you're ever in Seattle look me up. I'll be living on the family farm on Bainbridge Island."

"I'll do that. You take care now, son."

As the orderlies carried Paul off to the awaiting ship the doctor watched for moment then turned and headed back to the hospital. There were still a lot of other men that needed saving.

By medical standards Paul wasn't considered ambulatory while on board a ship so he spent the three plus day sailing back to England in the cradle. It was like half a straightened peanut shell with curved-up sides, gimbaled to reduce swaying and rocking while underway; Sort of half hammock, half Iron Maiden. In England he was transferred to another medical facility where he waited for air transport stateside. He thought about writing Mary a letter and realized he'd be back in the U.S. before she would get it. *I'll wait and hope she forgives me.* He knew the Army would have notified her of his being wounded but had no idea if they would update her on his status. He wasn't dead so at least she wouldn't have gotten a 'regret to inform you he's killed' telegram. He thought maybe he would send his own telegram when he got back but rejected that idea almost instantly when he realized such a thing would probably send shock waves through her before she even opened it. And he knew more about shock waves than he ever wanted to remember again.

On July 21 Paul was boarded on a C-54 long range cargo plane refitted for transport of wounded personnel and took to the sky. Seven hours to a refueling stop at Narsarsuaq Air Base in Greenland, another seven hours to Otis Army Air Base and just like that he was at the Camp Edwards Convalescent Hospital about fifty miles west of Providence, back in the USA.

Letters

My dearest Mary,

I hardly know where to begin. First, I'm stateside again in a convalescent center at Camp Edwards in Massachusetts. They don't have a specific timeline for me but the docs warn me it takes some time for my injury to heal well enough to be released. I'm hopeful that I may be out of here before Halloween. Where they send me after that is anyone's guess but for certain not to an active combat zone. My glorious military career was pretty short but I'm not complaining. I suppose you can tell the editor of the Irrigator that I'm on the mend and happy to be back in the states.

I'm sure you must have sent letters that never reached me. From the moment we stepped off the boat in Italy we were on the move and in contact with the enemy. So, truthfully, I didn't send another letter after the last one from Camp Shelby. We were weeks at sea as it was. The short version of what happened was I was on a dozer plowing a bypass for the troops to move supplies to the front lines. In comes an artillery shell and whammo I'm on the ground and unconscious. The doc said the field medics saved my life by getting me back to triage as fast as they did. From the time I hit the ground until I woke up three weeks later is a total blank. I was in a coma so they say due to blood loss and concussion so tell the editor of the paper to push those blood drives, they are saving lives over there.

It's been difficult knowing how you must have felt being in the dark about my status, doubly so since I am missing you and the rest of my family so much. I'm aching to hold you in my arms again, to smell your hair and kiss your nose. But we have endured so much in such a compressed time frame that we just need to hold on a few more months, I'm sure of it. When all this is over a quiet life on a farm will be such a blessing. I can barely wait. My very best to the family, and while my kidney belongs to the army, my whole heart belongs to you.

Love, Paul

PS My Purple Heart too!

Mary could barely breathe. Her sobs of relief had become hiccups as she read the letter for the third time. Her worries had melted away in a moment. *He's alive and recuperating! Dear God, thank you.* Benjamin was returning from school and noticed his sister was deep in concentration over something in her hand. "Whatcha got, Sis?" She startled upright at his voice.

"It's a letter from Paul(hic). He's back in the US on medical rehab back east(hic)."

"Wow, that's swell! Who else knows?"

"Just you(hic), I only got the mail a few minutes ago."

"Lemme dump these books, I'll go find everybody and bring them home." Mary just nodded as Benjamin dashed out the door to search for the family.

It was a grand evening of celebration. Smiles graced all the faces and as word traveled among the Bainbridge Island contingent neighbors and friends came to share in the good news. For the first time in a long while it seemed that the war was at last put aside for one family for a day and the barbed wire fences forgotten.

Dear Paul,

It was quite a party we had when we got your letter. The Bainbridge crew commandeered the mess hall for two hours and—no surprise here—they scrounged up some weenies to make appetizers. As you can imagine that elicited plenty of groans, especially since supper had been Spam and boiled cabbage again. I think half the population over fifty would kill for some good tofu and those under would do likewise for a decent steak. They were singing and dancing, the radio was cranked up high. KTFI was playing swing, and wow, we were swinging for sure. Now that you're safe all I want is for you to get well and come back to us.

Little Tom is a fully functional toddler now. We have to be careful, he wants to put everything in this mouth, climb up the stools and chairs and down the outside stairs. I'm considering buying a bell at the feed store next time I go to Twin Falls. We really do have to keep an eye out, not just for him but for all the other kids around the camp. It has become great fun for some of them to crawl under the barracks and hide while half the population is looking for them. Being missing is bad enough, but rattlesnakes hide under there as well. They killed a bullsnake over by the motor pool just yesterday.

Life here hasn't changed much. Blistering hot during the day, quite chilly overnight. Mess hall, laundry, mess hall, three hours working at the canteen, mess hall, bathe baby, take a shower, read a little then lights out. Occasionally we take the bus into town to watch a movie or do some shopping but so many things are in short supply or rationed that there isn't much to buy. Anyway, so glad you're healing. I can barely wait until we can hold each other in our arms alone together again.

Sloppy kisses and warm hugs,
Mary

Camp Edwards Convalescence Hospital
Mashpee, Rhode Island
September 11, 1944

It had been nearly three months since Paul caught shrapnel in the back and over two since he had awoken from his coma. All things considered he counted himself lucky. Yes, his back still hurt, yes they were still finding blood in his urine and the hearing in his right ear was still not quite right, but he was alive when so many of his fellow soldiers in the 442nd weren't. As best he could he followed their progress in Italy. Elements had crossed the river Arno and captured Pisa toward the end of August and apparently now they were reforming in Naples, probably to go into Europe through southern France.

Recovery had been slow initially but now he was moving more freely with fewer restrictions. He wasn't going to be playing baseball or tennis any time soon but he was ambulatory and regaining his strength each day.

Walking back to his barracks from the base post exchange he could tell something was up. Hospital staffers were rushing around barking out orders to a steady stream of ambulance drivers, patients were being loaded and driven off to be replaced by another. Deuce-and-a-halfs were being pressed into service as medical equipment and supplies were hurriedly loaded to follow the convoy of ambulances. Base G.I.s were taking down tents and other portable shelters too.

"Hey sarge," Paul yelled as a man hurried by, "what's going on?"

"Hurricane warning Corporal, you better find your unit assignment right now."

"No kidding! I've never been in a hurricane."

"I have and you want nothing to do with them. Find your group and catch the first ride out of here."

"Thanks, Sarge, that's a roger." It was about two hundred yards to his quarters and he could see a beehive of activity in the distance. It turned out he wouldn't be on a truck, he was boarded on a med plane at nearby Otis Army Airfield and touched down in Aurora, Colorado several hours later. His new assignment was Fitzsimons Army Medical Center.

Minidoka War Relocation Center
Hunt, Idaho
October 29, 1944

The beginning of the end of the war was nearing, as all wars do when belligerents are sufficiently destroyed, resources are devoured and enough pretty little towns and huge metropolitan manufacturing areas and their citizens have been reduced to blood stains and rubble. The Allied forces were driving Germans relentlessly back to the motherland. Soldiers could see in the eyes of the captured the shock of defeat, the weariness of war, their fear about the future and the yearning for home. Likewise, the war in the Pacific Theater was pushing Imperial Japanese forces in duress to *en extremis* efforts. Kamikaze planes sacrificed pilots to inflict minimal damage on an overwhelmingly superior naval force. The army invoked the *bushido* code calling for every soldier to fight to the death for the sake of the Emperor. For the Axis powers time was running out as they pushed the last of their chips into the poker pot, winner take all.

As it was in the field of battle, so it was in the relocation camps. Letters to friends back home asked about how things were in the neighborhood. Was there any work available, any housing? In so many words, was there any reason to return? Sadly for many the answer was no. Clouded with shame some would return to Japan, most would find somewhere else to live and small numbers would return to their pre-war homes to fight the war beyond the war for the respect and dignity that was their due.

The War Relocation Authority was making plans to turn over administration of the camps to the Department of Interior for disposition after closure. When the last of the prisoners were released they were mostly the infirm, elderly, mentally disabled, fearful and sick with nowhere to go and no one to go to. America's most recent official embrace of racism and prison camps as public policy had played out as a pitiable disruption of 120,000 innocent lives.

Bainbridge Island
Washington State
February 9, 1945

It was a gloomy Friday afternoon when the ferry tied up near the old Anderson pier. A damp chilling breeze greeted the members of the Sakai family, the Akagis and a dozen or so others returning from the relocation camp. For the Island Farms people, except for the clothes on their back, and a few pictures and toiletries, they had walked away from everything in the barracks. Steven had summed up the feelings of the group succinctly when he observed he wanted to take nothing that reminded him of his time as a prisoner of war.

Joshua was waiting nearby with the pickup. Stan, with the old Dodge, stood next to him. The reunions were warm and heartfelt but not in the least triumphant. It was as if everyone had been unable to rest for three straight years and now, finally, it was time for a deep, comforting slumber.

The short drive back to the farm was done in silence mostly, the time spent looking out the window at what seemed the same and what was unfamiliar. Here and there crocuses poked through toward the light, daffodils and tulips would follow soon thereafter. It was a flicker of light in a darkened room, the hope of better things to come.

Moriko finished her days in her husband's favorite chair on the porch of the old house in the warmth of a July afternoon. Stan and Leta gathered their family and moved to Astoria, Oregon, where he worked as a load-master on the docks, away from the bitter memories of their lost home. Steven finished his degree and accepted an associate designer offer with a Chicago architectural firm. A decade later he opened his own practice specializing in major public works including bridges and the new initiatives to build freeways.

Frank turned the farm over to Paul and became involved in the effort to garner reparations for prisoners and an apology from the U.S. Government. His efforts combined with many more voices would eventually prevail decades later. Eleanor succumbed to liver disease within a few years of returning home. Benjamin fell in love with food and spent a career washing the taste of spam and canned beans out of his mouth with *haute cuisine* eventually garnering a Michelin star for his restaurant in San Francisco.

Joshua and his son spent another year on the farm to help with the transition and so Rick, having abandoned the childish name Ritchie, could finish high school. Afterwards Joshua returned to Whidbey Island to spend his career working for the school district. Rick went to college on a scholarship offered by Stanford University studying computational science, eventually returning to Seattle to a comfortable retirement.

Paul and Mary settled into the industrious but quiet life of farming. Considering how many stories he had that he could never tell, putting those times further in the past as the years went by was a blessing. The family and friends never again gathered to celebrate the Fourth of July.

Richard Pearson's Shop
Whidbey Island, Washington
January 2, 1997

Much of Richard Pearson's boyhood had been spent aboard the little sailboat now resting keel up on sawhorses in the back of his shop. When he closed his eyes he could almost feel the wind in his hair as he raced across the waves. The memory of salt rime and ocean spray coaxed him from across the years and revealed themselves through holes in the dusty covering tarp. Now, nearly half a century later, it was time to unlimber his past.

A dozen or more unfinished projects in stasis at some stage of incompletion stood between Richard and the boat. Gingerly he picked his way through the shop pondering how the tyranny of *now*, that pilferer of time, had strangled each task in its moment and swept him past. Here was a chair, in its twentieth year of patiently waiting for a new cane seat. Next to it was a partially disassembled Honda Gold Wing. He had intended to restore it five—or maybe ten—years ago so he could finally take that motorcycle road trip for which he yearned. There was a toy for a grandchild now approaching adulthood, an antique clock, a ship model and three bicycles. Here and there lay a smattering of specialty tools for the repair of things now hopelessly obsolete. All this populated a neglected space in the cluttered shop, and a similar space in his brain.

When at last he reached his goal, he pulled back the cover from the sloop. The action sent clouds of dust into the air, to resettle as another archaeological layer. He stared for a long moment at the faded yellow paint. Peeling with age, splotched black in places with remnants of moss and algae near the waterline, the tiny vessel evoked countless memories. Hot dogs and crab pots swarmed into his consciousness, as did storms, baseball games, friends, fireworks and half-drowned strangers washed ashore. Images of his father and grandfather flashed through his head and he smiled. The tumult of long-ago wars, of unreasonable fears, and a mother gone too soon filtered back as well. He saw the patched old sail in a heap on the floor. He reached out and touched his sturdy little childhood companion, a sad smile crossing his face. Richard sighed, tested the condition of the sandpaper and satisfied, began stripping the old finish.

Threatening clouds outside were gray and gloomy, and smelled of rain. They sharply contrasted with the cheerful clouds of yellow dust plumes arising from the palm sander he wielded. Hours of tedious work had revealed the cedar substrate of his boyhood sailboat, and the final patches were being removed in preparation for a new application of modern marine paint.

Rick was a study in jonquil. Safety goggles and a respirator covered his face and he was swathed in gloves and coveralls all sporting, to varying degrees, a layer of micro-fine yellow dust. Hair sticking out from under an old Seattle Pilots baseball cap, along with the cap, was similarly coated. He thought he heard his name, so he switched off the sander and listened a moment.

"Rick!" his wife was shouting.

"What?" He muffled back from under the dust mask.

"Mary is trying to reach you."

"What?" He repeated.

"Take off that damn stuff so you can hear."

Richard knew that exasperated tone well enough to guess at the meaning and took off the respirator and goggles. "Okay, what?"

"I said Mary has been trying to reach you all day. Something about Paul, she wants you to call right away."

"Okay, but I've been here all afternoon, she could have just called."

"Like there's a chance you could have heard the phone," his spouse retorted sarcastically.

"Point made and taken, I'll call her now." Pearson opened the main door to the workshop. The cool wind and occasional raindrops felt good on his face as he retrieved his shiny new cellular phone. Six missed calls, it reported. Richard pushed the recall button on the phone, Mary Akagi answered on the second ring.

"Rick, thank God you called back. It's Paul, he's taken a turn for the worse and he's asking for you." Her voice was unmistakably tense with strain and worry.

"Where are you now?" Rick asked.

"In Poulsbo at the hospice," she replied. "Please hurry."

"Is there anything I can do, anything you need?"

"No, just get here as fast as you can."

"Will do, I'm on my way." Richard made a call to the Washington State Ferries: Yes, the Seattle to Bainbridge was still running, no, they don't think the weather will close the run today. The next ferry leaves in an hour and ten minutes.

He dashed into the house shedding yellow dust and sweaty garments as he headed for the shower. He'd have to hurry but he would make the sailing.

In-Patient Hospice
Poulsbo, Washington
January 2, 1997

It was always surprising to Richard that the hospice smelled so innocuous. He expected, well, he wasn't sure what he expected, but he imagined there should be some taint of death hanging in the air. He thought it should be palpable, but it never was. Around several corners and down a couple of long corridors he found Paul's room. Inside were Mary, one of their children, all three grandkids and even one of the great grands. In this room, bright and cheerful though the decor was, despondency was indeed present. The focus, of course, was Paul. The once robust man, reduced to a withered shell by cancer, lay helpless in bed, his breathing ragged and labored, his eyes perpetually half open.

Mary stood up and crossed to Richard as he came in. "I'm so glad you came," she said. Her eyes were tired and red and her voice was listless. All the emotion had been wrung from her. Resignation and acceptance had begun to sink in. She took Pearson to the bedside and offered the chair in which she had been sitting. Mary leaned over her husband stroking his head.

"Paul, Rick is here to see you." For a moment there was no reaction; then startlingly, the skeletal figure roused and opened his eyes wide. "Rick?" He croaked.

"Yes Paul, I'm here."

"Alone, I want to speak alone." He gave Mary an intense look.

She was surprised but offered no resistance.

"Come along kids, Paul wants to speak to Rick alone." Rick thought he could detect a weary hurt in her voice. His heart ached for his lifelong friends in this moment. Quietly they collected themselves and streamed out of the room to re-establish their dignified vigil in the corridor.

"Rick," Paul said urgently, "you remember our special secret?"

"Of course I do, Paul. Blood brothers forever, but your episode is water long under the bridge. No one needs to know about that."

"You deserve to know the whole story. After you hear it, you may make your decision. Then if you are still willing, I want you to do something." He rested for a moment before continuing. "After I'm gone, I want you to do something for me."

"Certainly, whatever you want. Just ask."

"Lean closer," Paul was losing his strength and Rick had to put his ear next to the dying man's mouth to hear his whispered confession.

It was eight more agonizing days before the disease took its final toll, draining the life force from Paul Akagi. Even when death is closing in with grim certainty the actual moment is always a shock and the wails of anguish from his devoted wife and family echoed down the hallways. Richard had visited with them when he could as his old friend slipped away. Each time he headed home his heart was burdened with grief. He had one more task to perform for his friend. It was a request as old as the Japanese culture itself, and he would see to its completion. He would repay Paul's debt of honor on his life.

Old Briarwood School
Whidbey Island
Washington State
January 14, 1997

A howling gale tossed dangling chains on old tether ball poles creating muted echoes like weirdly tuned wind chimes. Pearson was standing on the playground of Briarwood School in a bone-chilling January rainstorm. Skeletons of abandoned playground equipment fallen into neglect marched toward the horizon like old whale ribs bleached by years of weather. The wind whistled through the merry-go-round reminding him of the squeals of delighted children now long since grown. Restless sentinels of trees surrounded the perimeter of the grounds, the smooth red bark and the green waxy leaves of madronas contrasted starkly with the dominant grays and whites of the storm. The trees seemed to shiver while standing.

He gathered his heavy parka tightly around his rotund figure pulling the hood strings taut until only his blue eyes, bulbous nose and bushy gray mustache were visible. He hefted a crowbar onto his shoulders eyeballing the grounds. *I can't believe I came back here, not after all these years. Hell, it's probably not even here. It must be gone by now!*

Richard scanned his surroundings to get his bearings. Things were different of course, it had been fifty-two years since he left his school but most of the landmarks were still here. The three feathery western hemlock trees were now reduced to two, but had grown huge. The main building, built more on the expectation of, rather than actual need looked almost the same. 'Briarwood 1912' still carved in the gray-brown Chuckanut sandstone pediment. Some of the old wooden sash windows had tatters of peeling white paint and were broken and boarded over in places. A heavily rusted steel chain with a padlock secured the main entrance. Time and weather were sending dull reddish streaks bleeding down the doors.

A wave of sentimentality engulfed him as he recalled how he and his friends filled with the hopeful exuberance of youth would burst out on bright spring days racing to claim a spot on the now moldering equipment. His rain saturated deerskin gloves left him fumbling with a set of worn keys attached to an old ring. Awkwardly his cold fingers manipulated the keys. *This is for Paul,* he reminded himself. He searched his memory for any recollection of which key might fit and his eyes fell upon one with a tri-lobed head. *This is it! Dad always told me he remembered this key by the shape.* The odds, of course, were against any of the keys working, but his father Joshua, who had been custodian here for many years, had been the last one out when they shuttered the place. He brushed aside a layer of grime and slid in the key. He twisted and it moved slightly. *Amazing, this might actually work!* He worked the lock back and forth, withdrew the key and squirted some graphite lubricant into the keyway and tried again.

Pearson glanced up to survey the schoolyard. The Victorian style building was situated in a clearing on a small dun colored bluff overlooked his youthful haunts around Useless Bay along the southwestern shore of Whidbey Island. He wasn't expecting to be seen by anyone on a day like this. It would certainly be hard to explain, however, exactly what an aging fat guy was doing clawing through the nearly frozen lock of an abandoned school in a driving Pacific Northwest rainstorm. Even as the weather raged about him he continued his effort. *I'll probably have a heart attack breaking in here. In the spring they'll find my body in a heap at the bottom of the stairs. Crow bait.*

Finally the key moved more freely and the lock yielded. He prised the old door open while it protested with loud groans & screeches that echoed down empty hallways. Closing it behind him Richard beamed a flashlight against the enveloping gloom and made his way down dusty hallways toward the stairs. The *scriffling* sound of rodents scurrying into hiding was just discernible as his steps reverberated back to his ears from well-worn maple floors. He trained the beam along walls and into empty classrooms. Old-fashioned Victorian gas lamps were attached to the walls. Remarkably, most of their chimneys were intact, instant relics when the excitement of electric lights had supplanted them. There were faded construction paper trees and flowers on some of the bulletin boards. Vandals had ruined most of the equipment left behind. Time and the elements were finishing the job.

Stairs creaked dangerously as he made his way to the second floor and then into the old biology lab. This room, somehow, seemed to have been spared. Perhaps the menacing ambiance and whiff of decay had spooked away interlopers. Now it was just a fading time capsule. There was a carefully hand printed paper sign on the front of the desk; *Science & Chemistry - Mr. Fritz*. Along the walls, shelves held jars and bottles of all sizes and colors, each carefully labeled in ghostly Spenserian longhand recording the scientific nomenclature, date and location where the specimen had been obtained. Also noted was the collector that had found the long-dead embryo, animal or plant now floating serenely in formaldehyde. Black soapstone lab counters had flasks and Bunsen burners strewn about. High upon a perch of driftwood secured to the wall a bald eagle with eternally outspread wings clutched a salmon in one talon.

Pearson went to the back of the room to another door and unlocked it using the same key. Swinging wide, the door revealed more steep stairs. Sighing, he trudged to the top. The attic of the old school was a dust-covered, spider web draped curiosity shop of educational tools shunted aside through the decades. Broken file cabinets, desks of assorted types in varying states of disrepair were abundant. Long forgotten boxes of permanent records, with which administrators had long threatened recalcitrant students, were stacked away haphazardly. Off to the right was a shelf of old-fashioned silver-plate trophies tarnished with age, and a rolling chalkboard slightly canted due to a missing caster. Several old textbooks supported the compromised corner, forestalling a collapse.

Under the feeble winter light, struggling to penetrate a begrimed gable window, Richard took his crowbar and began prying on a loose floorboard. When he got good leverage on the old timber he got to his knees and jerked the plank aside. In spite of himself his heart was pounding and his hands shook as he looked between the scantlings of the floor. He plucked a package from its secret resting place. The timeworn string parted easily and he removed a faded old Gold Medal flour sack. Training the flashlight on the contents another flood of memories washed over him as he looked at the salt-rimed, dark blue Imperial Japanese Navy uniform and 7mm Baby *Nambu* pistol he had carefully hidden away so many years before.

Kingston Ferry

Puget Sound Washington

January 15, 1997

From behind the safety of the glass in the warmth of the passenger cabin Julie looked up from her magazine occasionally to glance at her husband. They had been married for forty years and had shared everything in life and love but in many ways her husband was still an enigma to her. She had no clue what he found so endlessly fascinating about cold winter weather or why he occasionally went trekking for hours in the middle of the night during the most frightening storms.

Even with freezing raindrops pelting his face like ten thousand icy needles Frank Pearson loved to stand on the forward observation deck while the ferry crossed the sound. He didn't think much about it, but his childhood exuberance at racing in the rain with his sailboat probably accounted for this compulsion. There were a few other hardy souls sharing in silence, for their own reasons, his predilection.

Visibility was perhaps a few miles forward toward the Kitsap Peninsula side, but Richard's mind was occupied with the task at hand. Under his heavy parka he was wearing a blue serge suit. An Oxford cloth dress shirt, whose neck was uncomfortably tightened by a dark silk tie, finished the ensemble. The package he had retrieved from the old school was carefully stowed away from prying eyes. Unconsciously he felt for the thousandth time the small object he was carrying in his pocket, and finding it, felt reassured for a moment or two.

As the Keystone terminal revealed itself from the mists he retreated to the lounge. With Julia in tow they headed back down to the car deck and sat in silence as the vehicles disembarked, falling in line as their turn came. Past the terminal they headed southwest toward Poulsbo, where Paul Akagi lay in repose. The funeral was scheduled in about two hours, with burial later that day on Bainbridge Island. Afterward, Richard imagined everyone would gather at the farm for a while before breaking up and heading home. He felt for the small object once again, fingering the hard surface, treating it like a talisman; tracing his finger around the perimeter. His mission was to pay respects to his dearest friends and their family, and this he would do with his presence. His final mission for the deceased was about to begin. Maybe, when Pearson was finished, Paul's soul would finally be released for eternal rest.

Useless Bay
Whidbey Island, WA
February 12, 1997

The funeral had been a somber, well attended event. Paul Akagi was respected in the community as both a friend and leader. His obituary was front page news in the island paper and highlighted his many years as a supporter of the arts and innovator in local agriculture. It briefly mentioned his service in WWII.

Richard, like most of the rest of Paul's family and close friends, had shed his tears before the service and it wasn't until he had walked down the church aisle behind the coffin as an honorary pall bearer that he began to choke up. But that had been nearly two weeks before and now he had a single request to honor.

Repainted in bright yellow marine paint, with a new rudder, aluminum alloy mast and nylon mainsail, the little sailboat of his youth bobbed alongside the dock, reborn to be handed down to another generation tomorrow.

Frank tossed a bag into the bow and stepped into the tiny vessel. As a child he had maneuvered it with ease, but it became clear immediately that his now adult size and ample girth would present a greater challenge when he had to come about in the wind. It was a cold, steady breeze laced with bone-chilling volleys of rain that filled the sail as he pushed away from the private floating pier. Rudder in hand he pointed the bow and set sail. It took about an hour to sail out of Useless Bay. An hour filled with nostalgia and a longing for the simpler days of his youth, but finally he rounded the northern point of the bay, slackened the sail and tossed a sea anchor from the stern.

Richard retrieved the flour sack from the bow and took the contents and laid them across the seat. Wrapped in stout twine was a vintage Japanese naval uniform with an old holstered pistol. He prepared the homage Paul had requested to honor his shipmates whose fate was now known only to him. Their honor restored, their sacrifices remembered. He gently placed it in the inky waters and watched as it swirled away into the depths to rejoin the sailors of the ruined submarine hidden in inky depths below. Then he placed a small wreath of chrysanthemums on the sea and watched silently as they floated away.

The button he had removed from the uniform and carried as a reminder for the last few weeks rested in his hand. He rubbed his thumb over it one last time and cast it away.

Rest your soul, Paul. The war is over.

ACKNOWLEDGEMENTS

Writers of historical fiction stand on the shoulders of our more disciplined colleagues, historians and librarians. The tireless efforts of professionals and dedicated amateurs to peel back the past to reveal and preserve its component parts made my work easier and allowed me to examine a story that didn't happen, but could have.

I must take a moment to express my deep appreciation to the librarians of the Special Collections Archive at the Allen Library of the University of Washington in Seattle. They were unfailing courteous and helpful, not only supplying documents I requested, but suggesting others that might be relevant as well. In each case their offerings were insightful and helpful.

Also invaluable were the small but industrious staffs and volunteers of the Wing Luke Museum in Seattle and the Bainbridge Island Historical Society.

A particularly special note of gratitude is due to Beth Sennett Porter of the Eastern California Museum of Inyo County, California. On a very special day spent in their archives and with her special knowledge of the Manzanar War Relocation Center, which I was visiting at the time, she opened my eyes and lead me to appreciate insights not widely known by the public. I hope my efforts do her justice.

A heartfelt note of gratitude is given to my spouse Nancy Pace, whose enduring patience has been sorely tested by this journey. Her encouragement, editing skills and willingness to grant the time-measured in years-needed for this effort have been invaluable.

Thanks also are due to my publisher Deep7 Press and Todd Downing for jacket cover art and formatting.

Thanks to the late David Deacon and his surviving spouse Betty. Their decades of friendship and early financial and practical support of my research efforts launched this book.

Finally my sincere appreciation is given for the now moribund Seattle 7 Writers group, including but not limited to, Garth Stein, Robert Dugoni, Jennie Shortridge, Kevin O'Brien, Laurie Frankel, Dave Boling and Deb Caletti for unflagging encouragement, insightful tips and education, and friendship most of all. You make my work a joy, and immeasurably better.

ABOUT THE AUTHOR

R.L. Pace has had a widely diversified career ranging from circus ringmaster and radio broadcaster to financial planner and rocket fuel researcher. That rich background has served as a springboard and catalyst for his writing, which in addition to this volume, includes multiple short stories in the *AEGIS Tales* pulp anthologies (volumes 1 & 2), essays, short stories, and political commentary.

He lives with his wife and dog in the Puget Sound area of Washington State.

Milton Keynes UK
Ingram Content Group UK Ltd.
UKHW020109041224
451896UK00013B/161/J